WAR STORY GUIDE

An annotated bibliography of military fiction

MYRON J. SMITH, JR.

The Scarecrow Press, Inc.
Metuchen, N.J., & London
1980

Library of Congress Cataloging in Publication Data

Smith, Myron J
    War story guide.

    Includes indexes.
    1. War stories--Bibliography. L   Title.
Z5917. W33S57   [PN3448. W3]   016. 823'008'0358   79-26740
ISBN 0-8108-1281-9

In memory of West Virginia boys
who died in Indochina

FOREWORD

Nearly 35 years have passed since the end of World War II, the greatest conflict in recorded history, one whose scope extended to virtually every continent on the globe. Those of us who fought that war cherished the hope that it would be the world's last. Of course, it has not been. A whole generation has grown up since then in years troubled by war in Asia, the Middle East, and Africa. Since 1950 the perceptions of people in America and the Western world in general regarding these strange and confusing wars have derived more and more from television news coverage and less and less from careful historical assessments or sober accounts by participants. But for earlier wars the written word remains the basis for our impressions.

Since the appearance in the last century of Stephen Crane's novel about the Civil War, The Red Badge of Courage, one of the most important ways Americans have attempted to gauge the thrust and reality of human conflict is through literature. At their best, accounts such as Crane's may be timeless, revealing aspects of soldiers' courageous grappling with the fear, stress, and suffering that together comprise the battlefield environment. Others seem to miss that essence entirely, reducing war to a stereotypical backdrop useful primarily for presenting shallow characters and implausible actions.

In recent years there has been no shortage of such accounts --whether of the useful and timeless or of the shallow sort--that have used World War II as their focus. Indeed, during the past two decades an enormous amount of fiction has been written to describe for Americans a war whose goals and objectives seemed, relative to more recent conflicts, clear and worthwhile.

v

With so many of these works in existence, and with tales of action and war forming such a significant part of English literature in the twentieth century, there has been an obvious need for a guide to what we might term "military fiction."

Myron J. Smith, Jr., who has already published a number of useful bibliographies dealing with the influence of sea power upon history, has now met that need. His hope is that the works listed in the pages to follow might help to "unlock for you certain pictures of life and death that, in real life, have often been startlingly similar to the imaginings of fiction writers." That is my hope as well.

Mark W. Clark
General, U.S. Army (Ret.)
Charleston, S.C.

TABLE OF CONTENTS

INTRODUCTION

Speaking before a group in Columbus, Ohio, on August 12, 1880, the brilliant Civil War general William T. Sherman told his listeners: "There is many a boy here today who looks on war as all glory, but, boys, it is all hell." After the recent experience in Southeast Asia, few Americans would now disagree with that assessment. So why, you ask, should anyone want to compile a guide to military fiction? The answers are varied.

Organized armed conflict is perhaps the oldest profession; if not that, at least the second most ancient. The Old Testament can be viewed as a series of interconnected war stories; Homer's Iliad is filled with the great fights of the Trojan War. War has always been a way of obtaining by force or power that which could not be obtained otherwise. Any student of history must acknowledge that combat between peoples, nations, or parties has played a very prominent part in human affairs. There is validity in the words of Prussian military thinker Karl von Clausewitz, who wrote in his 1833 classic On War: "War is not merely a political act, but also a political instrument, a continuation of political relations, a carrying out of the same by other means." In the more succinct definition of General Sherman: "War is simply power unrestrained by constitution or compact."

Given that wars have always existed in some larger or smaller form from antiquity to the latest crisis reported by television in our homes nightly, it would seem valuable that we learn more about it. The ancient writer Pindar suggested that "war is sweet to those who have never experienced it." In this generation, as in others, far less than a majority of Americans have such war experience. The war story, often brutal in its combat passages, allows us at least some vicarious acquaintance with what George Herbert in his 1640 Outlandish Proverbs called "death's feast." Given such under-standing as one might obtain from an easy-chair experience, perhaps we will begin to appreciate a remark made by von Clausewitz in his Principles of War (1812): "Only the study of military history is capable of giving those who have no experience of their own a clear picture...." The general, we hope, would allow us to add military fiction as an educational tool.

Despite the fact--and maybe because of it--that most of us agree that war is a dirty business, combat continues to fascinate the fiction readers of each new generation. Hardly an issue of Pub-lishers Weekly or Library Journal is published without at least one review of a war story. For those who write to entertain us, there is much truth in Thomas Hardy's comment in The Dynasts: "War makes rattling good history; but peace is poor reading."

This volume is divided into historical periods and ranges of years according to the following geographical areas: Europe, includ-ing Great Britain, Russia, and the Mediterranean; Central and South America; Asia, Africa, and the Pacific; and North America. With-in each time frame, following a brief introductory statement, war stories--defined here as novels or story collections about, or having significant passages devoted to, combat--are entered alphabetically by author. Readers should note that these tales relate to military operations only on the ground or in the air. Those seeking stories of nautical warfare should consult Myron J. Smith, Jr., and Robert C. Weller, Sea Fiction Guide (Metuchen, N.J.: Scarecrow Press, 1976). The 3916 titles in this compilation were written for the most part during the century between 1878 and 1978; many are now out of print, and users should check Books in Print or Forthcoming Books to ascertain current availability. Only those books thought to be of interest to adult and young adult readers are included in our listings.

Every title cited herein is annotated. It was a difficult task to decide in a very short space how much of a book's flavor could be revealed. Nevertheless, the notes should reveal something of the plot, characters, wars, or combats making volumes unique. In reading these you will quickly discover, as I did, that many themes repeat themselves from book to book or from author to author, usually with somewhat different twists in plot or character. I offer these as content annotations only; users must determine for themselves which tales are "best" to their own way of thinking.

A number of scholars have attempted to analyze military fiction through the years. I would like to call the following to your attention:

Aichinger, Peter. The American Soldier in Fiction, 1880-1963: A History of Attitudes Towards Warfare and the Military Establishment. Ames: Iowa University Press, 1975.

Bunting, Josiah, III. "The Military Novel." Naval War College Review, XXVI (Nov.-Dec. 1973), 30-38.

Cooperman, Stanley. World War I and the American Novel. Baltimore: Johns Hopkins University Press, 1970.

Jones, Peter G. War and the Novelist: Appraising the American War Novel. Columbia: University of Missouri Press, 1976.

Kotz, Marvin. "The Imitation of War, 1800-1900: Realism in the American War Novel." Unpublished Ph.D. dissertation, New York University, 1958.

Lively, Robert A. Fiction Fights the Civil War: An Unfinished Chapter in the Literary History of the American People. Chapel Hill: University of North Carolina Press, 1957.

Spindler, Russell S. The Military Novel. Madison, Wis.: United States Armed Forces Institute, 1964.

Wilson, Edmund. Patriotic Gore. New York: Oxford University Press, 1962.

The titles herein cited are each given a serial entry number keyed to the indices. In addition three other symbols are employed. Books aimed primarily at, or suitable for, young adult readers and possibly for less-than-tenth-grade readers have a "y" after the publication date. These should be checked for local standards of taste, etc., before handing out. Violence, bloodletting, and some sex are features of this genre and are present in varying degree in almost every story. A "P" after the publication data shows a book to have been published exclusively in paperback. "Rpr." and a date indicate the latest reprint date we have been able to uncover. Cross-references between authors and pen names and joint authors are provided within the body of the text.

In 1965 U.S. Marine Corps Colonel F. B. Nihart prepared a penetrating note on the value of understanding the past. "Military history," he began, "is the account of how force served political ends and how men, individual hero or leader or aggregated professionals, conscripts, or irregulars, accomplished this service." I hope that this exercise will help to unlock for you certain pictures of life and death that, in real life, have often been startlingly similar to the imaginings of fiction writers.

Myron J. Smith, Jr.
Salem, West Virginia
December 7, 1978

PART I

BEFORE THE TWENTIETH CENTURY

EUROPE: TO A.D. 400

The stories in this section cover events in the ancient world of
Europe and the Mediterranean, the majority relating to the Roman
Empire. Here the user will find tales of Caesar and Spartacus,
Gaul and Britain, Thermopylae and Canae. Such events as the con-
quests of Alexander and the Trojan War will be found in our section
on Africa, Asia, and the Pacific to the year 1000, entered below.

1 Anderson, Paul L. For Freedom and for Gaul. Appleton,
       1935. y.
       Young Taranis joins Vercingetorix's forces opposing Caesar's
       invasion of ancient Gaul, 46-40 B.C.

2 _____. Swords in the North. Appleton, 1931. y.
       A young Roman aristocrat joins Caesar's Tenth Roman Legion
       and participates in the conquests of Gaul and Britain.

3 _____. With the Eagles. Appleton, 1929. y.
       A Gallic lad joins Caesar's forces in Gaul, eventually winning
       a place in the famous Tenth Roman Legion.

4 Atherton, Mrs. G. F. The Jealous Gods. Liveright, 1928. y.
       The exploits of Alcibiades.

5 Ayrton, Michael. The Maze Maker. Holt, 1967. Rpr. 1975.
       y.
       The "autobiography" of the Greek engineer and military genius
       Daedalus.

6 Baumann, Hans. I Marched with Hannibal. Trans. from the
       German. Walck, 1962. y.
       A first-person account of the Carthaginian general's crossing
       of the Alps and descent on Italy during the Second Punic War.

7 Baxter, J. Dowling. The Meeting of the Ways. Greening,
       1908. y.
       Focuses on the struggle between Picts and Romans in Britain,
       A.D. 367-369.

8 Bentley, Phyllis. Freedom, Farewell! Macmillan, 1936. y.
       Examines the military and political life of Julius Caesar.

9 Bevan, Tom. <u>A Hero in Wolfskin.</u> G. W. Jacobs, 1904. y.
   Focuses on the struggle between the Romans and Goths in the
   Danubian district, A. D. 250-251.

10 Bishop, Farnham, and Arthur G. Brodeur. <u>Altar of the Legion.</u>
      Little, 1926. y.
   The heroic Roman, Drusus of Lyonesse, aids King Owan of
   Wales against the Saxons.

11 Blasco-Ibáñez, Vincente. <u>Sounica.</u> Trans. from the Spanish.
      Duffield, 1912. y.
   Focuses on Hannibal's three-month siege of the Italian town
   of Saguntum during the Second Punic War.

   Brodeur, Arthur G., jt. author. <u>See</u> Bishop, Farnham.

12 Bromby, Charles H. <u>Alcibiades.</u> Simpkin, 1905. y.
   Socrates, Alcibiades, and the Peloponnesian War between
   Athens and Sparta.

12a Brown, Esther F. <u>Gaul Is Divided.</u> William Frederick, 1952.
      y.
   Caesar versus Vercingetorix in 45 B. C.

13 Brun, Vincenz. <u>Alcibiades.</u> Putnam, 1935. y.
   Focuses on the Athenean general-leader in the Peloponnesian
   War.

   Bryher, Winifred, pseud. <u>See</u> Macpherson, Annie W.

14 Buchan, John. <u>The Lemnian.</u> Blackwoods, 1912. y.
   The gallant 300 Spartans versus the Persians in the Battle
   of Thermopylae.

15 Burke, John. <u>The Three Hundred Spartans.</u> New American
      Library, 1961. y. P.
   The Battle of Thermopylae; based on the script for a movie
   of the same title.

16 Challans, Mary. <u>The King Must Die.</u> By Mary Renault, pseud.
      Pantheon, 1958. Rpr. 1974. y.
   Theseus is sent to destroy the matriarchal pattern of Eleusis
   of Crete.

17 _____. <u>The Last of the Wine.</u> By Mary Renault, pseud.
      Pantheon, 1956. Rpr. 1975. y.
   Two lads grow up and experience the final phase of the Third
   Peloponnesian War.

18 _____. <u>The Lion in the Gateway.</u> By Mary Renault, pseud.
      Harper, 1964. y.
   The Greeks defy the Persians at Marathon and Thermopylae.

19 Church, Alfred J. The Fall of Athens. Jacobs, 1895. Rpr.
        1977. y.
    Alcibiades and the Peloponnesian War.

20 _____. Two Thousand Years Ago. Dodd, Mead, 1886. y.
    The slave revolt led by Spartacus.

21 _____, and Ruth Putnam. The Count of the Saxon Shores.
        Putnam, 1887. y.
    Examines the military withdrawal of Roman forces from
    Britain in the fourth century A. D.

22 Coolidge, Olivia. Marathon Looks on the Sea. Houghton Mif-
        flin, 1967. y.
    The Greek Miltiades opposes his son Metiochos, one of the
    Persian King Darius's generals, at the Battle of Marathon.

23 Cooper, Jefferson. Slave of the Roman Sword. Paperback Li-
        brary, 1965. P.
    A young gladiator and his followers defy the Roman Empire.

24 Dahn, Felix. Felicitas. Trans. from the German. McClurg,
        1883. y.
    Examines the barbarian invasion of the Roman-held Danubian
    area.

25 Davis, William S. A Friend of Caesar: A Tale of the Fall of
        the Roman Republic, 50-47 B. C. Macmillan, 1919. Rpr.
        1977. y.
    Caesar's crossing of the Rubicon and the Battle of Pharsalia.

26 _____. A Victor of Salamis. Macmillan, 1907. Rpr. 1925.
        y.
    Also pays attention to the Battles of Thermopylae and Plataea.

27 DeBeer, G. R. Alps and Elephants. Dutton, 1955. y.
    Hannibal invades Italy during the Second Punic War.

28 DeCamp, L. Sprague. The Arrows of Hercules. Doubleday,
        1965. y.
    Ordinance expert Zopyros and his catapult in the service of
    Dionysius of Syracuse in the fourth century B. C.

29 _____. The Bronze God of Rhodes. Doubleday, 1960. y.
    Chares reveals the fourth-century B. C. siege of Rhodes by
    the Macedonians and the erecting of the famed "Colossus. "

30 Dodd, Anna B. On the Knees of the Gods. Dodd, Mead, 1908.
        y.
    Focuses on Alcibiades's expedition against Sicily, c. 400 B. C.

31 Dolan, Mary. Hannibal of Carthage. Macmillan, 1955. y.
    The Greek freedman Sosylos relates Hannibal's famous march

over the Alps and campaign in Italy during the Second Punic War.

32 Donauer, Fredrich. Swords Against Carthage. Trans. from the German. Longmans, Green, 1933. y.
Scipio Africanus vs. Hannibal in the Second Punic War, 218-201 B. C.

33 Duggan, Alfred. Children of the Wolf. Coward-McCann, 1959. y.
Romulus defeats Remus and establishes the city of Rome.

34 _____. Winter Quarters. Coward-McCann, 1956. y.
Two Gauls join Caesar's army and help the Roman soldiers repulse a Germanic surge across the Rhine.

35 Eckstein, Ernst. Prusias. Trans. from the German. W. S. Gottsberger, 1884. y.
Spartacus and the slave revolt against Rome.

36 Fast, Howard. Spartacus. Citadel, 1952.
Focuses on the glory and sorrow of the rebels during the great slave revolt against Rome.

37 Fenn, George M. Marcus; or, The Young Centurian. E. Nister, 1904. y.
Pictures a boy's adventures in Caesar's Gallic Wars.

38 Gaines, Charles K. Gorgo. Lothrop, 1903. Rpr. 1976. y.
Alcibiades and the Peloponnesian War.

39 Gedge, Pauline. The Eagle and the Raven. Dial, 1978.
Briton Caradoc and his warriors bottle the Roman legions of Claudius in the first century A. D.

40 Gerard, Francis. Scarlet Beast. Longmans, Green, 1935. y.
A pro-Roman view of Hannibal and the Second Punic War.

41 Ghnassia, Maurice. Arena Viking, 1969.
A straightforward retelling of the 73 B. C. slave revolt in Capua led by Spartacus the gladiator.

42 Gilkes, A. H. Four Sons. G. A. Symcox, 1909. y.
Focuses on the 338 B. C. Samnite War in southern Italy.

43 _____. Kallistratus. Frowde, 1897. y.
Hannibal versus the Romans during the Second Punic War, told in autobiographical form.

44 Gloag, John. Caesar of the Narrow Seas. St. Martin's, 1972.
The battles of Roman general Carausius, governor of Britain from A. D. 286-293.

45 _____ . The Eagles Depart. St. Martin's, 1973.
Follows the fourth-century A. D. Roman military pullout from
Britain.

46 Godwin, Stephai. Roman Eagles . Oxford University Press,
    1951. y.
A tale about the Roman Army in Gaul, 80-60 B. C.

47 Graves, Ralph A. Lost Eagles. Knopf, 1955. y.
During the first century A. D. three golden eagles, symbols
of various legions, are lost in battle to the German barbarians; a kinsman of the defeated general in the house of
Varius vows their return.

48 Gray, Ernest A. Roman Eagle and Celtic Hawk. Barnes,
    1959. y.
Three Romans in Britain escape the clutches of the king of
the Brigantes in A. D. 69.

49 Grazebrook, O. F. Nicanor of Athens. Macmillan, 1947. y.
A tale of the 431-421 B. C. Peloponnesian War.

50 Green, Peter. Achilles, His Armor. Doubleday, 1967.
Alcibiades's disastrous Athenian expedition against Syracuse
during the Peloponnesian War.

51 _____ . The Sword of Pleasure. World, 1958.
The "autobiography" of the Roman general-dictator Lucius
Cornelius Sulla.

52 Gudmundsson, Kristmann. Winged Citadel. Trans. from the
    Norwegian. Holt, 1940. y.
In ancient Crete, a young Macedonian becomes the last Minos
and falls in combat when barbarians destroy Cnossus.

53 Hastings, Peter. S. P. Q. R. Holden, 1926. y.
How a barbarian gladiator becomes a Praetorian guard under
the Roman Emperor Domitian.

54 Henty, George A. Beric the Briton. Scribner's 1893. y.
Pictures native resistance to Caesar's invasion of Britain.

55 _____ . The Young Carthaginian. Scribner's 1887. y.
Rome versus Carthage, 218-183 B. C., with emphasis on the
exploits of Hamilcar and Hannibal.

56 Hood, Alexander N. Tales of Old Sicily. Hurst and Blackett,
    1906. y.
Alcibiades's expedition against Syracuse in 450 B. C.

57 Houghton, Eric. They Marched with Spartacus. McGraw-
    Hill, 1963. y.
A young slave searches for his mother during the slave
rebellion of 73 B. C.

58 _____. The White Wall. McGraw-Hill, 1961. y.
Hannibal crosses the Alps and descends on Italy.

59 Household, Geoffrey. The Exploits of Xenophon. Random
House, 1955. y.
The famous Athenian leader of 13,000 soldiers was defeated
in battle by the Persians and forced to make a hazardous
1000-mile retreat.

60 Jeske-Choinski, Teodor. The Last Romans. Trans. from the
Polish. Duquesne University Press, 1937.
The fourth-century A.D. victory of Emperor Theodosius over
Arbogast in the Battle on the Frigidus.

61 Kent, Louise A. He Went with Hannibal. Houghton Mifflin,
1964. y.
The second Punic War as seen by the Carthaginian general's
messenger boy.

62 Kingsley, Florence M. The Star of Love. D. Appleton, 1909.
y.
Includes a picture of the Battle of Thermopylae.

63 Koestler, Arthur. The Gladiators. Macmillan, 1939. Rpr.
1967. y.
Spartacus and the slave revolt of 73-71 B.C.

64 Lewis, Hugh. Gladiators' Revolt. Holt, 1934. y.
Theos, a Parthian slave, recalls the revolt led by Spartacus
in 73 B.C.

65 Lindsay, Jack. Rome for Sale. Harper, 1934. y.
Pictures Catiline's revolt against Rome.

66 Mabie, Mary L. Prepare Them for Caesar. Little, Brown,
1949. y.
The conquests of Julius Caesar in Britain, Gaul, and
Germany.

67 MacPherson, Annie W. The Coin of Carthage. By Winifred
Bryher, pseud. Harcourt, 1963. y.

68 _____. Gate to the Sea. By Winifred Bryher, pseud.
Pantheon, 1958. y.
Two tales of Hannibal and the Second Punic War.

69 _____. Roman Wall. By Winifred Bryher, pseud. Pantheon, 1954. y.
Roman officer Valerius escapes a Helvetian outpost in third-
century Britain when it is overrun by the Alemanni.

70 Marston, William M. Venus with Us. Sears, 1932. y.
The battles and loves of Julius Caesar.

71   Maxwell, Herbert. A Duke of Britain. Blackwoods, 1895.   y.
     Presents the struggle between the Picts and the Romans
     during the first century A. D.

72   Merejkowski, Dmitri. The Death of the Gods.   Trans. from
        the Russian. H. Altemus, 1889.   y.
     The emperor Julian campaigns on the Rhine border, finding
     victory at Argentoratum over Alemanni but death when he
     moves on the Persians.

73   Merrell, Leigh. Prisoner of Hannibal. Nelson, 1958.   y.
     A Roman POW reveals Hannibal's victory in the 216 B. C.
     Battle of Canae.

74   Mitchison, Naomi M. Cloud Cuckoo Land. Harcourt, 1926.
        y.
     Pictures the Spartan victory over Athens in the last of the
     Peloponnesian Wars.

75   _____. The Conquered. Harcourt, 1923. Rpr. 1959. y.
     An enslaved Gaul tells of Caesar's Gallic War in 58 B. C.

76   Mundy, Talbot. Tros of Samothrace. Appleton, 1934. Rpr.
        1978. y.
     One of Caesar's generals attempts to block the Roman in-
     vasion of Britain in 55 B. C.

77   Nathan, Robert. The Fair. Knopf, 1964. y.
     Celts battle Saxons in ancient Britain.

78   Osborne, Duffield. The Lion's Brood. Doubleday, Page, 1901.
        y.
     Hannibal wins the smashing victory at Canae in 216 B. C.

79   Perdue, Jacques. Slave and Master. Macaulay, 1960. y.
     In 73 B. C., Spartacus and his gladiator colleagues lead a
     slave revolt against Rome.

80   Plowman, Stephanie. The Road to Sardis. Houghton Mifflin,
        1965. y.
     The exploits of Athenian general Alcibiades in the Pelopon-
     nesian War.

81   Polland, Madeleine. To Tell My People. Holt, 1968. y.
     Britons view Caesar's 55 B. C. invasion.

82   Poole, Lynn and Gray. The Magnificent Traitor. Dodd, Mead,
        1968. y.
     The further problems of Alcibiades in the Peloponnesian War.

83   Powers, Alfred. Hannibal's Elephants. Longmans, Green,
        1944. y.
     Young assistant elephant keeper Agenor tells of the Cartha-
     gian general's crossing of the Alps and descent on Italy.

Putnam, Ruth, jt. author. See Church, A. J.

84 Read, Opio.   The Son of the Swordmaker.   Laird & Lee, 1905.
    y.
    Follows the exploits of a Roman soldier in Britain at the time
    of Caesar's invasion.

Renault, Mary, pseud. See Challans, Mary.

85 Roberts, Keith.   The Boat of Fate.   Prentice-Hall, 1974.   y.
    The Celtic invasion of Britain in the days of Rome's decline.

86 Schurfranz, Vivian.   Roman Hostage.   Follett, 1975.   y.
    Frithgeru's fourth-century A. D. Visigoths versus the Romans
    in the Battle of Adrianople.

87 Seton, Anya.   The Mistletoe and the Sword.   Doubleday, 1955.
    Rpr. 1976.   y.
    Roman legions versus Queen Boadicea's British tribes in 60
    A. D.

88 Shipway, George.   The Imperial Governor.   Doubleday, 1968.
    y.
    Nero sends General Paulinus to Britain to raise more cash
    for Rome, but ends up evacuating his forces from the island.

89 Sinclair, James.   Warrior Queen.   St. Martin's, 1978.   y.
    Boadicea of the Iceni leads the last serious British rebellion
    against the conquering Romans in A. D. 60.

90 Slaughter, Frank G.   Constantine.   Doubleday, 1967.   Rpr.
    1974.   y.
    The battles and problems of the first Christian Emperor of
    Rome.

91 Smith, E. M.   Aneroestes the Gaul.   Unwin, 1899.   y.
    Pictures Hannibal's invasion of Italy via the Alps.

92 Snedeker, Caroline D.   The Spartan.   Doubleday, Page, 1912.
    y.
    Aristodemos is the only survivor of the gallant 300 Spartans
    who fought the Persians at Thermopylae in 480 B. C.; return-
    ing to Athens, the soldier is accused of cowardice.

93 _____.   The Perilous Seat.   Doubleday, Page, 1923.   y.
    Greeks versus Persians in the Battle of Marathon.

94 Solon, Gregory.   The Three Legions.   Random House, 1956.   y.
    Roman-trained Arminius wins the A. D. 9 Battle of Teuto-
    burger Wald over Proconsul Varus.

95 Spurrell, Herbert.   At Sunrise.   Greening, 1904.   y.
    The problems of Roman soldiers in Britain, A. D. 59-62,
    including the revolt led by Queen Boadicea.

96 Sutcliff, Rosemary. The Eagle of the Ninth. Walck, 1954. y.
    A young Roman Centurion seeks the standard of the Ninth
    Roman Legion, which disappeared in Britain about A. D. 117.

97 _____ . The Flowers of Adonis. Coward, McCann, 1970.
            y.
    Presents another look at the Syracuse expedition undertaken
    by Athenian general Alcibiades during the Peloponnesian War.

98 _____ . The Mark of the Horse Lord. Walck, 1966. y.
    A former Roman gladiator helps a Scottish tribe overthrow
    an evil Queen in second-century Britain.

99 _____ . The Silver Branch. Walck, 1958. y.
    Follows the adventures of a young Roman army surgeon in
    Britain during the fourth century A. D.

100 Taylor, Anna. The Gods Are Not Mocked. Morrow, 1969. y.
    Roman soldier Lucius recalls Caesar's invasion of Britain.

101 Treece, Henry. The Centurian. Meredith, 1965. y.
    A retired officer of the Ninth Roman Legion recalls his ex-
    ploits in the defeat of Queen Boadicea's warriors in first-
    century Britain.

102 _____ . The Dark Island. Random House, 1952. y.
    Caesar's legions defeat native warriors in Britain, 55 B. C.

103 _____ . Golden Strangers. Random House, 1957. y.
    An account of Aryan people versus Neolithic men in southern
    England 4000 years ago.

104 _____ . Men of the Hills. Criterion, 1958. y.
    Hill-folk take on the warriors of the sun-worshippers in
    Neolithic England.

105 _____ . The Queen's Brooch. Putnam, 1967. y.
    A young Roman tribune witnesses the war between Roman
    legions and Queen Boadicea's British rebels.

106 _____ . Red Queen, White Queen. Random House, 1958. y.
    Queen Boadicea's warriors take on the Roman legions in
    Britain during the first century A. D.

107 Trevelyan, Marie. Britain's Greatness Foretold. John Hogg,
            1900. y.
    Another look at the revolt against Roman troops led by Queen
    Boadicea.

108 Walsh, Jill P. Farewell Great King. Coward, McCann, 1972.
            y.
    Greece versus Persia; the Battle of Marathon is featured.

109 Waltari, Mika. The Etruscan. Putnam, 1956. y.
      Greece beats off the attacks of Persia.

110 Warner, Rex. Imperial Caesar. Little, Brown, 1961. y.
      Traces the last 15 years in the life of Julius Caesar.

111 _____. Pericles the Athenian. Little, Brown, 1963. y.
      An Ionian Greek relates the life of the great statesman-
      general, including the Greek war with Darius's Persia.

112 _____. Young Caesar. Little, Brown, 1958. y.
      Pictures Julius and his warrior-uncle Marius.

113 Wells, R. F. On Land and Sea with Caesar. Lothrop, 1926.
      y.
      Caesar in Britain and Gaul, 80-60 B. C.

114 _____. With Caesar's Legions. Lothrop, 1923. y.
      A youth joins the Twelfth Roman legion in defense of the
      provinces, 58-49 B. C.

115 Williams, John. Augustus. Viking, 1972. y.
      Julius Caesar's nephew becomes Rome's great emperor;
      includes a look at the decisive Battle of Philippi.

116 Williamson, Joanne S. The Eagles Have Flown. Knopf, 1957.
      y.
      Young Lucius relates the defeat of Brutus in the Battle of
      Philippi.

EUROPE: 400 TO 1500

The stories from this period cover events in Europe and the Mediterranean from the time of Rome's decline through the Middle Ages
and into the later stages of the Renaissance. Because there are few
tales available on any given subject or century, we have placed them
all together here, despite the fact that we must cover a millenium
in time. Such events as the Crusades in the Middle East will be
found in our section on Africa, Asia, and the Pacific, 1000-1600.

117 Adams, Doris S. The Price of Blood. Scribner's, 1962. y.
      A Norse trader witnesses the Danish invasion of Wessex at
      the time of King Arthur.

118 Adams, J. D. The Mountains Are Free. Dutton, 1930. y.
      Rudolph of Hapsburg and the 1295-1350 Swiss struggle for
      independence.

119 Aguilar, Grace. Days of Bruce. Dutton, 1852. y.
     Robert the Bruce battles Edward I and II 1306-1314, ending
     with the latter's defeat at the Battle of Bannockburn.

120 Almedingen, E. M. A Candle at Dusk. Farrar, Straus, 1969.
     y.
     Charles Martel leads the Franks to victory over the Sara-
     cens in the 732 Battle of Poictiers.

121 Andrew, Prudence. The Constant Star. Putnam, 1946. y.
     Focuses on the Peasants' Revolt in the England of 1381.

122 _____. The Hooded Falcon. Putnam, 1961. y.
     A young English lord is torn by the fifteenth-century clashes
     on the Welsh border.

123 Ardagh, W. M. The Magada. Lane, 1910. y.
     How the Spanish captured the Canary Islands, 1482-1492.

124 Armitage, Alfred. Red Rose and White. J. Macqueen, 1901.
     y.
     Richard III loses the Battle of Bosworth Field, August 22,
     1485, and with it the War of the Roses.

125 Arnold, E. Lester. The Constable of St. Nicholas. Chatto &
         Windus, 1894. y.
     Pictures the fifteenth-century siege of Rhodes.

126 Babcock, William H. Cian of the Chariots. Lothrop, 1898.
     y.
     A look at the exploits of King Arthur and the Knights of the
     Round Table.

127 Bailey, H. C. The Fool. Dutton, 1927. y.
     Presents the twelfth-century English civil war between fol-
     lowers of King Stephen and Matilda, which ended in 1148
     when Matilda left England; her son, Henry of Anjou (later
     Henry II), forced Stephen to acknowledge him as successor
     to the throne.

128 Baker, Amy J. The King's Passion. Long, 1920. y.
     King Edmund and the Danish invasion of Britain, 866-870.

129 Baker, George. Hawk of Normandy. Roy, 1959. y.
     A biographical novel on the life of William the Conqueror.

130 Baker, James. The Cardinal's Page. Chapman & Hall, 1898.
     y.

131 _____. The Gleaming Dawn. Chapman & Hall, 1896. y.
     Two tales focusing on the 1419-1434 Hussite Wars in Bohe-
     mia; led by Ziska, the Bohemians, who followed the executed

John Hus, repeatedly defeated imperial armies of the Emperor Sigismund.

132 Balchin, Nigel. Borgia Testament. Houghton Mifflin, 1949.
     Cesare's fictional autobiography describing his wars and intrigues in Italy at the end of the fifteenth century.

133 Ballantyne, R. M. Erling the Bold. Burt, 1869. y.
     Viking activities in early tenth-century Norway.

134 Barnes, Margaret C. Isabel, the Fair. Macrae Smith, 1957.
     y.
     The Scottish wars of 1312-1377, including the Battle of Bannockburn.

135 _____. The King's Bed. Macrae Smith, 1961.
     Closes with the 1485 Battle of Bosworth Field.

136 _____. Passionate Brood. Macrae Smith, 1945. y.
     Focuses on Richard I of England, known as "The Lion Hearted. "

137 Barr, Robert. The Sword Maker. By Luke Sharp, pseud.
     Stokes, 1910. y.
     Prince Roland and the Robber Barons of the Rhine in the late fourteenth century.

138 Barroll, Clare. The Iron Crown. Scribner's, 1975. Rpr.
     1976.
     In the eleventh century, Eric the Viking helps Harald, heir to the Norwegian throne, escape from his captivity in Byzantium.

139 Beaty, J. C. Swords in the Dawn. Longmans, Green, 1937.
     y.
     The Anglo-Saxon conquest of England, 440-500.

140 Bengtssom, Frans G. Red Orm. Scribner's, 1943. y.
     The ninth-century Dane, Red Orm, moves into Britain.

141 Bennett, Robert A. For the White Christ. McClurg, 1905. y.
     Charlemagne's war with the Moors.

142 Bennetts, Pamela. The Barons of Runnymede. St. Martin's,
     1974. y.
     The military and political problems of John (called Lackland), King of England from 1199 to 1216.

143 _____. Don Pedro's Captain. St. Martin's, 1978.
     Edward, the Black Prince of England, aids Don Pedro of Castile in the fourteenth-century Battle of Najera.

144 Berger, Thomas. Arthur Rex: A Legendary Novel. Delacorte, 1978.

Follows Malory's (q. v.) outline in telling of the combats, loves, and derring-do of King Arthur and his Knights of the Round Table.

145   Berry, Erick. King's Jewel. Viking, 1957.   y.
      King Alfred fights the Danes.

146   Bevan, Tom.   The Lion of Wessex.   Partridge, 1902.   y.
      King Alfred versus the Danes in ninth-century Britain.

147   _____.   Red Dickon, the Outlaw.   Nelson, 1906.   y.
      Pictures Wat Tyler and the 1381 Peasants' Revolt in England.

148   Blake, M. M.   The Glory and Sorrow of Norwich.   Jarrold,
         1899.   y.
      Edward III and the Black Prince at Norwich and in the French wars, c. 1340.

149   _____.   The Siege of Norwich Castle.   Macmillan, 1893.   y.
      Battles during the Norman consolidation of Britain, 1073-1096.

150   Bolton, I. M.   The Lost Dragon.   Oxford University Press,
         1957.   y.
      King Alfred battles the Danes.

151   _____.   Son of the Land.   Messner, 1946.   y.
      Wat Tyler leads the English Peasants' Revolt.

152   _____.   The Young Knight.   Page, 1923.   y.
      The Hospitallers and the 1310-1350 defense of Rhodes against the Moslems.

153   Bonallack, Basil.   The Flame in the Dark.   St. Martin's,
         1976.   y.
      A squire tells of King Alfred's war with the Danes.

154   Borowsky, Marvin.   Queen's Knight.   Random House, 1955.   y.
      Projects King Arthur as a protector of the West Country commoners; the title refers to Sir Lancelot.

      Bowen, Marjorie, pseud.   See Long, Gabrielle C.

155   Bowers, Gwendolyn.   Brother to Galahad.   Walck, 1963.   y.
      Hengist, Horsa, and King Arthur.

156   Bowker, Alfred.   Armadin.   Causton, 1908.   y.
      Pictures the civil war between King Stephen and Matilda.

157   Brady, Charles A.   The Sword of Clontarf.   Doubleday, 1960.
         y.
      Brian Boru, High King of Ireland, versus the Norsemen in the 1014 Battle of Clontarf.

158   Braine, Sheila E.   The Adventures of Humphrey Chatteris.
        Dutton, 1902.   y.
        Simon de Montfort and the 1265 Battle of Evesham.

159   Bramston, M.   The Banner of St. George.   Duckworth, 1901.
        y.
        Another look at the 1381 Peasants' Revolt in England.

160   Bray, Anna E.   The White Hoods.   Chapman & Hall, 1884.   y.
        Philip van Artevelde's 1381-1382 revolt against the Count of
        Flanders.

161   Breem, Wallace.   Eagle in the Snow.   Putnam, 1970.   y.
        The Twentieth Roman Legion versus German barbarians on
        the Rhine in the fifth century A. D.

162   Breslin, Howard.   The Gallowglass.   Crowell, 1958.   y.
        Irish lords drive the Danes from ninth-century Dublin.

163   Brion, Marcel.   Alaric, the Goth.   McBride, 1930.   y.
        Barbarian invasion of Rome, A. D. 410.

164   _____.   Attila, the Scourge of God.   McBride, 1929.   y.
        A biographical novel about the Hun chieftain.

165   Buchan, John.   Midwinter.   Houghton Mifflin, 1923.   Rpr. 1971.
        y.
        Romance and combat during the English War of the Roses.

166   Buff, M. M. and Conrad.   The Apple and the Arrow.   Houghton
        Mifflin, 1951.   y.
        A biographical novel about Swiss archer William Tell.

167   Callcott, Frank.   When Spain Was Young.   McBride, 1932.   y.
        The Goths in Spain, A. D. 400-700.

168   Canning, Victor,   The Crimson Chalice.   Morrow, 1978.   y.
        Arthur rallies his men to meet a Saxon invasion of fifth-
        century Britain.

169   Carleton, Patrick.   Under the Hog.   Button, 1938.   y.
        King Richard III and the 1485 Battle of Bosworth Field.

170   Carter, R. G.   The King's Spurs.   Little, Brown, 1930.   y.
        The 1210-1215 Franco-English war, including the Battle of
        Bouvines.

171   Casey, Robert J.   Gentleman in Armor.   Sears, 1927.   y.
        The Duke of Lorraine finds love and battle during the Hun-
        dred Years War.

172   Chapman, A. Edwards.   Ready Blade.   Appleton, 1934.   y.
        A wandering minstrel leads commoners against the evil Sir
        Fulke de Maltroit in 1203 England.

173 Chapman, Vera. <u>King Arthur's Daughter</u>. Avon, 1978. P.
     The king's daughter Ursulet is crowned Queen upon his
     death, is involved with her half-brother Mordred in a civil
     war, and loses with him to invading Saxons.

174 Chetwode, R. D. <u>The Knight of the Golden Chain</u>. Appleton,
        1898. y.
     The twelfth-century civil war between Stephen and Matilda.

175 Chidsey, Donald B. <u>This Bright Sword</u>. Crown, 1957. y.
     With Richard I a hostage in Austria, his knight, Sir Guy
     fitz Warin, leads the fight in England against John's
     attempted usurpation of the throne.

176 Close, Hannah. <u>High Are the Mountains</u>. Vanguard, 1957. y.
     The siege of Carcassonne during the thirteenth-century
     Albigensian Crusade, directed by Pope Innocent III against
     heretics in southern France.

177 Collingwood, W. G. <u>Thorstein of the Mere</u>. E. Arnold,
        1895. y.
     Norse activities in Lakeland, c. 930.

178 Collins, Wilkie. <u>Antonia</u>. Harper, 1850. y.
     The Goths invade Italy and besiege Rome.

179 Conan Doyle, Arthur. <u>Sir Nigel</u>. McClure, 1906. Rpr. 1971.
        y.
     Edward II and the Black Prince in the French War of 1348-
     1356; features the siege of Calais and the Battle of
     Poictiers.

180 _____. <u>The White Company</u>. Harper, 1891. Rpr. 1971.
        y.
     Sir Nigel's exploits in Spain, 1366-1367.

181 Conscience, Hendrick. <u>The Lion of Flanders</u>. Murphy, 1848.
        y.
     Features the 1302 Battle of Courtrai.

182 Converse, Florence. <u>Long Will</u>. Dutton, 1903. y.
     Great figures populate this fictional recreation of the 1381
     Peasants' Rebellion led by Wat Tyler in England.

183 Costain, Thomas B. <u>Below the Salt</u>. Doubleday, 1957. y.
     The Barons' War and the 1215 signing by King John of the
     Magna Carta.

184 _____. <u>The Darkness and the Dawn</u>. Doubleday, 1959. y.
     In the fifth century Attila the Hun marches on Rome and
     there confronts Pope Leo.

185 Crake, A. D. <u>Afgar the Dane</u>. E. & J. B. Young, 1875. y.
     Canute and the Danes in eleventh-century Wessex.

186 _____ . The Andredsweald. Parker, 1878. y.
Pictures the Norman invasion and battles of Hastings and
Stamford Bridge, as well as the consolidation of Britain to
the death of William the Conqueror, 1065-1087.

187 _____ . The House of Walderne. Longmans, Green, 1886.
y.
The English Barons' War, 1253-1265, ending with the Battle
of Lewes.

188 _____ . The Rival Heirs. E. & J. B. Young, 1882. y.
William versus Harold at the 1066 Battle of Hastings.

189 Creswick, Paul. Hastings the Pirate. Dutton, 1902. y.

190 _____ . In Alfred's Days. Dutton, 1900. y.

191 _____ . Under the Black Raven. Dutton, 1901. y.
Three tales describing King Alfred's ninth-century war with
the Danes.

192 Crichton, Michael. Eaters of the Dead. Knopf, 1976. y.
Tenth-century Norsemen battle a race of cannibals attacking
King Rothgar's mead hall; partly based on the saga of
Beowulf.

193 Crockett, Samuel R. Joan of the Sword-Hand. Dodd, Mead,
1900. y.
Pictures a princess-warrior in northern Germany during the
fifteenth century.

194 Crosfield, Truda H. A Love in Ancient Days. Mathews, 1907.
y.
Love and war against the background of the Saxon invasion of
southwest Britain.

195 Curtis, A. C. The Good Sword Belgrade. Dodd, Mead, 1908.
y.
King John's disastrous thirteenth-century war with France,
featuring the siege of Dover.

196 Dahn, Felix. The Scarlet Banner. Trans. from the German.
McClurg, 1885. y.
The overthrow of the Vandal king Gelimer by the famous
Byzantine general Belisarius in 533-534.

197 _____ . A Struggle for Rome. Trans. from the German.
Bentley, 1876. y.
The Ostrogoths take on Belisarius and his Byzantine troopers.

198 Daniel, Hawthorne. Honor of Dunmore. Macmillan, 1927. y.
King Henry VI and the siege of Southwark Castle, early in
the English War of the Roses.

199 _____. Shuttle and Sword. Macmillan, 1932. y.
Pictures the revolt of Flanders against France and the
Flemish trade alliance with England in the days of
Edward III.

200 Davies, Naunton. The King's Guide. Simpkin, 1911. y.
Prince Llewelyn ap Gruffydd and the thirteenth-century
Welsh War of Independence.

201 Davis, Christopher. Belmarch: A Legend of the First Crusade. Viking, 1964.
A 1096 Crusader participates in the slaughter of the Jews
of Mainz; wounded in action, he falls into the hands of the
survivors.

202 Davis, William S. Beauty of the Purple. Macmillan, 1924. y.
Leo saves eighth-century Constantinople from the Saracens.

203 _____. The Saint of the Dragon's Dale. Macmillan, 1903.
y.
Rudolf I and the suppression of Germany's Robber Knights in
the thirteenth century.

204 DeAngeli, Marguerite. Black Fox of Lorne. Doubleday, 1956.
y.
Vikings raid the English and Scottish coasts during the eighth
century.

205 Debenham, Mary H. Conan the Wonder Worker. Whittaker,
1902. y.
Britons versus the Norsemen, 912-913; sequel to the next
citation.

206 _____. Keepers of England. Whittaker, 1900. y.
King Alfred and his army battle the Danes.

207 Deeping, Warwick. The Man Who Went Back. Cassell, 1940.
y.
Injured in an auto accident, the narrator dreams he is in
ancient Britain helping to hold back a Germanic invasion.

208 _____. Martin Valliant. McBride, 1939. y.
A monk becomes a mighty soldier during England's War of
the Roses.

209 _____. The Red Saint. Cassell, 1909. y.
Denise of the Red Hair and the gallant Lord Aymery join
Simon de Montfort in the 1264 Battle of Lewes.

210 Dehkes, Evelyn S. Young Viking Warrior. Bobbs-Merrill,
1953. y.
A youth joins the Vikings on their ninth-century raids along
the English coast.

211 DeWohl, Louis. Throne of the World. Lippincott, 1949. y.
Attila the Hun's invasion of the Western Roman Empire,
425-452.

212 Donauer, Freidrich. The Long Defense. Trans. from the
German. Longmans, Green, 1931. y.
The unsuccessful defense of Constantinople, 1450-1453.

213 Douglas, Donald. The Black Douglas. Doran, 1927. y.
The wars of Robert the Bruce.

214 Drummond, Hamilton. The Grain of Mustard. Paul, 1916. y.
Ferdinand and Isabella conquer Granada for Spain in 1492.

215 _____. Sir Galahad of the Army. Paul, 1913. y.
Exploits of a warrior for French King Charles VIII during
the latter's Italian campaigns, ending with the conquest of
Naples in 1495.

216 Druon, Maurice. The Lily and the Lion. Trans. from the
French. Scribner's, 1962. y.
King Edward III of England wins the Hundred Years War
battles of Sluys, Crecy, and Poictiers while also securing
the homage of the Scots.

217 DuBois, Theodora. The High King's Daughter. Farrar, Straus
1965. y.
Ninth-century Vikings under Turgesius invade Ireland.

218 _____. Love of Fingin O'Lea. Appleton, 1957. y.
A medical student accompanies Irish regional king Dermot
on a twelfth-century raid, instigating an invasion by the army
of English king Henry II.

219 Duggan, Alfred L. Lady for Ransom. Coward-McCann, 1954.
y.
Norman knight Roussel de Balliol, a mercenary paid by the
Byzantine emperor, participates in the eleventh-century
Battle of Manzikert.

220 _____. Leopards and Lilies. Coward-McCann, 1954. y.
Simon de Montfort, the Battle of Lewes, and the English
Barons' War.

221 _____. Lord Geoffrey's Fancy. Pantheon, 1963. y.
Sir Geoffrey de Bruyere and the thirteenth-century conflict
between the Byzantines and Franks in Morea (Greece).

222 _____. The Right Line of Cerdic. Pantheon, 1962. y.
King Alfred battles the Danes in ninth-century Britain.

223 Dunkerley, William A. Hawk of Como. By John Oxenham,
pseud. Longmans, Green, 1928. y.

Medieval soldier of fortune Gian Giacomo Medici captures
and holds the castle of Como in Italy.

224 Durbin, Charles. The Mercenary. Houghton Mifflin, 1963. y.
     The exploits of Italian soldier of fortune Gianpaolo Baglioni,
     1471-1520.

225 Echols, U. W. Knights of Charlemagne. Longmans, Green,
     1928. y.
     Roland and the Battle of Roncesvalles, 770.

226 Eckerson, Olive. The Golden Yoke. Coward-McCann, 1961.
     y.
     A tale of the English War of the Roses.

227 Edgar, J. G. Crecy and Poictiers. Harper, 1865. y.
     A fictional recreation of the fourteenth-century English
     victories over the French.

228 _____. How I Won My Spurs. Harper, 1863. y.
     Romance and combat with Simon de Montfort in the English
     Barons' War of the thirteenth century.

229 Edwards, Rhoda. The Broken Sword. Doubleday, 1976.
     Follows the life and exploits of King Richard III and the
     people around him, ending with the 1485 Battle of Bosworth
     Field.

229a _____. Fortune's Wheel. Doubleday, 1979.
     Edward IV is killed trying to invade Britain in the late
     1400's, in an unsuccessful effort to regain his throne.

230 Ellis, J. Breckenridge. The Soul of a Serf. Lee & Laird,
     1910. y.
     Saxons versus Angles on the shores of the Baltic at the
     beginning of the seventh century.

231 Ellis, Kenneth M. Guns Forever Echo. Messner, 1941. y.
     A tale of Yarmouth during the Hundred Years War.

232 Erskine, John. Galahad. Bobbs-Merrill, 1926. y.
     Pictures the exploits of one of King Arthur's knights.

233 Estrange, H. O. M. Mid Rival Roses. Selwyn & Blount,
     1922. y.
     York versus Lancaster in the English War of the Roses.

234 Evernden, Margery. The Sword with the Gold Hilt. Caxton,
     1950. y.
     King Olaf II of Norway and the Battle of Stikklestad, 1015-
     1030.

235 Fairburn, Eleanor. The Rose at Harvest End. Reader's
     Digest, 1975.

Love and combat during the War of the Roses.

236 Farnol, Jeffrey. The King Liveth. Doubleday, 1944. y.
     King Alfred struggles to save his Wessex kingdom from the
     Danes.

237 Farrington, Robert. The Killing of Richard the Third. Scrib-
          ner's, 1972. y.
     Events leading up to the king's death in the Battle of Bos-
     worth Field.

238 _____. The Traitors of Bosworth. St. Martin's, 1978. y.
     Some of Richard III's men betray him.

239 Fenton, Ronald O. The Bowmen of Crecy. By Ronald Welch,
          pseud. Criterion, 1966. y.
     An outlaw band of English archers save the Black Prince
     during the 1346 Battle of Crecy.

240 Fergusson, Adam. Roman Go Home. Putnam, 1969. y.
     Celtic guerrillas attack Roman positions in Britain, A.D. 408.

241 Finkel, George. The Long Pilgrimage. Viking, 1967. y.
     Focuses on Charlemagne's 778 advance into Spain and the
     794 Viking raids on Tyne and Wear.

242 _____. Watch Fires to the North. Viking, 1967. y.
     King Arthur and a young companion travel to Byzantium in
     the sixth century are trained in cavalry tactics by General
     Belisarius, and taking Thracian horses, return to Britain
     to engage the invading Saxons.

243 Forrest, Thorpe. Builders of the Waste. Duckworth, 1899.
          y.
     King Arthur and his knights engage the Anglians in sixth-
     century Britain.

244 Forster, R. H. In Steel and Leather. Long, 1904. y.
     King Henry VI escapes to Scotland following the 1461 York-
     ist victory at St. Albans during the early years of the War
     of the Roses.

245 _____. The Mistress of Aydon. Long, 1907. y.
     Pictures border clashes in Northumberland during the four-
     teenth century.

246 Foster, Hal. Prince Valiant: Adventures in Two Worlds.
          Crown, 1977. y.

247 _____. Prince Valiant: Companions in Adventure. Crown,
          1975. y.

248 _____. Prince Valiant: In the Days of King Arthur. Crown,
          1975. y.

249 _____. Prince Valiant: In the New World. Crown, 1976.
          y.

250 _____. Prince Valiant: Queen of the Misty Isles.   Crown,
        1977. y.

251 _____, and Max Trell. Prince Valiant and the Golden
        Princess. Crown, 1976. y.

252 _____. Prince Valiant's Perilous Voyage.   Crown, 1976.
          y.
          Seven tales recalling the adventures of a Viking youth from
          his early years to early middle age as a squire and knight
          of Camelot and through many adventures; these are oversize
          large books reprinting the comic strips made famous by the
          author in newspapers over the last 40 years.

253 Fotheringhame, Josephine. Sir Valdemar the Ganger. Low,
        1905. y.
        Alexander III of Scotland defeats Hugo V of Norway in the
        1263 Battle at Largs.

254 Fox, Marion. The Seven Nights. Elliott Stock, 1910. y.
        Wat Tyler leads the 1381 Peasants' Revolt in England.

255 French, Allen. The Lost Baron. Houghton Mifflin, 1940. y.
        Strife in Britain during the reign of King John.

256 Fuller, Roger. Sign of the Pagan. Dial, 1954. y.
        Follows the fifth-century campaigns of Attila the Hun.

257 Gallizier, Nathan. Castel Del Monte. L. C. Page, 1905. y.
        Recreates the 1266 Battle of Benevento in Italy.

258 _____. The Crimson Gondola. Doubleday, Page, 1915. y.
        Presents the conflict between Venice and Constantinople at
        the time of the Fourth Crusade.

259 Gamo, Jean. The Golden Chain. Trans. from the French.
        David McKay, 1958. y.
        A squire recalls the deeds of valor in battle and jousts of
        the Medieval French fighter Bernat VIII, Comte de Heres-
        medan.

260 Gardonyi, Geza. Slave of the Huns. Trans. from the Hun-
        garian. Bobbs-Merrill, 1969. y.
        First published in Hungary in 1901, this tale is a depiction
        by a young slave attached to Attila's army of the barbarian
        sweep into Gaul during the mid-400's.

261 Garnier, Russell, When Spurs Were Gold. Allen, 1902. y.
        Recreates the famous victory won by Henry V of England
        over the French on October 14, 1415.

262 Gay, Geraldine M. A King's Thegn. Whittaker, 1900. y.
King Alfred battles the Danes.

263 Gedge, Pauline. The Eagle and the Raven. Dial, 1978. y.
Caradoc, son of a Celtic king, and later Boudicca, the warrior queen, fight against the Roman occupation of Britain.

264 Gee, Annie L. Through the Door of Hope. Gorham, 1900. y.
Kings Edmund and Alfred versus the Danes, A. D. 868-880.

265 Gellis, Roberta. The Sword and the Swan. Playboy, 1977.
Nobleman Rannulf takes part in the English civil war between
the forces of Stephen and Matilda.

Gerrare, Wirt, pseud. See Greener, William.

266 Gerson, Noel B. The Conqueror's Wife. Doubleday, 1957. y.
Portrays the success of William the Conqueror through the
eyes of his wife Matilda.

267 Gifford, Evelyn H. Provenzano the Proud. Smith, Elder, 1904.
y.
Focuses on the struggle between Sienna and Florence after
1268, especially the Battle of Tagliarozzo.

268 Gilliat, E. God Save King Alfred. Macmillan, 1901. y.
Recreates the ninth-century siege of Rochester.

269 _____. John Standish. Scribner's, 1889. y.
Wat Tyler's Rebellion of 1381.

270 _____. The King's Reeve. Dutton, 1898. y.
Edward I, King of England, and the thirteenth-century Welsh
border war.

271 Gissing, George. Veranilda. Dutton, 1905. y.
Follows the Byzantine war with Rome.

272 Gladd, Arthur A. Galleys East. Dodd, Mead, 1961. y.
The 1431 Battle of Lepanto between Christians and Moslems.

273 _____. The Saracen Steed. Dodd, Mead, 1960. y.
Charles Martel and the 732 Battle of Tours-Poictiers.

274 Gloag, John. Artorius Rex. St. Martin's, 1977.
A sixth-century king vainly tries to unite Roman Britain;
later, he becomes the legendary King Arthur of song and
fable.

275 Goldston, Robert. The Legend of the Cid. Bobbs-Merrill,
1963. y.
How Rodrigo Diaz de Vivar's exploits for King Fernando I of
Castile against the Moors of Spain in 1032-1065 won him the
title "El Mio Cid Campeador."

276 Gordon, Samuel. The Lost Kingdom. Shapiro, Vallentine,
        1926. y.
        Problems of the kingdom of Khazaria in medieval Crimea.

277 Graham, Alice W. Shield of Honor. Doubleday, 1957. y.
        How Edward I and Gloucester defeated and killed Simon de
        Montfort in the 1265 Battle of Evesham in England.

278 Graves, Robert. Count Belisarius. Cassell, 1938. y.
        Presented as a contemporary chronicle, this tale details
        the life of the military exploits of the famous sixth-century
        Byzantine general.

279 Green, E. Everett. Cambria's Chieftain. Nelson, 1904. y.
        Owen Glendower and the fifteenth-century Battle of Shrews-
        bury.

280 _____. A Clerk of Oxford. Nelson, 1898. y.
        Simon de Montfort fights the 1264 Battle of Lewes during
        the English Barons' War.

281 _____. In the Days of Chivalry. Nelson, 1893. y.
        Features the fourteenth-century battles of Crecy and Poic-
        tiers.

282 _____. In the War of the Roses. Nelson, 1899. y.
        Henry VI and the early days of the conflict.

283 _____. The Lord of Dyneover. Nelson, 1892. y.
        King Edward I and the thirteenth century Welsh wars.

284 Greener, William. The Men of Harlech. By Wirt Gerrare,
        pseud. Ward & Downey, 1896. y.
        Concentrates on the siege of Harlech Castle during the
        English War of the Roses.

285 Greenleaf, Margery. Banner Over Me. Follett, 1968. y.
        Two brothers fight on opposite sides during the 1066 Battle
        of Hastings, won by William the Conqueror over Harold the
        Saxon.

286 Gull, C. Ranger. The Serf. Greening, 1902. y.
        Pictures the first revolt of the peasants in England during
        the twelfth century.

287 Haggard, H. Rider. Red Eve. Doubleday, Page, 1911. y.
        How the archers of English King Edward III defeated the
        French knights in the 1346 Battle of Crecy.

288 Hamilton, Bernard. Coronation. Ward, Lock, 1902. y.
        English king Henry V defeats the French in the Battle of
        Agincourt.

289 Hamilton, Franklin. 1066. Dial, 1964. y.

A fictional recreation of the Battle of Hastings and the subsequent Norman victory and invasion of England.

290 Harris, Edwin. William D'Albini. Harris, 1901. y.
During his dispute with the English barons, King John besieges Rochester Castle.

291 Harrison, Frederick. De Montfort's Squire. Gorham, 1909. y.
A youth tells us of Simon de Montfort in the 1264-1265 battles of Lewes and Evesham.

292 Hawtrey, Valentina. Suzanne. Holt, 1906. y.
Includes a look at the 1381-1382 revolt by Philip van Artevelde against the Count of Flanders.

293 Haycraft, Molly C. The Lady Royal. Lippincott, 1964. y.
Includes fictional recreations of the fourteenth-century battles of Crecy and Poictiers, won by the English over the French.

294 Henty, George A. At Agincourt. Scribner's, 1897. y.
Henry V's great victory over the French on October 25, 1415.

295 _____. Both Sides of the Border. Scribner's, 1899. y.
While Owen Glendower is successful in maintaining Welsh independence, King Henry IV of England defeated a combined Scots, Welsh, and English rebel army in the 1403 battle of Shrewsbury recreated here.

296 _____. The Dragon and the Raven. Scribner's, 1886. y.
The Danes unsuccessfully take on King Alfred and his army.

297 _____. In Freedom's Cause. Scribner's, 1885. y.
Wallace and Bruce battle for the Scots against the English late in the thirteenth century.

298 _____. A Knight of the White Cross. Scribner's, 1896. y.
Features a look at the Battle of Tewkesbury and the first siege of Rhodes, 1470-1480.

299 _____. A March on London. Scribner's, 1898. y.
Wat Tyler and the 1381 English Peasants' Revolt.

300 _____. Sir George for England. Scribner's, 1885. y.
Edward III's victories at Crecy and Poictiers.

301 _____. Wulf the Saxon. Scribner's, 1895. y.
The Norman conquest and 1066 Battle of Hastings from the Saxon viewpoint.

302 Hewlett, Maurice. The Life and Death of Richard Yea-and-Nay. Macmillan, 1900. y.

Follows the life and combats of English king Richard I.

Heyer, Georgette, pseud. <u>See</u> Rougier, G. R.

303 Heygate, W. E. <u>The Black Danes</u>. Parker, 1860. y.
    English kings Edmund and Alfred fight the Danes in the
    ninth century.

303a Hibbert, Eleanor. <u>The Bastard King</u>. By Jean Plaidy, pseud.
    Putnam, 1979.
    Robert, Duke of Normandy, and his son, William the
    Conqueror.

304   . <u>The Goldsmith's Wife</u>. By Jean Plaidy, pseud.
    Putnam, 1974. Rpr. 1978. y.
    Jane Shore, King Edward IV, and the early years of the
    War of the Roses.

305   . <u>Isabella and Ferdinand</u>. By Jean Plaidy, pseud.
    Hale, 1970. y.
    An omnibus volume of three previously published accounts
    of the Spanish unification and war on the Moore: <u>Castile</u>
    <u>for Isabella</u>, <u>Spain for the Sovereigns</u>, and <u>Daughters of</u>
    <u>Spain</u>.

306 Hoare, E. N. A Turbulent Town. Young, 1879. y.
    Philip van Artevelde versus the Count of Flanders in the
    1380 Battle of Rosebecque.

307 Hodges C. Walter. <u>The Marsh King</u>. Coward-McCann, 1967.
    y.
    Guthoim the Dane seeks King Alfred; sequel to the next
    title.

308   . <u>The Namesake</u>. Coward-McCann, 1964. y.
    Scribe Alfred-the-one-Legged, namesake of King Alfred,
    tells how Alfred became king and drove the Danes out of
    England.

309 Holland, Cecelia. The Death of Attila. Knopf, 1973. y.
    Upon the death of the famous leader, two friends must fight
    when the alliance between the Huns and Goths disolves.

310   . The Earl. Knopf, 1971. y.
    Fulk, Earl of Stafford, is caught in the war between King
    Stephen and Henry Plantagenet.

311   . The Firedrake. Atheneum, 1968. y.
    The adventures of Irish mercenary knight, Lear the Fear-
    less, in the army of William the Conqueror.

312   . Great Maria. Knopf, 1974. Rpr. 1975. y.
    In politically divided eleventh-century Sicily, a young knight
    fights for power and unification.

313 _____ . The Kings in Winter. Atheneum, 1968. Rpr. 1969.
         y.
     The king of Leinster joins the invading Danes against the
     Irish at the Easter 1014 Battle of Clontarf.

314 Hollis, Gertrude. Jenhyn Clyffe, Bedesman. Gorham, 1910.
         y.
     An old man remembers his service under King Henry V in
     the French wars, especially the Battle of Agincourt.

315 Holt, Emily S. Behind the Veil. J. F. Shaw, 1890. y.
     Begins with the Battle of Hastings, 1066, and ends with the
     First Crusade, 1096-1097.

316 Horne, Roland. The Lion of De Montfort. Dent, 1909. y.
     Pictures the English Barons' War, ending with the 1264
     Battle of Lewes.

317 Hosford, Dorothy. By His Own Might. Holt, 1964. y.
     The Anglo-Saxon hero Beowulf battles Grendel.

318 Hughes, Beatrix. Joan of St. Albans. Heath, Cranton, 1926.
         y.
     King Edward IV and the second Battle of St. Albans during
     the War of the Roses.

319 Hyde, M. P. The Singing Sword. Little, Brown, 1930. y.
     The life and exploits of Charlemagne.

320 Hyman, Freda. Who's for the North. Roy, n. d. y.
     A biographical novel concerning the English fighter Harry
     Hotspur, 1366-1403.

321 Ingram, Grace. Gilded Spurs. Stein & Day, 1978. y.
     Guy Armourer wins knighthood in the brutal world of Eng-
     land in the days just before the reign of King Henry II.

322 Ipcar, Dahlov. The Warlock of the Night. Viking, 1969. y.
     Tale of a medieval battle refought in 1949 by two chess
     grandmasters.

323 Israel, Charles E. Who Then Was the Gentleman? Simon &
         Schuster, 1963. y.
     Wat Tyler leads the 1381 English Peasants' Revolt.

324 Jackson, Dorothy V. S. Walk With Peril. Putnam, 1959. y.
     A youth seeks knighthood from King Henry V and partici-
     pates in the Battle of Agincourt.

325 James, G. P. R. Agincourt. Warne, 1844. y.
     Henry V wins his great victory over the French.

326 _____ . Attila. Dutton, 1837. y.

A young Roman witnesses the exploits of the famous Hun leader.

327 _____. The Castle of Ehrenstein. Routledge, 1847. y.
Pictures the Robber Knights of thirteenth-century Germany.

328 _____. Forest Days. Dutton, 1843. y.
Robin Hood and others opposed Prince John's attempted usurpation of King Richard's throne.

329 _____. The Jacquerie. Dutton, 1841. y.
Focuses on the 1358 Peasants' Insurrection in France.

330 _____. The Woodman. Newby, 1849. y.
King Richard III loses the 1485 Battle of Bosworth Field.

331 Jarman, Rosemary H. The King's Grey Mare. Little, Brown, 1973. y.
Another look at how King Richard III lost the crown in the War of the Roses.

332 _____. We Speak No Treason. Little, Brown, 1971. y.
A young knight remembers Richard III and Bosworth Field.

333 Jeffries, Ian. A Kingdom for a Song. By Ira J. Morris, pseud. Dutton, 1963. y.
Pictures the medieval military exploits of Charles, Duke of Burgundy, in the Low Countries.

334 Johnston, Mary. The Fortunes of Garin. Houghton Mifflin, 1915. y.
A look at the French court under siege in medieval days.

335 Johnstone, Paul. Escape from Attila. Criterion, 1969. y.
Two Frankish hostages escape from the Huns to warn their people of the impending invasion of Gaul.

336 Jósika, Nicholas. 'Neath the Hoof of the Tartar; or, The Scourge of God. Trans. from the Hungarian. Jarrold, 1856. y.
A fictional recreation of the thirteenth-century Mongol invasion of Hungary.

337 Keith, Chester. Queen's Knight. Allen, 1920. y.
A look at the combats of Sir Lancelot.

338 Kelland, C. B. Merchant of Valor. Harper, 1947. y.
The 1455-1465 wars of the Medici in Italy.

339 Keneally, Thomas. Blood Red, Sister Rose. Viking, 1974. Rpr. 1976. y.
Fictionalized account of the battles and problems of Joan of Arc.

340 Ketchem, Philip. Great Axe Bretwalda. Little, Brown, 1955.
       y.
     The warrior Wilton, with his mighty battle-ax and band of
     followers, supports King Alfred against the Danes.

341 Kidwell, Carl. Granada! Surrender! Viking, 1968. y.
     Ferdinand and Isabella capture the city from the Moors in
     1492.

342 Kiely, Mary. O'Donnell of Destiny. Oxford University Press,
       1939. y.
     Scottish hero Hugh Roe O'Donnell, Prince of Triconnel, and
     the fifteenth-century Battle of Kinsale.

343 Kingsley, Charles. Hereward the Wake. Macmillan, 1874. y.
     Story about an unruly warrior who refused to accept the out-
     come of the Norman invasion of England.

344 Knapp, Adeline. The Boy and the Baron. Century, 1902. y.
     Focuses on the suppression of the Robber Knights of Ger-
     many by Rudolf I of Hapsburg in 1260-1268.

345 Knowles, Mabel W. Let Erin Remember. By May Wynne,
       pseud. Greening, 1908. y.
     A fictional account of the Norman invasion of Ireland in the
     1170's.

346 Koningsberger, Hans. A Walk with Love and Death. Simon &
       Schuster, 1961. y.
     Romance of two doomed lovers during the 1358 Peasants'
     Insurrection in France.

347 Lansing, M. F. Page, Esquire, Knight. Ginn, 1910. y.
     Chivalry and knightly combat at the court of Charlemagne.

348 Lawrence, George A. Brahespeare. Routledge, 1868. y.
     Edward III and the Black Prince in the French Wars with
     emphasis on the battles of Crecy, Calais, and Poictiers.

349 Leary, Francis W. Fire and Morning. Putnam, 1957. y.
     Bosworth Field and the death of King Richard III.

350 _____. The Swan and the Rose. Wyn, 1954. y.
     A Lancastrian soldier relates events that took place during
     three weeks in 1471.

351 Lee, Albert. The Black Disc. Digby & Long, 1897. y.
     Ferdinand and Isabella versus the Moors in fifteenth-cen-
     tury Spain.

352 Leighton, Margaret. Journey for a Princess. Farrar, 1960.
       y.
     King Alfred's daughter witnesses his great combat with the
     Danes at Louvain.

353 Leighton, Robert. Olaf the Glorious. Scribner's, 1895. y.
       Pictures the eleventh-century Viking incursion into Russia.

354 _____. The Thirsty Sword. Scribner's, 1893. y.
       Combat during the 1262-1263 Norse invasion of Scotland.

355 Lenanton, Carola M. A. Crouchback. Holt, 1929. y.
       Richard III and the 1485 Battle of Bosworth Field.

356 Lewis, Hilda W. Harold Was My King. McKay, 1970. y.
       Harold versus William in the 1066 Battle of Hastings.

357 Lindsay, Philip. London Bridge Is Falling. Little, Brown,
       1934. y.
       Jack Cade or "Mortimer" occupies London for two days in
       1450 with 40,000 malcontents; the revolt is quickly put down.

358 Llywelyn, Morgan. The Wind from Hastings. Houghton Mif-
       flin, 1978. y.
       Pictures the Battle of Hastings and the Norman Conquest of
       England from the viewpoint of King Harold's widow.

359 Lofts, Nora. The Homecoming. Doubleday, 1976. Rpr.
       1977. y.
       Returning to domestic strife in England after adventures in
       Spain, a knight joins in the War of the Roses.

360 _____. Knights Acre. Doubleday, 1975. Rpr. 1976. y.
       When Sir Godfrey Tallboy's English knights arrive in Spain
       for a tournament, all are sacrificed in a hopeless battle
       against the Moors, c. 1400's.

361 Long, Gabrielle C. The Viper of Milan. By Marjorie Bowen,
       pseud. McClure, 1906. y.
       Gian Galeazzo Visconti, Duke of Milan, and his wars with
       the free towns of northern Italy late in the fourteenth cen-
       tury.

362 Ludlow, J. M. Captain of the Janizaries. Harper, 1887. y.
       The Turkish siege and capture of Constantinople, 1443-
       1456.

363 Lynn, Escott. Under the Red Rose. Cassell, 1910. y.
       Action in the War of the Roses, ending with the Battle of
       Bosworth Field.

364 _____. When Lion Heart Was King Blackie, 1907. y.
       Fictional recreation of the exploits of King Richard I.

365 Lytton, Edward Bulwer. Harold, the Last of the Saxon Kings.
       Longmans, 1848. Rpr. 1970. y.
       The Norman invasion, the Battle of Hastings, and the death
       in combat of the last Saxon king.

366 _____. Leila. Dutton, 1838.
Spanish Christians under Ferdinand and Isabella assault
Moorish Granada in 1492.

367 McCarthy, Justin H. The Dryad. Methuen, 1905. y.
French knights fight in Greece at the beginning of the fourteenth century.

368 McDermott, Gerald. The Knight of the Lion. Four Winds,
1978. y.
Yvain, Knight of the Lion, sets forth from Camelot to van-
quish the dreaded Black Knight.

369 MacFarlane, Charles. The Cap of Refuge. Longmans, 1846.
y.
Hereward the Wake resists the Norman consolidation after
Hastings.

370 MacKay, Charles. Longbeard. Routledge, 1841. y.
How William FitzOsbert, or "Longbeard," led the citizens
of London against William and his Norman knights.

371 MacPherson, Annie W. The Fourteenth of October. By Winifred Bryher, pseud. Pantheon, 1952. y.
A Saxon lad escapes the Normans to join King Harold in the
1066 Battle of Hastings.

372 _____. This January Tale. By Winifred Bryher, pseud.
Harcourt, 1966. y.
William the Conqueror besieges the city of Exeter in 1068.

373 Maiden, Cecil. Harp into Battle. Crowell, 1959. y.
Prince Llewelyn the Great leads the thirteenth-century
Welsh war of independence.

374 Malory, Thomas. Le Morte d'Arthur. Edited by Edward
Strachey. Scholarly, 1972. y.
Reprint of the 1899 edition; Malory is entered here as the
base upon which most stories of King Arthur are built.

375 Malvern, Gladys. Heart's Conquest. Macrae Smith, 1962. y.
Pictures the Saxon insurrection against Norman overlords
following the Conquest.

376 Marshall, Edison. The Pagan King. Doubleday, 1959. y.
King Arthur and the barbarian invasions of Britain during
the sixth century.

377 Masefield, John. Conquer. Macmillan, 1941. y.
General Belisarius saves the Emperor Justinian during the
Nika uprising in 532 Byzantium.

378 Maugham, A. Margery. Harry of Monmouth. Sloane, 1956.
y.

The life and battles of English King Henry V, including the Battle of Agincourt.

379 Maxwell, Herbert. The Chevalier of the Splendid Cross. Blackwoods, 1900. y.
      Robert the Bruce defeats the English army of Edward II in the 1314 Battle of Bannockburn.

380 Mayer, A. I. Defense of the Castle. Harper, 1937. y.
      The 900-1000 wars in Germany.

381 Meyer, Annie N. Robert Annys, Poor Priest. Macmillan, 1901. y.
      Focuses on the English Peasants' Revolt of 1381.

382 Minto, William. The Meditation of Ralph Hardelot. Harper, 1888. y.
      Another look at the 1381 English rebellion.

383 Monaco, Richard. Parsival; or, A Knight's Tale. Macmillan, 1977. Rpr. 1978. y.
      Sir Parsival seeks the Holy Grail and engages in chivalric combat and knightly adventures.

Morris, Ira J., pseud. See Jeffries, Ian.

384 Morris, William. The Dream of John Ball. Longmans, Green, 1888. y.
      John Ball joins Wat Tyler in leading the 1381 Peasants' Revolt in England.

385 Muntz, Hope. Golden Warrior. Scribner's, 1949. Rpr. 1978. y.
      The problems and battles of Harold the Saxon, including his death in 1066 Battle of Hastings.

386 Napier, Charles. William the Conqueror. Routledge, 1858. y.
      An early biographical novel concerning the victor in the 1066 Battle of Hastings.

387 Nathan, Robert. The Fair. Knopf, 1964. y.
      King Arthur's defeat at Salisbury Plain allows the Anglo-Saxon invasion of Britain.

388 Neale, J. M. Theodora Phranza. Young, 1857. y.
      Pictures the 1453 fall of Constantinople to the Turks.

389 Newbolt, Henry. The New June. Blackwoods, 1909. y.
      Henry IV versus the Scots, Welsh, and Hotspur in the 1403 Battle of Shrewsbury.

390 Norton, Alice M. Huon of the Horn. By Andre Norton, pseud. Harcourt, 1951. y.
      Legends of Charlemagne.

391 O'Byrne, Miss M. L. The Court of Rath Croghan. Simpkin,
       1887. y.
       Focuses on the 1070's Norman conquest of Ireland from the
       Irish viewpoint.

392 O'Byrne, W. L. The Falcon King. Blackie, 1907. y.
       King Henry II and the Anglo-Norman invasion of Ireland in
       1171.

393 O'Connor, Richard. The Vandal. Doubleday, 1960. y.
       Adjutant Marius, a Vandal, and the great Byzantine general
       Belisarius lead a mixed force of Goths, Moors, and Vandals
       against the invading army of Khusrau I of Persia in A. D.
       451.

394 Oldenbourg, Zoe. Destiny of Fire. Trans. from the French.
       Pantheon, 1962. Rpr. 1976. y.
       The Seigneur de Montgell and his family suffer when the
       barons of northern France answer Pope Innocent III's call
       for a crusade against the Albigensians early in the thir-
       teenth century.

    Oliver, Jane, pseud. See Rees, Helen C. E.

395 Olsen, T. V. Brothers of the Sword. Berkley, 1962. y. P.
       Follows the adventures of two young Viking warriors.

396 Oman, Carola. Crouchback. Holt, 1929. y.
       Warwick, Richard, and the War of the Roses.

397 O'Meara, Walter. The Duke of War. Harcourt, 1966. y.
       King Arthur versus the Saxons in sixth-century Britain.

398 Osgood, Claude J. Eagle of the Gredos. Reynal, 1942. y.
       Ramon del Aguila versus the Moors in thirteenth-century
       Spain.

399 Oswald, E. J. The Dragon of the North. Seeley, 1888. y.
       Fighting between the Norman rulers of southern Italy and
       the Saracens, 1020-1056.

    Oxenham, John, pseud. See Dunkerley, William A.

400 Palmer, Marion. The Wild Boar. Doubleday, 1968. y.
       King Richard III loses the 1485 Battle of Bosworth Field.

401 _____. The Wrong Plantagenet. Doubleday, 1972. y.
       Perkin Warbeck's attempt to overthrow King Henry VII of
       England.

402 Pargeter, Edith. The Bloody Field. Viking, 1973. y.
       Hotspur and the Welsh battle King Henry IV in the 1403
       Battle of Shrewsbury.

403 Park, Mrs. Kendall. Requilda. Murray, 1912. y.
     Focuses on the tenth-century Moorish drives on Christian
     Catalonia and Barcelona.

404 Peart, Hendry. Red Falcons of Tremoine. Knopf, 1956. y.
     Knightly combat between two noble houses in twelfth-century
     Britain.

405 Pei, Mario A. Swords of Anjou. Day, 1953. y.
     Thierry of Anjou, a follower of Roland, versus the Moors
     in Spain; based on the "Song of Roland."

     Plaidy, Jean, pseud. See Hibbert, Eleanor.

406 Pollard, Eliza F. A Hero King. Partridge, 1898. y.
     King Alfred fights the ninth-century Danes.

407 _____. Soldiers of the Cross. Nelson, 1905. y.
     Ferdinand and Isabella versus the Moors in Spain.

408 Porter, Jane. The Scottish Chiefs. Scribner's, 1950. y.
     A reprinting of the 1810 edition; William Wallace and Robert
     the Bruce of Scotland versus the English, 1296-1314.

409 Pottinger, Henry. Blue and Green. Chapman & Hall, 1879.
     y.
     General Belisirius and the bloody 532 Nika insurrection
     against Byzantine emperor Justinian.

410 Powers, Anne. The Gallant Years. Bobbs-Merrill, 1946. y.
     The fifteenth-century English invasion of Ireland.

411 _____. Ride East! Ride West! Bobbs-Merrill, 1947. y.
     Combat in Europe during the 1340-1350 phase of the Hundred
     Years War.

412 _____. Ride with Danger. Bobbs-Merrill, 1958. y.
     Edward III and Ireland, 1312-1377.

413 Powys, John C. Owen Glendower. Simon & Schuster, 1940.
     y.
     Exploits of the Welsh leader in the revolt against King Henry
     IV.

414 _____. Porius. Macdonald, 1952. y.
     King Arthur and his knights repel a Saxon invasion and put
     down a rebellious Welsh tribe.

415 Price, Eleanor C. The Queen's Men. Constable, 1905. y.
     Includes the battles of Wakefield and St. Albans during the
     English War of the Roses.

416 Prior, Loveday. A Law Unto Themselves. Little, Brown,
        1934. y.

A look at the Robber Knights in the thirteenth-century Austrian Tyrol.

417 Pyle, Howard. The Champions of the Round Table. Scribner's, 1905. y.
A well-illustrated tale of King Arthur's knights.

418 _____. The Grail and the Passing of Arthur. Scribner's, 1910. y.
Two well-illustrated tales based on the Malory account.

419 _____. The Merry Adventures of Robin Hood of Great Renown in Nottinghamshire. Scribner's, 1946. Rpr. 1968. y.
A classic adaptation of the ballads concerning the English outlaw-noble who battled the soldiers of Prince John during King Richard's absence.

420 _____. Otto of the Silver Hand. Scribner's, 1948. Rpr. 1967. y.
A well-illustrated look at the Robber Knights of medieval Germany.

421 _____. Sir Lancelot and His Companions. Scribner's, 1907. y.
A well-illustrated tale about some of King Arthur's knights.

422 _____. The Story of King Arthur and His Knights. Scribner's, 1903. Rpr. 1978. y.
How King Arthur came to Camelot and formed the Round Table for his knights.

423 Pyle, Katherine. Charlemagne and His Knights. Lippincott, 1932. y.
The battles of the eighth-century Frankish leader and his followers.

424 Raine, Allan. Heart of Wales. Hutchinson, 1905. y.
Owen Glendower battles the English of King Henry IV.

425 Rees, Helen C. E. Lion Is Come. By Jane Oliver, pseud. Putnam, 1957. y.
The thirteenth-century exploits of Robert the Bruce and the Scots.

426 _____. Young Man with a Sword. By Jane Oliver, pseud. Macmillan, 1955. y.
The military adventures of the young Robert the Bruce.

427 Reinherz, Nathan. Trumpets at the Crossroads. Crowell, 1948. y.
Good descriptions of medieval battles.

428 Roberts, Dorothy J. Lancelot, My Brother. Appleton, 1954.
     y.
     The Camelot story as revealed by Bors de Ganis.

429 Robinson, Mabel L. King Arthur and His Knights. Random
        House, 1953. y.
     A fictionalized view of Camelot.

430 Rofheart, Martha. Fortune Made His Sword. Putnam, 1972.
     y.
     The battles and complicated personality of English King
     Henry V.

431 _____. Glendower Country. Putnam, 1973. Rpr. 1978.
     y.
     The Welsh national hero Owen Glendower leads his ill-fated
     revolt against English king Henry IV.

432 Rolt-Wheeler, Francis. In the Time of Attila. Lothrop, 1928.
     y.
     The A.D. 451 Battle of Chalons.

433 Ross, Charles. Edward the Fourth. University of California
        Press, 1975. y.
     A biographical novel concerning the politics and battles of
     the first English king from the house of Lancaster.

     Ross, Robert, jt. author. See Woodhouse, Martin.

434 Roth, Richard. King Otto's Crown. Concordia, 1917. y.
     How the German king defeated the Hungarians in the great
     955 battle on the Lechfeld.

435 Rougier, G. R. My Lord John. By Georgette Heyer, pseud.
        Dutton, 1975. y.
     John of Lancaster, First Duke of Bedford, and Harry, the
     future Henry V, battle invading Scots, and Owen Glen-
     dower's rebellious Welsh, on behalf of their father, King
     Henry IV.

436 Sabatini, Rafael. Bellarion the Forturnate. Houghton Mifflin,
        1926. y.
     Pictures the wars of fifteenth-century Italy and the rise of
     a prince.

437 _____. Love at Arms. Hutchinson, 1907. y.
     The military and political exploits of Cesare Borgia, 1498-
     1503.

438 _____. The Shame of Motley. Hutchinson, 1908. y.
     The further adventures of Cesare Borgia.

439 Samuel, Maurice. Web of Lucifer. Knopf, 1947. y.
     A young peasant becomes a noted soldier for Cesare Borgia.

440 Schoonover, Laurence. The Burnished Blade. Macmillan,
     1948. y.
     A young French knight's activities in the Hundred Years
     War, including his witnessing of the exploits and death of
     Joan of Arc.

441 _____. Gentle Infidel. Macmillan, 1950. y.
     A Christian orphan is kidnapped by the Turks, inducted into
     their Janissary Corps, and participates in Mohammed II's
     1453 conquest of Constantinople.

442 _____. Golden Exile. Macmillan, 1951. y.
     Military and political problems of a knight returning home
     from the Crusades to reclaim his lands.

443 _____. The Queen's Cross. Sloane, 1955. y.
     The military and political problems of Isabella of Spain.

444 _____. The Spider King. Macmillan, 1954. y.
     King Louis XI of France versus Charles the Bold of Bur-
     gundy, 1467-1477.

444a Schrieber, Harvey K. The Eagle and the Sword. Fawcett,
     1979. P.
     Attila the Hun portrayed as "the noble savage."

445 Scollard, Clinton. A Man at Arms. Page, 1898. y.
     Gian Galeazzo Visconti, Duke of Milan, makes war on the
     free Italian cities.

446 Scott, Walter. The Betrothed. Lovell, 1885. y.
     Romance and warfare along the Welsh border during the
     reign of English King Henry II.

447 _____. Castle Dangerous. A. & C. Black, 1832. y.
     Pictures the Scotch Wars, c. 1306.

448 _____. Ivanhoe. A. & C. Black, 1819. Rpr. 1970.
     The often-reprinted story of Wilfred, knight of Ivanhoe, who
     loves the ward of his father; conspiracy and battles with the
     supporters of "evil" Prince John in the twelfth century
     complicate their prospective union.

449 _____. Quentin Durwood. Constable, 1910. Rpr. 1957.
     y.
     Tale of a Scottish archer's service in the army of Louis XI,
     the "Spider King," in his war with Charles the Bold.

450 Scott-Giles, C. W. The Wimsey Family. Harper, 1978.
     Tells of one man who encouraged Richard I's siege of Acre
     and of another who followed Duke William's Norman inva-
     sion of England in 1066.

451 Senior, Dorothy. The Clutch of Circumstance. Macmillan,
        1908. y.
     King Arthur and his men battle the Saxons in sixth-century
     Britain.

452 Serrailier, Ian. The Challenge of the Green Knight. Walck,
        1967. y.
     The exploits of Sir Gawain of King Arthur's Camelot.

453 _____. Robin and His Merry Men. Walck, 1970. y.

454 _____. Robin in the Greenwood. Walck, 1968. y.
     Robin Hood, Little John, and Company versus the followers
     of "evil" Prince John and the Sheriff of Nottingham.

455 Seth-Smith, E. K. A Son of Odin. Jarrold, 1909. y.
     Tale of a Norseman and his followers in 861 Britain.

     Sharp, Luke, pseud. See Barr, Robert.

456 Shelby, Graham. The Devil Is Loose. Doubleday, 1974.
     The lives and power struggles between Richard I and Prince
     John.

457 Shellabarger, Samuel. Prince of Foxes. Little, Brown, 1947.
        Rpr. 1976. y.
     Follows a friend of Cesare Borgia during the latter's Italian
     wars.

458 Sherwood, Merriam. The Tale of the Warrior Lord. Long-
        mans, Green, 1930. y.
     El Cid battles the Moors in Spain.

459 Shipway, George. The Knight. Doubleday, 1970. y.
     A young English knight unknowingly serves as a traitor, al-
     ternately to King Stephen and Queen Matilda.

460 _____. The Paladin. Harcourt, 1973. y.
     Norman knight Walter Tirel aids Rufus, son of William the
     Conqueror, but then accidentally kills him.

461 Sienkiewicz, Henryk. The Knights of the Cross. Trans. from
        the Polish. Little, 1897. y.
     The Teutonic Knights assail Poland and Lithuania.

462 Simms, John K. Gibral-Taric. Avon, 1963. P.
     The Moors conquer Spain in the eighth century.

463 Sprague, Rosemary. Red Lion and Gold Dragon. Chilton,
        1965. y.
     The Norman Conquest and 1066 Battle of Hastings told from
     both Norman and Saxon viewpoints.

464 Stephens, Peter J. Battle for Destiny. Atheneum, 1967. y.
A Welsh boy aids Henry Tudor to land at Milford Haven and
defeat King Richard III in the 1485 Battle of Bosworth Field.

465 Stevenson, Robert Louis. The Black Arrow. Scribner's, 1888.
Rpr. 1964. y.
The often-reprinted tale of military action in the early years
of the War of the Roses, when Henry VI was the English
monarch.

466 Stoddard, W. O. With the Black Prince. Appleton, 1898. y.
How the eldest son of King Edward III distinguished himself
in the battles at Crecy and Poictiers.

467 Strang, Herbert. Claud the Archer. Hodder, 1909. y.
An English archer fights for King Henry V in the Battle of
Agincourt.

468 _____. In the New Forest. Hodder, 1910. y.
Duke William versus King Harold in the 1066 Battle of
Hastings.

469 _____. Lion Heart. Hodder, 1910. y.
Follows the adventures of King Richard I.

470 _____. With the Black Prince. Hodder, 1910. y.
Edward III's son fights at Crecy and Poictiers.

471 Stubbs, Jean. The Unknown Welshman. Stein & Day, 1972.
Henry Tudor versus King Richard III in Battle of Bosworth
Field.

472 Sutcliff, Rosemary. The Chronicles of Robin Hood. Oxford
University Press, 1950. Rpr. 1978. y.
Robin, Little John, and the Merry Men of Sherwood versus
Prince John and the Sheriff.

473 _____. Dawn Wind. Walck, 1962. Rpr. 1973. y.
Pictures the battle of Aquae Sulis during the sixth-century
Anglo-Saxon invasion of Britain.

474 _____. The Hound of Ulster. Dutton, 1964. y.
Recounts the exploits of the medieval Irish hero Cuchulainn.

475 _____. Knight's Fee. Walck, 1960. y.
A youth rises from a lowly position to become a knight in
Norman England.

476 _____. The Lantern Bearers. Walck, 1959. y.
The last defense of the Roman-British leader Ambrosius
against the Saxons in fifth-century Britain.

477   _____ .   The Shield Ring.   Oxford University Press, 1956.
          Rpr. 1972.   y.
       Demonstrates Saxon-Viking defenses against the Norman
       conquerors in England's Lake Country.

478   _____ .   Sword at Sunset.   Coward-McCann, 1963.   y.
       Portrays King Arthur as a Camelot-less figure, Artos the
       Bear, in combat with the Saxons in fifth-century Britain.

479   Swann, Edgar.   The Sword and the Cowl.   Digby & Long,
          1909.   y.
       The 1066 Battle of Hastings and the Norman Conquest.

480   Taylor, Anna.   Drustan the Wanderer.   Saturday Review, 1972.
          y.
       Tristan and the sixth-century Saxon invasion of Cornwall.

481   Taylor, Georgia E.   The Infidel.   St. Martin's, 1978.   y.
       The wife of Rodrigo Diaz is captured by Hasan the Moor,
       bringing a response from the legendary El Cid.

482   Tranter, Nigel.   Robert the Bruce.   3 vols.   St. Martin's,
          1972-1973.
       Traces the life of the Scottish hero-king who defeated the
       English in the famous 1314 Battle of Bannockburn.

483   Trease, Geoffrey.   The Baron's Hostage.   Nelson, 1975.   y.
       A page helps Prince Edward Longshanks escape from prison
       and win the Battle of Evesham.

484   _____ .   Escape to King Alfred.   Vanguard, 1958.   y.
       Several young Englishmen escape the Danes to join King
       Alfred.

485   Treece, Henry.   The Great Captains.   Random House, 1956.
          y.
       King Arthur and his knights face the invading Saxons.

486   _____ .   The Green Man.   Putnam, 1966.   y.
       Pictures the brutality and combat in northern Europe after
       the fall of Rome.

487   _____ .   The Last Viking.   Pantheon, 1966.   y.
       King Harald of Norway invades England, but is killed in the
       Battle of Stamford Bridge.

488   _____ .   Man with a Sword.   Pantheon, 1964.   y.
       Hereward, a young warrior, fights for King Harold during
       the Battle of Hastings.

489   _____ .   Ride into Danger.   Criterion, 1959.   y.
       During the 1346 Battle of Crecy, a young English soldier

learns how he will later defend his home against Welsh
raiders.

490 _____. Road to Miklagard. Criterion, 1957. y.
Harald of Norway battles and wanders his way through
eighth-century Iceland, Moorish Spain, Russia, Byzantium,
and Scandinavia.

491 _____. Splintered Sword. Duell, Sloan, 1966. y.
Young Runolf of Orkney is disappointed after joining a band
of Viking adventurers.

492 _____. Swords from the North. Pantheon, 1967. y.
Viking King Harald Hardrada and his followers serve as the
Byzantine emperor's guards at Constantinople.

Trell, Max, jt. author. See Foster, Hal.

493 Trevor, Meriol. The Last of Britain. St. Martin's, 1956. y.
The 577 defeat of the Romanized princes of Bath, Glouces-
ter, and Cirencester by Saxon invaders.

494 Turton, Godfrey. The Emperor Arthur. Doubleday, 1967. y.
King Arthur is seen as a product of Roman civilization.

495 Tyler-Whittle, Michael S. Richard III: The Last Plantagenet.
By Tyler Whittle, pseud. Chilton, 1970. y.
A sympathetic portrayal of King Richard III in the War of
the Roses.

496 Underdowne, Emily. Christina. Sounenschein, 1903. y.
Includes a look at the 1268 Battle of Tagliacozzo in Italy.

497 Vidal, Gore. Search for the King. Dutton, 1950.
Blondel searches Europe for the imprisoned Richard I.

498 Wallace, Lew. The Prince of India. Harper, 1893. y.
Features description of the 1453 fall of Constantinople to the
Turks.

499 Walsh, Gillian P. Hengest's Tale. St. Martin's, 1967. y.
Jutes, Saxons, and Frisians battle one another in fifth-century Britain.

500 Waltari, Mika T. The Dark Angel. Trans. Putnam, 1953.
y.
A fictional recreation of the Turkish siege of Constantinople,
1452-1453.

501 Walworth, Alice. Shield of Honor. Doubleday, 1957. y.
Sir Andrew de Astley serves with Simon de Montfort and is
killed with his leader in the 1265 Battle of Evesham.

502 Ward, Bryan W. The Forest Prince. Digby & Long, 1903.
     y.
     Simon de Montfort battles King Edward I in the thirteenth
     century.

503 Weenolsen, Hebe. The Last Englishman. Doubleday, 1951.
     y.
     Hereward the Wake takes on the followers of William the
     Conqueror.

504 _____. To Keep This Oath. Doubleday, 1958. y.
     Henry Plantagenet versus King Stephen.

     Welch, Ronald, pseud. See Felton, Ronald O.

505 Westcott, Jan. Hepburn. Crown, 1950. y.
     Patrick Hepburn aids James IV, who became King of Scot-
     land upon the defeat of his father in 1489.

506 Wheeler, Thomas G. All Men Tall. Phillips, 1969. y.
     Hugh the Armorer develops new weapons for King Edward III
     to take into the Battle of Crecy.

507 Whishaw, F. Harold the Norseman. Nelson, 1897. y.
     Harold of Norway engages in the 1066 Battle of Stamford
     Bridge.

508 Whistler, C. W. For King or Empress? Nelson, 1904.
     Pictures the twelfth-century English civil war between fol-
     lowers of King Stephen and Queen Matilda.

509 _____. Havelok the Dane. Nelson, 1900. y.
     King Alfred resists the ninth-century Danish invasion of
     Britain.

510 _____. King Olaf's Kinsman. Blackie, 1898. y.
     The eleventh-century battles of Ethelred the Unready.

511 _____. Wulfric, the Weapon Thane. Scribner's, 1897. y.
     Edmund Ironside and the Danes in eleventh-century East
     Anglia.

512 White, T. H. The Book of Merlyn: The Unpublished Conclu-
          sion of the Once and Future King. University of Texas
          Press, 1977. Rpr. 1978. y.
     Imbued with pacifist sentiment, this tale tells how King
     Arthur, Queen Guenever, and Sir Lancelot came to their
     ends.

513 _____. The Ill-Made Knight. Putnam, 1940. y.
     The adventures of Sir Lancelot in the days of King Arthur.

514 _____. The Once and Future King. Putnam, 1958. Rpr.
          1963. y.

The adventures of King Arthur from his youth onward.

515 Whittington, Harry. The Fall of the Roman Empire. Fawcett,
        1964. P.
     Romans versus German barbarians in the fifth century; based
     on the script for a movie of the same title.

     Whittle, Tyler, pseud. See Tyler-Whittle, Michael S.

516 Wilbraham, Frances M. The Queen's Badge. Milner, 1878.
        y.
     Pictures Queen Margaret during the War of the Roses; cov-
     ers the various battles in some detail.

517 Williams, Jay. The Siege. Little, Brown, 1955. y.
     Pope Innocent III sends Crusaders against the Albigensian
     heretics of southern France during the thirteenth century.

518 Williams, Patry. Alfred the King. Faber & Faber, 1951. y.
     King Alfred battles the Danes in ninth-century Britain.

519 Wilson, Sandra. The Lady Cicely. St. Martin's, 1975.

520 _____. Less Fortunate Than Fair: The Story of Cicely
        Plantagenet. St. Martin's, 1975.

521 _____. The Queen's Sister. St. Martin's, 1975.
     Three tales depicting the battles and problems of the War of
     the Roses from the fictional viewpoint of the second daughter
     of Edward IV.

522 _____. Wife to the Kingmaker. St. Martin's, 1975.
     The struggle of Richard Neville, Earl of Warwick, to over-
     throw King Edward IV and place Henry VI back on his
     throne.

523 Woodhouse, Martin, and Robert Ross. The Medici Guns. Dut-
        ton, 1975. y.
     As the papal armies advance on Florence in 1477, Lorenzo
     de Medici turns to young Leonardo da Vinci for a military
     miracle.

524 _____. The Medici Hawks. Dutton, 1978. y.
     When Otranto is sacked by Sultan Mohammed II in 1480,
     Lorenzo de Medici sends the gunners of Florence to halt the
     invasion, defeating the Turkish Army with the world's first
     airborne operation!

525 Woods, William H. Riot at Gravesend. Duell, Sloane, 1952.
        y.
     A nobleman's son sides with the peasants in Wat Tyler's
     1381 revolt in England.

526 Wright, Sydney F. Elfwin. Longmans, Green, 1930. y.
       Focuses on the battles of Ethelfleda, daughter of King Al-
       fred, with the Danes.

     Wynne, May, pseud. See Knowles, Mabel W.

527 Younge, Charlotte M. The Constable's Tower. Whittaker,
       1891. y.
       King John, Magna Carta, and the siege of Dover.

528 _____. Grisley Grissell. Macmillan, 1893. y.
       Love and combat during the English War of the Roses.

529 _____. The Lances of Lynwood. Macmillan, 1855. y.
       The military exploits of the English Black Prince in four-
       teenth-century Spain.

530 _____. The Little Duke. Macmillan, 1854. y.
       The battles of Richard the Fearless in tenth-century Nor-
       mandy.

EUROPE: 1500 TO 1700

The tales in this section cover military events in Europe and the
Mediterranean from the later stages of the Renaissance to the time
of Marlborough. Prominent in this period, from the viewpoint of
those who have written military fiction, are the English Civil War
of 1642-1646 and the Dutch revolt against King Philip II of Spain.

531 Achard, Amédée. The Golden Fleece. Trans. from the
       French. L. C. Page, 1875. y.
       Focuses on King Louis XIV and France's seventeeth-century
       Turkish wars.

532 Anderson, Paul L. The Knights of St. John. Appleton, 1932.
       y.
       Their combats with the Moslems, 1560-1570.

533 Andrews, Marion. Cousin Isabel. Wells Gardner, 1892. y.
       A picture of Ireland from 1688 to 1691, when James II was
       attempting to regain his throne; includes the siege of Lon-
       donderry and William of Orange's 1690 victory in the Bat-
       tle of the Boyne.

     Anthony, Evelyn, pseud. See Stephens, Eve.

534 Arthur, Mary L. The Baton Sinister. By George David Gil-
       bert, pseud. Long, 1903. y.

Military exploits of the English Duke of Monmouth, 1674-1686.

535 Bailey, H. C. <u>Raoul, Gentleman of Fortune.</u> Appleton, 1907. y.
Examines the 1573-1584 revolt of the Netherlands against Spain.

536 Baker, H. Barton. <u>For the Honour of His House.</u> Long, 1906. y.
Monmouth's rebellion and the Battle of Sedgemoor.

537 Barrington, Michael. <u>The Knight of the Golden Sword.</u> Chatto & Windus, 1909. y.
The exploits of John Graham, Claverhouse, 1683-1689; ends with the Battle of Killiecrankie.

538 Bartos-Hoppner, B. <u>The Cossacks.</u> Trans. from the German. Walck, 1963. y.
Portrays the Cossack conquest, led by Yarmack, of the capital of Siberia, 1580-1584.

539 _____. <u>Save the Khan.</u> Trans. from the German. Walck, 1964. y.
Duritai, the Tartar prince, battles Kuchum Khan for control of Siberia at the end of the sixteenth century.

540 Beatty, John and Patricia. <u>King's Knights.</u> Morrow, 1971. y.
Cromwell's Roundheads massacre Irish and English Royalists at Drogheda.

541 Bedford-Jones, Henry. <u>The Black Bull.</u> By John Wycliffe, pseud. Putnam, 1928. y.
A seventeenth-century Irish cavalier battles the evil Duke of Corthia in southern Italy.

542 _____. <u>D'Artagnan.</u> By John Wycliffe, pseud. Covici, 1928. y.
Covers the periods between Dumas's <u>Three Musketeers</u> and <u>Twenty Years After</u>.

543 _____. <u>King's Passport.</u> By John Wycliffe, pseud. Putnam, 1928. y.
Battles and adventures of a friend of D'Artagnan and Cyrano de Bergerac versus Cardinal Richelieu.

544 Bennetts, Pamela. <u>The Borgia Prince.</u> St. Martin's, 1975.
Cesare Borgia and his soldiers capture Savarno castle early in the sixteenth century.

545 Bevans, Tom. <u>The "Grey Fox" of Holland.</u> Nelson, 1908. y.
A tale of the 1576 Dutch revolt against Spain.

546 Binns, Ottwell. The Sword of Fortune. By Ben Bolt, pseud.
        Ward, Lock, 1927.   y.
     The Duke of Monmouth's rebellion against English King
     James II, 1685.

547 Blackmore, Richard D. Lorna Doone. Putnam, 1869.   y.
     The often-reprinted story of the outlaw Doones of the north
     Devon coast with attention to plain John Redd's service to
     James II during the Monmouth Rebellion.

548 Blake-Forster, Charles F. The Irish Chieftains. Whittaker,
        1874. y.
     William of Orange takes on the forces of James II in the
     Battle of the Boyne.

549 Blayney, Owen. The Macmahon. Constable, 1898.   y.
     Features the 1690 Battle of the Boyne.

     Bolt, Ben, pseud. See Binns, Ottwell.

     Bowen, Marjorie, pseud. See Long, Gabrielle C.

550 Brebner, Percy J. The Brown Mask. Cassell, 1910.   y.
     A highwayman becomes involved in Monmouth's rebellion,
     1685.

551 Brereton, Frederick S. A Knight of St. John. Blackie, 1906.
        y.
     The 1564 Turkish siege of Malta.

552 Briggs, Jean. The Flame of the Borgias. Harper, 1975.
     Love and war in sixteenth-century Italy.

553 Burton, John Bloundelle. The Clash of Arms. Methuen, 1897.
        y.
     The battles of General Turenne for King Louis XIV; Briton
     John Churchill is a noted opponent.

554 _____. The King's Mignon. Everett, 1909. y.
     France and the War of the League, 1588.

555 _____. Knighthood's Flower. Hurst & Blackett, 1906.   y.
     The 15-month siege of Huguenot-held La Rochelle, which
     ends in 1628 with victory to the forces of Cardinal Riche-
     lieu.

556 Caine, O. V. The Coming of Navarre. Nisbet, 1909.   y.
     Looks at the French Huguenot victories of 1590.

557 Chalmers, Stephen. When Love Calls Men to Arms. Rich-
        ards, 1912. y.
     Pictures the border clashes in sixteenth-century Scotland
     under James VI.

558 Charques, Dorothy. The Dark Stranger. Coward-McCann,
         1957. y.
     Royalists versus Roundheads in the English Civil War.

559 Church, Alfred J. With the King at Oxford. Dodd, Mead,
         1886. y.
     Charles I and his Cavaliers in the early stages of the Eng-
     lish Civil War.

560 Church, Samuel H. John Marmaduke. Putnam, 1889. y.
     Cromwell's forces capture Drogheda, Ireland, in 1649.

561 Clarke, Henry. In Jacobite Days. Nelson, 1904. y.
     Pictures Devonshire from the landing of William of Orange
     to the burning of Teignmouth.

562 Comstock, Seth C. Monsieur le Capitaine Douay. J. Long,
         1904. y.
     The defense of Antwerp against the Spaniards in 1576.

563 Conan Doyle, Arthur. Micah Clarke. Murray, 1950.
     First published in 1889, this tale details the 1685 Monmouth
     Rebellion against King James II, including the Battle of
     Sedgemoor.

564 _____. Refugees. Harper, 1891. y.
     A tale of the Huguenot wars at the time of King Louis XIV.

565 Conscience, Hendrick. The Lion of Flanders. Trans. from
         the Dutch. Kelly, 1838. y.
     Portrays the Flemish uprising against France, including the
     Battle of Courtrai and the Massacre of Bruges.

566 Cornfold, L. Cape. Sons of Adversity. L. C. Page, 1898.
         y.
     The 1574 Dutch revolt against the Spaniards of Philip II.

567 Crake, E. E. The Royalist Brothers. Gorham, 1908. y.
     Includes the 1648 siege of Colchester.

568 Crockett, Samuel R. Lockinvar. Harper, 1897. y.
     Features the seventeenth-century Battle of Killiecrankie.

569 _____. The White Plume. Dodd, Mead, 1906. y.
     Henry of Navarre and the French religious wars of 1568-
     1570.

570 Crosfield, H. C. For Three Kingdoms. Elliott Stock, 1909.
         y.
     The English campaign in Ireland, 1688-1691, including the
     Battle of the Boyne.

571 Curties, Henry. Renée. Richards, 1908. y.

The sixteenth-century conflict between France and England-Austria; battles covered include Marignano and the Field of the Cloth of Gold.

572 Daive, Carlton. One Fair Enemy. J. Long, 1908. y.
Cromwell's Roundheads defeat the Cavaliers of Charles I in the decisive 1645 Battle of Naseby.

573 Daniel, Hawthorne. Broken Dykes. Macmillan, 1934. y.
The siege of Leyden during the Dutch revolt against Spain.

574 Deeping, Warwick. Bertrand of Brittany. Harper, 1908. y.
The 1520-1544 exploits of Bertrand de Guesclin, military leader of Holy Roman Emperor Charles V in his wars with France.

575 Defoe, Daniel. Memoirs of a Cavalier. Macmillan, 1720. Rpr. 1972.
Military journal of an Englishman who fought in the seventeenth-century wars in Germany (Gustavus Adolphus) and England (Charles I).

576 Dekker, Maurits. Beggars' Revolt. Trans. from the Dutch. Doubleday, 1938. y.
The sixteenth-century Dutch revolt against the Spaniards.

577 DeWohl, Louis. The Last Crusader. Lippincott, 1957. y.
The military operations of John of Austria, including his victory at Lepanto in 1531 and his campaign on behalf of Philip II in the Netherlands.

578 Dix, Beulah M. The Fighting Blade. Holt, 1912. y.
Tale of a German soldier of fortune in the service of Charles I.

579 _____. Hugh Gwyeth: Round-Head Cavalier. Macmillan, 1899. y.
Includes the 1642 English Civil War battle of Edgehill.

580 _____. Merrylips. Macmillan, 1906. y.
A girl masquerades as a boy during the English Civil War.

581/2 Douglas, Alan. For the King. Macrae Smith, 1926. y.
How a Cromwellian soldier finds himself protecting Charles I during the English Civil War.

583 Dumas, Alexandre. The Three Musketeers. Trans. from the French. Taylor, Wilde, 1846. Rpr. 1974. y.
This often-reprinted story shows young D'Artagnan and his companions involved in duels, swordfighting, battles, and conspiracy in the France of 1625.

584 _____. Twenty Years After. Trans. from the French. Taylor, Wilde, 1846. y.

This often-reprinted sequel to the above tale finds D'Artagnan and his companions involved in the insurrection of Fronde and the English Civil War.

585 DuMaurier, Daphne. The King's General. Doubleday, 1946. Rpr. 1978. y.
The military exploits of Sir Richard Grenville, general for King Charles I in the west during the English Civil War.

586 Dunnett, Dorothy. The Disorderly Knights. Putnam, 1966. y.
Scottish prince Francis Crawford of Lymond joins the Knights of St. John in defending Malta against the Turks in 1551.

587 _____ . The Ringed Castle. Putnam, 1972. y.
A Scottish mercenary becomes commander of the Russian armies of Ivan the Terrible in the wars with Khazan and Astrakhan, 1552-1556.

588 Durych, Jaroslav. Descent of the Idol. Trans. from the Slovak. Dutton, 1936. y.
The exploits of Wallenstein in the Thirty Years War in Germany in the seventeenth century.

589 Eaton, Evelyn S. M. In What Torn Ship? Harper, 1944. y.
Pascal Paoli frees Corsica from the Genoese in the seventeenth century.

590 Eccott, W. J. Fortune's Castaway. Blackwoods, 1904. y.
A tale of the 1683-1685 Monmouth Rebellion against England's James II.

591 Eckerson, Olive. My Lord Essex. Holt, 1955. y.
Includes Robert Devereux's military campaigns in Ireland, sixteenth century.

Edwards, Samuel, pseud. See Gerson, Noel B.

592 Ellis, Beth. Barbara Winslow, Rebel. Blackwoods, 1903. y.
A girl's role in the Monmouth Rebellion, including the Battle of Sedgemoor.

593 Eyre-Todd, G. Cavalier and Covenant. Routledge, 1895. y.
Cromwell invades Scotland in 1650.

594 Faulkner, Nancy. Knights Besieged. Doubleday, 1964. y.
A young eyewitness describes the downfall of the Knights of St. John on Rhodes to the Turks in 1522.

595 Fea, Allen. My Lady Wentworth. Mills & Boone, 1909. y.
The Duke of Monmouth, his rebellion and romance with Lady Wentworth.

596   Fecher, Constance. Traitor's Son. Dell, 1976. P.
         The role of Carew, son of Sir Walter Raleigh, in the Eng-
         lish Civil War.

597   Felton, Ronald O. For the King. By Ronald Welch, pseud.
            Criterion, 1962. y.
         The son of a Welsh noble fights for King Charles I during
         the English Civil War.

598   Finlay, T. A. The Chances of War. Gill (Dublin), 1877. y.
         The 1646-1649 war in Ireland, including the Battle of Ben-
         burb and Cromwell's advance on Limerick.

599   Fitzpatrick, Thomas. The King of Claddagh. Sands, 1899. y.
         How Cromwell's soldiers occupied Galway.

600   Fletcher, J. S. Mistress Spitfire. McClurg, 1896. y.
         A girl's role in the English Civil War.

601   _____. When Charles I Was King. McClurg, 1892. y.
         Recreates the Battle of Marston Moor and the siege of
         Pontefrait in the English Civil War.

602   Forster, R. H. The Arrow of the North. Long, 1906. y.
         War between England and Scotland, ending with the Battle of
         Flodden Field in 1513.

603   Freshfield, F. H. At All Hazards. George Allen, 1910. y.
         The Duke of Monmouth rebels against English King James II.

604   Frith, Henry. Under Bayard's Banner. Cassell, 1886. y.
         The Chevalier de Bayard and the sixteenth-century Battle of
         Ravenna.

605   Fulton, D. Kerr. The Witch's Sword. E. Arnold, 1908. y.
         War between England and Scotland, ending with the 1513
         Battle of Flodden Field.

606   Galt, John. Ringan Gilhaize. Greening, 1899. y.
         Recalls the Scottish uprising of 1688 and the Battle of Killie-
         crankie.

607   Garnett, Henry. Gamble for a Throne. Barnes, 1958. y.
         An attempted Royalist uprising against Cromwell's Protec-
         torate.

608   Garnier, Russell M. His Counterpart. Harper, 1898. y.
         John Churchill and the seventeenth-century Wars of Turenne.

609   Gerson, Noel B. The Queen's Husband. By Samuel Edwards,
            pseud. McGraw-Hill, 1960. y.
         William the Silent leads the Dutch revolt against the Spanish
         of the Duke of Alva.

610 _____. The White Plume. By Samuel Edwards, pseud.
        Morrow, 1961. y.
        The military exploits of Prince Rupert of the Rhine under
        the English kings Charles I and II.

Gilbert, George David, pseud. See Arthur, Mary L.

611 Gogol, Nikolai V. Taras Bulba, a Tale of the Cossacks.
        Trans. from the Russian. Knopf, 1915. Rpr. 1972. y.
        This often-reprinted tale recalls the wars and battles of the
        Cossacks against the Christian Poles and Moslem Tartars
        during the sixteenth century.

612 Goudge, Elizabeth. The White Witch. Coward-McCann, 1958.
        Rpr. 1976. y.
        A noble posing as a painter is caught up in the battles and
        skirmishes of the English Civil War.

613 Graeme, David. The Sword of Monsieur Blackshirt. Lippin-
        cott, 1937. y.
        A French swordsman aids the King during the days of the
        religious wars led by Henry of Navarre.

614 Grant, James. The Scottish Cavalier. Routledge, 1850. y.
        A picture of the seventeenth-century Battle of Killiecrankie.

615 Grattan, Thomas C. Agnes de Mansfelt. Saunders & Otley,
        1835. y.
        The Dutch revolt against Spain during the sixteenth century.

616 Green, E. Everett. In Taunton Town. Nelson, 1896. y.
        A story of Monmouth's Rebellion.

617 _____. Shut In. Nelson, 1894. y.
        Recreates the 1585 Spanish siege of Antwerp.

618 _____. Under Two Queens. J. F. Shaw, 1904. y.
        Lady Jane Grey and Thomas Wyatt's rebellion in England,
        1551-1554.

619 Gresley, L. The Siege of Lichfield. Masters, 1840. y.
        Recreates the English Civil War battles after 1642, including
        the contest at Edgehill.

620 Grierson, Edward. Dark Torrent of Glencoe. Doubleday,
        1960.
        A fictional account of the feud between the MacDonald and
        Campbell clans of Scotland and the infamous Glencoe Mas-
        sacre of 1692.

621 Griffin, Gerald. Duke of Monmouth. R. Bentley, 1836. y.
        An early biographical novel, including the great Rebellion
        of 1674-1686.

622 Grogan, Walter E. The King's Cause. J. Milne, 1909. y.
     Prince Rupert of the Rhine captures Bristol for Charles I
     during the English Civil War and later surrenders to Fair-
     fax.

623 Habeck, Fritz. Days of Danger. Harcourt, 1963. y.
     The Turks besiege Vienna in 1683.

624 Haggard, H. Rider. Lysbeth. Longmans, Green, 1901. y.
     The sixteenth-century sieges of Leyden and Haarlem in the
     Dutch revolt against Spain.

625 Hales, A. G. Maid Molly. Treherne, 1907. y.
     The 1645 Battle of Naseby during the English Civil War.

626 Hart, J. Wesley. In the Iron Time. Robert Culley, 1907. y.
     The battles of Edgehill and Marston Moor during the English
     Civil War.

627 Harwood, Alice. Lily and the Leopards. Bobbs-Merrill, 1949.
     y.
     The July 1553 struggle of Lady Jane Grey to succeed Ed-
     ward VI.

628 _____. Seats of the Mighty. Bobbs-Merrill, 1957. y.
     Turmoil in Scotland, 1567-1578.

629 Haugaard, Erik C. Cromwell's Boys. Houghton Mifflin, 1978.
     y.

630 _____. A Messenger for Parliament. Houghton Mifflin,
     1977. y.
     Two tales of young Oliver Cutter, a courier for Roundhead
     forces during the English Civil War.

631 Haverfield, E. L. Stanhope. Nelson, 1903. y.
     The English Civil War battle of Naseby.

632 Haynes, Herbert. For Rupert and the King. Gorham, 1910.
     y.
     Cavaliers versus Roundheads in 1642-1646 England.

633 Helm-Pirgo, Marian. Royal Dragoons. Bicentennial Publishing
         Corps., 1977. y.
     A tale of the cavalry in seventeenth-century Poland.

634 Henty, George A. By England's Aid. Scribner's, 1891. y.
     Queen Elizabeth's support of the Dutch revolt against Spain.

635 _____. By Pike and Dyke. Scribner's, 1890. y.
     Recreates the Spanish sieges of Haarlem, Leyden, and An-
     twerp during the revolt of the Netherlands.

636 _____ . Orange and Green. Scribner's, 1888. y.
     Ireland, 1688-1691, featuring the sieges of Derry and Lime-
     rick and the Battle of the Boyne.

637 _____ . St. Bartholomew's Eve. Scribner's, 1894. y.
     France and the religious wars of 1567-1572, including fights
     at Jarnac and Moncontour.

     Heyer, Georgette, pseud. See Rougier, G. R.

638 Hibbert, Eleanor. Evergreen Gallant. By Jean Plaidy, pseud.
     Putnam, 1973. y.
     The battles and problems of Henry of Navarre.

639 _____ . Queen Jezebel. By Jean Plaidy, pseud. Appleton,
     1953. Rpr. 1977. y.
     Catherine de Medici and the sixteenth-century religious wars
     in France, including a number of battles and skirmishes.

640 Hillary, Max. The Blue Flag. Ward, Lock, 1898. y.
     Presents the Monmouth Rebellion in Somersetshire.

641 Hinkson, Henry A. Silk and Steel. Chatto & Windus, 1902.
     y.
     Combat in Ireland at the time of English King Charles I.

642 Hocking, Joseph. Follow the Gleam. Hodder & Stoughton,
     1903. y.
     Cromwell, Charles I, and the 1642 Battle of Marston Moor.

642a Holland, Cecelia. City of God. Knopf, 1979.
     The military and political intrigues of Cesare Borgia, cen-
     tering around Rome.

643 _____ . Rakossy. Atheneum, 1967. y.
     A minor Magyar noble and warrior knight attempts to alert
     Vienna officials to the 1526 invasion by Sulieman the Mag-
     nificent's Turks.

644 Hope, Graham. A Cardinal and His Conscience. Smith, Elder,
     1901. y.
     The Guises and the sixteenth-century French religious wars.

645 Horton, S. For King or Parliament? Robert Culley, 1909. y.
     A Yorkshire Parliamentarian's adventures in the English
     Civil War Battle of Marston Moor.

646 Houston, June D. Faith and the Flame. Sloane, 1959. y.
     Cardinal Richelieu's war on the French Huguenots.

647 Hunter, Mollie. The Ghosts of Glencoe. Funk & Wagnalls,
     1969. y.
     In 1692 William of Orange secretly orders the Campbells to
     massacre the MacDonalds at Glencoe.

648 Innes, Norman. My Lady's Kiss. Rand McNally, 1908. y.
     Love and combat in Germany's Thirty Years War.

649 Irwin, Margaret E. F. Proud Servant. Harcourt, 1934. y.
     The Earl of Montrose conquers Scotland for King Charles I.

650   . Stranger Prince. Harcourt, 1937. y.
     Prince Rupert of the Rhine and his service to Charles I
     during the English Civil War.

651 James, G. P. R. The Man at Arms. Dutton, 1840. y.
     Recreates the sixteenth-century Huguenot wars in France.

652   . One in a Thousand. Harper, 1835. y.

653   . Rose D'Albert. Dutton, 1844. y.
     Two tales concerning the victory by King Henry IV of France
     in the 1590 Battle of Ivry against the Huguenots.

654 Jessop, George H. Desmond O'Connor. Long, 1914. y.
     A captain of the Irish Brigade in combat--and in love with
     a ward of French king Louis XIV.

655 Jokai, Maurus. 'Midst the Wild Carpathians. Trans. from the
     Hungarian. Jarrold, 1894. y.

656   . The Slaves of the Padishah. Trans. from the Hun-
     garian. Jarrold, 1902. y.
     Two stories about the war between the Turks and Hungarians
     in Transylvania in the seventeenth century.

657 Kenny, Louise M. S. Love Is Life. Greening, 1910. y.
     The exiled soldier, Sarsfield, fights for French king Louis
     XIV.

658 Kenyon, Frank W. The Glory and the Dream. Dodd, Mead,
     1963. y.
     The exploits of John Churchill, First Duke of Marlborough.

659 Kerr, Robert. The Stuart Legacy. Stein & Day, 1973. y.
     Border clashes and besieged castles follow the return of
     James II to Scotland after the Glorious Revolution.

660 Keyes, Frances P. I, the King. McGraw-Hill, 1966. y.
     The reign of Spanish King Philip IV, 1621-1665, and his
     disastrous wars with France, Germany, and Holland.

661 Keynes, Helen M. Honour the King. Chatto & Windus, 1914.
     y.
     The siege of Bristol during the English Civil War.

662 Kiely, Mary. O'Donel of Destiny. Oxford University Press,
     1939. y.
     Strife and combat in Ireland, 1565-1579.

663 Kirke, Violet T. Brothers Five. Gorham, 1910. y.
The Netherlands revolt against Spain, 1568-1574; includes
the battles of Heiligerlee, Ems, and Mookerhyde.

664 Kimmel, Eric A. The Tartar's Sword. Coward-McCann, 1974.
Cossacks battle the Poles in the Ukraine of 1623.

Knight, Brigid, pseud. See Sinclair, Kathleen.

665 Knight, Frank. The Last of the Lallows. Macmillan, 1961.
y.
A girl's father and uncle fight on opposite sides during the
English Civil War.

666 Knightley, S. R. The Cavaliers. Harper, 1896. y.
The English Civil War from the viewpoint of the followers
of King Charles I.

667 _____. The Crimson Sign. Harper, 1895. y.
Pictures the 1689 siege of Derry.

668 Knowles, Mabel W. For Church and Chieftain. By May Wynne,
pseud. Mills & Boone, 1909. y.
The sixteenth-century Geraldine rebellion in Ireland.

669 _____. Hey for Cavaliers. By May Wynne, pseud. Green-
ing, 1912. y.
Looks at the siege of Pontefract Castle during the English
Civil War.

670 _____. Ronald Lindsay. By May Wynne, pseud. J. Long,
1904. y.
The exploits of Claverhouse in Scotland, 1684-1689, to the
Battle of Killiecrankie.

671 Krasnov, Petr N. Kostia the Cossack. Trans. from the
Russian. Duffield, 1930. y.
Cossacks battle Turks in the seventeenth century.

672 Krepps, Robert W. Taras Bulba. Fawcett, 1962. P.
Cossacks versus Poles; a tale based on the movie screen-
play, which in turn was based on the novel by Russian author Nikolai Gogol cited above.

673 Kulish, Panteleimon. The Black Council. Trans. from the
Ukrainian. Classics in Translation Series. Libraries
Unlimited, 1973.
Originally published in Russia in the nineteenth century, this
story describes Cossacks in battle with Poles in the Ukraine
of the seventeenth century.

674 Lamb, Harold. The Curved Sabre. Doubleday, 1964. y.
Short stories about the seventeenth-century Cossack, Khlit
of the Curved Sabre.

675 Lang, Angela. The Priceless Passion. Ballantine, 1978. P.
     First published in France in 1974, this tale recounts love
     and battle during the 1572 French religious war.

676 Lawless, Emily. Mallcho. Appleton, 1890. y.
     The Earl of Essex and the Irish rebellion of 1579.

677 _____. With Essex in Ireland. J. W. Lovell, 1894. y.
     Robert Devereux's campaign of 1599.

678 Lederer, Charlotte. The Eagle's Quest. Doubleday, 1939. y.
     Rakoczy's attempt to free Hungary from Austria, 1660-1664.

679 LeFanu, J. Sheridan. The Fortunes of Colonel Torlogh
        O'Brien. Routledge, 1847. y.
     An Irish commander during the war of 1688-1691; ends with
     the Battle of Aughrim.

680 Lindsay, Philip. The Knights at Bay. Loring & Mussey, 1935.
        y.
     In the sixteenth century the Turks finally gain the upper hand
     over the warrior Knights Hospitallers.

681 Linington, Elizabeth. The Kingbreaker. Doubleday, 1958. y.
     After the 1645 Battle of Naseby, Royalist Ivor ap Maddox
     consents to impersonate Thomas Dennistown, killed on his
     way to join Cromwell.

682 _____. The Proud Man. Viking, 1955. y.
     Shane O'Neill, Prince of Ulster, almost succeeds in driving
     the English out during the sixteenth century and becoming
     king of a united Ireland.

683 Long, Gabrielle C. Kings-At-Arms. By Marjorie Bowen,
        pseud. Dutton, 1919. y.
     The conflicts and battles of the seventeenth century between
     Peter the Great of Russia and Karl XII of Sweden.

684 _____. A Knight of Spain. By Marjorie Bowen, pseud.
        Methuen, 1913. y.
     Don Juan of Austria at Lepanto and in the Netherlands.

685 _____. Prince and Heretic. By Marjorie Bowen, pseud.
        Dutton, 1915. y.
     William the Silent and the Dutch revolt against Spain.

686 _____. "William, by the Grace of God." By Marjorie
        Bowen, pseud. Dutton, 1917. y.
     William of Orange and the English Glorious Revolution of
     1688.

687 Lons, Hermann. Harm Wulf. Trans. from the German.
        Minton, 1931. y.
     The saga of a peasant leader who tries to protect his people

from marauding soldiers and cavalry of both sides during the seventeenth-century conflict in Germany known as the Thirty Years War.

688 McChesney, Dora. Cornet Strong of Ireton's House. Lane, 1903. y.
Follows the English Civil War from the Battle of Marston Moor to the fall of Bristol.

689 _____. Miriam Cromwell. Blackwoods, 1897. y.
Follows the English Civil War from the Battle of Edgehill to the decisive fight at Naseby.

690 MacDonald, George. St. George and St. Michael. Munro, 1875. y.
A story of the English Civil War, featuring the fights at Raglan Castle and Newbury.

691 MacDonald, Ronald. My Sword for Patrick Sarsfield. Gill (Dublin), 1907. y.
General Sarsfield's exploits during the 1688-1691 English campaign in Ireland, with special attention to the siege of Limerick.

692 _____. The Sword of the King. Century, 1900. y.
William of Orange and the Glorious Revolution of 1688.

693 McDonnell, Randal. When Cromwell Came to Drogheda. Gill (Dublin), 1906. y.
Cromwell's subjugation of Ireland, 1648-1649.

694 Macken, Walter. Seek the Fair Land. Macmillan, 1959. y.
Cromwell's invasion of Ireland.

Maclaren, Ian, pseud. See Watson, John.

695 McManus, Miss L. In Sarsfield's Days. Gill (Dublin), 1906. y.
General Patrick Sarsfield and the 1690 siege of Limerick.

696 _____. The Wager. Buckles, 1906. y.
The 1690 siege of Limerick and Sarsfield's midnight cavalry action.

697 Mally, Emma L. Tides of Dawn. Sloane, 1949. y.
Pictures the 1574 liberation of Leyden, Netherlands, from the Spanish.

698 Mann, Henry. Young Henry of Navarre. Trans. from the German. Knopf, 1937. y.
The military and political career of Navarre to 1589 when he became King Henry IV of France.

699 Marriott-Watson, H. B. Captain Fortune. Methuen, 1904. y.
     Focuses on the Cornish Rising of 1643.

700 Marshall, Beatrice. An Old London Nosegay. Seeley, 1903.
     y.
     London and Oxford during the first year of the English Civil
     War, 1642.

701 _____. The Siege of York. Seeley, 1902. y.
     Fairfax in the English Civil War, 1642.

702 Marshall, Rosamund. None but the Brave. Houghton Mifflin,
     1942. y.
     Recreates the Spanish siege of the Dutch in Leyden, 1574-
     1575.

703 Masefield, John. Martin Hyde. Wells Gardner, 1910. y.
     A young man serves the Duke of Monmouth during the lat-
     ter's English rebellion.

704 Mills, J. M. A. The Way Triumphant. Hutchinson, 1926. y.
     Royalists under Montrose fight Cromwell's Protectorate from
     the Scottish highlands.

705 Molander, Harald. The Fortune Hunter. Heinemann, 1905.
     y.
     Recreates the siege of Magdeburg during the Thirty Years
     War.

706 Morley, Iris. We Stood for Freedom. Morrow, 1942. y.
     Monmouth's rebellion against King James II.

707 Neill, Robert. Traitor's Moon. Doubleday, 1952. y.
     The Titus Oates uprising against English king Charles II.

708 Nicholls, William J. The Daughters of Suffolk. Lippincott,
     1910. y.
     Lady Jane Grey and Wyatt's rebellion in the sixteenth cen-
     tury.

709 O'Grady, Standish. Ulrich the Ready. Downey, 1896. y.
     Recreates the 1602 Battle of Kinsale in Ireland.

     Oliver, Jane, pseud. See Rees, Helen C. E.

710 Orczy, Emmuska. The First Sir Percy: An Adventure of the
     Laughing Cavalier. Doran, 1921. y.
     Sir Percy Blakeney fights for the Dutch during their revolt
     against Spain.

711 _____. Flower o' the Lily. Doran, 1919. y.
     The Duke of Parma besieges Cambrai in 1581.

712 Paterson, A. Cromwell's Own. Harper, 1899. y.
     Roundhead forces in the 1642 Battle of Marston Moor.

713 Pauli, Hertha. The Two Trumpeters of Vienna. Doubleday,
     1961. y.
     Recreates the 1683 Turkish invasion of Austria and the siege
     of Vienna.

714 Pick, John B. Last Valley. Little, Brown, 1960. y.
     Vogel the Wanderer persuades a band of mercenaries to
     spare a rich German valley village during the Thirty Years
     War.

715 Pickering, Edgar. True to the Watchword. Warne, 1903. y.
     William of Orange's forces and the 1689 siege of Derry in
     Ireland.

     Plaidy, Jean, pseud. See Hibbert, Eleanor.

716 Polland, Madeline. Shattered Summer. Doubleday, 1969. y.
     An English girl is drawn into Monmouth's rebellion of 1685.

717 Price, Anthony. War Game. Doubleday, 1977. y.
     Although this is a spy story of the twentieth century, it is
     entered here for its extensive information on the English
     Civil War, especially the storming of Standingham Castle.

718 Pugh, John J. Captain of the Medici. Little, Brown, 1954.
     y.
     Pietro Lucca rises to become an officer in the Bande Nere
     of sixteenth-century Florence.

719 Purtscher, Nora. Woman Astride. Appleton, 1934. y.
     Tale of a woman warrior during the Thirty Years War in
     Germany.

720 Quiller-Couch, Arthur T. Splendid Spur. Doubleday, 1889. y.
     Adventures of an Army courier during the English Civil War,
     1642-1643.

721 Ramsden, Lewis. Red Cavalier. Sisleys, 1907. y.
     Exploits of a horseman with Monmouth during the revolt of
     1685.

722 Rees, Helen C. E. Sunset at Noon. By Jane Oliver, pseud.
     Putnam, 1963. y.
     Scottish king James IV invades England only to be killed by
     the troops of Henry VIII in the 1513 Battle of Flodden Field.

723 Rhoscomyl, Owen. Battlement and Tower. Longmans, 1876.
     y.
     Recreates the 1645 Battle of Naseby during the English
     Civil War.

724   Rhys, Grace.   The Charming of Estercel.   Dutton, 1913.   y.
      Lord Essex's attempt to put down a revolt in Ireland late in
      the sixteenth century.

725   Ritchie, Rita.   The Enemy at the Gate.   Dutton, 1959.   y.
      Gunsmith's apprentice Michael devises a plan to halt the
      Turkish tunneling under the walls of Vienna in 1529.

726   Roberts, Margaret.   In the Olden Time.   Holt, 1882.   y.
      The sixteenth-century Peasants' War in Germany.

727   Rougier, G. R.   Royal Escape.   By Georgette Heyer, pseud.
          Doubleday, 1939.   y.
      The flight and pursuit of English King Charles II from Wor-
      cester.

728   Runkle, Bertha.   Helmet of Navarre.   Century, 1901.   y.
      A young soldier follows Henry of Navarre as the Protestant
      leader entered Paris.

729   Sabatini, Rafael.   Anthony Wilding.   Putnam, 1910.   y.
      A tale of adventure, sword-fighting, derring-do, and mili-
      tary operations during Monmouth's rebellion of 1685.

730   _____.   Bardelys the Magnificent.   E. Nash, 1906.   y.
      Recreates the Orleanish Revolt in France in 1632.

731   _____.   Hounds of God.   Houghton Mifflin, 1928.   y.
      An English soldier of fortune rescues an English lady from
      the Spanish Inquisition in the days of Queen Elizabeth I.

732   _____.   Mistress Wilding.   Houghton Mifflin, 1924.   Rpr.
          1976.   y.
      Another tale of adventure and derring-do during Monmouth's
      rebellion.

733   _____.   The Sword of Islam.   Houghton Mifflin, 1939.   y.
      Genoa's relations with the Turks, 1527-1580.

734   Scott, Walter.   The Legend of Montross.   Lovell, 1885.   y.
      Royalists in Scotland oppose Cromwell's Protectorate.

735   Sienkiewicz, Henryk.   The Deluge.   Trans. from the Polish.
          2 vols.   Little, 1890.   y.
      Recreates the Swedish-Polish conflict of 1665.

736   _____.   On the Field of Glory.   Trans. from the Polish.
          Little, 1906.   y.
      King John Sobieski of Poland opposes the Turkish invasion
      of 1672-1673.

737   _____.   With Fire and Sword.   Trans. from the Polish.
          Little, 1890.   y.
      Cossacks rebel along the Dneiper in the seventeenth century.

738 Sinclair, Kathleen. The Valiant Lady. By Brigid Knight,
    pseud. Doubleday, 1948. y.
    Focuses on the sixteenth-century revolt of the Netherlands
    against Spain.

739 Speas, Jan C. Bride of the Machugh. Bobbs-Merrill, 1954.
    y.
    A seventeenth-century Scottish clan refuses to submit to
    James VI.

740 _____. My Lord Monleigh. Bobbs-Merrill, 1956. y.
    The adventures of the outlawed Simon, Earl of Monleigh, in
    Scotland at the time of Cromwell's Protectorate.

741 Stephens, Eve. Charles the King. By Evelyn Anthony, pseud.
    Doubleday, 1963. Rpr. 1976. y.
    The military and political problems of Charles I during the
    English Civil War.

742 Stephens, R. N. An Enemy to the King. L. C. Page, 1897.
    y.
    The role of Henry of Guise in the sixteenth-century French
    Huguenot wars.

743 Stevenson, John P. Captain General. Doubleday, 1956. y.
    Duke Alva of Spain is sent to Holland by King Philip II to
    stamp out the English-supported Protestant Revolt.

744 Stevenson, Philip L. The Black Cuirassier. Hurst & Blackett,
    1906. y.
    General Pappenheim's Cuirassiers in the Thirty Years War
    in seventeenth-century Germany.

745 _____. The Rose of Dauphiny. Stanley Paul, 1909. y.
    The role of Henry of Navarre in the French religious wars
    of the sixteenth century.

746 Strain, E. H. A Man's Foes. Ward, Lock, 1895. y.
    Recreates the 1689 English siege of Derry in Ireland.

747 Stuart, Henry L. The Weeping Cross. Regnery, 1954. y.
    Combat in Germany during the Thirty Years War, 1618-
    1648.

748 Surry, George. Mid Clash of Swords. Hodder & Stoughton,
    1908. y.
    Pictures the 1527 sack of Rome.

749 Sutcliff, Rosemary. Rider on a White Horse. Coward-
    McCann, 1959. y.
    In 1642 Sir Thomas Fairfax and his family join the Round-
    heads in the Civil War against the Cavaliers of King
    Charles I.

750 _____ . Simon. Oxford University Press, 1953. y.
     Includes a look at the English Civil War battle of Torring-
     ton.

751 Sutcliffe, Halliwell. The Crimson Field. Ward, Lock, 1916.
     y.
     The English versus the Scots in the 1513 Battle of Flodden
     Field.

752 _____ . The White Horses. Ward, Lock, 1915. y.
     A tale of Royalist cavalry in the English Civil War.

753 Taylor, Irene S. True Gold. Marshall Bros., 1910. y.
     Follows the exploits of a captain in Cromwell's Horse, 1642-
     1645.

754 Thompson, E. Perronet. A Dragon's Wife. Greening, 1907.
     y.
     French efforts to subdue the Huguenots near Fontevrault,
     1685-1687.

755 Trease, Geoffrey. Trumpets in the West. Harcourt, 1947.
     y.
     Monmouth's rebellion.

756 Vansittart, Peter. The Siege. Walker, 1962. y.
     Catholics and Anabaptists battle for Munster, Germany, in
     the 1530's.

757 Vaughan, Owen. Sweet Rogues. Duckworth, 1907. y.
     Follows the adventures of one of Prince Rupert's captains
     on the Welsh border in 1645.

758 Walsh, Maurice. Blackcock's Feather. Grosset, 1934. y.
     The English campaigns in Ireland, 1565-1579.

759 _____ . The Dark Rose. Stokes, 1938. y.
     Martin Somers fights with Montrose's Irish and Highland
     troops in the Scottish revolt against the Covenanters, 1644-
     1645.

760 Waltari, Mika. The Adventurer. Putnam, 1950. y.
     A soldier's exploits during the Thirty Years War.

761 Watson, H. B. Marriott. The Rebel. Harper, 1900. y.
     The Duke of Monmouth and the 1684 rising at Taunton.

762 Watson, John. Graham of Claverhouse. By Ian Maclaren,
     pseud. J. Murray, 1908. y.
     John Graham's Scottish exploits, 1684-1689, ending with
     the Battle of Killiecrankie.

    Welch, Ronald, pseud. See Felton, Ronald O.

763 Westcott, Jan. The Hepburn. Crown, 1950. y.
Border warfare between Scotland and England, ending with
the 1513 Battle of Flodden Field.

764 Weyman, Stanley J. The Long Night. McClure, 1903. y.
Recreates the 1602 attack on Geneva by the Savoyards.

765 Whislaw, Frederick J. Mazeppa. Chatto & Windus, 1902. y.
Examines the warfare among the Cossacks in the seventeenth
century.

766 White, Leslie T. Highland Hawk. Crown, 1952. y.
Scottish guerrilla warfare against Cromwell's attempt to win
Scotland for Parliament.

767 Wilkinson, Burke. The Helmet of Navarre. Macmillan, 1965.
y.
A biographical novel about Henry of Navarre (later Henry
IV) and the French-Huguenot wars of the late 1500's.

768 Williams, Jay. The Sword and the Scythe. Oxford University
Press, 1947. y.
Combat during the Peasants' War in Germany, 1524-1535.

769 Wohl, Burton. Soldier of Fortune. Putnam, 1977. y.
An English youth becomes a captain fighting in the eastern
European wars against the Turks in the sixteenth century.

Wycliffe, John, pseud. See Bedford-Jones, Henry.

Wynne, May, pseud. See Knowles, Mabel W.

770 Zara, Louis. Against This Rock. Creative Age, 1943. y.
Follows the sixteenth-century wars of Holy Roman Emperor
Charles V against the French and Italians.

EUROPE: 1700 TO 1800

The tales in this section cover military events in Europe and the
Mediterranean from the time of Marlborough's premier victories into the time of Napoleon Bonaparte. Despite the almost unending
conflict between the various European powers throughout this century, the majority of the campaigns are not well covered. Fiction
writers have seized upon the romantic and underdog aspects of the
1745 Jacobite rising in Scotland as their first and easiest subject
around which to build stories. Readers will find references to
British activities in India and Napoleon's campaign in Egypt in our
section on Africa, Asia, and the Pacific: 1600-1800.

771 Adams, H. C. In the Fifteen. Hodder & Stoughton, 1893. y.
     Recreates the Scottish uprising of 1715.

     Anthony, Evelyn, pseud. See Stephens, Eve.

772 Austin, Frederick B. The Road to Glory. Stokes, 1935. y.
     Focuses on Napoleon's 1796-1797 Italian campaign.

773 Bailey, H. C. The God of Clay. Brentano, 1908. y.
     Traces the military and political career of Bonaparte from
     1785, when he became a lieutenant of French artillery, to
     1799 when he became First Consul.

774 Balfour, Andrew. To Arms! Page, 1898. y.
     A medical student becomes involved in the Scottish uprising
     of 1715.

775 Barker, John and Patricia. The Royal Dirk. Morrow, 1966.
        y.
     In 1745 Charles Edward Stuart, the "Young Pretender," who
     is better known as "Bonnie Prince Charlie," arrives in
     Scotland, where a few Scottish lords and clans join him in
     an unsuccessful Jacobite rebellion. After some initial suc-
     cess, Stuart and his followers were routed by English troops
     in the April 16, 1746 Battle of Culloden. This tale con-
     cerns a Scottish boy's efforts to help his prince escape af-
     ter that fight, a flight that proved successful.

776 Belloc, Hilaire. The Girondin. Nelson, 1911. y.
     An adventurer is pressed into the army of Revolutionary
     France.

777 Bennett, Louie. A Prisoner of His Word. Maunsel (Dublin),
        1908. y.
     An Englishman joins the United Irishmen in their ill-fated
     rebellion of 1798, which might have been more successful
     if promised French aid had been delivered.

778 Blake, Bass. A Lady's Honour. Appleton, 1902. y.
     John Churchill, first Duke of Marlborough, defeats the
     French in the 1704 Battle of Blenheim.

779 Bodkin, M. McDonnell. The Rebels. Ward, Lock, 1899. y.
     Pictures the Irish revolt of 1798.

     Bowen, Marjorie, pseud. See Long, Gabrielle C.

780 Braine, Sheila E. The King's "Blue Boys." Jarrold, 1902.
        y.
     King Frederick II of Prussia and his giant Grenadiers defeat
     the French in pitched battles during the Seven Years War,
     1756-1763.

781   Broster, Dorothy K.   The Dark Mile.   Coward-McCann, 1934.
      y.

782   _____.   The Flight of the Heron.   Dodd, Mead, 1926.   y.

783   _____.   The Gleam in the North.   Coward-McCann, 1931.
      y.
      Three tales describing the 1745 Jacobite rising in Scotland,
      from the landing of the "Young Pretender" to his escape af-
      ter the Battle of Culloden.

      Bryher, Winifred, pseud.   See MacPherson, Annie W.

784   Burgess, Anthony.   Napoleon Symphony.   Knopf, 1974.   y.
      Contrasts Napoleon's Italian victories to the moods of
      Beethoven's Eroica symphony.

785   Burton, John Bloundelle.   Across the Salt Seas.   Methuen,
      1898.   y.
      Marlborough wins the 1704 Battle of Blenheim.

786   _____.   The Right Hand.   Everett, 1911.   y.
      Recreates the Battle of Dettingen during the French Revo-
      lutionary days of the 1790's.

787   _____.   The Scourge of God.   Appleton, 1898.   y.
      Jean Cavalier in the eighteenth-century Cevennes Revolt.

788   _____.   The Sword of Gideon.   Cassell, 1905.   y.
      Austria, England, and Holland are allied against France in
      1702 in the War of Spanish Succession; Prince Eugene and
      Marlborough succeed in driving French forces out of Ger-
      many (1704), Italy (1706), and the Netherlands (1706-1708).

789   _____.   The Last of Her Race.   J. Milne, 1908.   y.
      Peterborough's victories over the French in Spain, 1705-
      1706.

790   Campbell, Grace M.   Torbeg.   Duell, 1953.   y.
      With 5000 loyal Scots, Bonnie Prince Charlie attempts to
      regain the English throne in 1745.

791   Carmichael, Miss E. M.   The House of Delusion.   Melrose,
      1925.   y.
      Lord Lovat and the Jacobite uprising of 1745 in Scotland.

792   Cordell, Alexander.   The Healing Blade.   Viking, 1971.   y.

793   _____.   The White Cockade.   Viking, 1970.   y.

794   _____.   Witche's Sabbath.   Viking, 1970.   y.
      A trilogy concerning Lord Edward Fitzgerald and Wolfe
      Tone, the Society of United Irishmen, and the 1798 rebel-
      lion against Britain.

795 Crosbie, W. J. David Maxwell. Jarrold, 1902. y.
     Presents a Loyalist's view of the Irish rebellion of '98.

796 Daly, Robert W. Soldier of the Sea. Morrow, 1942. y.
     Lieutenant Peter leads his Royal Marines into combat during
     the early stages of England's war with Napoleon.

797 Defoe, Daniel. Memoirs of an English Officer and Other Sto-
         ries. 1728.
     Contents. --Memoirs of a Military Officer (The Military
     Memoirs of Captain George Carleton). --The History of the
     Remarkable Life of John Sheppard. --The Memoirs of Major
     Alexander Ramkins, a Highland Officer.

798 De La Torre, Lillian. White Rose of Stuart. Nelson, 1954.
         y.
     Bonnie Prince Charlie and the "Rising of '45. "

799 Dill, Bessie. The Silver Glen. Digby, Long, 1909. y.
     Bonnie Prince Charlie and the "Rising of '45. "

800 Duke, Winifred. Heir to Kings. Stokes, 1926. y.
     A sympathetic view of Bonnie Prince Charlie's problems in
     Scotland.

801 _____. Scotland's Heir. Chambers, 1925. y.
     Bonnie Prince Charlie.

802 Dundas, Norman. Castle Adamant. Murray, 1927. y.
     Exploits of a Jacobie Scots lord during the "Rising of '45. "

803 Eccott, W. J. The Heart of Hutton. Blackwoods, 1906. y.
     The Jacobite march to Derby and back during the 1745 up-
     rising, ending with the Battle of Falkirk.

     Edwards, Samuel, pseud. See Gerson, Noel B.

804 Fenton, Ronald O. Captain of the Dragoons. By Ronald
         Welch, pseud. Oxford University Press, 1957. y.
     A young English cavalry officer is involved with Marlborough
     in the War of the Spanish Succession.

805 Findlay, J. T. A Deal with the King. Digby, Long, 1901. y.
     James Stuart, the "Old Pretender, " leads the Jacobite up-
     rising in Scotland in 1715 in protest of the 1707 Scottish
     union with England.

806 Forbes, Eveline L. Loroux. Greening, 1908. y.
     Follows the career of a French Republican soldier from the
     noncommissioned ranks to his promotion as a general.

807 Forster, R. H. Strained Allegiance. Long, 1905. y.
     English and loyal Scottish troops put down the "Rising of
     '15. "

808 Gartner, Chloe. The Woman from the Glen. Morrow, 1973.
     y.
     Two twins join Bonnie Prince Charlie in the 1745 Rebellion.

     Gerard, Maurice, pseud. See Teague, J. J.

809 Gerson, Noel B. Mohawk Ladder. Doubleday, 1951. y.
     A small band of American colonials skilled in Indian fighting
     join the Duke of Marlborough's campaigns against the troops
     of Louis XIV.

810 _____. The Scimitar. By Samuel Edwards, pseud. Far-
     rar, Straus, 1955. y.
     An English soldier of fortune aids Prince Eugene of Savoy
     to defeat the Turks at Belgrade.

811 Gibbs, Willa. Tell Your Sons. Farrar, Straus, 1946. y.
     Lieutenant Paul d'Aunay's fortunes in love and war as he
     follows Napoleon.

812 Gogarty, Oliver St. J. Mad Grandeur. Lippincott, 1941. y.
     Recreates the United Irish revolt of 1798.

813 Gough, George W. Yeoman Adventurer. Putnam, 1917. y.
     A Stratfordshire farmer becomes a soldier under Bonnie
     Prince Charlie in the "Rising of '45. "

814 Grant, James. The Adventures of Rob Roy. O. S. Felt, 1865.
     y.
     The military exploits of Robert Macgregor, called Rob Roy,
     to 1734.

815 _____. Second to None. Dutton, 1864. y.
     The Duke of Cumberland's military exploits in Hanover.

816 Gras, Felix. Reds of the Midi. Trans. from the French.
     Appleton, 1896. y.
     The Marseilles Battalion marches on Paris during the French
     Revolution.

817 _____. The White Terror. Trans. from the French. Ap-
     pleton, 1899. y.
     Pictures the French Revolutionary battles of Valmy and
     Jemappes and the rise of Napoleon through his victory at
     Marengo, June 14, 1800.

818 Green, E. Everett. The Defence of the Rock. Nelson, 1907.
     y.
     The Franco-Spanish siege of English-held Gibraltar, 1779-
     1783.

819 _____. Fallen Fortunes. Nelson, 1903. y.
     The Duke of Marlborough blunts French expansion in the
     1706 Battle of Ramillies.

820 _____. A Hero of the Highlands. Nelson, 1903. y.
Bonnie Prince Charlie loses the Battle of Culloden.

821 Griffiths, Arthur. Thrice Captive. F. V. White, 1908. y.
Peterborough's actions at Barcelona, Montjuich, and Alman-
sa in Spain, 1705-1706.

822 Hardwick, Mollie. Charlie Is My Darling. Coward-McCann,
1977. y.
A sympathetic view of the aims of Bonnie Prince Charlie.

823 Henry, George A. The Coronet of the Horse. Scribner's,
1881. y.
The military exploits of the Duke of Marlborough in the War
of the Spanish Succession.

824 _____. Held Fast for England. Scribner's, 1892. y.
The siege of Gibraltar, 1779-1783.

825 _____. In the Irish Brigade. Scribner's, 1901. y.
Irish soldiers fight with Prince Eugene in Italy, 1706.

826 _____. With Frederick the Great. Scribner's, 1898. y.
The Prussian military genius, though vastly outnumbered,
defeats the French during the Seven Years War.

827 Hinkson, Henry A. Up for the Green. Lawrence & Bullen,
1898. y.
Focuses on the Irish revolt of 1798.

828 Innes, Norman. The Lonely Guard. Jacobs, 1908. y.
Adventures of a Scot in Bavaria during the 1740-1748 War
of Austrian Succession.

829 _____. The Surge of War. E. Nash, 1906. y.
Focuses on the military victories of Frederick the Great in
the Seven Years War.

830 Jacob, Violet. Flemington. Murray, 1911. y.
A tale of the Jacobite Rebellion of 1745 in Scotland.

831 Johnston, Mary. The Laird of Glenfernie. Harper, 1919. y.
Scottish lords aid Bonnie Prince Charlie.

832 Keddie, Henrietta. The Macdonald Lass. By Sarah Tytler,
pseud. Chatto & Windus, 1895. y.
The role of Flora MacDonald in the rescue and escape of
Bonnie Prince Charlie after the Battle of Culloden in 1746.

833 Knowles, Mabel W. Foes of Freedom. By May Wynn, pseud.
Chapman & Hall, 1916. y.
Recreates the revolt of the Belgian provinces against the
rule of the Austrian emperor Joseph II.

834 _____ . The King of a Day. By May Wynn, pseud. Jar-
       rolds, 1918. y.
       King Stanislaus I of Poland is driven from his country in
       1734 by a Russian invasion that places Augustus III of Saxony
       on the throne and brings on the brief War of Polish Succes-
       sion.

835 _____ . The Red Fleur-De-Lys. By May Wynn, pseud.
       Chapman & Hall, 1911. y.
       French aristocrats oppose the revolutionaries in 1791.

836 Lederer, Charlotte. The Eagle's Quest. Doubleday, 1939. y.
       György Rákóczy leads a Hungarian revolt against Austria.

837 Linklater, Eric. The Prince in the Heather. Harcourt, 1965.
       y.
       A day-by-day account of Bonnie Prince Charlie's escape af-
       ter the Battle of Culloden to August 1746.

838 Long, Gabrielle C. Kings-at-Arms. By Marjorie Bowen,
       pseud. Dutton, 1919. y.
       Charles XII of Sweden versus Peter the Great of Russia,
       1700-1721.

   McAuley, Allan, pseud. See Stewart, Charlotte.

839 McIlwraith, Jean. The Curious Career of Roderick Campbell.
       Constable, 1901. y.
       Tale of a Scotsman in the "Rising of '45."

840 MacKaye, D. L. Silver Disk. Longmans, Green, 1955. y.
       The exploits of Frederick II of Prussia.

841 McKown, Robin. The Ordeal of Anne Devlin. Messner, 1963.
       y.
       A courageous young woman's involvement in the Irish revolt
       of 1798.

842 McManus, L. Lally of the Brigade. L. C. Page, 1899. y.
       A young man serves with the Irish Brigade fighting with
       Prince Eugene of Savoy in Italy during the War of the Span-
       ish Succession.

843 MacPherson, Annie W. The Colors of Vaud. By Winifred
       Bryher, pseud. Harcourt, 1969. y.
       Focuses on the liberation of the Swiss canton of Vaud during
       the days of the French Revolution.

844 Macquoid, Katherine S. Captain Dallington. Arrowsmith, 1907.
       y.
       A highwayman helps the Duke of Marlborough against the
       French.

845 Marshall, Emma. <u>An Escape from the Tower</u>. Seeley, 1896.
     y.
     A story of the "Rising of '15. "

846 Milne, James. <u>The Black Colonel</u>. Lane, 1921. y.
     Adventures of a Scottish Jacobite during and after the "Ris-
     ing of '45. "

847 Muddock, J. E. <u>For the White Cockade</u>. J. Long, 1906. y.
     The role of Simon Fraser, Lord Lovat, in the 1745 Rebel-
     lion.

848 Murphy, James. <u>The Shan Van Vocht</u>. Gill (Dublin), 1883.
     y.
     Minor French aid to the United Irish in the rebellion of
     1798.

849 Murray, David L. <u>Commander of the Mists</u>. Knopf, 1938. y.
     Charles Edward Stuart and the gallant Highlanders who tried
     to help him in 1745.

     Oliver, Jane, pseud. <u>See</u> Rees, Helen C. E.

850 Parker, Gilbert. <u>The Battle of the Strong</u>. Harper, 1898. y.
     French revolutionary troops invade Jersey.

851 _____. <u>No Defence</u>. Lippincott, 1920. y.
     Minimum French aid to the Irish in 1798.

852 Pease, Howard. <u>The Burning Cresset</u>. Constable, 1908. y.
     The exploits of the Earl of Derwentwater during the "Rising
     of '45. "

853 Peck, Theodore. <u>The Sword of Dundee</u>. Duffield, 1908. y.
     Scottish warriors try to aid Bonnie Prince Charlie.

854 Pemberton, Max. <u>Beatrice of Venice</u>. Dodd, Mead, 1904. y.

855 _____. <u>Paulina</u>. Cassell, 1922. y.
     A pair of stories focusing on Napoleon's Italian campaign.

856 Pender, Mrs. M. T. <u>The Green Cockade</u>. Downey, 1898. y.
     The United Irish and the rebellion of 1798.

857 Pickering, Edgar. <u>King for a Summer</u>. Hutchinson, 1896. y.
     Portrays the 1735 revolt on Corsica.

858 Preddy, George. <u>General Crack</u>. Dodd, Mead, 1928. y.
     A mercenary fights to put Leopold, Elector of Bavaria, on
     the Imperial throne of Austria.

859 Pushkin, Alexander. <u>The Captain's Daughter</u>. Trans. from
     the Russian. Viking, 1928. Rpr. 1961.

First published in 1836, this account tells of the 1773-1774 rebellion against Catherine the Great by Pugachev the Pretender and his peasant followers.

860 Raine, William M. For Love and Hanover. Isbister, 1904. y.
An Englishman's adventures during the "Rising of '45."

861 Rees, Helen C. E. Candleshine No More. By Jane Oliver, pseud. Putnam, 1967. y.
Bonnie Prince Charlie attempts to recover the English throne from the Hanoverians in 1745.

862 Salmon, Geraldine G. Corsican Justice. By J. G. Sarasin, pseud. Doubleday, Doran, 1927. y.
Gaston de Saulx, no friend of Napoleon, accepts the Consul's soldiers to help him track down the Italian brigand Mazzarda.

Sarasin, J. G., pseud. See Salmon, Geraldine G.

863 Scalzo, John R. A Prince, a Piper, and a Rose. McKay, 1976. y.
Focuses on a Highland piper in the service of Bonnie Prince Charlie.

864 Scott, Walter. Rob Roy. Dutton, 1931. Rpr. 1973. y.
Recalls the adventures of Robert Macgregor in Scotland during the early years of the century; first published in 1817.

865 _____. Waverly. Dutton, 1929. Rpr. 1976. y.
Love and conflict during the "Rising of '45"; first published in the 1820's.

866 Seaton, Paul. For Love and Loyalty. Simpkin, 1905. y.
Prince Charles Edward loses the 1746 Battle of Culloden.

867 Seawell, Molly E. The Rock of the Lion. Harper, 1899. y.
The British defense of Gibraltar, 1779-1783.

868 Sheehan, Vincent. A Day of Battle. Doubleday, 1938. y.
The Anglo-French battle at the Flanders village of Fontenoy, May 11, 1745, in the War of Austrian Succession.

869 _____. Sanfelice. Doubleday, 1936. y.
Pictures the unsuccessful 1799 rebellion in Naples.

870 Sheehy-Sheffington, Francis. In Dark and Evil Days. Duffy (Dublin), 1919. y.
The United Irish attempt to rebel against Britain in 1798.

871 Smith, Arthur D. H. Claymore. Sheffington, 1918. y.
Bonnie Prince Charlie at Derby and Culloden.

872 Stephens, Eve. Clandara. By Evelyn Anthony, pseud. Double-
        day, 1964. y.
        Charles Edward Stuart returns to Scotland in 1745 and calls
        on the clans for help.

873 Stevenson, Philip L. A Gendarme of the King. Hurst & Black-
        ett, 1905. y.
        A Prussian soldier recalls the genius of Frederick the Great
        in the Seven Years War.

874 Stevenson, Robert Louis. Kidnapped. Scribner's, 1886. Rpr.
        1971. y.
        David Balfour, a Lowlander and a Whig, becomes involved
        with the "Rising of '45. "

875 _____. The Master of Ballantrae. Scribner's, 1889. Rpr.
        1972. y.
        A faithful steward recalls the downfall of a noble Scottish
        family involved in Bonnie Prince Charlie's 1745 Rebellion.

876 Stewart, Charlotte. Poor Sons of a Day. By Allan McAulay,
        pseud. Nisbet, 1902. y.
        The problems of Highlanders who supported Charles Edward.

877 Strang, Herbert. The Adventures of Harry Rochester. Put-
        nam, 1906. y.
        Marlborough and the 1704 Battle of Blenheim.

878 _____. With Marlborough to Malplaquet. Hodder & Stough-
        ton, 1910. y.
        The Duke's battles in the War of the Spanish Succession,
        with special focus on Blenheim and Malplaquet.

879 Sutcliffe, Halliwell. The Lone Adventure. Doubleday, Doran,
        1911. y.
        Bonnie Prince Charlie and the "Rising of '45. "

880 _____. Under the White Cockade. Cassell, 1902. y.
        A Jacobite's adventures in the 1745 Scottish Rebellion.

881 Tarbet, W. G. A Loyal Maid. Arrowsmith, 1908. y.
        A girl becomes involved with Bonnie Prince Charlie and the
        "Rising of '45. "

882 Teague, J. J. Rose of Blenheim. By Maurice Gerard, pseud.
        Hodder & Stoughton, 1907. y.
        John Churchill, Duke of Marlborough, campaigns in 1704,
        winning his most famous battle, that at Blenheim.

883 Vaughan, C. A. The Charlatan. Doubleday, 1959. y.
        A tale of the 1701-1714 War of Spanish Succession.

884 Von Heidenstram, Verner. The Charles Men. Trans. from

the Swedish. 2 vols. American Scandanavian Founda-
tion, 1920. y.
The military exploits and defeats of King Charles XII of
Sweden in the war with Peter the Great of Russia.

885 Watson, Sally. Highland Rebel. Holt, 1954. y.
Scots attempt to put Charles Stuart on the English throne in
1745.

Welch, Ronald, pseud. See Fenton, Ronald O.

886 Wheelwright, Jere H. Draw Near to Battle. Scribner's, 1953.
y.
An American serves in the French Army under Napoleon.

887 Wright, Constance. A Chance for Glory. Holt, 1957. y.
Pictures the rescue of Lafayette from prison at Olmutz in
1794.

Wynn, May, pseud. See Knowles, Mabel W.

EUROPE: 1800 TO 1900

The tales in this section cover military operations throughout the
nineteenth century. Here one will find stories about Napoleon's losing battle at Waterloo, the charge of the Light Brigade in the Crimean War, the struggles for Italian and German unification, Germany's
quick victories in the Franco-Prussian War, and various struggles
marking unrest in a number of countries. Such events as the British
wars in India will be found in our section on Africa, Asia, and the
Pacific, 1800-1900.

888 Alcock, Deborah. The Czar. Nelson, 1882. y.
Alexander I and Napoleon's war, 1806-1815.

Aldanov, M. A., pseud. See Landau, Mark A.

889 Alington, Argentine F. Gentlemen--The Regiment! By Hugh
Talbot, pseud. Dent, 1934. y.
Two families bound up in the honor and glory of two British
regiments find their sons in combat in the Crimean War.

890 Aminoff, Constance L. C. Retreat! Dutton, 1938. y.
Napoleon's army must withdraw from Moscow in 1812, its
Russian campaign a costly failure.

Anthony, Evelyn, pseud. See Stephens, Eve.

891   Aragon, Louis. <u>Holy Week.</u> Putnam, 1961. y.
      On Palm Sunday, 1815, Napoleon began his 100 Days Cam-
      paign, which ended in the Battle of Waterloo.

892   Armstrong, Thomas. <u>The Ring Has No End.</u> Sloane, 1958.
      y.
      A tale of the Crimean War.

893   Avery, Harold. <u>Firelock and Steel.</u> Nelson, 1907. y.
      Sir John Moore's campaign in Spain, ending with the affair
      at Corunna in 1809.

894   _____. <u>With Wellington at Waterloo.</u> Wells Gardner, 1901.
      y.
      Focuses on the English army, June 14-18, 1815, and Wel-
      lington's great victory over Napoleon.

895   Bailey, H. C. <u>The Pillar of Fire.</u> Methuen, 1918. y.
      Follows Garibaldi and the Italian liberation movement.

896   _____. <u>The Rebel.</u> Methuen, 1923. y.
      Garibaldi is defeated at Mentana.

897   _____. <u>The Young Lovers.</u> Methuen, 1918. y.
      Love and warfare in Spain's Peninsular War.

898   Barry, William. <u>The Dayspring.</u> Fisher, Unwin, 1903. y.
      Action in the Franco-Prussian War of 1870.

899   Bartos-Hoppner, B. <u>Storm Over the Caucasus.</u> Walck, 1968.
      y.
      Moslem leader Iman Shamyl defends the Caucasus against
      Russian invasion.

900   Benson, Edward F. <u>The Capsina.</u> Harper, 1899. y.

901   _____. <u>The Vintage.</u> Harper, 1898. y.
      Two tales, told from the Christian viewpoint, about the bat-
      tles and sieges of the Greek War of Independence in the
      1820's.

902   Bloem, Walter. <u>The Iron Year.</u> Trans. from the German.
      Lane, 1914. y.
      A pro-Prussian view of the victories of Germany over
      France in the 1870 war.

903   Brady, Cyrus T. <u>The Eagle of the Empire.</u> Doran, 1915. y.
      Wellington and his men versus Napoleon's troops at Water-
      loo.

904   _____. <u>The Sword Hand of Napoleon.</u> Dodd, Mead, 1914.
      y.
      The French emperor's disastrous Russian invasion of 1812.

905   Brereton, Frederic S.   A Gallant Grenadier.   Scribner's, 1902.
      y.
      Recreates the Crimean War battles of Sevastopol and Bala-
      clava.

906   _____.   A Hero of Sedan.   Blackie, 1909.   y.
      The Battle of Sedan and the Siege of Paris, 1870-1871.

907   Butler, Suzanne.   Vale of Tyranny.   Little, Brown, 1954.   y.
      Napoleon III and the Franco-Prussian War of 1870-1871.

908   Campbell, A. Gordic.   Fleur-De-Camp.   Chatto & Windus,
            1905.   y.
      One of Napoleon's aides follows his emperor's military ca-
      reer from Austerlitz to Waterloo, 1805-1815.

909   Caprina, Luigi.   Nimble Legs.   Trans. from the Italian.   Long-
            mans, Green, 1927.   y.
      Garibaldi and the unification of Italy.

910   Chambers, Robert W.   Ashes of Empire.   Stokes, 1898.   y.

911   _____.   Lorraine.   Harper, 1898.   y.

912   _____.   The Maids of Paradise.   Harper, 1902.   y.

913   _____.   The Red Republic.   Putnam, 1895.   y.
      Four novels depicting the military, political, and social life
      of France and Germany during the Franco-Prussian War.

      Chatrian, Alexandre, jt. author.   See Erckmann, Emile.

914   Chavadze, Paul.   Mountains of Allah.   Doubleday, 1952.   y.
      A look at the Crimean War from the Russian viewpoint.

915   Conan Doyle, Arthur.   The Adventures of Gerard.   McClure,
            1903.   Rpr. 1971.   y.

916   _____.   The Exploits of Brigadier Gerard.   McClure, 1896.
            Rpr. 1971.   y.

917   _____.   Gerard at Waterloo.   Harper, 1892.   y.
      Three tales about an English soldier in the Napoleonic wars.

918   _____.   The Green Flag and Other Stories of War and
            Sport.   McClure, 1900.   Rpr. 1970.   y.
      A collection of 13 tales, many published earlier in various
      English magazines.

919   Costain, Thomas B.   Ride with Me.   Doubleday, 1944.   Rpr.
            1965.   y.
      A crusading news reporter finds himself drawn into the
      1808-1812 Peninsular War in Spain.

920 Cowper, Edith E. "Viva Christina." Lippincott, 1904. y.
    Carlos I revolts against his brother, Ferdinand the Spanish
    king, in 1833 and through four years of warfare unsuccess-
    fully attempts to seize the throne.

921 Crockett, Samuel R. A Silver Skull. Smith, Elder, 1901. y.
    Englishman Richard Church, acting as a general in the Nea-
    politan service, suppresses the brigands in southern Italy,
    1815-1820.

922 _____. Strong Mac. Dodd, Mead, 1904. y.
    Pictures the Peninsular War in 1812-1813, ending with the
    Battle of Vittoria.

923 Danilevski, Grigovil P. Moscow in Flames. Trans. from the
    Russian. Brentano's, 1917. y.
    A Russian view of Napoleon's unsuccessful 1812 invasion.

924 Daudet, Alphonse. Monday Tales. Trans. from the French.
    Little, Brown, 1927. y.
    Short stories about incidents in the Franco-Prussian War.

925 Deeping, Warwick. The Lame Englishman. Cassell, 1910.
    y.
    Portrays the Roman defense against the French in 1849.

926 DeLaguna, Frederica. The Thousand March. Little, Brown,
    1930. y.
    An American youth serves with Garibaldi in the wars of
    Italian unification.

927 Delderfield, Ronald F. Seven Men of Gascony. Simon &
    Schuster, 1949. Rpr. 1975. y.
    A group of men from Gascony fight with Napoleon in his
    Austrian, Spanish, and Russian campaigns; when captured
    by the British, they begin to disappear--one by one.

928 _____. Too Few for Drums. Simon & Schuster, 1972.
    Rpr. 1974. y.
    During the Napoleonic war in Spain, eight British soldiers
    are trapped inside the French lines; together with their
    young ensign, the men must find a way to the safety of
    Lisbon.

929 Delves-Broughton, Josephine. Officer and Gentleman.
    McGraw-Hill, 1951. y.
    The son of an unsavory English officer is wounded in the
    Crimean War battle of Balaclava.

930 DeVigny, Alfred V. Military Necessity. Trans. from the
    French. Grove, 1953.
    Three tales about the French Army in the last century form
    a timeless commentary on the profession of war.

931 Dicker, Stefan K. Kali. Stackpole, 1961. y.
Looks at the beginnings of the Bulgarian uprising against the
Turks in 1876.

932 Djilas, Milovan. Under the Colors. Trans. from the Serbo-
Croat. Harcourt, 1971. y.
The bloody struggle of the Radah clan, in what is now Yugoslavia, to free itself from Turkish rule in the last quarter
of the century.

933 Drummond, Emma. Scarlet Shadows. Dell, 1978. P.
Problems in love and war of English soldiers during the
Crimean conflict of the 1850's.

934 Dunkerley, William A. Broken Shackles. By John Oxenham,
pseud. Lane, 1915. y.
General Bourbaki's attack on and retreat from the Prussians
in the Franco-Prussian War.

935 _____. The Coil of Carne. By John Oxenham, pseud.
Methuen, 1911. y.
Recreates the Crimean War battles of Alma, Balaclava,
Inkerman, and Sevastopol.

936 _____. Great Heart Gillian. By John Oxenham, pseud.
Hodder & Stoughton, 1909. y.
A tale about the French defeat at Sedan in 1870.

937 _____. John of Gerisau. By John Oxenham, pseud.
Hurst & Blackett, 1902. y.
Tales of the Italian and German wars of the 1860's.

938 _____. Under the Iron Flail. By John Oxenham, pseud.
Cassell, 1902. y.
Pictures the Battle of Metz and the Siege of Paris during
the Franco-Prussian War.

939 Erckmann, Emile, and Alexandre Chatrian. History of a Conscript of 1813. By Erckmann-Chatrian, pseud. Trans.
from the French. Dutton, 1940. y.
Depicts French soldiers in the defeat at Leipzig.

940 _____. Waterloo. By Erckmann-Chatrian, pseud. Trans.
from the French. Dutton, 1940. y.
Depicts the great battle of 1815, which ended Napoleon's
dreams of empire.

Erckmann-Chatrian, pseud. See Erckmann, Emile, and Alexandre Chatrian.

941 Fecher, Constance. The Night of the Wolf. Delacorte, 1974.
Napoleon invades Russia in 1812.

942 Fenton, Ronald O. <u>Captain of Foot.</u> By Ronald Welch, pseud.
      Oxford University Press, 1954. y.
      The adventures of a member of the British Cary family
      fighting under Wellington in the 1808-1812 Peninsular War.

943 Finnemore, John. <u>In the Trenches.</u> Nelson, 1904. y.
      Treats of the Crimean War siege of Sevastopol.

944 Fogazzaro, Antonio. <u>The Patriot.</u> Trans. from the Italian.
      Hodder & Stoughton, 1896. y.
      A sympathetic portrayal of Garibaldi and his 1848-1849
      struggle for a united Italy.

945 Ford, Ford Madox. <u>A Little Less Than Gods.</u> Viking, 1978.
      y.
      Napoleon's 100 Days and the Battle of Waterloo from the
      viewpoint of the coalition of armies out to end the French
      dreams of empire.

946 Foreman, Stephen. <u>The Fen Dogs.</u> Long, 1912. y.
      Two soldiers from the English Fens area participate in the
      Battle of Waterloo.

947 Forester, C. S. <u>Rifleman Dodd and The Gun: Two Novels of
      the Peninsular Campaign.</u> Little, Brown, 1943. y.
      Two short novels by the creator of naval hero Horatio Horn-
      blower; in the first an English soldier, cut off from his
      unit, wages several weeks of individual guerrilla warfare on
      the French; in the second the Spanish partisans employ a
      huge abandoned French siege cannon against French fortifi-
      cations. (Cary Grant and Frank Sinatra played the leads in
      the movie version of the latter title, which had the gun a
      32-pounder from a British warship.)

948 Forester, F. B. <u>Hostage for a Kingdom.</u> Nelson, 1907. y.
      Carlos III enters Spain and wages an unsuccessful civil war
      for the throne, 1973-1876.

949 Fraser, George M. <u>Flashman at the Charge.</u> Knopf, 1973.
      Rpr. 1974.
      Sequel to Flash for Freedom cited in our section on North
      America, 1861-1865; after leading the charge of the Light
      Brigade in the Crimea (quite by mistake!), Flashman is
      captured by the Russians, but turns this adversity to good
      advantage, foiling a Czarist plot against India.

950 _____. <u>Royal Flash.</u> Knopf, 1970. Rpr. 1971.
      Sequel to Flashman, in which our hero is involved in an
      intrigue engineered by Otto von Bismarck to disrupt the
      balance of power in Europe.

951 Gielgud, Val H. <u>White Eagles.</u> Constable, 1929. y.
      Russian forces harry Napoleon's retreat from Moscow.

952 Gilson, Charles. The Spy: A Story of the Peninsular War.
       Hodder & Stoughton, 1910. y.
       Pays particular attention to the 1809 Battle of Talavera and
       the 1812 assault on Badajoz.

953 Giono, Jean. Straw Man. Trans. from the French. Knopf,
       1960. y.
       Hussar colonel Angelo Pardi is involved in the Italian revolt
       against Austria in 1848.

954 Gorman, Herbert S. Brave General. Farrar, Straus, 1942.
       y.
       Military hero General Georges Boulanger almost becomes
       dictator of France during the late 1880's.

955 _____. Jonathan Bishop. Farrar, Straus, 1934. y.
       A young American is involved in the Battle of Sedan and the
       Siege of Paris during the Franco-Prussian War.

956 Grant, James. The Aide-de-Camp. Routledge, 1848. y.
       Subtitle: "A Campaign in Calabria"; a tale of the Napole-
       onic war.

957 _____. The "Black Watch"; Or, the Forty Second High-
       landers. Routledge, 1892. y.
       Fictional exploits of a Scottish regiment in the Peninsular
       War.

958 _____. Laura Everingham. Dutton, 1870. y.
       An almost contemporary view of regimental life in the Brit-
       ish army during the Crimean War.

959 _____. One of the Six Hundred. Dutton, 1875. y.
       Portrays the charge of the Light Brigade in the Crimean
       War.

960 _____. The Romance of War. Little, Brown, 1847.
       Scottish Highlanders battle the French in the Peninsular War.

961 _____. The Royal Regiment, and Other Novelettes. Rout-
       ledge, 188-. y.
       Six long tales about Scottish military life.

962 _____. With the Red Dragon. 3 vols. Tinsley, 1872. y.
       Military action in the Crimean War of the 1850's.

963 Green, E. Everett. Castle of the White Flag. Nelson, 1904.
       y.
       Pictures the Battle of Worth in the Franco-Prussian War.

964 _____. Ringed by Fire. Nelson, 1905. y.
       The Franco-Prussian War Battle of Gravelotte and the Siege
       of Paris.

965 Gregg, Hilda C. One Crowded Hour. By Sydney C. Grier,
        pseud. Blackwoods, 1912. y.
     A pair of Englishmen fight with Garibaldi against Austria.

966 Gribble, Francis. The Dream of Paris. Chatto & Windus,
        1904. y.
     General Bourbaki's retreat into Switzerland during the Fran-
     co-Prussian War.

     Grier, Sydney C., pseud. See Gregg, Hilda C.

967 Gunter, A. C. The Sword in the Air. Ward, Lock, 1904. y.
     Portrays the Milanese uprising of 1848.

968 Hales, A. G. The Watcher on the Tower. Fisher, Unwin,
        1904. y.
     Presents Napoleon's march on Moscow in 1812.

969 Hansard, Luke J. Flame in the South. Hutchinson, 1925. y.
     The Italian war of unification, 1848-1849.

970 Hartley, M. Beyond Man's Strength. Heinemann, 1909. y.
     Begins with the Piedmontese rising of 1821 and moves on to
     the 1848-1849 Italian war of unification, with particular em-
     phasis on the battles of Novara and Carlo Alberto.

971 _____. A Sereshan. Mill & Boon, 1911. y.
     Pictures the Hungarian revolt of 1848.

972 Haynes, Herbert. The British Legion. Nelson, 1900. y.
     British troops are sent to Spain to put down the 1833-1836
     rising led by Carlos I.

973 _____. Paris at Bay. Blackie, 1897. y.
     After the Battle of Sedan, the Prussians besiege Paris.

974 _____. Red, White, and Green. Nelson, 1901. y.
     Action during the Hungarian revolution of 1848.

974a Heaven, Constance. Heir to Kuragin. Coward-McCann, 1979.
     Love and warfare in the Caucasus of 1846.

975 Henty, George A. One of the 28th. Scribner's, 1889. y.
     An English boy fights with the 28th Regiment under Welling-
     ton at Waterloo.

976 _____. Out with Garibaldi. Scribner's, 1901. y.
     The Italian hero leads the war for unification, 1848-1849.

977 _____. Through Russian Snows. Scribner's, 1896. y.
     Napoleon's drive on Moscow and the Battle of Borodino.

978 _____. Under Wellington's Command. Scribner's, 1899. y.
     British troops fight the French in Spain, 1808-1812.

979 _____ . With Moore at Corunna. Scribner's, 1898. y.
Sir John Moore's troops in the Peninsular War.

980 _____ . With the British Legion. Scribner's, 1903. y.
Sir George de Lacey's British troops battle the rebels of
Carlos I in Spain in the 1830's Carlist uprising.

981 _____ . The Young Buglers. Hodder & Stoughton, 1880. y.
Covers the great battles of the Peninsular War from Tala-
vera to Vittoria.

982 _____ . The Young Franctireurs. Hodder & Stoughton, 1872.
y.
A tale of the Franco-Prussian War, ending with the fighting
around Orleans.

983 Herbert, Alan P. Why Waterloo? Doubleday, 1953. y.
Presents Napoleon's 100 Days in 1815.

Heyer, Georgette, pseud. See Rougier, G. R.

984 Hood, Alexander N. Adria: A Tale of Venice. J. Murray,
1904. y.
Presents the Venetian struggle against the Austrians, 1848-
1849.

985 Hopkins, Tighe. For Freedom. Chatto & Windus, 1899. y.
Garibaldi leads the war of Italian unification.

986 Huch, Ricarda O. Defeat. Trans. from the German, Knopf,
1928. y.
Covers Garibaldi's reunification attempt in Italy to his loss
of Rome in 1849.

987 _____ . Victory. Trans. from the German. Knopf, 1929.
y.
Follows Garibaldi from his victory at Solferino to his disaster at Aspromonte.

988 Huffaker, Clair. The Cowboy and the Cossack. Trident, 1973.
y.
An unusual adventure tale with some irregular military ac-
tion; in 1880 a group of Montana cowboys, escorted by anti-
Czarist Cossacks, drive a herd of cattle 1000 miles across
Siberia to the Tartar town of Bakaskaya.

989 Jeal, Tim. Until the Colors Fade. Delacorte, 1976.
A Victorian family saga that ends on the battlefields of the
Crimea.

990 Jeans, Alice. The Stronger Wings. Stock, 1909. y.
The 1848 uprising in Vienna.

991 Johnson, David. Proud Canaries. Sloane, 1959. y.
     A cavalryman relates Napoleon's campaigns from 1806-
     1809.

992 Johnston, Myrtle. The Rising. Appleton-Century, 1939. y.
     American Civil War veteran Wolfe Darragh joins the Irish
     Fenians in the 1867 revolt against the British; the patriots,
     armed with pikes, are halted by British artillery.

993 Jokai, Maurus. The Baron's Sons. Trans. from the Hungari-
     an. Page, 1900. y.

994 _____. The Day of Wrath. Trans. from the Hungarian.
     McClure, 1900. y.

995 _____. Debts of Honor. Trans. from the Hungarian.
     Doubleday, 1900. y.

996 _____. An Hungarian Nabob. Trans. from the Hungarian.
     Doubleday, 1898. y.

997 _____. Manasseh. Trans. from the Hungarian. Page,
     1901. y.
     Five tales of combat during the 1848 Magyar revolt against
     the Austrians.

998 Kazantzakis, Nikos. Freedom or Death. Trans. from the
     Greek. Simon & Schuster, 1956. y.
     The residents of Crete revolt against the Turks on 1889.

999 Kingsley, Henry. Silcote of Silcotes. Longmans, 1867. y.
     Includes detail of the battles in the Italian war of unifica-
     tion.

1000 _____. Valentin. Longmans, 1872. y.
     Battle of Sedan, 1870.

1001 Komroff, Manuel. Waterloo. Coward-McCann, 1936. y.
     Two boys, one English and one French, recall Napoleon's
     100 Days.

1002 Landau, Mark A. Devil's Bridge. By M. A. Aldanov, pseud.
     Trans. from the Russian. Knopf, 1928. y.
     Field Marshal Suvorov takes on Napoleon's troops in the
     1812 Battle of Devil's Bridge in Russia.

1003 Lansworth, Lew X. Over the River Charlie. Doubleday,
     1956. y.
     Depicts the Prussian Siege of Paris in 1871.

1004 Lee, Albert. The Emperor's Trumpeter. Shaw, 1907. y.
     A young French bugler recalls the French invasion of
     Russia.

1005 LeQueux, William. The Great War in England in 1897. Tow-
          er, 1894. y.
          An imaginary conflict in which Franco-Russian forces in-
          vade an unprepared Britain.

1006 Lever, Charles. Charles O'Malley, the Irish Dragoon. Lit-
          tle, 1841. y.

1007 _____ . Tom Burke of Ours. Macmillan, 1844. Rpr.
          1931. y.
          Two tales of Irish soldiers fighting for Napoleon and against
          the British in the Peninsular War.

1008 Lowe, Charles. A Linsay's Love. Werner, Laurie, 1905.
          y.
          Romance and fighting during the Prussian Siege of Paris
          in 1871.

1009 Lukash, Ivan S. Flames of Moscow. Trans. from the Rus-
          sian. Macmillan, 1930. y.
          Burning of Moscow in 1812 and Napoleon's retreat.

1010 Lundegard, Axel. The Storm Bird. Trans. from the German.
          Hodder & Stoughton, 1895. y.
          Portrays the 1848 rising in Vienna.

1011 Madden, Eva. Two Royal Foes. McClure, 1907. y.
          Napoleon invades Prussia.

1012 Manceron, Claude. So Brief a Spring. Putnam, 1958. y.
          Napoleon's 100 Days, ending with the Battle of Waterloo.

1013 Marsh, Frances. The Iron Game. Fifield, 1909. y.
          Combat in the Franco-Prussian War.

1014 Maxwell, Anna. Pietro the Garibaldian. Parsons, 1925. y.
          An Italian soldier recalls the war of unification.

1015 Maxwell, W. H. Stories of Waterloo. Routledge, 1834. y.
          Tales depicting various aspects of the great 1815 fight.

1016 Meding, Oskar. For Sceptre and Crown. By Gregor Sama-
          row, pseud. King, 1875. y.
          An almost contemporary fictional recreation of the war
          between Austria and Prussia in 1866.

       Merriman, H. Seton, pseud. See Scott, Hugh S.

1017 Mockler-Ferryman, A. F. Lads of the Light Division. Nel-
          son, 1909. y.
          Young English soldiers participate in the Peninsular War
          battles of Talavera, Torres Vedras, and Cindad Rodrigo.

1018   Morgan, Michaela. Zanzara. Pinnacle, 1978. P.
       Nobility and revolutionaries clash in Sicily.

1019   Murray, D. Christie. VC: A Chronicle of Castle Barfield.
          Chatto & Windus, 1904. y.
       A young English soldier wins the Victoria Cross for brav-
       ery in the Crimean War battles of Sevastopol and Scutari.

1020   Murray, David. Trumpeter, Sound! Putnam, 1923. y.
       Two English half-brothers see service in the Crimean War,
       especially the Battle of Balaclava.

1021   Neumann, Alfred. The Rebels. Trans. from the German.
          Knopf, 1929. y.
       Looks at the Carbonari revolt in Tuscany in the 1830's.

1022   Odell, Katherine. Mission to Circassia. Harper, 1977.
       An Englishman joins the Circassians in their effort to hold
       back a Russian invasion.

       Oxenham, John, pseud. See Dunkerley, William A.

1023   Pemberton, Max. The Garden of Swords. Dodd, Mead, 1899.
          y.
       The Franco-Prussian War battles of Worth and Strasburg.

1024   _____. The Great White Army. Cassell, 1915. y.
       Napoleon's invasion of and retreat from Russia in 1812.

1025   _____. The Hundred Days. Cassell, 1915. y.
       Napoleon's 1815 campaign from Elba to Waterloo.

1026   _____. The Virgin Fortress. Cassell, 1912. y.
       The siege and capture of Metz in the Franco-Prussian War.

1027   Perutz, Leo. Marquis De Bolibar. Trans. from the Spanish.
          Viking, 1927. y.
       Problems of a German coalition regiment attempting to
       hold the Spanish town of La Bisbal for Napoleon.

1028   Petrakis, Harry M. The Hour of the Bell. Doubleday, 1976.
          y.
       Follows the battles of the Greek War of Independence to
       the insurgent conquest of Turkish-held Tripolitsa.

1029   Pollard, Eliza F. For the Emperor. Nelson, 1909. y.
       Napoleon's retreat from Moscow in the winter of 1812.

1030   Powers, Anne. A Thousand Fires. Bobbs-Merrill, 1958. y.
       Alan de Lacey, an engineer on Napoleon's staff, recalls
       the emperor's battles following the 1809 fight at Wagram.

       Presland, John, pseud. See Skelton, Gladys.

1031   Quiller-Couch, Arthur, T.   Rain of Dollars.   Longmans,
            Green, 1908.   y.
       Sir John Moore's retreat upon Corunna in 1809.

1032   Ralli, Constantine S.   The Wisdom of the Serpent.   Griffith,
            1907.   y.
       Depicts the Franco-Prussian War Battle of Vionville-Mars
       la Tour.

1033   Rascovich, Mark.   Falkenhorst.   Holt, 1974.   Rpr. 1975.   y.
       Military, political, and social problems of a German fam-
       ily during the Franco-Prussian War of 1870-1871.

1034   Reuter, Fritz.   In the Year '13.   Trans. from the German.
            Sampson, Low, 1860.   y.
       Pictures the French occupation of Mecklenburg.

1035   Rougier, G. R.   An Infamous Army.   By Georgette Heyer,
            pseud.   Doubleday, 1938.   Rpr. 1977.   y.
       Napoleon's 100 Days and the Battle of Waterloo.

1036   _____ .   The Spanish Bride.   By Georgette Heyer, pseud.
            Dutton, 1965.   y.
       A young Spanish bride follows her soldier husband into the
       fighting of the Peninsular War.

1037   Rudigos, Roger.   French Dragoon.   Trans. from the French.
            Coward-McCann, 1960.   y.
       The adventures of a French cavalry captain, Claude Solas-
       sier, during and after the 1813 Battle of Leipzig.

1038   Sabatini, Rafael.   Snare.   Lippincott, 1917.   y.
       When an English soldier muffs one of Wellington's plans
       against the French in Portugal, his brother-in-law, the
       Adjutant General, is ordered to track the offender down.

       Samarow, Gregor, pseud.   See Meding, Oskar.

1039   Scott, Hugh S.   Barlasch of the Guard.   By H. Seton Merri-
            man, pseud.   McClure, 1903.   y.
       Depicts the Battle of Danzig and Napoleon's Russian inva-
       sion.

1040   _____ .   In Kedar's Tents.   By H. Seton Merriam, pseud.
            Dodd, Mead, 1897.   y.
       Carlos I attempts to win the throne of Spain during the
       1830's.

1041   _____ .   The Velvet Glove.   By H. Seton Merriam, pseud.
            Dodd, Mead, 1902.   y.
       Carlos III attempts to win the throne of Spain during the
       1870's.

1042 Skelton, Gladys. Barricade. By John Presland, pseud.
      Philip Allan, 1926. y.
      Love and fighting during the 1848 uprising in Vienna.

1043 Smith, Frederick E. Waterloo. Award, 1970. P.
      The great battle of 1815 as adapted from the screenplay
      of a movie of the same title.

1044 Stephens, Eve. Far Flies the Eagle. By Evelyn Anthony,
      pseud. Crowell, 1955. y.
      Alexander I and the defeat of Napoleon, 1806-1815.

1045 Strachey, J. S. The Madonna of the Barricade. Harcourt,
      1925. y.
      A tale built around the 1848 uprising in Vienna.

1046 Strang, Herbert. Boys of the Light Brigade. Putnam, 1905.
      y.
      Young English soldiers participate in the Peninsular War
      battles of Corunna and Saragossa.

1047 Stuart, Esmé. For Love and Ransom. Jarrold, 1904. y.
      Murat is overthrown in southern Italy by the Austrians in
      1815.

1048 Styles, Showell. Greencoats Against Napoleon. Vanguard,
      1960. y.
      A young British ensign, aided by a Yankee backwoodsman
      and Cockney riflemen, help Sir John Moore in the 1809
      Peninsular War battle at Corunna.

1049 _____. His Was the Fire. Vanguard, 1957. y.
      The exploits of Sir John Moore in the Peninsular War.

      Talbot, Hugh, pseud. See Alington, Argentine F.

1050 Taylor, H. C. Chatfield: The Crimson Wing. Grant, Rich-
      ards, 1902. y.
      A tale of fighting during the Franco-Prussian War.

1051 Thomas, Donald. Flight of the Eagle. Viking, 1976. y.
      The adventures of Captain Charles Tollemache of His Maj-
      esty's 18th Light Dragoons in Napoleonic Europe and the
      Battle of Waterloo.

1052 Tolstoy, Leo. War and Peace. Trans. from the Russian.
      Harper, 1886. Rpr. 1976. y.
      An often-reprinted and lengthy tale of love and war from
      the Russian viewpoint during Napoleon's 1812 invasion; the
      Battle of Borodino and the burning of Moscow are vividly
      presented.

1053 Trease, Geoffrey. Follow My Black Plume. Vanguard, 1963.
      y.

A young Englishman becomes involved in Garibaldi's war
of Italian unification.

1054   Trevelyan, Robert.   The Montenegran Plot.   St. Martin's,
          1976.
          An unusual military tale; to blunt the mad plans of Janez
          Krakar against Queen Victoria, British officer Pendragon
          finds himself in battle near the Tower of London (receiv-
          ing aid from a unit of U. S. Marines) and leading a caval-
          ry battle in St. James' Park.

1055   Vazov, Ivan.   Under the Yoke.   Trans. from the Russian.
          Heinemann, 1893.   y.
          Examines the revolt of the Bulgarians against the Turks.

          Welch, Ronald, pseud.   See Fenton, Ronald O.

1056   Westall, William.   A Red Bridal.   Chatto & Windus, 1898.
          y.

1057   _____.   With the Red Eagle.   Chatto & Windus, 1897.   y.
          Two accounts of how Hofer led the people of Tyrol in an
          1809 revolt against the French and Bavarians.

1058   Wheeler, Thomas G.   A Fanfare for the Stalwart.   S. G.
          Phillips, 1967.   y.
          A young French soldier describes the French retreat from
          Moscow to Warsaw.

1059   Wheelwright, J. H.   Draw Near to Battle.   Scribner's, 1953.
          y.
          Napoleon's Russian campaign.

1060   Whishaw, F.   Moscow.   Longmans, Green, 1905.   y.
          Burned by Napoleon in 1812.

1061   Wibberley, Leonard.   Kevin O'Connor and the Light Brigade.
          Farrar, Straus, 1967.   y.
          A young English horseman recalls the October 20, 1854
          charge of the Gallant Six Hundred at Balaclava during the
          Crimean War.

1062   Woods, Margaret L.   Sons of the Sword.   McClure, 1901.   y.
          The troops of Sir John Moore fight in the Peninsular War.

1063   Younge, Charlotte M.   Kenneth.   Macmillan, 1850.   y.
          Action during Napoleon's Russian campaign of 1812.

1064   Zola, Emile.   Downfall.   Trans. from the French.   Macmil-
          lan, 1893.   y.
          Two French privates witness the disastrous campaign of
          their army, ending in defeat in the Battle of Sedan in
          1870.

NORTH AMERICA: TO 1754

The stories in this section concern English- and French-colonized
America from the time of the Pilgrims to the opening of the French
and Indian War, known as the Seven Years War in Europe.   Throughout this period American colonials, the English, French, and native
Indians fought several wars among themselves, either as a result of
settlement problems or as the outgrowth of European conflicts.   Tales
concerning Spanish activities in the New World will be found in our
Latin America section.

1065 Barbour, R. H.   Metipom's Hostage.   Houghton Mifflin, 1921.
          y.
      Whites are captured during King Philip's War of 1675.

1066 Buchan, John.   Salute to Adventurers.   Houghton Mifflin, 1915.
          y.
      Adventure in Virginia at the time of the most prominent of
      colonial revolts, Bacon's Rebellion.   Beginning as an unau-
      thorized war on the Indians on Virginia's northwest fron-
      tier, the followers of Nathaniel Bacon took on the forces
      of Governor Berkeley in 1676, seized the colonial govern-
      ment, defeated the governor's troops, and burned James-
      town to the ground.   After the death of Bacon from expo-
      sure and exhaustion during a confused campaign, the rebel-
      lion faded out.

1067 Catherwood, Mary H.   Romance of Dollard.   Century, 1889.
          y.
      Sixteen French soldiers hold a small fort on the Ottawa
      River against a determined assault by Iroquois Indians in
      1660.

1068 Coatsworth, Elizabeth J.   Sword of the Wilderness.   Macmil-
          lan, 1966.   y.
      During the Indian wars of 1689, Seth Hubbard is captured
      by the Abenakis and spends a bitter winter with them.

1069 Coryell, Hubert B.   Indian Brother.   Harcourt, 1935.   y.
      Catholic Father Rale incites the Indians against English
      settlers in Maine in 1713.

1070 _____ . Scalp Hunters. Harcourt, 1936. y.
     Canadian Indians attack English settlements in Queen Anne's
     War, the colonial phase of Europe's War of the Spanish
     Succession.

1071 Crowley, Mary C. Daughter of New France. Little, 1901.
     y.
     Follows military, political, and social events in French
     Canada from 1687 to 1735.

1072 Eaton, Evelyn S. M. Restless Are the Sails. Harper, 1941.
     y.
     In 1745 a French POW escapes his British captors, but
     cannot convince the residents of Louisbourg to heed his
     warning of a colonial attack on their Cape Breton Island
     fortress.

1073 Ellis, Edward S. The Cromwell of Virginia. Coates, 1904.
     y.
     Nathaniel Bacon leads his rebellion of 1676.

1074 _____ . Uncrowning a King. Cassell, 1899. y.
     English-French-Indian conflict during King Philip's War of
     1675-1676 in New England.

1075 Field, Rachel. Calico Bush. Macmillan, 1966. y.
     A servant girl saves her employers from attacking Indians
     in Maine during Queen Anne's War.

1076 Finney, Gertrude E. Muskets Along the Chickahominy. Long-
     mans, Green, 1953. y.
     Andrew Shields becomes involved in Indian warfare and
     Bacon's Rebellion in Virginia.

1077 Flannagan, Roy C. Forest Cavalier. Bobbs-Merrill, 1952.
     y.
     Nathaniel Bacon and his 1676 rebellion against Governor
     Berkeley.

1078 Fox, John, Jr. Erskine Dale, Pioneer. Scribner's, 1920.
     y.
     Captured by Indians, an English boy is raised with the
     benefits of both the Red and White worlds; in time he saves
     a group of colonials from an Indian attack on their Virginia
     settlement.

1079 Fuller, Hulbert. Vivian of Virginia. Page, 1900. y.
     Love and conflict during Bacon's Rebellion.

1080 Gerson, Noel B. The Highwayman. Doubleday, 1956. y.
     A criminal becomes involved in the successful colonial
     attack on Louisbourg in 1745.

1081 _____ . The Invincibles. By Carter A. Vaughan, pseud.
Doubleday, 1958. y.
Colonial troops, with little aid from the English, storm
and capture the important French fortress of Louisbourg
in 1745.

1082 _____ . Roanoke Warrior. By Carter A. Vaughan, pseud.
Doubleday, 1965. y.
A former debtor, now a colonial leader, leads English at-
tacks on Virginia Indians.

1083 _____ . Savage Gentlemen. Doubleday, 1950. y.
The adventures of Jeffrey Wyatt as an Indian fighter in
Queen Anne's War.

1084 Goodwin, Maud W. White Aprons. Little, 1896. y.
Female supporters of Nathaniel Bacon form a defensive
line to hold off Governor Berkeley's troops.

1085 Hinsdale, Harriet. Be My Love. Creative Age, 1951. y.
Love and conflict during the 1745 siege of Louisbourg.

1086 Kaler, James O. The Boys of '45. By James Otis, pseud.
Estes, 1898. y.
How colonial troops captured Louisbourg from the French.

1087 Lobdell, Helen. Captain Bacon's Rebellion. Macrae-Smith,
1959. y.
A fictional recreation of the 1676 unpleasantness in Virginia.

1088 MacDonald, Z. K. Courage to Command. Winston, 1953. y.
The 1745 colonial capture of Louisbourg.

1089 Malkus, Alida S. There Really Was a Hiawatha. Grosset &
Dunlap, 1963. y.
A biographical novel built around the life of Great White
Eagle, the Onondaga warrior who helped form the Iroquois
Confederacy and served as the model for Longfellow's epic
poem.

1090 Mason, Francis Van Wyck. Rascal's Haven. Doubleday,
1964. y.
General James Oglethorpe's Georgia settlers battle Indians
and the Spanish from St. Augustine in the late 1730's.

1091 _____ . Young Titan. Doubleday, 1960. y.
The most historically accurate recounting of the 1745 colo-
nial capture of Louisbourg during King George's War, the
American phase of the War of Austrian Succession. Led
by popular Maine merchant and militia colonel William
Pepperrell, 4000 New England troops were landed on Cape

Breton Island, where they seized a French battery and
turned it on the fortress. After two and a half months of
siege, the French surrender the "Gibraltar of the New
World" on June 17.

1092 Miers, Earl S. Valley in Arms. Westminster, 1943. y.
A look at Connecticut in colonial times, with emphasis on
the Wethersfield massacre and the colonial campaign
against the Pequot Indians in the 1630's.

1092a Moore, Arthur. The Sword and the Cross. Popular Library,
1979. P.
A young Spanish lieutenant is sent to build a fort in California.

Otis, James, pseud. See Kaler, James O.

1093 Oxley, J. MacDonald. Fife and Drum at Louisbourg. Little,
1899. y.
General Pepperrell's men take the French fortress in 1745.

1094 Riggs, Sidney H. Arrows and Snakeskins. Lippincott, 1962.
y.
Portrays the English defeat of the Pequot Indians.

1095 Ritchie, Cicero T. The Willing Maid. Abelard, 1958. y.
Love and conflict during the siege of Louisbourg.

1096 Sass, Herbert R. Emperor Brims. Doubleday, 1941.
A picture of the so-called Yamassee War of 1715, in which
the South Carolina Indians of the Creek Confederacy under
Brims of Coweta rose against the English settlers.

1097 Schachner, Nathan. The King's Passenger. Lippincott, 1942.
y.
Adventure and military action in Bacon's Rebellion of 1676,
with emphasis on the burning of Jamestown.

1098 Schofield, William G. Ashes in the Wilderness. Macrae
Smith, 1942. y.
Captain Benjamin Church leads colonial forces against the
French and Indians in King William's War in Massachusetts
and Rhode Island, 1675-1676.

1099 Scruggs, Philip L. Man Cannot Tell. Bobbs-Merrill, 1942.
y.
An indentured servant becomes involved in Bacon's Rebellion.

1100 Shafer, Donald C. Smokefires in Schoharie. Longmans,
Green, 1938. y.
Chronicles the defenses of the Palatine Germans in the
Schoharie Valley against the Indians, 1713 to 1782.

1101 Simms, William G.   The Yemassee, a Romance of Carolina.
      Twayne, 1964.   y.
      Originally published in 1835 and regarded by most as the
      author's best work, this tale tells of the Creek Confeder-
      acy's uprising under Emperor Brims against colonists in
      South Carolina in 1715.

1102 Spector, Robert M.   The Greatest Rebel.   Walck, 1969.   y.
      Nathaniel Bacon and his 1676 rebellion.

1103 Stillman, A. L.   Drums Beat in Old Carolina.   Winston, 1939.
      y.
      A tale of the Indian War of 1715.

1104 Stone, Grace Z.   The Cold Journey.   Morrow, 1934.   y.
      Pictures the Indian attack on Deerfield, Massachusetts, in
      January 1704 and the journey of the captive survivors to
      Quebec.

1105 Stuart, Henry L.   Weeping Cross.   Doubleday, 1908.   y.
      Recreates the Indian massacre of English settlers in Long
      Meadow, Massachusetts, in 1652.

1106 Sublette, Clifford.   The Bright Face of Danger.   Little,
      Brown, 1926.   y.
      Combat and vengeance in Bacon's Rebellion.

1107 Travers, Milton A.   The Last of the Great Wampanoag Indian
      Sachems.   Christopher, 1963.   y.
      A short tale about King Philip (Metacomet) in the 1675-
      1676 war against the whites in Massachusetts.

      Vaughan, Carter A., pseud.   See Gerson, Noel B.

1108 Wells-Smith, Mary P.   Boys of the Border.   Little, 1907.   y.
      Indian fighting on the northwest frontier of Massachusetts,
      1746-1755.

1108a Wilson, Derek.   Her Majesty's Captain.   Little, Brown, 1979.
      Elizabeth I sends the son of Sir Robert Dudley to find El
      Dorado.

NORTH AMERICA: 1754 TO 1775

The stories in this section cover the French and Indian War (1756-
1763), the colonial phase of Europe's Seven Years War, Pontiac's
Indian rebellion in the Ohio Valley (1763), and miscellaneous tales
of colonist-Indian combat.   The European phase of the Seven Years
War is covered in our section on Europe, 1700-1800.

1109 Alderman, Clifford L. <u>To Fame Unknown</u>. Appleton, 1955.
      y.
      Reveals the exploits of Esek Warren in the last days of
      the French and Indian War.

1110 Allen, Hervey. <u>Bedford Village</u>. Rinehard, 1944. Rpr. 1978.
      y.
      Sequel to the next title; portrays the activities of Salathiel
      Albine, a ranger of the "Mountain Foxes," and life at a
      Pennsylvania military outpost in 1763.

1111 _____. <u>Forest and the Fort</u>. Rinehart, 1943. Rpr. 1978.
      y.
      Salathiel Albine is involved in Chief Pontiac's 1763 siege
      of Fort Pitt.

1112 Allen, Merritt P. <u>Black Rain</u>. Longmans, Green, 1939. y.
      Pontiac and the siege of Detroit.

1113 _____. <u>Flicker's Feather</u>. Longmans, Green, 1953. y.
      A New Hampshire youth scouts for Robert's Rangers in
      the French and Indian War.

1114 Alter, Robert E. <u>Time of the Tomahawks</u>. Putnam, 1964.
      y.
      Chief Pontiac's Indians take many English strongholds in
      the years between 1762 and 1766, but cannot capture Fort
      Pitt.

1115 Althsheler, Joseph A. <u>The Hunters of the Hills</u>. Appleton,
      1916. y.
      Colonial rangers battle savage Indians on the frontier in
      the French and Indian War.

1116 _____. <u>The Masters of the Peaks</u>. Appleton, 1918. y.
      Another tale of Indian warfare in the French and Indian
      War.

1117 _____. <u>The Rulers of the Lakes</u>. Appleton, 1917. y.
      Braddock's 1755 defeat near Fort Duquesne.

1118 _____. <u>A Soldier of Manhattan</u>. Appleton, 1897. y.
      A colonial soldier participates in the French and Indian
      War battles of Ticonderoga and Quebec.

1119 _____. <u>The Sun of Quebec</u>. Appleton, 1919. y.
      General Wolfe's English troops defeat the soldiers of Mont-
      calm in the 1759 Battle of the Plains of Abraham.

1120 Baines, Annie M. <u>The Little Lady at the Fall of Quebec</u>.
      Penn, 1909. y.
      A girl helps Wolfe take Quebec in 1759.

1121 Best, Herbert. The Long Portage. Viking, 1948. y.

1122 _____. Ranger's Ransom. Aladdin, 1953. y.
      Two tales built around the 1758 Battle of Fort Ticonderoga.

      Bowen, Marjorie, pseud. See Long, Gabrielle C.

1123 Boyd, Thomas A. Shadow of the Long Knives. Scribner's,
          1928. Rpr. 1978. y.
      The adventures of British scout Angus McDermott on the
      Ohio Valley frontier in the years just before the American
      Revolution.

1124 Brereton, Frederic S. How Canada Was Won. Blackie, 1908. y.
      A fictional recreation of the French and Indian War, with
      emphasis on the defense of Fort William Henry, the Eng-
      lish attack on Louisbourg, and Wolfe versus Montcalm at
      Quebec.

1125 Breslin, Howard. Bright Battalions. McGraw-Hill, 1953. y.
      Irishman Kevin O'Connor fights for the French against the
      English in the French and Indian War battles up and down
      Lake Champlain and Lake George, 1756-1759.

1126 Brill, Ethel C. White Brother. Holt, 1932. y.
      Tale of a half-white Indian in Pontiac's revolt.

1127 Briton, E. Vincent. Amyot Brough. Houghton Mifflin, 1884. y.
      Pictures Wolfe's victory over Montcalm in the Battle of
      the Plains of Abraham.

1128 Browne, G. Waldo. With Roger's Rangers. L. C. Page,
          1906. y.
      Robert Rogers and his scouts battle the Indians in New
      England and New York in 1754.

1129 Buck, Elizabeth H. The Powder Keg. Penn, 1940. y.
      The French and Indian War on the Pennsylvania frontier.

1130 Burke, Wilfred L. Naked Days of the Lost Moon. Vantage,
          1970. y.
      Portrays Indian attacks on colonial settlements in western
      Pennsylvania.

1131 Chalmers, Harvey. Drums Against Frontenac. Richard R.
          Smith, 1949. y.
      The French and Indian War capture of Fort Frontenac by
      British colonel Bradstreet in 1760.

1132 Chambers, Robert W. War Paint and Rouge. Appleton, 1932.
          y.
      Love and combat during the French and Indian War.

1133 Coatsworth, Elizabeth J. The Last Fort. Winston, 1952. y.
      Indians attack settlers in the French and Indian War.

1134 Cooper, James Fenimore. The Deerslayer. Lea & Blanch-
            ard, 1841. Rpr. 1977. y.
      Brought up by the Delaware Indians, young Natty Bumppo
      wars on the Huron, defends a family, and meets his great
      friend Chingachgook.

1135 _____. The Last of the Mohicans. Carey & Lea, 1826.
            Rpr. 1977. y.
      Natty Bumppo, or Hawkeye the Scout, and Chingachgook
      rescue two women and a British major who is returning
      them to Fort William Henry; the fort surrenders to Mont-
      calm in 1758, and 400 people are killed or carried off by
      Montcalm's Indian allies.

1136 _____. The Pathfinder. Bentley, 1840. Rpr. 1973. y.
      Hawkeye and Chingachgook help defend a fort under attack
      by Iroquois on the shores of Lake Ontario.

1137 _____. Leatherstocking Saga. Ed. by Allan Nevins. Pan-
            theon, 1954. y.
      Presents the five Hawkeye stories, including the three from
      our period entered above, arranged chronologically with
      passages and scenes not related to Natty Bumppo's career or
      character eliminated.

      Craddah, Charles E., pseud. See Murfree, Mary N.

1138 Crawnfield, Gertrude. Alison Blair. Dutton, 1927. y.
      Captured by Indians in the French and Indian War, a lass
      finds an able ally in Sir William Johnson.

1139 Crowley, Mary C. Heroine of the Strait. Little, 1902. y.
      A young girl and white settlers become involved in the
      siege of Detroit by Pontiac's warriors.

1140 Curwood, James O. The Black Hunter. Cosmopolitan, 1922.
            y.
      Portrays military and other events in French Canada during
      the early phases of the French and Indian War.

1141 _____. Plains of Abraham. Doubleday, 1928. y.
      Sequel to the above title; General Wolfe captures Quebec
      in 1759.

1142 Dwight, Allan. Guns at Quebec. Macmillan, 1962. y.
      The French lose Quebec to the British in the 1759 Battle
      of the Plains of Abraham outside the city.

1143 Eckert, Allan. The Frontiersman. Little, Brown, 1967. y.
      The activities and Indian-fighting exploits of Simon Kenton
      on the American frontier.

1144 Edmonds, Walter D. <u>Matchlock Gun.</u> Dodd, Mead, 1941. y.
      Whites versus Indians in the French and Indian War.

1145 Ellis, Edward S. <u>Pontiac, Chief of the Ottawas.</u> Cassell,
      1897. y.
      Pays special attention to his 1763 siege of Detroit.

1146 Elwood, Muriel. <u>Web of Destiny.</u> Bobbs-Merrill, 1951. y.
      Focuses on the roles of the Marquis de Montcalm, General
      James Wolfe, and Sir William Johnson in the French and
      Indian War.

1147 Felton, Ronald O. <u>Mohawk Valley.</u> By Ronald Welch, pseud.
      Criterion, 1958. y.
      A young English aristocrat becomes involved in the 1758
      Battle of Ticonderoga and Wolfe's 1759 capture of Quebec.

1148 Frederic, Harold. <u>In the Valley.</u> Scribner's, 1890. y.
      White settlers battle hostile Indians along the Mohawk dur-
      ing the French and Indian War.

1149 Frey, Ruby. <u>Red Morning.</u> Putnam, 1946. y.
      The problems and combats of Jane Bell and other Ohio
      Valley settlers during the French and Indian War.

1150 Gay, Margaret C. <u>Hatchet in the Sky.</u> Simon & Schuster,
      1954. y.
      Pictures the activities of Chief Pontiac and the Ojibway
      Indians in the 1763 siege of Detroit.

1151 Gibbs, G. F. <u>The Flame of Courage.</u> Appleton, 1926. y.
      The military role of French leader Montcalm in the French
      and Indian War.

1152 Giles, Janice. <u>The Kentuckians.</u> Houghton Mifflin, 1953.
      Rpr. 1976. y.
      Daniel Boone and other settlers battle the Indians in the
      new Kentuck' from 1769 to 1777.

1153 Gordon, Caroline. <u>Green Centuries.</u> Scribner's, 1941. Rpr.
      1972. y.
      Hostile Indians attempt to halt the flow of settlers into
      Kentucky in the years just before the American Revolution.

1154 Green, E. Everett. <u>French and English.</u> Nelson, 1899. y.
      Focuses on the Indian massacre of English survivors at
      Fort William Henry and Wolfe's capture of Quebec.

1155 Gregor, Elmer R. <u>Mason and His Rangers.</u> Appleton, 1927.
      y.
      Jim Mason, Ranger captain, is ordered to clear the French
      and Indians out of the Lake George area in the 1754-1763
      conflict.

1156 Grey, Zane. <u>Spirit of the Border.</u> Grosset, 1905. Rpr.
      1976. y.
      Long rifles protect frontier settlers from the Delaware
      Indians and various renegade whites in the Ohio Valley.

1157 Gringhuis, Dirk. <u>Young Voyageurs.</u> McGraw-Hill, 1955. y.
      Young trappers are involved in Pontiac's siege of Detroit.

1158 Hamilton, Harry. <u>Thunder in the Wilderness.</u> Bobbs-Merrill,
      1949. y.
      A tale of Frenchmen and Indians in the Mississippi Valley
      during the 1760's.

1159 Haworth, Paul L. <u>The Path of Glory.</u> Little, 1911. y.
      Wolfe's 1759 victory over Montcalm in the Battle of the
      Plains of Abraham.

1160 Hays, Wilma P. <u>Drummer Boy for Montcalm.</u> Macmillan,
      1959. y.
      A young French drummer recalls his general's defeat by
      the British in the Battle of the Plains of Abraham.

1161 Henty, George A. <u>With Wolfe in Canada.</u> Scribner's, 1887.
      y.
      Actually a fictional recreation of many battles of the French
      and Indian War, including Braddock's defeat, Fort William
      Henry, Ticonderoga, and Quebec.

1162 Jennings, John E. <u>Gentleman Raker.</u> Reynal, 1942. y.
      The black sheep of an English aristocratic family enlists
      in Braddock's army and participates in the English disaster
      when that force is wiped out in its 1755 advance on Fort
      Duquesne.

1163 _____. Next to Valour. Macmillan, 1939. y.
      Jamie Ferguson's New Hampshire adventures with Robert's
      Rangers in the French and Indian War.

1164 Lodbell, Helen. <u>The Fort in the Forest.</u> Houghton Mifflin,
      1963. y.
      Young Andre becomes a French recruit in the French and
      Indian War and helps to strengthen Fort Niagara.

1165 Long, Gabrielle C. <u>Mr. Washington.</u> By Marjorie Bowen,
      pseud. Appleton, 1915. y.
      George Washington's military exploits in the French and
      Indian War and later in the American Revolution.

1166 Longstreet, Stephen. <u>War in the Golden Weather.</u> Doubleday,
      1965. y.
      Tale about a young artist who is caught up in various bat-
      tles of the French and Indian War.

1167 Meader, Stephen W. Rivers of the Wolves. Harcourt, 1948.
      y.
      Inland combat during the French and Indian War.

1168 Munroe, Kirk. At War with Pontiac. Scribner's, 1895. y.
      White settlers are attacked by the Indians in 1763.

1169 Murfree, Mary N. The Amulet. By Charles Egbert Craddah,
      pseud. Macmillan, 1906. y.
      English settlers at Fort Prince George battle Pontiac's
      Indians in 1763.

1170 _____. The Story of Old Fort Loudon. By Charles Egbert
      Craddah, pseud. Macmillan, 1899. y.
      An English settlement/stronghold is attacked by Cherokees
      in 1758.

      Nevins, Allan, ed. See Cooper, James Fenimore.

1171 Page, Elizabeth. Wilderness Adventure. Rinehart, 1946. y.
      Frontiersmen rescue a girl captured by the Indians.

1172 Parker, Gilbert. Seats of the Mighty. Appleton, 1896. y.
      A tale of the French and Indian War in Canada, with em-
      phasis on the 1759 Battle of the Plains of Abraham.

1173 _____. The Trial of the Sword. Appleton, 1896. y.
      Another look at the French Canadian side of the French
      and Indian War.

1174 Parrish, Randall. A Sword of the Old Frontier. McClurg,
      1905. y.
      Presents Pontiac's rebellion of 1763, paying special atten-
      tion to Indian attacks on Detroit and Fort Chartres, Illi-
      nois.

1175 Patterson, Burd S. The Head of Iron. Walker, 1908. y.
      The head belongs to General Edward Braddock who, not
      understanding colonial warfare, was badly defeated near
      Fort Duquesne in 1755; later, General John Forbes cap-
      tured the place and renamed it Fort Pitt.

1176 Peck, Robert N. Fawn. Little, Brown, 1975. y.
      An Indian boy and young Benedict Arnold participate in the
      1758 Battle of Fort Ticonderoga.

1177 Pendexter, Hugh. Red Road. Bobbs-Merrill, 1927. y.
      Black Brond, an English scout, recalls Braddock's defeat
      along the Monogahela in 1755.

1178 Pike, R. E. Fighting Yankee. Abelard-Schuman, 1955. y.
      English colonials battled the Indians in the French and
      Indian War.

1179   Provan, Eldoris A. Drummer for the Americans.   Chilton,
         1965. y.
         A young drummer serves with the Royal American troops
         in the Ohio Valley in the French and Indian War.

1180   Pryor, Elinor. Double Men. Norton, 1967. y.
         Baron Mark Caldwell becomes the Cherokee chief Tsani,
         but despite victories, cannot hold his Indians to their al-
         liance with the British.

1181   Quiller-Couch, Arthur T. Fort Amity. Scribner's, 1904. y.
         Focuses on the 1758-1759 French and Indian War battles
         of Fort Ticonderoga and Quebec.

1182   Richardson, John. Wacousta. McClurg, 1882. y.
         Pontiac's Indians succeed against minor posts, but fail in
         their attempt to take Detroit.

1183   Richter, Conrad. A Light in the Forest. Knopf, 1953. Rpr.
         1966. y.
         Pictures Bouquet's expedition, undertaken in 1765, to free
         captives of the Tuscarawas.

1184   Roberts, Kenneth L. Northwest Passage. Doubleday, 1937.
         Rpr. 1972. y.
         The most noteworthy account of the activities of Robert's
         Rangers in the French and Indian War.

1185   Schumann, Mary. Strife Before Dawn. Dial, 1939. y.
         Pontiac's warriors attack frontier outposts.

1186   Seifert, Shirley. Never No More. Lippincott, 1964. y.
         Examines the effects on Rebecca and Daniel Boone of the
         death of their son by Indian arrows, 1773.

1187   Settle, Mary L. O Beulah Land. Viking, 1956. Rpr. 1974.
         y.
         Virginia settlers in the wilderness beyond the Allegheny
         Mountains battle the Indians from 1754 to 1774.

1188   Singmaster, Elsie. High Wind Rising. Houghton Mifflin,
         1942. y.
         Conrad Weiser, the Pennsylvania Dutch, and the French
         and Indian War.

1189   Spicer, Bart. The Tall Captain. Dodd, Mead, 1957. y.
         The Battle of the Plains of Abraham.

1190   Stevenson, Burton E. A Soldier of Virginia. Houghton Mif-
         flin, 1901. y.
         Following Braddock's 1755 defeat, Colonel George Wash-
         ington leads the pell-mell British retreat, buried his gen-
         eral in a secret grave, and establishes the temporary
         stronghold of Fort Necessity.

1191 Stover, Herbert E. Song of the Susquehanna. Dodd, Mead,
         1949. y.
      Peter Grove tells of Indian/white battles in Pennsylvania
      during the French and Indian War.

1192 Stratemeyer, Edward. On the Trail of Pontiac. Lothrop,
         1904. y.
      A tale of adventure and combat set in the 1763 Indian up-
      rising.

1193 _____. With Washington in the West. Lee & Shepard,
         1901. y.
      Washington's role following Braddock's 1755 defeat near
      Fort Duquesne.

1194 Swanson, Neil. The First Rebel. Farrar, Straus, 1937. y.
      James Smith's Scotch-Irish rebellion against the British in
      Pennsylvania and his capture by Indians, 1763-1767.

1195 _____. The Judas Tree. Putnam, 1935. y.
      Pontiac besieges Fort Pitt in 1763.

1196 _____. Unconquered. Doubleday, 1947. y.
      Fort Pitt proves too tough a nut for Pontiac's Indians to
      crack.

1197 Taylor, Richard. Girty. Turtle Island, 1978.
      Simon Girty, white renegade, terrorizes the frontier be-
      fore the American Revolution.

1198 Tebbel, John W. Conqueror. Dutton, 1951. y.
      Sir William Johnson, British Superintendent of Indian af-
      fairs in North America, and his role in the French and
      Indian War.

1199 Thomas, Donald. Prince Charlie's Bluff: a novel of the
         Kingdom of Virginia. Viking, 1974. y.
      Assuming that the French under Montcalm won the Battle
      of the Plains of Abraham at Quebec in 1759, Highland
      troops transferred to Virginia revolt and set up a province
      under Charles Edward Stuart, in hiding as a result of his
      defeat in the "Rising of '45."

1200 Tomlinson, Everett T. The Fort in the Forest. W. A.
         Wilde, 1904. y.
      After Montcalm's victory at Fort William Henry in August
      1757, his Indian allies massacre a large number of the
      surrendering English.

1201 _____. A Soldier in the Wilderness. W. A. Wilde, 1905.
         y.
      A British soldier remembers the 1758 capture of Fort
      Frontenac.

1202 Tracy, Don. Cherokee. Dial, 1957. y.
     Pictures the wars of Chief Suti and the Cherokee with white
     settlers in the Great Smokies.

     Welch, Ronald, pseud. See Felton, Ronald O.

1203 Wheelwright, Jere H. Kentucky Stand. Scribner's, 1951. y.
     Settlers battle Indians in the years before the American
     Revolution.

1204 White, Leslie T. Daniel Boone, Wilderness Scout. Double-
        day, Doran, 1935. y.
     Adventures of the "Long Knife" in early Kentucky, including
     many encounters with hostile Indians.

1205 _____. His Majesty's Highlanders. Crown, 1964. y.
     A fictional recreation of the role of Scottish soldiers in
     Wolfe's 1759 victory at Quebec.

1206 Whitson, Denton. The Governor's Daughter. Bobbs-Merrill,
        1953. y.
     Problems in New York during the French and Indian War.

1207 Widdemer, Margaret. The Golden Wildcat. Doubleday, 1954.
        y.
     A girl's adventures while both the British and French seek
     Indian support, 1754-1759.

1208 _____. Lady of the Mohawks. Doubleday, 1951. y.
     Molly Brant and Sir William Johnson.

NORTH AMERICA: 1775 TO 1782

The stories in this section, concerning military operations of the
American Revolution, make up the second largest part of our North
American segment. Tales about fighting in other countries during
what became, in fact, a world war will be found in our sections on
Europe, 1700-1800, and Asia, Africa, and the Pacific, 1600-1800.

1209 Albrecht, Lillie V. Hannah's Hessians. Hastings, 1958. y.
     German conscripts fight for King George III.

1210 Alderman, Clifford L. Arch of Stars. Appleton, Century,
        1950. y.
     Ethan and Seth Allen and Seth Warner take part in Revo-
     lutionary War activities in Vermont.

1211 _____. The Way of Eagles. Doubleday, 1965. y.

A young colonial tries to save the day in the unsuccessful Montgomery-Arnold assault on Quebec in 1775.

Alexander, William P., jt. author. See Cormack, Maribelle.

1212 Allen, Merritt P. Battle Lanterns. McKay, 1949. y.
A young white man and a black support the activities of Francis Marion, "the Swamp Fox," in his guerrilla campaign in the Carolinas.

1213 _____. Green Cockade. Longmans, Green, 1942. y.
Ethan Allen and his Green Mountain Boys.

1214 _____. Red Heritage. McKay, 1946. y.
Chief Joseph Brant's Mohawks defeat General Herkimer's followers in the Battle of Oriskany; young Cobus Derrick, the book's hero, becomes a P. O. W.

1215 Altsheler, Joseph A. The Forest Runners. D. Appleton, 1908. y.
Indians battle settlers along the great war trails in Revolutionary War Kentucky.

1216 _____. In Hostile Red. Doubleday, Page, 1900. y.
Focuses on Washington's 1778 Monmouth campaign in New Jersey.

1217 _____. The Sun of Saratoga. D. Appleton, 1897. y.
Colonial forces under General Horatio Gates force the surrender of General "Johnny" Burgoyne's Redcoats at Saratoga in 1777.

1218 Arnow, Harriette S. The Kentucky Trace: a Novel of the American Revolution. Knopf, 1974. y.
Settlers fight Indians, Redcoats, and renegades.

1219 Bacheller, Irving. Master of Chaos. Bobbs-Merrill, 1932. y.
Follows the generalship of George Washington in the early days of the Revolution.

1220 Bakeless, John. Fighting Frontiersman. Morrow, 1948. y.
A fictional biography of Daniel Boone.

1221 Barker, Shirley. Fire and the Hammer. Crown, 1953. y.
The five Tory Donan brothers prey on rebel American families in Bucks County, Pennsylvania.

1222 _____. The Road to Bunker Hill. Duell, Sloan, 1962. y.
A woman witnesses the colonial slaughter of British troops on Breed's Hill, Boston, in 1775.

1223 Barry, Jane. The Carolinians. Doubleday, 1959. y.

1224   _____. The Long March. Appleton, 1955. y.
          Two stories concerning General Daniel Morgan, his rifle-
          men, and the war in the South, culminating in the Battle
          of Cowpens.

1225   Beebe, Elswyth T. Dawn's Early Life. By Elswyth Thane,
          pseud. Duell, Sloane, 1943. y.
          Portrays Williamsburg and the Revolutionary War cam-
          paigns in the south.

1226   Beers, Lorna. The Crystal Cornerstone. Harper, 1953. y.
          Examines the experiences of a young Continental soldier
          in Washington's Army.

1227   Bell, Kensil. Jersey Rebel. Dodd, Mead, 1951. y.
          Jeff Lundy aids colonial forces in the 1777 campaign along
          the Delaware River.

1228   _____. Secret Missions for Valley Forge. Dodd, Mead,
          1955. y.
          Raids by troops under "Mad" Anthony Wayne.

1229   Best, Allena C. Horses for the General. Macmillan, 1956.
          y.
          Young people help provide them for Washington's Army.

1230   Boyce, Burke. The Man from Mount Vernon. Harper, 1961.
          y.
          A biographical novel about George Washington, including
          his 1775-1783 service as commander-in-chief of the Con-
          tinental Army.

1231   _____. The Perilous Night. Viking, 1941. y.
          Military and political problems of settlers in the Hudson
          River Valley.

1232   Boyd, James. Drums. Scribner's, 1925. y.
          Scotsmen participate in the Revolutionary War fighting in
          the Carolinas.

1233   Boyd, Thomas A. Shadow of the Long Knives. Scribner's,
          1928. Rpr. 1970. y.
          Indian warfare in the Ohio country.

1234   Brady, Cyrus T. When Blades Are Out and Love's Afield.
          Lippincott, 1901. y.
          British versus colonials in the Carolinas, 1780-1781.

1235   Brick, John. Ben Bryan, Morgan Rifleman. Duell, Sloan,
          1963. y.
          A young soldier participates in the 1775 colonial attack on
          British Quebec.

1236 _____. Captives of the Senacas. Duell, Sloan, 1964. y.
Two young hunters are taken by British Indians during the
Revolutionary War.

1237 _____. Eagle of Niagara. Doubleday, 1955. y.
Chief Joseph Brant's Revolutionary War exploits are witnessed by his captive, Continental soldier Daivd Harper.

1238 _____. King's Rangers. Doubleday, 1954. y.
Colonel Walter Butler's Tory woodsmen fight the colonials
in upper New York.

1239 _____. The Raid. Straus, 1951. y.
Chief Joseph Brant's Indians and the Tory Butler's Rangers
attack a village in the Hudson River Valley, capturing a
young girl who must survive until her rescue.

1240 _____. The Rifleman. Doubleday, 1953. y.
New York rifleman Tim Murphy and Pennsylvania troops
participate in the 1777 Battle of Saratoga.

1241 _____. Strong Man. Doubleday, 1960. y.
A young Continental soldier from New York participates in
the 1778 Battle of Monmouth.

1242 Bristow, Gwen. Celia Garth. Crowell, 1959. Rpr. 1974.
y.
Seamstress Garth records the successful British siege of
Charleston, 1780.

1243 Brooks, Elbridge S. In Blue and White. Lothrop, 1899. y.
The Marquis de Lafayette and his men pursue Arnold, now
a British general, in Virginia in 1781.

1244 Brown, M. M. Swamp Fox. Westminster, 1950. y.
A fictional biography of Francis Marion.

Buntline, Ned, pseud. See Judson, Edward Z. C.

1245 Cannon, LeGrande. Look to the Mountains. Holt, 1942.
Rpr. 1976. y.
Pictures the New Hampshire frontier aflame during the
Revolutionary War.

1246 Carter, Jefferson. Madam Constantia. Longmans, Green,
1919. y.
A girl is faced with betraying a Revolutionary War soldier/
spy into British hands in return for the release of her
father.

1247 Chalmers, Harvey. West of the Setting Sun. Macmillan,
1944. y.

Chief Joseph Brant leads the Iroquois of the Six Nations
against white settlers in New York.

1248   Chambers, Robert W. Cardigan. Harper, 1901. y.
The hero, a nephew of Sir William Johnson, witnesses
Brant's activities in the Mohawk Valley.

1249   _____. Little Red Foot. Doran, 1921. y.
John Drogue, former overseer for Sir William Johnson,
fights with the Oneidas on the side of the Americans
against the Iroquois and Tories in the Mohawk Valley,
1774-1782.

1250   _____. Love and the Lieutenant. Appleton, 1935. y.
Pictures British recruitment of Hessians and Burgoyne's
disaster at Saratoga in 1777.

1251   Chapman, Ann S. Mary Derwent. Burt, 1909. y.
Portrays the Revolutionary War Indian massacre of settlers in New York's Wyoming Valley.

Chapman, Maristan, pseud. See Chapman, Mary and Stanton.

1252   Chapman, Mary and Stanton. Rogue's March. By Maristan
Chapman, pseud. Lippincott, 1949. y.
A fictional recreation of the 1780 Battle of King's Moun-
tain.

1253   Churchill, Winston. The Crossing. Macmillan, 1904. y.
David Ritchie joins George Rogers Clarke's expedition to
Vincennes and Kaskaskia.

1254   Cobb, Sylvanus J. Karmel the Scout; or, The Rebel of the
Jerseys. Cassell, 1888. y.
Describes Washington's military operations in New Jersey,
1776-1777.

1255   Coffman, Virginia. Fire Dawn. Arbor House, 1977. Rpr.
1978. y.
Conflict between a colonial scout and British officer seeking an alliance with the Indians in 1775.

1256   Cooke, John E. Canolles, the Fortunes of a Partisan of '81.
E. B. Smith, 1877. y.
Follows the activities of colonial guerrillas in Virginia in
1781.

1257   Cormack, Maribelle, and William P. Alexander. Land for
My Sons. Appleton, 1939. y.
Experiences of a Pennsylvania militiaman in the Battle of
Bunker Hill.

1258   Davis, Burke. The Ragged Ones. Rinehart, 1951. y.

Generals Morgan and Nathanael Greene harry Cornwallis in 1781.

1259 _____ . Yorktown. Rinehart, 1952. y.
Escaping from a New York prison ship, a Continental sergeant takes part in the climactic battle of the Revolution.

1260 Doughty, W. Dyre. Crimson Mocassins. Harper, 1966. y.
George Rogers Clark versus the Miami Indians.

1261 Eastman, Edward R. The Destroyers. American Agricultur-
ist, Inc. , 1947.
A recreation of the 1778 Indian attack on Fort Alden, lo-
cated in the Cherry Valley south of the Mohawk in New
York.

1262 Eckert, Allan W. The Court Martial of Daniel Boone. Little, Brown, 1973. y.
In 1778 "the Long Knife" is tried for treason for alleged
collusion with the British and Shawnees; based on an actual
case involving Boone.

1263 Edmonds, Walter D. Drums Along the Mohawk. Little,
Brown, 1936. y.
Colonials in the Mohawk Valley resist British and Indian
attacks, 1776-1784; the Battle of Oriskany is prominent in
this tale.

1264 _____ . In the Hands of the Senacas. Little, Brown, 1947.
y.
In 1778 Indians raid the town of Dygartsbush, in New
York's Finger Lake area, and carry off a number of people.

1265 _____ . Wilderness Clearing. Dodd, Mead, 1944. y.
Chief Brant's braves win the Battle of Oriskany.

1266 Eggleston, George C. A Carolina Cavalier. Lothrop, 1901.
y.
Francis Marion's guerrilla activities.

1267 _____ . Long Knives. Lothrop, 1907. y.
George Rogers Clark takes Vincennes.

1268 Ellis, Edward S. Patriot and Tory. Estes, 1904. y.
Two brothers fight on opposite sides.

1269 Epstein, Samuel. Change for a Penny. Coward-McCann,
1959. y.

1269a _____ . Jackknife for a Penny. Coward-McCann, 1958.
y.
Two tales about the war on Long Island.

1270 Farmer, James E. Brinton Eliot. Macmillan, 1902. y.
      A Harvard student joins Washington's army and fights
      through the Revolution to Yorktown.

1271 Fast, Howard. April Morning. Crown, 1961. Rpr. 1970.
      y.
      Two youths become involved in the April 19, 1775 Battle
      of Lexington and Concord.

1272 _____. Conceived in Liberty. Simon & Schuster, 1939.
      Rpr. 1974. y.
      Pictures the difficulties of Washington's army at Valley
      Forge.

1273 _____. The Hessian. Morrow, 1972. y.
      Connecticut militiamen subject a captured German drummer
      boy to a kangaroo court for "war crimes."

1274 _____. The Proud and the Free. Little, Brown, 1950.
      Rpr. 1977. y.
      General Anthony Wayne quells the January 1, 1781 revolt
      of the 11th Regiment of the Pennsylvania Line.

1275 _____. The Unvanquished. Duell, Sloane, 1942. y.
      Washington's 1776 campaign on Long Island, in Manhattan
      and Westchester, and in New Jersey.

1276 Fenner, Phyllis R., comp. The Price of Liberty: Stories
      of the American Revolution. Morrow, 1960. y.
      Contains a dozen tales by various authors.

1277 Fleming, Thomas J. Now We Are Enemies. St. Martin's,
      1960. y.
      The story of the Battle of Bunker Hill from both sides.

1278 Fletcher, Inglis. Toil of the Brave. Bobbs-Merrill, 1947.
      Rpr. 1976. y.
      Washington's liaison officer in the Carolinas, Capt. Hunt-
      ley, takes part in the 1780 Battle of King's Mountain.

1279 Flood, Charles B. Monmouth. Houghton Mifflin, 1962. Rpr.
      1977. y.
      Captain Allen McLane's American cavalry participates in
      the 1778 battle.

1280 Forbes, Esther. Johnny Tremain. Houghton Mifflin, 1943.
      Rpr. 1969. y.
      A young Boston apprentice participates in the Battle of
      Lexington.

1281 Forbes-Lindsay, C. H. Daniel Boone. Lippincott, 1908. y.
      "Long Knive's" Revolutionary War exploits.

1282 Ford, Paul L.   Janice Meredith.   Dodd, Mead, 1899.   y.
      Focuses on Washington's 1776 campaigns in New York and
      New Jersey.

1283 Fox, Erskine.   Ershine Dale, Pioneer.   Scribner's, 1920.   y.
      Revolutionary War Indian warfare on the Virginia-Kentucky
      border.

1284 Frederick, Harold.   In the Valley.   Scribner's, 1890.   y.
      Chief Brant's Indians versus settlers in the Mohawk Valley.

1285 French, Allen.   The Colonials.   Doubleday, 1902.   y.
      Washington's siege of British-occupied Boston.

1286 Gerson, Noel B.   Fortress Fury.   By Carter A. Vaughan,
            pseud.   Doubleday, 1966.   Rpr. 1977.   y.
      Frontier fighting in the Detroit area.

1287 _____.   I'll Storm Hell.   Doubleday, 1967.   y.
      A biographical novel about General "Mad" Anthony Wayne.

1288 _____.   The Swamp Fox.   Doubleday, 1967.   y.
      A biographical novel about Francis Marion.

1289 _____.   The Yankee Rascals.   By Carter A. Vaughan,
            pseud.   Doubleday, 1963.   y.
      American POW's are freed by a guerrilla leader.

1290 Gessner, Robert.   Treason.   Scribner's, 1944.   y.
      Benedict Arnold's West Point treason as viewed by one of
      his aides.

1291 Goll, Reinhold W.   Valley Forge Rebel.   Dorrance, 1974.   y.
      Too young to join the Continental Army, a 15-year-old
      youth finds other ways to help Washington at Valley Forge.

1292 Gordon, Charles W.   The Rebel Loyalist.   Dodd, Mead, 1935.
      y.
      A Tory fighting for King George changes sides.

1293 Graves, Robert.   Proceed, Sergeant Lamb.   Random House,
            1941.   y.
      Pictures a British noncom's P. O. W. experiences and his es-
      cape to serve under Cornwallis in the Battle of Yorktown.

1294 Green, Marjorie S.   Cowboy of the Ramapos.   Abelard-Schu-
            man, 1956.   y.
      A story about one of Washington's scouts.

1295 Grey, Zane.   Betty Zane.   Harper, 1903.   Rpr. 1978.   y.
      An Ohio Valley heroine in battles with the Indians.

1296 Griffis, William E.   The Pathfinders of the Revolution.   W.
            A. Wilde, 1900.   y.

Portrays General Sullivan's campaign against the Indians
in New York, 1779.

1297 Hall, Marjory. A Hatful of Gold. Westminster, 1964. y.
       Molly Pitcher becomes a heroine in the Battle of Monmouth.

1298 Harris, Cyril. Trumpets at Dawn. Scribner's, 1938. y.
       A fictional recreation of the Battle of Trenton.

1299 Havinghurst, Walter. Proud Prisoner. Holt, Rinehart, 1964.
       y.
       George Rogers Clark captures Vincennes.

1300 Haycox, Ernest. Winds of Rebellion: Tales of the American
           Revolution. Criterion, 1964. y.
       Contents:--Winds of Rebellion. --The Drums Roll. --A
       Deserter at Valley Forge.

1301 Henri, Florette. King's Mountain. Doubleday, 1950. y.
       Carolina patriot Reece MacDermott and English officer
       Colonel Ferguson meet in the great 1780 clash.

1302 Henty, George A. True to the Old Flag. Scribner's, 1885.
       y.
       A fictional recreation of the battles of the Revolution, from
       Bunker Hill to Yorktown.

1303 Hopkins, Joseph G. E. Patriots' Progress. Scribner's, 1961.
       y.
       A Harvard medical doctor serves with Washington's forces
       at the siege of Boston.

1304 _____. The Price of Liberty. Scribner's, 1976. y.
       Recreates the trials and tribulations of surgeon John Frayne
       in caring for General Washington's wounded.

1305 Hoppus, Mary A. M. A Great Treason. Macmillan, 1883.
       y.
       Benedict Arnold tries to turn over West Point to the Brit-
       ish in 1780.

1306 Horan, James D. King's Rebel. Crown, 1953. y.
       Ex-British officer Robert Carhampton participates in the
       Indian-white battles in New York's Cherry Valley.

1307 Horne, Howard. Concord Bridge. Bobbs-Merrill, 1952. y.
       Focuses on the first fight of the Revolutionary War.

1308 Hough, Frank O. If Not Victory. Carrick, 1939. y.
       A Quaker youth of Weschester County deserts his pacifist
       faith to serve in the Continental Army, 1776-1778.

1309 _____. Renown. Lippincott, 1938. y.

A sympathetic view of the deeds and misdeeds of Benedict
Arnold.

J. S. of Dale, pseud. See Stimson, Frederic J.

1310 Jahoda, Gloria. Delilah's Mountain. Houghton Mifflin, 1963.
      y.
      British and Cherokees raid settlers in the Clinch River
      Valley of the Tennessee frontier.

1311 Jennings, John E. Shadow and the Glory. Reynal, 1943. y.
      Follows the exploits of James Ferguson, from an attack
      on a British fort at the mouth of Portsmouth harbor in
      1774 to the Battle of Bennington in 1777.

1312 Johnston, Mary. Hunting Shirt. Little, Brown, 1931. y.
      Life in a Cherokee village in the Virginia woods from 1775
      to 1780, including raids on colonists.

1313 Jones, Peter. Rebel in the Night. Dial, 1971. y.
      A Long Island farmboy fights for the Continental Army.

1314 Judson, Edward Z. C. Thayendanegea, the Scourge; or, The
      War Eagle of the Mohawks. By Ned Buntline, pseud.
      F. A. Brady, 1858. y.
      Chief Joseph Brant's activities in New York.

1315 Kaler, James O. Across the Delaware: a Boy's Story of the
      Battle of Trenton in 1777, as Set Down by Lieut. George
      Wentwort. By James Otis, pseud. A. L. Burt, 1903.
      y.
      Washington crosses the river and takes the British by sur-
      prise.

1316 _____ . Amos Dunkel, Oarsman. By James Otis, pseud.
      A. L. Burt, 1901. y.
      A young man serves with the "amphibious" Marblehead
      Regiment in the crossing of the Delaware and the Battle
      of Trenton.

1317 _____ . At the Siege of Quebec. By James Otis, pseud.
      Penn, 1897. y.
      Arnold and Montgomery in Canada, 1775.

1318 _____ . Boston Boys of 1775; or, When We Besieged Bos-
      ton. By James Otis, pseud. D. Estes, 1900. y.
      Young men participate in Washington's endeavor to force
      out the British occupiers.

1319 _____ . Corporal 'Lige's Recruit, a Story of Crown Point
      Ticonderoga. By James Otis, pseud. A. L. Burt,
      1898. y.
      Young people join the Green Mountain Boys in 1775 ex-
      ploits.

1320   .   The Defense of Fort Henry, a Story of Wheeling
             Creek in 1777.   By James Otis, pseud.   A. L. Burt,
             1900.   y.
             Patriot settlers versus Indians on the Ohio frontier.

1321   .   How the Twins Captured a Hessian, a Story of
             Long Island in 1776.   By James Otis, pseud.   T. Y.
             Crowell, 1902.   y.
             Young people participate in Washington's New York cam-
             paign.

1322   .   The Minute Boys of Boston.   By James Otis,
             pseud.   D. Estes, 1910.   y.
             Young people participate in the opening rounds of the Revo-
             lution.

1323   .   The Minute Boys of New York City.   By James
             Otis, pseud.   D. Estes, 1909.   y.
             Young people participate in Washington's campaign and de-
             fense.

1324   .   The Minute Boys of Philadelphia.   By James Otis,
             pseud.   D. Estes, 1911.   y.
             Young people participate in combat around the city and
             witness activities of the American Congress.

1325   .   The Minute Boys of South Carolina, a Story of
             How We Boys Aided Marion, the "Swamp Fox," as
             Told by Rufus Randolph.   By James Otis, pseud.   D.
             Estes, 1907.   y.
             Young people participate in the guerrilla warfare of 1781.

1326   .   The Minute Boys of the Green Mountains.   By
             James Otis, pseud.   D. Estes, 1905.   y.
             Activities of young people with Ethan Allen's men.

1327   .   The Minute Boys of the Mohawk Valley.   By James
             Otis, pseud.   D. Estes, 1905.   y.

1328   .   The Minute Boys of the Wyoming Valley.   By
             James Otis, pseud.   D. Estes, 1906.   y.
             Two tales in which young people participate in the Indian
             battles in New York State.

1329   .   The Minute Boys of York Town.   By James Otis,
             pseud.   D. Estes, 1912.   y.
             Lafayette and young friends participate in the climactic
             battle of the conflict.

1330   .   Morgan, the Jersey Spy: A Story of the Siege of
             Yorktown in 1781.   By James Otis, pseud.   A. L.
             Burt, 1899.   y.
             A young man becomes involved in the climactic engage-
             ment.

1331 _____ . Sarah Dillard's Ride, a Story of the Carolinas in
1780. By James Otis, pseud. A. L. Burt, 1898. y.
A girl helps the "Swamp Fox," Francis Marion.

1332 _____ . The Signal Boys of '75: A Tale of Boston During
the Siege. By James Otis, pseud. D. Estes, 1897. y.
Young people participate in Washington's siege of the city.

1333 _____ . With Lafayette at Yorktown: A Story of How Two
Boys Joined the Continental Army. By James Otis,
pseud. A. L. Burt, 1895. y.
Two colonial boys participate in the final battle of the war.

1334 _____ . With the "Swamp Fox." By James Otis, pseud.
A. L. Burt, 1899. y.
Young men aid Francis Marion in South Carolina.

1335 _____ . With Warren at Bunker Hill: A Story of the Siege
of Boston. By James Otis, pseud. A. L. Burt, 1898. y.
Young people participate in the Battle of Bunker Hill.

1336 _____ . With Washington at Monmouth. By James Otis,
pseud. A. L. Burt, 1897. y.
Several young men join in the 1778 New Jersey fight.

1337 Kantor, MacKinley. Valley Forge. Evans, 1975. Rpr. 1976. y.
Washington's encampment as seen by various soldiers.

1338 Kennedy, John Pendleton. Horse-Shoe Robinson: A Tale of
the Tory Ascendency. Rev. ed. Putnam, 1852. Rpr.
1977. y.
First published in 1835, this story concerns Carolina partisan activities in the 1780's.

1339 Kenyon, Charles R. Won in Warfare. Nelson, 1904. y.
Colonial troops defeat British regulars and Tories in the
1780 Battle of King's Mountain.

1340 King, Charles. Cadet Days. Harper, 1894. y.
Arnold and West Point, 1780.

1341 Kjelgaard, J. A. Rebel Siege. Holiday, 1943. y.
Carolina mountain boy fights for freedom with colonial
forces.

1342 Lancaster, Bruce. The Big Knives. Little, Brown, 1964.
Rpr. 1978. y.
George Rogers Clark takes Detroit with 200 men in 1778.

1343 _____ . The Blind Journey. Little, Brown, 1953. Rpr.
1976. y.
Benjamin Franklin's courier lands in Virginia from France
with money and supplies for Washington just before the
Battle of Yorktown.

1344 _____. Guns of Burgoyne. Stokes, 1939. Rpr. 1977. y.
A young Hessian in command of some of Burgoyne's cannon
is a party to the great British defeat at Saratoga in 1777.

1345 _____. Phantom Fortress. Little, Brown, 1950. Rpr.
1976. y.
Rhode Island cavalry captain Ross Pembroke serves with
Marion's guerrillas in the Carolinas.

1346 _____. The Secret Road. Little, Brown, 1952. Rpr.
1976. y.
Examines Washington's move toward Long Island in 1781.

1347 _____. Trumpet to Arms. Little, Brown, 1944. Rpr.
1976. y.
John Glover's Marblehead Regiment in the battles of Tren-
ton and Princeton.

1348 Lay, Elery A. Trek to King's Mountain. Moore, 1976. y.
Focuses on American pioneers in the great 1780 battle.

1349 Leland, John A. Othneil Jones. Lippincott, 1957. y.
A half-Cherokee fights with the "Swamp Fox."

1350 Lender, C. F. Down the Ohio with Clark. Crowell, 1937.
y.
A youth accompanies George Rogers Clark to Vincennes.

1351 Lippard, George. Washington and His Generals; or, Legends
of the Revolution. Arno, 1976. y.
A series of short tales originally published in 1847 as The
Legends of the American Revolution, 1776.

1352 Longstreet, Stephen. Eagles Where I Walk. Doubleday, 1961.
y.
Experiences of an upper-class doctor in Washington's
Army.

1353 _____. A Few Painted Feathers. Doubleday, 1964. y.
Portrays the exploits of Dr. David Courtlandt, surgeon
general of Continental forces in the South late in the Revolutionary War.

1354 Lynde, Francis. Mr. Arnold. Bobbs-Merrill, 1923. y.
In 1780 Benedict Arnold leads British troops on a raid into Virginia.

1355 McCants, Elliott C. Ninety Six. Crowell, 1930. y.
Revolutionary War action at Frontier Post 96 in South
Carolina.

1356 McIntyre, John T. The Young Continentals at Bunker Hill.
Penn, 1910. y.
Young American soldiers participate in the Boston contest.

1357 _____ . The Young Continentals at Lexington.   Penn, 1909.
       y.
       Young Americans engage in firing the "shot heard 'round
       the world. "

1358 Mason, Francis Van Wyck.   Guns for Rebellion.   Doubleday,
       1977. y.
       Ethan Allen and Benedict Arnold take Ticonderoga, and
       our hero helps Henry Knox transport the fortress's guns
       overland to Washington at Boston.

1359 _____ . Rivers of Glory.   Lippincott, 1942.   y.
       Recreates the 1778-1779 siege of Savannah.

1360 _____ . Valley Forge.   Doubleday, 1951.   y.
       A small book (only thirty pages) that portrays the near-
       resignation of General Washington in late December 1777.

1361 _____ . Wild Horizons.   Little, Brown, 1966.   y.
       Carleton's raids and the Scots-Irish in Eastern Tennessee,
       ending with the 1780 Battle of King's Mountain.

       Mayrant, Drayton, pseud.   See Simons, Katherine D. M.

1362 Meadowcraft, Enicl M.   Silver for General Washington.   Cro-
       well, 1944. y.
       Youngsters near Valley Forge help alleviate the suffering
       of soldiers in the Continental Army.

1363 Miller, Helen T.   Slow Dies the Thunder.   Bobbs-Merrill,
       1955. y.
       Recreates Revolutionary War activities in the Carolinas,
       including the siege of Charleston and the Battle of King's
       Mountain.

1364 _____ . Sound of Chariots.   Bobbs-Merrill, 1947.   y.
       When Britain elects to abandon Augusta, Georgia, in 1780,
       Loyalists are forced to push inland to escape American
       guerrilla troops.

1365 Mitchell, S. Weir.   Hugh Wynne, Free Quaker, Sometime
       Brevet Lieutenant Colonel on the Staff of His Excellency
       General Washington.   Century, 1897.   y.
       Activities of a Free Quaker and his participation in the
       1777 Battle of Germantown.

1366 Orrmont, Arthur.   Diplomat in Warpaint.   Abelard, 1968.   y.
       Well-educated Creek chief Alexander McGillivray keeps
       his tribe neutral during the Revolution, despite various
       pressures.

       Otis, James, pseud.   See Kaler, James O.

1367	Paretti, Sandra. The Drums of Winter. Trans. from the
	German. Lippincott, 1974. y.
	Family problems come to a head in the split of loyalties
	between two brothers during Washington's Delaware Valley
	campaign.

1368	Partington, Norman. The Sunshine Patriot. St. Martin's,
	1975. y.
	The deeds and misdeeds of Benedict Arnold.

1369	Peck, Robert N. Hang for Treason. Doubleday, 1976. y.
	Able Booker joins Allen and Arnold in taking Fort Ticon-
	deroga in 1775.

1370	_____. The King's Iron. Little, Brown, 1977. y.
	Henry Knox brings Ticonderoga's guns to Boston; compare
	with Mason's Guns for Rebellion cited above.

1371	Pollard, Eliza P. The Green Mountain Boys. Dodd, Mead,
	1896. y.
	Carleton and Montgomery at Quebec in 1775.

1372	Pridgen, Tim. Tory Oath. Doubleday, 1941. y.
	Scottish Highlanders in the 1780 Battle of King's Mountain.

1373	Rayner, William. The World Turned Upside Down. Morrow,
	1970. y.
	British major James Blackford is the only survivor of a
	1781 rebel attack on his small force in Virginia; disguised
	as a slave, he must somehow regain his own lines.

1374	Roberts, Kenneth L. Arundel. Doubleday, Doran, 1930.
	Rpr. 1976. y.
	Fictional recreation of the Arnold-Montgomery campaign
	against Quebec in 1775.

1375	_____. Oliver Wiswell. Doubleday, 1940. Rpr. 1977.
	y.
	A famous portrayal of the problems of a Tory in the Ken-
	tucky and South Carolina of the Revolutionary War.

1376	_____. Rabble in Arms. Doubleday, 1934. Rpr. 1977.
	y.
	Sequel to Arundel; Maine soldiers participate in the 1777
	Battle of Saratoga.

1377	Robinson, Gertrude. Winged Feet. Dutton, 1939. y.
	Scouting for General Washington.

1378	Safford, Henry B. That Bennington Mob. Messner, 1935.
	y.
	Ethan Allen and the Green Mountain Boys.

1379 Schneider, Benjamin. Winter Patriot. Chilton, 1967. y.
        The son of a patriot killed early in the war joins a guer-
        rilla unit harassing the British.

1380 Scollard, Clinton. The Son of a Tory. Badyer, 1901. y.
        Centers on the British siege of Fort Stanwix.

1381 Seifert, Shirley. Let My Name Stand Fair. Lippincott, 1956.
        Rpr. 1976. y.
        A biographical novel about the exploits of American general
        Nathanael Greene.

1382 _____. Waters of the Wilderness. Lippincott, 1941. Rpr.
        1976. y.
        George Rogers Clark's 1778-1780 missions to Vincennes
        and Kaskaskia.

1383 Simms, William G. Eutaw, a Sequel to the Forayers; or,
        The Raid of the Dog-Days, a Tale of the Revolution.
        Widdleton, 1856. Rpr. 1970. y.
        Presents the 1781 Battle of Eutaw Springs in South Caro-
        lina.

1384 _____. The Forayers; or, The Raid of the Dog Days.
        Rev. ed. Donohue, Henneberry, 1890. Rpr. 1970. y.
        First published in 1855; patriot partisan activities in South
        Carolina in 1780.

1385 _____. Mellichampe: A Legend of the Santee. Harper,
        1836. Rpr. 1970. y.
        Follows military operations in South Carolina in the inter-
        val between the Battle of Camden and the coming of Gen-
        eral Nathanael Greene.

1386 _____. The Partisan: A Tale of the Revolution. Harper,
        1835. Rpr. 1970. y.
        Traces military operations in South Carolina from the fall
        of Charleston in 1780 to the defeat of General Horatio
        Gates at Camden.

1387 _____. The Scout; or, The Black Riders of Congaree.
        New and rev. ed. J. W. Lovell, 1885. Rpr. 1976.
        y.
        First published as The Kinsman in 1841, this story tells
        of General Greene's first victories in South Carolina.

1388 Simons, Katherine D. M. The Red Doe. By Drayton May-
        rant, pseud. Appleton, 1953. y.
        The exploits of "Swamp Fox" Francis Marion.

1389 Sinclair, Harold. Westward the Tide. Doubleday, 1940. y.
        George Rogers Clark and the capture of Vincennes.

1390 Singmaster, Elsie. <u>Rifles for Washington</u>. Houghton Mifflin,
      1939. y.
      Arming Continental troops for the Battle of Yorktown.

1391 Skinner, Constance L. <u>Silent Scout, Frontier Scout</u>. Mac-
      millan, 1925. y.
      Andy MacPhail's scouting activities on the Tennessee bor-
      der.

1392 Slaughter, Frank G. <u>Flight from Natchez</u>. Doubleday, 1955.
      Rpr. 1974. y.
      A doctor leads the evacuees from Natchez.

1393 Stanley, Edward. <u>Thomas Forty</u>. Duell, Sloan, 1947. y.
      A youth becomes a lieutenant in Armand's Partisan Legion
      in Westchester County, New York.

1394 Sterne, Emma G. <u>Drums on the Monmouth</u>. Dodd, Mead,
      1935. y.
      Focuses on Washington's 1778 New Jersey campaign.

1395 Stevenson, Burton E. <u>The Heritage</u>. Houghton Mifflin, 1903.
      y.
      The 1781 siege and Battle of Yorktown.

1396 Stimson, Frederic J. <u>My Story: Being the Memoirs of Bene-
      dict Arnold</u>. By J. S. of Dale, pseud. Scribner's,
      1917. y.
      A fictional autobiography that covers the military successes
      as well as the great West Point failure of America's best-
      known traitor.

1397 Stoddard, William O. <u>Dan Monroe</u>. Lothrop, 1905. y.
      A young man's participation in the Battle of Bunker Hill.

1398 _____ . <u>The Fight for the Valley</u>. Appleton, 1904. y.
      The siege of Fort Schuyler and the Battle of Oriskany.

1399 _____ . <u>On the Old Frontier</u>. Appleton, 1894. y.
      Pictures the last Revolutionary War raid of the Iroquois
      into the Onondaga Valley of New York.

1400 _____ . <u>Two Cadets with Washington</u>. Lothrop, 1906. y.
      The 1775 siege of British-occupied Boston.

1401 Stover, Herbert E. <u>Men in Buckskin</u>. Dodd, Mead, 1950.
      y.
      British-instigated Indian raids on Pennsylvania settlers in
      the Susquehanna area.

1402 _____ . <u>Powder Mission</u>. Dodd, Mead, 1951. y.
      An expedition from Fort Pitt to New Orleans to get gold
      and powder for Washington's army.

1403 Styles, Showell. Gentleman Johnny. Macmillan, 1963. y.
        The exploits of General John Burgoyne, including his 1777
        defeat at Saratoga.

1404 Sullivan, James A. Valley Forge. Dorrance, 1964. y.
        American troops suffer badly in their winter quarters.

1405 Swanson, Neil H. The Forbidden Ground. Farrar, Straus,
        1938. y.
        Military actions around Detroit in the Revolutionary War.

1406 Taylor, Allan. Morgan's Long Rifles. Putnam, 1965. y.
        Dan Morgan's riflemen participate in the 1775 assault on
        Quebec.

1407 Taylor, David. Farewell to Valley Forge. Lippincott, 1955.
        y.
        Virginia captain Jonathan Kimball at Valley Forge and the
        Battle of Monmouth.

1408 _____. Lights Across The Delaware. Lippincott, 1954.
        y.
        Washington takes Trenton on Christmas, 1776.

1409 _____. Storm the Last Rampart. Lippincott, 1960. y.
        The siege and Battle of Yorktown in 1781.

1410 _____. Sycamore Men. Lippincott, 1958. y.
        Colonel Dixon Blakely musters his irregulars to help Fran-
        cis Marion against Cornwallis and Tarleton, 1780-1781.

      Thane, Elswyth, pseud. See Beebe, Elswyth T.

1411 Thompson, Daniel P. The Green Mountain Boys. Nelson,
        1927. y.
        First published in Montpelier, Vermont, in 1839, this tale
        focuses on Vermonters under Ethan Allen in early cam-
        paigns of the Revolution.

1412 Thompson, Maurice. Alice of Old Vincennes. Cassell, 1901.
        Rpr. 1978. y.
        The best-remembered story about Clark's capture of Vin-
        cennes.

1413 Thompson, N. P. The Rangers. Nichols and Hall, 1851. y.
        Early fictional tale of George Rogers Clark's exploits.

1414 Tilton, Dwight. My Lady Laughter. C. M. Clark, 1905. y.
        Portrays the 1775 colonial siege of Boston.

1415 Todd, A. L. Richard Montgomery. McKay, 1967. y.
        A fictional biography of the U. S. leader instrumental in
        the defense of New York and in the assaults on St. John's
        Montreal, and Quebec.

1416   Toepfer, Ray G.   Liberty and Corporal Kincaid.   Chilton,
          1968.   y.
          The activities of a Virginia militia company and one of its
          men.

1417   _____.   The White Cockade.   Chilton, 1966.   y.
          Patriots fight the July 22, 1779 Battle of Minisink.

1418   Tomlinson, Everett T.   A Lieutenant Under Washington.
          Houghton Mifflin, 1903.   y.
          Follows Washington's campaigns from the Brandywine to
          Valley Forge.

1419   _____.   Marching Against the Iroquois.   Houghton Mifflin,
          1906.   y.
          General Sullivan's campaigns against the Indians in New
          York, 1779.

1420   _____.   The Red Chief.   Houghton Mifflin, 1905.   y.
          Recreates the Cherry Valley Massacre of 1778.

1421   _____.   Under Colonial Colors.   Houghton Mifflin, 1902.
          y.
          The 1775 attack by Arnold and Montgomery on Quebec.

1422   _____.   Washington's Young Aides.   Wilde, 1897.   y.
          How they viewed the 1776-1777 New Jersey campaign.

1423   True, John P.   On Guard Against Tory and Tarleton.   Little,
          1903.   y.
          Greene's defeat of Cornwallis in the Carolinas.

1424   Vail, Philip.   The Twisted Sabre.   Dodd, Mead, 1963.   y.
          The pre-1780 military successes of Benedict Arnold in the
          colonial cause and his great treason at West Point.

1425   Van de Water, Frederic F.   Catch a Falling Star.   Duell,
          Sloane, 1949.   y.
          Ethan Allen and the capture of Fort Ticonderoga.

1426   _____.   Day of Battle.   Washburn, 1958.   y.
          Lieutenant Jeremy Shaw of the Continental Army fights in
          the 1777 Battle of Bennington.

1427   _____.   Reluctant Rebel.   Duell, Sloan, 1948.   y.
          Allen and Arnold take Ticonderoga.

1428   _____.   Wings of the Morning.   Washburn, 1936.   y.
          Recreates the 1777 Battle of Bennington.

1429   Van Every, Dale.   Bridal Journey.   Messner, 1950.
          Problems of a girl on the Ohio frontier during 1781 and
          the exploits of George Rogers Clark in the same area.

1430   _____. Captive Witch. Messner, 1952. y.
        Begins with Clark's victory at Vincennes in 1778.

1431   _____. Scarlet Feather. Holt, 1959. Rpr. 1978. y.
        Indians versus settlers in Kentucky.

Vaughan, Carter A., pseud. See Gerson, Noel B.

1432   Wallace, Mary. Blue Meadow. Morrow, 1975. y.
        The Revolutionary War as viewed by farmers near Phila-
        delphia.

1433   Wallace, Willard M. East to Bagaduce. Regnery, 1963. y.
        British siege of Bagaduce (Castine), Maine, in 1779.

1434   Warren, C. E. The Musket Boys of Old Boston. Cupples &
        Leou, 1909. y.
        Washington's siege of Boston in 1775.

1435   _____. The Musket Boys Under Washington. Cupples &
        Leou, 1909. y.
        The battle for New York in 1776.

1436   Wellman, Manly W. Clash on the Catawba. Washburn, 1962.
        y.
        Carolina militiamen participate in the battles at Cowpens
        and on the Catawba, 1780-1781.

1437   Wheelwright, Jere. Kentucky Stand. Scribner's, 1951. y.
        Indian fighting on the Kentucky frontier in 1777.

1438   Wibberley, Leonard. John Treegate's Musket. Farrar,
        Straus, 1959. y.
        A young soldier participates in the Battle of Bunker Hill.

1439   _____. Peter Treegate's War. Farrar, Straus, 1960. y.
        The son of a Scots clansman is involved in the crossing
        of the Delaware and the battles of Trenton and Saratoga.

1440   _____. Treegate's Raiders. Farrar, Straus, 1962. y.
        A Colonial army captain leads his troops into battle at
        King's Mountain, Cowpens, and Yorktown.

1441   Wiener, Willard. Morning in America. Farrar, Straus,
        1942. y.
        One of General Charles Lee's soldiers recalls the battles
        of the Revolutionary War.

NORTH AMERICA: 1783 TO 1815

The stories in this section cover military events in the new United
States of America from the end of the Revolutionary War to Andrew
Jackson's victory at New Orleans in 1815.   Among the highlights of
these years were the Shays Rebellion, the St. Clair-Wayne campaign
against the Indians in Ohio, and the War of 1812.

1442 Allis, Marguerite. To Keep Us Free. Putnam, 1953. y.
      Love and combat in Ohio during the War of 1812.

1443 Altsheler, Joseph A. A Herald of the West. Appleton, 1898.
      y.
      Settlers and militia battle British and Indians on the north-
      west frontier during the War of 1812.

1444 _____. The Wilderness Road. Appleton, 1901. y.
      After St. Clair's militia is defeated by the Indians in 1791,
      General "Mad" Anthony Wayne is placed in charge of the
      western army and is victorious in the 1794 Battle of Fallen
      Timbers.   For another look at Wayne's Indian-fighting ex-
      periences, see Noel B. Gerson's I'll Storm Hell, cited in
      the previous section.

1445 Anness, Milford E. Song of Metamoris. Caxton, 1964. y.
      Metamoris and his brother Tecumseh are defeated by Gen-
      eral Harrison in the 1811 Battle of Tippecanoe.

1446 Bacheller, Irving. D'Ri and I. Harper, 1901. y.
      The War of 1812 in the St. Lawrence Valley.

1447 Banks, Polan. Black Ivory. Harper, 1926. y.
      Pirate Jean Lafitte helps Andrew Jackson win the 1815
      Battle of New Orleans.

1448 Beebe, Ralph. Who Fought and Bled. Coward-McCann, 1941.
      y.
      Boston heir Roderick Hale and scout Captain Abijah Stark
      fight the British and Indians in the west, witnessing Gen-
      eral Hull's surrender of Detroit on August 16, 1812.

1449 Bellamy, Edward. The Duke of Stockbridge. Silver, Burdett,
      1900. y.
      A realistic treatment of Daniel Shays's 1786 rebellion in
      western Massachusetts.

1450 Bird, Robert M. Nick o' the Woods; or, The Jibbenainosay.
      Armstrong, 1837. y.
      An early story about Indian fighting in Kentucky in the
      years just after the Revolution.

1451 Bontemps, Arna. Black Thunder. Macmillan, 1936. y.
      About 1800 a group of slaves try to capture Richmond in
      the so-called "Gabriel Insurrection."

1452 Burgoyne, Leon E. Ensign Ronan. Winston, 1956. y.
      At Fort Dearborn, in 1812, a young officer thirsts for
      Indian scalps.

1453 Campbell, Grace M. Higher Hill. Duell, Sloan, 1944. y.
      Warfare on both sides of the St. Lawrence River during
      the War of 1812.

1454 Campbell, Wilfrid. A Beautiful Rebel. Doran, 1909. y.
      Involves Sir Isaac Brock and the 1812 Battle of Queens-
      town Heights in upper Canada.

1455 Case, Josephine. Wind in the Sand. Houghton Mifflin, 1945.
      y.
      General William Eaton leads U.S. Marines to Tripoli in
      1805.

1456 Chambers, Robert W. The Rake and the Hussy. Appleton-
      Century, 1930. y.
      How gallant Joshua Brooke helped Jackson defend New
      Orleans.

      Chapman, Maristan, pseud. See Chapman, Mary and Stanton.

1457 Chapman, Mary and Stanton. Tennessee Hazard. By Mari-
      stan Chapman, pseud. Lippincott, 1953. y.
      Frontiersmen versus the Indians during the days of the
      Spanish Conspiracy.

      Connor, Ralph, pseud. See Gordon, Charles W.

1458 Cooper, Jamie L. The Horn and the Forest. Bobbs-Mer-
      rill, 1963. y.
      General Benjamin Harrison and his troops defeat Tecumseh
      in the 1811 Battle of Tippecanoe.

1459 Crowley, Mary C. Love Thrives in War. Little, 1903. y.
      General Brock forces Hull to surrender Detroit in 1812.

1460 Crownfield, Gertrude. When Glory Waits. Lippincott, 1934.
      y.
      Mary Vining, Anthony Wayne, and the 1794 Battle of Fallen
      Timbers.

1461 Degenhard, William. The Regulators. Dial, 1943. y.
      Recreates the 1786 Shays Rebellion in Massachusetts.

1462 Devereux, May. Lafitte of Louisiana. Little, 1902. y.

How the pirate chief aided General Jackson at New Orleans
in 1815.

1463 Downes, Anne M.   The Quality of Mercy.   Lippincott, 1959.
          y.
      Andrew Jackson and the Creek Indian War, ending with the
      1814 Battle of Horseshoe Bend.

1464 DuSoe, R. C.   Your Orders Sir!   Longmans, Green, 1953.
          y.
      A young soldier in the Battle of New Orleans.

1465 Elson, John M.   The Scarlet Sash.   Dent, 1925.   y.
      The War of 1812 Battle of Queenstown Heights in Canada.

1466 Evernden, Margery.   Wilderness Boy.   Putnam, 1955.   y.
      A youth is involved in the 1794 Whiskey Rebellion in west-
      ern Pennsylvania.

1467 Field, Dawn S.   Luise.   Putnam, 1974.   y.
      A Prussian exile experiences the fall of Washington to the
      British in 1814.

1468 Gerson, Noel B.   Cumberland Rifles.   Doubleday, 1952.   y.
      A soldier of fortune joins the American frontiersmen bat-
      tling the Spanish Conspiracy in Tennessee after the Revo-
      lution.

1469 _____.   Old Hickory.   Doubleday, 1964.   y.
      A biographical novel about Andrew Jackson, telling of his
      victories at Horseshoe Bend and New Orleans.

1470 Giles, Janice H.   Land Beyond the Mountains.   Houghton Mif-
          flin, 1958.   y.
      Indian fighting in Kentucky from 1783-1792.

1471 Gordon, Charles W.   Rock and the River.   By Ralph Connor,
          pseud. Dodd, Mead, 1931.   y.
      Tells of the battles of Lundy's Lane, Chippewa, and the
      Thames during the War of 1812; from the Canadian view-
      point.

1472 _____.   The Runner.   By Ralph Connor, pseud.   Double-
          day, Doran, 1930.   y.
      American soldiers battle the British at Lundy's Lane and
      Chippewa in 1814.

1473 Gordon, H. R.   Black Partridge.   W. & W. Chambers, 1908.
          y.
      Recreates the fall of Fort Dearborn.

1474 Hale, Edward Everett.   The Man Without a Country.   1863.
          Rpr. 1974.

A young U.S. Army officer is tried for treason as a result of his participation in the Burr Conspiracy; upon uttering a desire never to see the U.S. again, he is granted his wish by the court in a most unusual manner.

1475 Harper, Robert S. Trumpet in the Wilderness. M. S. Mill,
          1940. y.
      General Hull surrenders Detroit in 1812.

1476 Hodge, Jane A. Here Comes a Candle. Doubleday, 1967. y.
      American soldiers raid Canada in the War of 1812.

1477 Howard, Elizabeth. Candle in the Night. Morrow, 1952. y.
      Focuses on Hull's surrender of Detroit.

1478 Kaler, James O. At the Siege of Detroit, a Story of Two
          Ohio Boys in the War of 1812, as Set Down by David
          Bellinger. By James Otis, pseud. A. L. Burt, 1904.
      Hull surrenders Detroit in 1812.

1479 Kent, Madeline F. The Corsair. Doubleday, 1956. y.
      Lafitte aids Jackson at New Orleans.

1480 Kummer, Frederick A. For Flag and Freedom. Morrow,
          1942. y.
      The 1814 defense of Baltimore.

1481 Marshall, Bernard G. Old Hickory's Prisoner. Appleton,
          1926. y.
      Hubert Delaroche and an Indian friend provide valuable
      service to General Jackson just before the Battle of New
      Orleans.

1482 Mayer, Albert L. Follow the River. Doubleday, 1969. y.
      General Josiah Harmon's expedition against the Indians
      along the Maumee River in the 1790's.

1483 Moore, John T. Hearts of Hickory. Cokesbury, 1926. y.
      General Jackson and Davy Crockett fight in the Creek War
      of 1814.

1484 Muir, Robert. The Spring of Hemlock. Longmans, Green,
          1957. y.
      The menfolk of the Tucker family join in the 1786 Shays
      Rebellion.

1485 Nicholson, Meredith. The Cavaliers of Tennessee. Bobbs-
          Merrill, 1928. y.
      A fictional biography of Andrew Jackson, with attention
      paid to his generalship in the Creek War and the Battle
      of New Orleans.

1486 Orr, Myron D. Mission to Mackinac. Dodd, Mead, 1956.
          y.

The English-French conflict in northern Michigan prior to
the War of 1812.

Otis, James, pseud. See Kaler, James O.

1487 Palmer, Bruce. Horseshoe Bend. Simon & Schuster, 1962.
y.
How William Weatherford, leader of the Creeks, was defeated by General Jackson in Alabama on March 27, 1814.

1488 Parrish, Randall. When Wilderness Was King. McClurg,
1904. y.
The fall of Fort Dearborn, now Chicago, in 1812.

1489 Pendexter, Hugh. Red Belts. Doubleday, 1920. y.
Pioneer John Sevier aids settlers in fighting off Indians
and Spanish agents in 1784 Tennessee.

1490 _____. A Virginia Scout. Bobbs-Merrill, 1922. y.
Indian warfare on the Virginia border after the Revolution.

1491 Pridgen, Tim. West Goes the Road. Doubleday, 1944. y.
Frontiersmen battle Indians and foreign agents for the
lands between the Alleghenies and the Mississippi River.

1492 Read, Opie. By the Eternal. Laird & Lee, 1906. y.
General Jackson wins the January 1815 Battle of New Orleans.

1493 Reed, Myrtle. The Shadow of Victory. Putnam, 1903. y.
The massacre and fall of Fort Dearborn in 1812.

1494 Rickett, Edith. Out of the Cypress Swamp. Methuen, 1902.
y.
Jackson and the Battle of New Orleans.

1495 Root, Corwin. An American, Sir! Dutton, 1940. y.
Love and a young soldier's combat experiences in the War
of 1812.

1496 Schumann, Mary K. My Blood and My Treasure. Dial, 1941.
y.
The siege and fall of Detroit in 1812.

1497 Shepard, Odell and Willard. Holdfast Gaines. Macmillan,
1946. y.
Military and other U.S. events from 1783 to 1815, includ-
ing the Fort Mims Massacre, the defeat of Tecumseh at
Tippecanoe, the burning of Washington, and the Battle of
New Orleans.

1498 Sperry, Armstrong. Black Falcon. Winston, 1949. y.
Wade Thayer escapes the British to join Jean Lafitte in
the Battle of New Orleans.

1499   Stoddard, William O.   The Errand Boy of Andrew Jackson.
            Lothrop, 1902.   y.
       Old Hickory at Mobile and New Orleans, 1814 to 1815.

1500   Street, James.   Oh, Promised Land.   Dial, 1940.   y.
       Jackson and Crockett battle the Creeks in Alabama and
       Mississippi.

1501   Tracy, Don.   Crimson Is the Eastern Shore.   Dial, 1953.
            Rpr. 1978.   y.
       Dritish raiding parties pillage Maryland's Eastern Shore
       in the War of 1812.

1502   Van Every, Dale.   Captive Witch.   Messner, 1951.   y.
       Adventures of one of George Rogers Clark's scouts in Vir-
       ginia and Kentucky after the Revolution.

1503   Wood, Charles.   On the Frontier with St. Clair.   Wilde, 1902.
            y.
       St. Clair's motley collection of militia and levies is anni-
       hilated by the Northwestern Indians in the Ohio Territory
       in 1791.

NORTH AMERICA: 1815 TO 1860

The tales in this section cover an exciting period in North American
history.   Stories recreate for us the Black Hawk and Seminole wars,
the Texan War of Independence, the Canadian Rebellion of 1837,
"Bleeding Kansas," the war with Mexico, and various Indian fights.
Some of these accounts are contemporary with the occurrences they
portray and, although now difficult to locate, provide an interesting
flavor for those hardy enough to endure their antiquated style.

1504   Aimard, Gustave.   The Freebooters: A Story of the Texan
            War.   Ed. by St. Percy B. John.   Scholarly, 1976.   y.
       This edition adds much background to the 1887 original.

1505   Ainsworth, Edward.   Eagles Fly West.   Macmillan, 1946.   y.
       A newspaper reporter takes part in the fighting between
       U.S. troops and Spanish Californians during the Mexican
       War.

1506   Allen, Merritt P.   Out of a Clear Sky.   Longmans, Green,
            1938.   y.
       The Mountain Meadow massacre in Utah.

1507   Alter, Robert E.   Two Sieges of the Alamo.   Putnam, 1965.
            y.
       Texan defense of San Antonio, 1835-1836.

1508   Altsheler, Joseph A.   The Quest of the Four.   D. Appleton,
           1911.   y.
           Four Americans fight the Commanches and participate in
           the Mexican War Battle of Buena Vista.

1509   .   The Texan Scouts.   D. Appleton, 1921.   y.
           Ned Fulton and the 1836 defense of the Alamo against San-
           ta Anna.

1510   .   The Texan Star.   D. Appleton, 1912.   y.
           Ned Fulton becomes involved in the early stages of the
           Texan War.

1511   .   The Texan Triumphant.   D. Appleton, 1913.   y.
           Young Ned Fulton joins Sam Houston in defeating Santa
           Anna in the Battle of Jan Jacinto.

1512   Bailey, Paul D.   The Claws of the Hawk.   Westernlore, 1966.
           y.
           A fictionalized biography of the great Ute war chief, Wal-
           kara, c. 1808-1855.

1513   Baker, Betty.   The Dunderhead War.   Harper, 1967.   y.
           Recalls the adventures of a German immigrant and his
           nephew on the Santa Fe Trail during the Mexican War.

1514   Baker, Keith.   Star of the Wilderness.   By Charlotte Wilson,
           pseud.   Coward-McCann, 1942.   y.
           Two young men become involved in the Texan War of In-
           dependence.

1515   Barr, Amelia E.   Remember the Alamo.   Dodd, Mead, 1908.
           y.
           A portrayal of the Battle of the Alamo, March 6, 1836.

1516   Barrett, Monte.   Sun for Their Eyes.   Bobbs-Merrill, 1944.
           y.
           Texans revolt against Mexican rule in the 1820's.

1517   .   Tempered Blade.   Bobbs-Merrill, 1946.   y.
           A fictional biography of Jim Bowie, knife inventor, planter,
           and gambler, who died in defense of the Alamo.

1518   Bean, Amelia.   Francher Train.   Doubleday, 1958.   y.
           Recreates the 1857 massacre of a wagon train in southern
           Utah by Indians and Mormans.

1519   Brackett, Leigh.   Follow the Free Wind.   Doubleday, 1963.
           y.
           The son of a slave is adopted by the Crow Indians and
           joins them in fighting the whites.

1520   Brady, Cyrus T.   In the War with Mexico.   Scribner's, 1903.
           y.

Covers the entire war in fiction form, recreating most
battles.

1521 Brand, Anna. Thunder Before Seven. Doubleday, 1941. y.
      The Texas War of Independence, ending with the Battle of
      San Jacinto.

1522 Brown, Dee. Wave High the Banner. Macrae Smith, 1942.
      y.
      A fictional biography of Davy Crockett, ending with his
      death with Bowie, Travis, and the others at the Alamo in
      1836.

1523 Bryan, Jack Y. Come to the Bower. Viking, 1963. y.
      Another look at the Texan War of Independence, from the
      Alamo to San Jacinto.

      Buntline, Ned, pseud. See Judson, Edward Z. C.

1524 Burke, James W. The Blazing Dawn. Pyramid, 1975. y.
      P.
      Bowie, Crockett, and Travis defend the Alamo against
      Santa Anna.

1525 Cameron, W. B. The War Trail of Big Bear. Duckworth,
      1926. y.
      The Wood Cree Indian rebellion in northwest Canada, 1830-
      1860.

1526 Campbell, Walter S. Revolt on the Border. By Stanley Ves-
      tal, pseud. Houghton Mifflin, 1938. y.
      A look at General Kearney's annexation of New Mexico,
      1846-1847.

1527 Capron, Louis. White Moccasins. Holt, 1955. y.
      A tale of the Second Seminole War of 1835.

1528 Carhurt, Arthur H. Drum Up the Dawn. Dodd, Mead, 1937.
      y.
      Bill Meek's soldiers follow Zebulon Pike into the South-
      west in the early 1800's.

1529 Carlisle, Henry. The Land Where the Sun Dies. Putnam,
      1975. y.
      An epic tale of the Seminole Wars in Florida and the re-
      moval of the Eastern Indians to the American Southwest
      during the 1830's.

1530 Carpenter, E. Childs. Captain Courtesy. G. W. Jacobs,
      1906. y.
      Fremont and the American conquest of California in 1846.

1531 Chambers, Robert W. Gitana. Appleton, 1931. y.

Captain John Maddox witnesses the Mexican War from its
beginnings to the Battle of Buena Vista.

1532 Cheshire, Giff. Stronghold. Doubleday, 1963. y.
Focuses on U. S. Army efforts to displace the Modoc Indians of California.

1533 Choate, R. G. Phantom Hill. Doubleday, 1960. y.
Whites versus Indians in 1851 Texas.

1534 Clemens, Jeremiah. Bernard Lile; An Historical Romance
Embracing the Periods of the Texas Revolution and the
Mexican War. Lippincott, 1856.
Based on the author's experiences as a volunteer with the
Texan forces and as a major in the 13th U. S. Infantry.

1535 Coolidge, Dane. Under the Sun. Dutton, 1927. y.
Gilpin, known as Bajo Sol, the only survivor of a wagon
train massacre, becomes a Navajo warrior chief and leads
his people in battle against the Apache.

1536 Cousins, Margaret. We Were There at the Battle of the Alamo. Grosset & Dunlap, 1958. y.
A fictional recreation of the 1836 fight.

1537 Crowley, Mary C. In Treaty with Honor. Little, Brown,
1906.
Focuses on the Quebec revolt of 1837-1838.

1538 Culp, John H. Men of Gonzales. Sloane, 1961. y.
On March 1, 1836, 36 determined Texans from Gonzales,
guided by John W. Smith, reach the outskirts of San Antonio and attempt to reinforce the Alamo.

1539 Davis, James F. Road to San Jacinto. Bobbs-Merrill, 1936.
y.
A Georgia boy participates in the Texan War of Independence.

1540 Davis, Julia. Ride with the Eagle. Harcourt, 1962. y.
Based on diaries kept by the men of the 1st Missouri Volunteers during lulls in Mexican War action.

1541 Derleth, August W. Wind Over Wisconsin. Scribner's, 1938.
y.
The Black Hawk War of the 1830's.

1542 Duffus, Robert L. Jornada. Covici, 1935. y.
General Kearney versus Armijo in the Mexican War.

1543 Dunsing, Dee. War Chant. Longmans, Green, 1954. y.
A young Florida woodsman becomes an Army scout against
Osceola in the Second Seminole War of 1835.

1544 Duval, John C. <u>Early Times in Texas; or, The Adventures</u>
         <u>of Jack Dobell.</u> Tardy, 1936. y.
         First published in 1892, this story concerns the 1836 Fan-
         nin Expedition to Goliad.

1545 Ehrlich, Leonard. <u>God's Angry Man.</u> Simon & Schuster,
         1932. y.
         John Brown of Osawatomie wreaks Abolitionist terror in
         Kansas and tries to free the slaves by seizing the federal
         arsenal at Harpers Ferry; taken by troops under Robert E.
         Lee, he is executed for treason.

1546 Embree, Charles F. <u>A Dream of a Throne.</u> Little, 1900.
         y.
         Love and combat during the Mexican War.

1547 Everett, Wade. <u>First Command.</u> Ballantine, 1959. y. P.
         A U.S. Dragoon officer's first task is to keep order in
         1850's Kansas.

1548 Fisher, Vardis. <u>Mountain Man.</u> Morrow, 1966.
         Sam Minard declares a one-man war on Crow Indians, who
         have murdered a white family in the Rocky Mountains dur-
         ing the early 1830's.

1549 Fleischmann, Glen. <u>While Rivers Flow.</u> Macmillan, 1963.
         y.
         The U.S. Army removes the Cherokees from Georgia and
         Tennessee to the Southwest during the 1830's.

1550 Foreman, Leonard L. <u>The Road to San Jacinto.</u> Dutton,
         1943. y.
         Focuses on military operations in the Texan War of Inde-
         pendence.

1551 Forrest, William. <u>Trail of Tears.</u> Crown, 1958. y.
         Despite John Ross's best efforts, the U.S. Army evicts
         the Eastern Cherokee during the 1830's.

1552 Frazee, Steve. <u>The Alamo.</u> Avon, 1960. y. P.
         The 1836 battle; adapted from the John Wayne movie
         screenplay.

1553 Frost, T. G. <u>The Man of Destiny.</u> Gramercy, 1909. y.
         Follows the exploits of U. S. Grant in the Mexican War.

1554 Fuller, Iola. <u>Shining Trail.</u> Duell, Sloan, 1943. y.
         Black Hawk leads the last major Indian war against whites
         east of the Mississippi River.

1555 Gant, Matthew. <u>The Raven and the Sword.</u> Coward-McCann,
         1960. y.
         A fictional biography covering the life and combats of Sam
         Houston, especially during the Texan War of Independence.

1556 Garner, Claud. Sam Houston, Texas Giant. Naylor, 1969.
        y.
        A biographical novel.

1557 Gerson, Noel B. Golden Eagle. Doubleday, 1953. y.
        A fictional novel about the life of Winfield Scott, especially
        his Mexican War campaign in Vera Cruz.

1558 _____. The Sad Swashbuckler. Nelson, 1976. y.
        William Walker unsuccessfully attempts to take over Latin
        American countries in the 1850's.

1559 _____. Sam Houston, a Biographical Novel. Doubleday,
        1968. y.
        Includes his victory at San Jacinto during the Texas War.

1560 Giles, Janice H. The Great Adventure. Houghton Mifflin,
        1966. y.
        Captain Benjamin Bonneville, the soldier-explorer, is sent
        by the U. S. government to pry into Britain's activities in
        the Pacific Northwest.

1561 Gorman, Herbert S. Wine of San Lorenzo. Farrar, Straus,
        1945. y.
        An American boy, captured at the Alamo, fights for Santa
        Anna in the Mexican War until the Mexicans surrender to
        General Winfield Scott.

1562 Gunter, A. C. The Spy Company. Ward, Lock, 1903. y.
        Love, combat, and espionage during the Mexican War.

1563 Hall, Rubylea. Flamingo Prince. Duel, Sloan, 1954. y.
        Chief Osceola and the Second Seminole War.

1564 Hallet, Richard. Michael Beam. Houghton Mifflin, 1939. y.
        Recreates the Black Hawk War of the 1830's.

1565 Harris, John. Chant of the Hawk. Random House, 1959. y.
        Indian warfare and mountain men along the Oregon Trail.

        Hazel, Harry, pseud. See Jones, Justin.

1566 Hogan, Pendleton. The Dark Comes Early. Washburn, 1934.
        y.
        Romance and fighting during the Texan War of Independ-
        ence.

1567 Ingram, Hunter. The Trespassers. Ballantine, 1965. y.
        P.
        Portrays the war between Mormons and Gentiles in the
        Utah area.

1568 Jennings, John E. Shadows in the Dusk. Little, Brown,
        1955. y.

Following the 1837 capture of Sante Fe by Taos Indians
and Mexicans, José Gonzales becomes head of the free
government.

1569 Jones, Justin. The Flying Artillerist; or, The Child of the
Battlefield. By Harry Hazel, pseud. H. Long, 1853.
y.
Military action in the Mexican War.

1570 _____. The Light Dragoon; or, The Rancheros of the Poi-
soned Lance. By Harry Hazel, pseud. Star Spangled
Banner Office, 1848. y.
Cavalry action in the early phases of the Mexican War.

1571 _____. The Rival Chieftains; or, The Brigands of Mexico:
A Tale of Santa Anna and His Times. By Harry Hazel,
pseud. F. Gleason, 1847. y.
An unflattering account of the Mexican leader's actions
during the wars with Texas and the U.S.

1572 Judson, Edward Z. C. The Volunteer; or, The Maid of Mon-
terey. By Ned Buntline, pseud. F. Gleason, 1852. y.
Love and combat during Fremont's expedition into California.

1573 Kantor, MacKinley. Spirit Lake. World, 1961. y.
How the Wakpekate Indians massacred white settlers in
1857 Iowa.

1574 Knaggs, John R. The Bugles Are Silent. Shoal Creek, 1977.
y.
Fictional recreation of the 1835-1836 Texan revolt against
Mexico.

1575 Kreuger, Carl. St. Patrick's Battalion. Dutton, 1960. y.
Irish members of the U.S. Army declare the Mexican War
to be immoral and switch sides to fight with Santa Anna.

1576 Krey, Laura L. On the Long Tide. Houghton Mifflin, 1940.
y.
Combat and romance during the Texan War of Independence.

1577 L'Amour, Louis. The Ferguson Rifle. Bantam, 1973. y.
P.
A mountain man fights off Crow Indians with a new long-
range rifle.

1578 Lancaster, Bruce. Bright to the Wanderer. Little, Brown,
1942. y.
The Stensrood family in the Canadian Rebellion of 1837.

1579 Latham, Jean L. Retreat to Glory. Harper, 1965. y.
Sam Houston leads Texas forces in the war of independence.

1580   Lutz, Giles A. The Bleeding Land. Doubleday, 1965. y.
        A homesteader is caught up in the feuding between pro-
        and anti-slavery nightriders in 1850's Kansas.

1581   Lyle, Eugene P., Jr. The Lone Star. Doubleday, Page,
            1907. y.
        Military action in the Texan War of Independence.

1582   Lynn, Margaret. Land of Promise. Little, Brown, 1927. y.
        Neighbor against neighbor in "Bleeding Kansas," 1850's.

1583   McGiffin, Lee. The Fifer of San Jacinto. Lothrop, 1956. y.
        A youth participates in the Texan War of Independence.

1584   McNeil, Everett. Fighting with Fremont. Dutton, 1910. y.
        The American conquest of California in 1846.

1585   Maher, Ramona. Their Shining Hour. John Day, 1960. y.
        Santa Anna's victory over the defenders of the Alamo is
        recalled by a young wife, Susanna Dickinson, who refused
        to leave the makeshift fort, was captured, and released
        by the Mexican forces.

1586   Mott, F. B. Before the Crisis. J. Lane, 1904. y.
        Irregular military action in Kansas during the 1850's.

1587   Munroe, Kirk. Through the Swamp and Glade. Scribner's,
            1896. y.
        Army forces pursue Indians in the Second Seminole War
        of the 1830's.

1588   _____. With Crockett and Bowie. Scribner's, 1897. y.
        The two heroes, together with Travis and the others, de-
        fend the Alamo.

1589   Nelson, Truman J. The Surveyor. Doubleday, 1960. y.
        Traces John Brown's activities in Kansas, 1854-1856.

        North, Anison, pseud. See Wilson, May.

1590   Norton, Alice M. Stand to Horse. By Andre Norton, pseud.
            Harcourt, 1956. y.
        The adventures of Ritchie Peters with the 1st US Dragoons
        at Santa Fe, 1846-1861; Indian fighting and other activities
        based on actual officers' diaries.

        Norton, Andre, pseud. See Norton, Alice M.

1591   O'Dell, Scott. Hill of the Hawk. Bobbs-Merrill, 1947. y.
        In 1847 Kit Carson and the U.S. Army of the West march
        on Los Angeles.

1592   Olsen, Theodore V. Mission to the West. Doubleday, 1973.
            y.

Indian fighting breaks out when officers of the U.S. 1st
Dragoons are unable to convince the Indians that a peace
treaty should be signed.

1593   . Summer of the Drums. Doubleday, 1972. y.
White settlers fight off attacks by Sac Indians in Wisconsin
during the 1830's.

1594 Parker, Gilbert. The Pomp of the Lavilettes. Appleton,
      1897. y.
Papineau leads the 1837 rebellion in French-speaking Quebec.

1595 Parrish, Randall. The Devil's Own. McClurg, 1917. y.
Pictures the Balck Hawk War of 1832 in the upper Mid-
west.

1596 Pearce, Richard E. The Impudent Rifle. Lippincott, 1951.
      y.
A U.S. Army officer is transferred to the Arkansas Territory in the 1830's, where he battles Commanches and
participates in the enforced migration of a Choctaw band.

1597   . Restless Border. Lippincott, 1953. y.
Captain Alex Prince and a Dragoon unit are sent to protect Texas from Santa Anna and the Commanches in 1839.

1598 Pope, Edith E. River in the Wind. Scribner's, 1954. y.
Romance and fighting in the Second Seminole War.

1599 Potter, David. The Eleventh Hour. Dodd, Mead, 1910. y.
Zachary Taylor and the Mexican border dispute of the
early 1840's.

1600 Regli, Adolph. Partners in the Saddle. Watts, 1950. y.
Pictures cavalry skirmishes with the Indians near Fort
Sill, Oklahoma.

1601 Sabin, Edwin L. Rio Bravo. Macrae Smith, 1926. y.
A tale of the border war between U.S. and Mexican forces
and the adventures of a brevet second lieutenant in Zachary
Taylor's army.

1602 Savage, Les. Doniphan's Ride. Doubleday, 1960. y.
A boy's life with the 1st Missouri Volunteers in the Mexican War, 1846.

1603 Seifert, Shirley. Captain Grant. Lippincott, 1946. y.
The earlier years of U.S. Grant, from West Point to his
leading of an Illinois regiment in 1861.

1604   . Turquois Trail. Lippincott, 1950. y.
A tale of the Mexican War.

1605   Slate, Sam J. Satan's Backyard. Doubleday, 1974. y.
       The American effort to win Florida as viewed by an aide
       to U. S. Secretary of War Crawford.

1606   Slaughter, Frank G. Fort Everglades. Doubleday, 1951. y.
       A doctor becomes involved in the Second Seminole War of
       1835-1840.

1607   _____. Warrior. Doubleday, 1957. Rpr. 1977. y.
       Osceola and the Second Seminole War as seen by his white
       blood brother.

1608   Stratemeyer, Edward. For the Liberty of Texas. Lothrop,
          1909.
       Focuses on the Texan War of Independence, 1835-1836.

1609   _____. Under Scott in Mexico. Lothrop, 1909. y.
       Military action in the Mexican War.

1610   _____. With Taylor on the Rio Grande. Lothrop, 1909.
          y.
       Skirmishes on the Mexican border prior to the Mexican
       War.

1611   Styron, William. The Confessions of Nat Turner. Random,
          1967.
       Fictional reminiscences of the leader of the 1831 slave
       revolt in Southampton, Virginia.

1612   Taylor, Robert L. Two Roads to Guadalupe. Doubleday,
          1965. y.
       Two young men and a disguised girl join the U. S. Army
       and participate in the Mexican War.

1613   Venable, Clarke. All the Brave Rifles. Reilly & Lee, 1929.
          y.
       The Texan War of Independence, from the Alamo to San
       Jacinto.

       Vestal, Stanley, pseud. See Campbell, Walter S.

1614   Warren, Robert Penn. Remember the Alamo! Random
          House, 1958. y.
       Recreates the 1836 defense of the San Antonio fortress.

1615   Wilder, Robert. Bright Feather. Putnam, 1948. y.
       The white's attempt to evict the Seminoles from Florida
       brings war.

       Wilson, Charlotte, pseud. See Baker, Keith.

1616   Wilson, May. Forging of the Pikes. By Anison North,
          pseud. Doran, 1920. y.
       The Upper Canadian Rebellion of 1837.

1617 Wormster, Richard E. <u>Battalion of Saints</u>. David McKay,
          1961. y.
          Mountainman Ned Springer leads Morman and Missouri
          volunteers to fight with U. S. troops in the Mexican War.

1618 Wyatt, Geraldine. <u>Sun Eagle</u>. Longmans, Green, 1952. y.
          Commanche Indian raids in Texas, 1839-1850.

NORTH AMERICA: 1861 TO 1865

The stories in this, our largest North American section, concern
military operations in the U. S. Civil War. These tales represent a
rather large body of literature, which, were it to include naval and
home-front accounts, would be worthy of a separate compilation.
Until recently many of the authors prepared their offerings with certain biases in mind, mostly pro-Union. This was in keeping with
the winner-loser perspective that existed in this country until the
early decades of the twentieth century.

1619 Allen, Henry. <u>Journey to Shiloh</u>. By Will Henry, pseud.
          Random House, 1960. y.
          The Battle of Shiloh as seen by the Concho County Com-
          manches, seven young Confederate soldiers from Texas.

1620 Allen, Hervey. <u>Action at Aquila</u>. Rinehart, 1938. y.
          Colonel Franklin's 6th Pennsylvania Cavalry in the 1864
          action.

1621 Allen, Merritt P. <u>Blow Bugles, Blow</u>. Longmans, Green,
          1956. y.
          A farmboy serves with General Sheridan in the Battle of
          the Wilderness.

1622 _____. <u>Johnny Reb</u>. David McKay, 1952. y.
          Focuses on Confederate cavalry during the conflict, espe-
          cially that of Wade Hampton.

1623 _____. <u>The White Feather</u>. David McKay, 1944. y.
          A Kentucky mountain boy joins Morgan's Raiders in 1863.

1624 Althsheler, Joseph A. <u>Before the Dawn</u>. Doubleday, Page,
          1903. y.
          A story of the 1865 fall of Richmond, the Confederate
          capital.

1625 _____. <u>The Guns of Bull Run</u>. Appleton, 1914. y.
          Recreates the Confederate victory in the first Virginia
          battle.

1626 _____ . The Guns of Shiloh. Appleton, 1914. y.
      Union troops recoup to win the great 1862 battle in west-
      ern Tennessee.

1627 _____ . In Circling Days. Appleton, 1900. y.
      The 1863 Battle of Gettysburg.

1628 _____ . The Rock of Chickamauga. Appleton, 1915. y.
      General Thomas in the September 19-20, 1863 Georgia
      fight.

1629 _____ . The Scouts of Stonewall. Appleton, 1914. y.
      A youth serves with Stonewall Jackson during his Shenan-
      doah Valley campaign.

1630 _____ . The Shades of the Wilderness. Appleton, 1916.
      y.
      Focuses on General Lee's Confederate soldiers and their
      suffering during the 1864 Wilderness fighting in Virginia.

1631 _____ . The Star of Gettysburg. Appleton, 1915. y.
      General Pickett unsuccessfully charges the Union line.

1632 _____ . The Sword of Antietam. Appleton, 1914. y.
      Lee and McClellan meet in western Maryland in 1862.

1633 _____ . The Tree of Appomattox. Appleton, 1916. y.
      Presents the final campaign of the war and Lee's surrender
      to Grant.

1634 Anderson, Alston. All God's Children. Bobbs-Merrill, 1965.
      y.
      An escaped Negro slave fights for the Union.

1635 Andrews, Mary R. S. The Perfect Tribute. Scribner's,
      1906. y.
      A wounded Union soldier in hospital speaks well of Lin-
      coln's Gettysburg Address.

1636 Appell, George C. The Man Who Shot Quantrill. Doubleday,
      1958. y.
      Curtis Blackman's Union soldiers seek Rebel raiders under
      William Clarke Quantrill.

1637 Ashley, Robert. The Stolen Train. Winston, 1953. y.
      Andrew's Raiders seek to make off with a Confederate
      train.

1638 Ballard, Willis T. Trials of Rage. Doubleday, 1975. y.
      Union Army captain Jack Price and his men seek Confed-
      erate raiders preying on homesteaders and instigating the
      Indians to open a second front against the federal govern-
      ment.

1639   Bechdolt, Frederick R.   Bold Raiders of the West.   Double-
         day, 1940. y.
         A tale of cavalry action in New Mexico during the conflict.

1640   Becker, Stephen.   When the War Is Over.   Random House,
         1969. y.
         Based on a true incident of 1865, during the hysteria over
         Lincoln's assassination; a Confederate youth in Kentucky
         shoots a Union lieutenant 16 days after Appomattox and al-
         though the officer lives and befriends him, the boy is
         court-martialled and executed.

1641   Bell, John.   Moccasin Flower.   Bookmasters, 1936.   y.
         A tale of the Sioux uprising in Minnesota in 1862.

1642   Bellah, James W.   Ordeal at Blood River.   Ballantine, 1959.
         y.   P.
         Cavalry action in Colorado during the war.

1643   _____ .   The Valiant Virginians.   Ballantine, 1953.   y.   P.
         General Early's Confederate cavalry fights in the Shenan-
         doah Valley.

1644   Benner, Judith A.   Lone Star Rebel.   J. F. Blair, 1971.   y.
         Focuses on a young courier to Colonel Lawrence S. Ross,
         commander of the 6th Texas Cavalry.

1645   Benson, Blackwood K.   Bayard's Courier.   Macmillan, 1902.
         y.
         Tale about a Union cavalryman's love and adventures dur-
         ing the war's first year.

1646   _____ .   Friend with the Countersign.   Macmillan, 1901.
         y.
         Love, combat, and espionage after the Battle of Gettys-
         burg.

1647   _____ .   Old Squire.   Macmillan, 1903.   y.
         Records a black man's role in the Battle of Gettysburg.

1648   _____ .   Who Goes There?   Macmillan, 1900.   y.
         A Union spy with amnesia serves in the Confederate Army
         from the Battle of Bull Run through Gettysburg.

1649   Bierce, Ambrose.   In the Midst of Life: Tales of Soldiers
         and Civilians.   Rivercity Press, 1964.   y.
         First published in 1891 as Tales of Soldiers and Civilians;
         Contents:--A Horseman in the Sky. --An Occurrence at Owl
         Creek Bridge. --Chickamauga. --A Son of Gods. --The Af-
         fair at Coulter's Notch. --The Coup de Grace. --Parker
         Addison, Philospher. --An Affair of Outposts. --The Story
         of a Conscience. --One Kind of Officer. --One Officer, One
         Men. --George Thurston. --The Mocking Bird. --The Man

Out of the Nose. --An Adventure at Brownville. --The Famous Gilson Bequest. --The Applicant. --A Watcher by the
Dead. --The Man and the Snake. --A Holy Terror. --The
Suitable Surroundings. --The Boarded Window. --A Lady
from Red Horse. --The Eyes of the Panther.

1650 · Borland, Hal G. The Amulet. Lippincott, 1958. y.
A Missourian takes a long trip to join Confederate Quincy
Scott's volunteers in the skirmish at Wilson's Creek, Col-
orado.

1651 Boyd, James. Marching On. Scribner's, 1927. y.
A Confederate soldier is taken as a P. O. W. during Sherman's
march to the sea.

1652 Brady, Cyrus T. The Last Hope. Dodd, Mead, 1906. y.
Lee's surrender to Grant at Appomattox.

1653 _____. The Patriots of the South. Dodd, Mead, 1906. y.
General Lee and the Army of Northern Virginia at Appomattox.

1654 _____. The Southerners. Scribner's, 1903. y.
Confederate military action.

1655 Branson, H. C. Salisbury Plain. Dutton, 1966. y.
Looks at the disintegration of morale and discipline in a
Union division before it is defeated by the Confederates
somewhere in western Virginia.

1656 Brick, John. Jubilee. Doubleday, 1956. y.
Lieutenant Jeff Barnes and the 195th New York Volunteer
Infantry participates in Sherman's march to the sea, in-
cluding the Battle of Lookout Mountain and the burning of
Atlanta.

1657 _____. The Richmond Raid. Doubleday, 1963. y.
Colonel Dahlgren's cavalry unsuccessfully attempts to raid
the Confederate capital and release Union P. O. W. 's.

1658 _____. Yankees on the Run. Duell, Sloane, 1961. y.
Two Union soldiers escape Andersonville prison in Georgia
and attempt to make it back to the northern lines.

1659 Brier, Royce. Boy in Blue. Appleton, 1937. y.
Adventures of a youth in the Army of the Cumberland,
ending with the Battle of Chickamauga.

1660 Bromfield, Louis. Wild Is the River. Harper, 1941. y.
The capture and occupation of New Orleans by Union forces
in 1862.

1661 Bronson, Lynn. The Runaway. Lippincott, 1953. y.
A youth witnesses the generalship of U. S. Grant.

1662   Brooks, Asa P.   The Reservation.   Brooks, 1908.   y.
           Minnesota whites battle the Sioux uprising of 1862.

1663   Buck, Irving A.   Cleburne and His Command.   D. C. Neale,
           1909.   y.
           A Confederate soldier remembers the Battle of Shiloh.

1664   Burchard, Peter.   North by Night.   Coward-McCann, 1962.
           y.
           Two Yankee soldiers escape a rebel POW camp and seek
           northern lines.

1665   _____ .   Rat Hall.   Coward-McCann, 1971.   y.
           Over 100 Yankee soldiers escape Libby Prison in Rich-
           mond in 1864; based on a true event.

1666   Burnett, William R.   The Dark Command.   Knopf, 1938.   y.
           Military action in Kansas and Missouri in 1861.

1667   Burow, Daniel R.   Sound of the Bugle.   Concordia, 1973.   y.
           A German immigrant in Georgia learns the horrors of war
           during Sherman's march to the sea.

1668   Burress, John.   Bugle in the Wilderness.   Vanguard, 1958.
           y.
           Farm life and armed conflict in Missouri during the war.

1669   Cable, George W.   The Cavalier.   Scribner's, 1901.   y.
           Cavalry action in Mississippi.

1670   _____ .   Kinkaid's Battery.   Scribner's, 1908.   y.
           Artillery and occupation, New Orleans, 1861-1862.

       Carroll, Gordon, ed.   See Saturday Evening Post.

1671/2 Castor, Henry.   The Spanglers.   Doubleday, 1948.   y.
           Includes a look into Andersonville prison.

1673   Catton, Bruce.   Banners at Shenandoah.   Doubleday, 1955.
           y.
           A young Union soldier, Bob Hayden, joins Sheridan in the
           battles at Booneville, Missionary Ridge, and Cedar Creek.

1674   Chambers, Robert W.   Whistling Cat.   Appleton, 1932.   y.
           A pair of Texans serve as telegraphers for the Union
           Army.

1675   Christgau, John.   Spoon.   Viking, 1978.
           Pictures the 1862 Sioux uprising in Minnesota.

1676   Cooke, John E.   Hilt to Hilt; or, Days and Nights on the
           Banks of the Shenandoah in the Autumn of 1864.   Carle-
           ton, 1871.
           Cavalry action in western Virginia.

1677 _____. Mohun; or, The Last Days of Lee and His Pala-
        dins. G. W. Dillingham, 1893. y.
        Portrays the Appomattox campaign and meeting of 1865.

1678 _____. Surrey of Eagle's Nest; or, The Memoirs of a
        Staff Officer Serving in Virginia. Bunce & Huntington,
        1866. Rpr. 1968. y.
        A Confederate view of the eastern cavalry war, focusing
        on the leadership of Stonewall Jackson and J. E. B. Stuart;
        the author based these three tales on his service as a
        captain under Stuart late in the conflict.

1679 Corrington, John W. And Wait for the Night. Putnam, 1964.
        y.
        The federal occupation of Shreveport, Louisiana, in Janu-
        ary 1865.

1680 Crabb, Alfred L. Dinner at Belmont. Bobbs-Merrill, 1942.
        y.
        The 1864 Battle of Nashville predominates.

1681 _____. Home to Tennessee. Bobbs-Merrill, 1952. y.
        The Army of Tennessee fights to regain Nashville in 1864.

1682 _____. Lodging at the St. Cloud. Bobbs-Merrill, 1946.
        y.
        The Union occupation of Nashville and the activities of
        Nathan Bedford Forrest.

1683 _____. The Mockingbird Sang at Chickamauga: A Tale of
        Embattled Chattanooga. Bobbs-Merrill, 1949. y.
        Lieutenant Beasley Nichol helps Nathan Bedford Forrest
        win the Battle of Chickamauga.

1684 Crane, Stephen. Little Regiment, and Other Episodes of the
        American Civil War. Arno, 1977. y.
        Reprints a collection of short stories first published in
        1896.

1685 _____. The Red Badge of Courage. Appleton, 1895. Rpr.
        1977. y.
        A dispirited Union soldier finds courage during the Battle
        of Chancellorsville; using epic devices, a romantic pro-
        tagonist, psychological aspects, and naturalistic action,
        Crane here provides us with the first modern war story.
        Readers might also consult Bradley, Sculley, et al. (eds.),
        The Red Badge of Courage: An Annotated Text with Crit-
        ical Essays. Rev. ed. Norton Critical Editions Series
        (New York: Norton, 1977).

1686 Dahlinger, Charles W. Where Red Volleys Poured. G. W.
        Dillingham, 1907. y.
        A German exile serving as a Union soldier takes part in
        the battles of Centreville, Fredericksburg, and Gettysburg.

1687 Daringer, Helen F. Mary Montgomery, Rebel. Harcourt,
          1948. y.
      A young girl is involved in the burning of Atlanta.

1688 Davis, Burke. To Appomattox. Rinehart, 1959. y.
      A fictional recreation of the nine last days of the war, in-
      cluding Lee's surrender.

1689 Davis, Hazel H. General Jim. Bethany, 1950. y.
      The role of James A. Garfield as a Union officer.

1690 Davis, Maggie. The Far Side of Home. Macmillan, 1963.
          y.
      Depicts the trials and privations of a Georgia soldier and
      his wife during the war.

1691 Davis, Paxton, The Seasons of Heroes. Morrow, 1968. y.
      A three-part tale, the first section of which deals with
      Confederate cavalry leader McNaught's 1864 raid into
      Pennsylvania.

      Dean, Jauchins, jt. author. See Rhodes, James. A.

1662 DeForest, John W. Miss Revenel's Conversion from Secession
          to Loyalty. Ed. by Gordon S. Haight. Rinehart, 1957.
      The effects of combat on Captain Colburne and his men;
      published in 1867, this title is one of the first to deal
      realistically with military and sanitary conditions of the
      war.

1693 _____ . A Volunteer's Adventures: A Union Captain's Rec-
          ord of the Civil War. Ed. by James H. Croushore.
          Yale University Press, 1946. y.
      Lt. Col. Carter leads his men through the horrors of bat-
      tle in the first novel to deal realistically with the military
      events of the conflict.

1694 DeLeon, T. Cooper. Crag-Nest. G. W. Dillingham, 1910.
          y.
      Focuses on Sheridan's 1864 campaign in the Shenandoah
      Valley.

1695 Demarest, Phyllis G. Wilderness Brigade. Doubleday, 1957.
          y.
      A Southern girl rescues an escaped Yankee P.O.W. from
      bushwackers.

1696 Devon, Louis. Aide to Glory. Crowell-Collier, 1953. y.
      A biographical novel about John Rawlings, General Grant's
      aide-de-camp.

1697 Dillon, Mary. In Old Bellaire. Century, 1906. y.
      Focuses on the Battle of Gettysburg.

1698 Dixon, Thomas. The Man in Gray. Appleton, 1922. y.
      Depicts real events of the conflict in a biographical novel
      spun around Robert E. Lee.

1699 Doneghy, Dagman. The Border, a Missouri Saga. Morrow,
           1931. y.
      Irregular action on the Kansas-Missouri border in 1861.

1700 Dowdey, Clifford. Bugles Blow No More. Little, Brown,
           1937. Rpr. 1967. y.
      Life in Richmond during the war, from Virginia's seces-
      sion to the evacuation and burning of the city.

1701 _____. Proud Retreat. Doubleday, 1953. y.
      Raider Francis Malvern accompanies the Confederate gold
      out of Richmond in the last days of the war.

1702 _____. Tidewater. Little, Brown, 1943. y.
      Another tale of people living in Richmond during the fight-
      ing.

1703 _____. Where My Love Sleeps. Little, Brown, 1945. y.
      A young Confederate captain in the 1864-1865 Battle of
      Petersburg.

1704 Dwight, Allan. Linn Dickson, Confederate. Macmillan, 1934.
           y.
      Tale of a Confederate soldier; based on authentic accounts.

1705 Eaton, Jeanette. Lee, the Gallant General. Morrow, 1953.
           y.
      The leadership of the South's most famous general.

1706 Edgerton, Lucille. Pillars of Gold. Knopf, 1941. y.
      Secessionist and cavalry action in the Southwest.

1707 Edmonds, Walter D. Cadmus Henry. Dodd, Mead, 1949. y.
      A Confederate youth becomes a balloonist for the Army of
      Northern Virginia.

1708 Ehle, John. The Time of Drums. Harper, 1970. y.
      Two brothers, the Wrights, fight for the Confederacy in
      the battles of Chancellorsville and Gettysburg.

1709 Epstein, Samuel. The Great Locomotive Chase. Coward-
           McCann, 1956. y.
      The Andrews Raiders unsuccessfully attempt to steal a
      train.

1710 Erdman, Loula G. Another Spring. Dodd, Mead, 1966. y.
      Raiders in 1863 Missouri force citizens from their home
      into a cold winter.

1711   Faulkner, William.   The Unvanquished.   Random House, 1938.
        Rpr. 1965.   y.
        Life and raids on a Mississippi plantation at war's end.

1712   Fenner, Phyllis R. , comp.   Brother against Brother: Stories
        of the War Between the States.   Morrow, 1957.   y.
        An action-packed anthology containing a dozen short tales.

1713   Ferrell, Elizabeth and Margaret.   Full of Thy Riches.   Mill,
        1944.   y.
        Rebel troops raid the oil wells of West Virginia.

1714   Fisher, Clay.   The Crossing.   Houghton Mifflin, 1958.   y.
        A tale of Rebel-Yankee cavalry action in the Southwest.

1715   Foote, Shelby.   Shiloh.   Dial, 1952.   Rpr. 1976.   y.
        The great battle of 1862 as it appeared to six soldiers,
        Union and Confederate.

1716   Ford, Jesse H.   The Raider.   Little, Brown, 1975.   Rpr.
        1976.   y.
        Civil War cavalry raids in western Tennessee; suggested
        by the operations of Nathan Bedford Forrest.

1717   Fordyce, W. C. , Jr.   Civil War Dragoon.   Exposition, 1965.
        y.
        Adventures of a Union cavalry soldier.

1718   Fowler, Robert H.   Jim Mundy.   Harper, 1977.   y.
        Captured at Gettysburg, Confederate soldier Mundy is sent
        to the Johnson Island P. O. W. camp, from which he escapes
        to Canada; in the north, he joins the St. Albans raiders,
        eventually returning south in time to fight in the Battle of
        Petersburg.

1719   Fox, John.   Little Shepherd of Kingdom Come.   Scribner's,
        1903.   y.
        A tale of Morgan's raiders in Kentucky in 1863.

1720   Fraser, George M.   Flash for Freedom.   Knopf, 1972.
        Sequel to Royal Flash; English officer Flashman becomes
        involved in the slave trade and the American Civil War.

1721   Gardiner, Dorothy.   The Great Betrayal.   Doubleday, 1949.
        y.
        Colonel John M. Chivington leads the whites in a massacre
        of the Cheyenne at Sand Creek in 1864.

1722   Garlin, Hamlin.   Trail-Makers of the Middle Border.   Mac-
        millan, 1926.   y.
        A fictional biography of the author's father who met Grant
        in Illinois before the war, joined his regiment, and went
        on to participate in the siege of Vicksburg.

1723   Garth, David. Gray Canaan. Putnam, 1947. y.
       A Confederate captain takes part in the 1862 Second Battle
       of Bull Run.

1724   Glasgow, Ellen A. G. Battle Ground. Doubleday, 1920. y.
       Focuses on the fighting in Virginia.

1725   Goodrich, Arthur. The Sign of Freedom. Appleton, 1916.
       y.
       A "bound boy" finds achievement as a Union soldier.

1726   Gordon, Caroline. None Shall Look Back. Scribner's, 1937.
       y.
       Outlines the effects of the war on the border states, with
       attention to the battles at Fort Donelson and Chickamauga
       and the cavalry exploits of Nathan Bedford Forrest.

1727   Green, Homer. A Lincoln Conscript. Houghton Mifflin, 1909.
       y.
       A draftee fights for the Union in the Battle of Gettysburg.

1728   Gruber, Frank. The Bushwackers. Rinehart, 1959. y.
       Examines the massacre in Lawrence, Kansas, perpetrated
       by Quantrill and his men on August 21, 1863.

1729   _____. Outlaw. Bantam, 1963. y. P.
       When his best friend is killed, a Rebel declares his own
       personal war on Union troops.

1730   Haas, Ben. The Foragers. Simon & Schuster, 1962. y.
       A Confederate captain assigned to pillage a southern plan-
       tation meets unsuspected obstacles.

1731   Hanson, Joseph M. With Sully into the Sioux Lands. McClurg,
       1910. y.
       Depicts the dealings between General Sully and the Dakota
       Indians in 1864.

1732   Harben, William N. Triumph. By Will N. , pseud. Harper,
       1917. y.
       Andrew Merlin, of Union sympathy, flees his brother
       Thomas in Georgia, escapes a Confederate ambush, and
       joins the Yankee army.

1733   Harrison, Constance. The Carlyles. Appleton, 1905. y.
       A story about the fall of Richmond.

1734   Hart, Scott. Eight April Days. Coward-McCann, 1949. y.
       Follows the retreat of the Confederate Army from Peters-
       burg to Appomattox in the spring of 1865.

1735   Havill, Edward. Big Ember. Harper, 1947. y.
       Whites battle Indians: the 1862 Sioux uprising in Minnesota.

1736 Haycox, Ernest. The Border Trumpet. Little, Brown, 1939.
      y.
      Life and fights at a frontier Army post in Arizona.

1737 _____. Long Storm. Little, Brown, 1946. y.
      Copperhead violence in Seattle.

      Henry, Will, pseud. See Allen, Henry.

1738 Henty, George A. With Lee in Virginia. Scribner's, 1890.
      y.
      A young soldier participates in the victories of 1862.

1739 Hicks, John. The Long Whip. David McKay, 1969. y.
      Includes a picture of black service with the Union army.

1740 Hoehling, Mary D. Girl Soldier and Spy. Messner, 1959.
      y.
      A young woman aids the Union Army in Virginia.

1741 Hogan, Ray. The Ghost Rider. Pyramid, 1960. y. P.
      John Singleton Mosby and his Rangers capture Union gen-
      eral Stoughton behind federal lines in 1863.

1742 _____. Hell to Hallelujah. Macfadden, 1962. y. P.
      A small Confederate guerrilla band battles Yankee troops
      and renegades.

1743 _____. Mosby's Last Ride. Mcfadden, 1966. y. P.
      Follows the last mission of the intrepid Confederate raider.

1744 _____. Night Raider. Avon, 1964. y. P.
      Mosby's Rangers take an important Union figure.

1745 _____. Rebel Ghost. Macfadden, 1964. y. P.
      The Yankees finally capture the elusive John S. Mosby.

1746 _____. Rebel Raid. Berkeley, 1961. y. P.
      Southern patriots stage a dangerous mission to rescue a
      young woman spy.

1747 Hooper, Byrd. Beef for Beauregard. Putnam, 1959. y.
      Texas troops "round-up" food for Confederate forces.

1748 Horsley, Reginald. Stonewall's Scout. Harper, 1896. y.
      Battle of Antietam.

1749 Hosmer, George W. As We Went Marching On: A Story of
      the War. Arno, 1973. y.
      A reprinting of a tale first published in 1885.

1750 Icenhower, Joseph B. The Scarlet Raider. Chilton, 1961.
      y.
      A 16-year-old joins Mosby's Rangers.

1751   Jacobs, Thornwell. Red Lanterns on St. Michaels. Dutton,
            1940. y.
            Events in Charleston, South Carolina during the war.

1752   Jakes, John W. The Texans Ride North. Winston, 1952. y.
            Texas troops join the Confederacy for the Battle of Bull
            Run.

1753   Johnson, C. F. A Hand Raised at Gettysburg. Bruce, 1950.
            y.
            General Lee unsuccessfully attempts to take the Pennsyl-
            vania town.

1754   Johnston, Mary. Cease Firing. Houghton Mifflin, 1912. y.
            A sequel to the next title, continuing the story of Stone-
            wall Jackson.

1755   _____. The Long Roll. Houghton Mifflin, 1911. y.
            The activities of Stonewall Jackson from a southern view-
            point.

1756   Kaler, James O. With Grant at Vicksburg, a Boy's Story of
            the Siege of Vicksburg. By James Otis, pseud. A. L.
            Burt, 1910. y.
            A Union boy is involved in the 1862-1863 siege.

1757   _____. With Sherman to the Sea, a Boy's Story of Gen-
            eral Sherman's Famous March and Capture of Savannah.
            By James Otis, pseud. A. L. Burt, 1911. y.
            A Union soldier is involved in the exploit.

1758   Kane, Harnett T. Bride of Fortune. Doubleday, 1948. y.
            Jefferson Davis's problems as seen by his wife.

1759   _____. The Gallant Mrs. Stonewall: A Novel Based on
            the Lives of General and Mrs. Stonewall Jackson.
            Doubleday, 1957. y.
            The general's campaigns are described in part.

1760   _____. The Lady of Arlington: A Novel Based on the
            Life of Mrs. Robert E. Lee. Doubleday, 1953. y.
            Lee's military operations form part of the book.

1761   _____. The Smiling Rebel: A Novel Based on the Life of
            Belle Boyd. Doubleday, 1955. y.
            The exploits of a young woman spy for the South.

1762   Kantor, MacKinley. Andersonville. World, 1955. y.
            Ira Claffey and the infamous Confederate prison built on
            his Georgia property.

1763   _____. Arouse and Beware. Coward-McCann, 1936. y.
            Two Yankee soldiers escape the southern prison at Belle
            Island in 1864 and head for northern lines on the Rapidan.

1764   _____. If the South Had Won the Civil War. Bantam,
                1965. y. P.
            Suggests an outcome if Lee had won at Gettysburg.

1765   _____. Long Remember. Coward-McCann, 1932. y.
            A pacifist becomes involved in the 1863 Battle of Gettys-
            burg and later enters the Union Army.

1766 Keith, Harold. Rifles for Watie. Crowell-Collier, 1957. y.
            Stand Watie leads the Cherokee Indians fighting for the
            Confederacy; Union soldier Jess Busey is sent to find
            out the source of the Rebel's repeating rifles.

1767 Kennedy, Sara B. Cicely. Doubleday, 1911. y.
            Focuses on Sherman's march to the sea and the burning
            of Atlanta.

1768 Keyes, Frances P. Madame Castel's Lodger. Farar, Straus,
                1962. y.
            A fictional biography about Confederate general Pierre G.
            T. Beauregard.

1769 King, Charles. Between the Lines. Harper, 1888. y.
            A Union soldier's mission for the Army of the Potomac.

1770   _____. A Broken Sword. Hobart, 1905. y.
            Depicts McClellan's campaign at Antietam in 1862.

1771   _____. The Deserter and From the Ranks, Two Novels.
                Lippincott, 1893. y.
            A pair of action tales from the Union Army viewpoint.

1772   _____. From School to Battlefield, a Story of the War
                Days. Lippincott, 1899. y.
            A youth enlists in the Yankee Army early in the conflict.

1773   _____. The General's Double. Lippincott, 1898. y.
            A young man poses as General McClellan during the Army
            of the Potomac's advance on Antietam in 1862.

1774   _____. The Iron Brigade, a Story of the Army of the
                Potomac. G. W. Dillingham, 1902. y.
            A fictional history of an actual unit in Grant's army.

1775   _____. A Knight of Columbia, a Story of the War. Ho-
                bart, 1904. y.
            Cavalry action by Union troopers in Virginia.

1776   _____. The Medal of Honor, a Story of Peace and War.
                Hobart, 1905. y.
            A young Union soldier wins the Congressional Medal of
            Honor for bravery.

1777   . Norman Holt. G. W. Dillingham, 1901. y.
              A tale of combat with the Army of the Cumberland.

1778   . The Rock of Chickamauga. G. W. Dillingham,
              1907. y.
              General George H. Thomas commands Union troops in the
              battles of Chickamauga and Nashville.

1779   . Trials of a Staff Officer. Lippincott, 1896. y.
              Difficulties of a Union Army officer in the East.

1780   . A War-Time Wooing. Harper, 1888. y.
              A Union officer in love and combat.

1781 Kirkland, Joseph. The Captain of Company K. Dibble, 1891.
              y.
              Experiences of a Union unit in heavy combat in Virginia.

1782 Lagard, Gerald. The Scarlet Cockerrel. Morrow, 1948. y.
              Surgeon Lane Byrn accompanies the raids led by John S.
              Mosby.

1783 Lancaster, Bruce. Night March. Little, Brown, 1958. Rpr.
              1977. y.
              Two Yankee soldiers captured in Dalgren's Richmond Raid
              are cast into Libbey Prison.

1784   . No Bugles Tonight. Little, Brown, 1948. Rpr.
              1977. y.
              A dashing Yankee officer fights in Tennessee.

1785   . Roll Shenandoah. Little, Brown, 1956. Rpr.
              1977. y.
              Young trooper Ellery Starr views General Sheridan's cam-
              paign in Shenandoah valley in 1864.

1786   . Scarlet Patch. Little, Brown, 1947. Rpr. 1977.
              y.
              Virginia combat with the foreign-born volunteers of the
              Union Army's Rocheambeau Rifles.

1787 Lanier, Sidney. Tiger-Lilies and Southern Prose. Johns
              Hopkins University Press, 1945. y.
              Originally published in 1867, this novel contains some of
              the most incisive descriptions of Civil War horrors and
              is the only southern effort to approach the realistic battle
              descriptions of Crane's The Red Bad of Courage (q. v.).

1788 LeMay, Alan. By Dim and Flaring Lamps. Harper, 1962.
              y.
              Combat on the Missouri border in 1861.

1789 Lentz, Perry. The Falling Hills. Scribner's, 1967. y.

The Fort Pillow massacre of 1864 is recalled by Union and Confederate officers.

1790   _____. It Must Be Now the Kingdom Coming. Crown, 1973. y.
A Yankee patrol raids a southern plantation during the war.

1791 Longstreet, Stephen. Gettysburg. Farrar, Straus, 1961. y.
Centers around the activities of several Union officers and townspeople during the great three-day battle.

1792   _____. Three Days. Messner, 1947. y.
The Battle of Gettysburg, July 1-3, 1863.

1793 Lowden, Leone. Proving Ground. McBride, 1946. y.
Indiana soldiers at Shiloh and in Morgan's 1863 Raid.

1794 Lytle, Andrew. The Long Night. Bobbs-Merrill, 1936. y.
The protagonist participates in the 1862 Battle of Shiloh.

1795 McCord, Joseph. Red House on the Hill. Macrea Smith, 1938. y.
Action in Maryland.

1796 McElroy, Lee. Long Way to Texas. Doubleday, 1976. y.
Lieutenant David Buckalew returns to Texas with 19 soldiers, after suffering the first great defeat of the Texas Confederates in the Southwest.

1797 McGiffin, Lee. Rebel Rider. Dutton, 1959. y.
A Confederate youth scouts for General Wade Hampton.

1798 MacGowan, Alice. The Sword in the Mountains. Putnam, 1910. y.
Depicts the Battle of Chattanooga.

1799 Mackey, Morris. The Band Played Dixie. Harcourt, 1927. y.
Examines the battles of Fredericksburg, Savannah, and Richmond.

1800 McNicol, J. M. Ride for Old Glory. McKay, 1964. y.
A youth serves as an aide to Union cavalry general James Wilson in the 1864 Battle of Nashville.

1801 Mason, Francis Van Wyck. Hang My Wreath. By Ward Weaver, pseud. Funk & Wagnalls, 1941. y.
A look at Union troopers battling J. E. B. Stuart's horse cavaliers in Virginia and Maryland before the 1862 Battle of Antietam.

1802   _____. The Trumpets Sound No More. Little, Brown, 1975. y.

The last days of the war and the financial-defense problems
of a Confederate colonel and his company mustered out at
Appomattox.

1803   Meader, Stephen.   The Muddy Road to Glory.   Harcourt, 1963.
       y.
       A youth joins the 20th Maine Regiment and fights with the
       Army of the Potomac at Spotsylvania, Cold Harbor, and
       in the Wilderness.

1804   Mellard, Rudolph.   Across the Crevasse.   Sage, 1966.   y.
       Experiences of a Confederate guerrilla fighter.

1805   Miers, Earl S.   The Guns of Vicksburg.   Putnam, 1957.   y.
       Grant besieges the Mississippi fortress.

1806   Miller, Helen T.   Sing One Song.   Appleton, 1956.   y.
       Organized combat and guerrilla raids in "neutral" Ken-
       tucky.

1807   Miller, May M.   First the Blade.   Knopf, 1938.   y.
       Focuses on the 1861 guerrilla war in Missouri.

1808   Mitchell, Margaret.   Gone with the Wind.   Macmillan, 1936.
       y.
       The most famous romantic story set in the War Between
       the States also contains sequences about the burning of
       Atlanta.

1809   Moberg, Vilhelm.   The Last Letter Home.   Simon & Schuster,
       1961.   y.
       Depicts the 1862 Sioux uprising in Minnesota.

1810   Moore, Arthur.   Look Down, Look Down.   Powell, 1970.   y.
       P.
       A few hundred untrained southern recruits led by a mad-
       man defend a small fort against a Yankee regiment.

1811   Mordecai, Alfred.   The Uncommon Soldier.   Farrar, Straus,
       1959.   y.
       Examines the backgrounds of various soldiers.

1812   Morrison, Gerry.   Unvexed to the Sea.   St. Martin's, 1961.
       y.
       The siege of Vicksburg in the spring and summer of 1863.

1813   Morrow, Honoré.   Great Captain.   Morrow, 1935.   y.
       A trilogy about the leadership of Abraham Lincoln, in-
       cluding: Forever Free, With Malice Toward None, and
       The Last Full Measure.

       N., Will, pseud.   See Harben, William N.

1814 Noble, Hollister. Woman with a Sword. Doubleday, 1948.
        y.
        Anna Ella Carroll and the 1862 battles of Forts Henry and
        Donelson.

1815 Norton, Alice M. Ride Proud Rebel. By Andre Norton,
        pseud. World, 1961. y.
        A young confederate scout with Morgan's Raiders joins
        Nathan Bedford Forrest in attacks on Union supply lines.

      Norton, Andre, pseud. See Norton, Alice M.

1816 O'Connor, Richard. Company Q. Doubleday, 1957. y.
        A group of deranked Union officers is assigned to unwel-
        come infantry tasks; sort of a Civil War Dirty Dozen.

1817 _____. Guns of Chickamauga. Doubleday, 1955. y.
        A cashiered Chicago news reporter is involved in the
        great battle.

1818 Odom, John D. Hell in Georgia. Corlies, Macy, 1960. y.
        Recreates Sherman's march to the sea.

1819 Oldham, Henry. The Man from Texas. Petersen, 1887. y.
        The exploits of a Confederate guerrilla chief.

      Otis, James, pseud. See Kaler, James O.

1820 Page, T. N. Two Little Confederates. Scribner's, 1932. y.
        Action with the Army of Northern Virginia.

1821 Palmer, Bruce. Many Are the Hearts. Simon & Schuster,
        1961. y.
        Four tales dealing with individual responsibility during the
        conflict; Contents. --The Butcher's Bill. --My Brother's
        Keeper. --The Rooster. --The Short Straw.

1822 Parrish, Randall. My Lady of the North. McClerg, 1904.
        y.
        The adventures of one of Lee's couriers and Phil Sheri-
        dan's 1864 campaign in the Shenandoah Valley.

      Pendleton, Tom, pseud. See Van Zandt, Edmund.

1823 Pereny, Eleanor. Bright Sword. Rinehart, 1955. y.
        The 1864 campaigns of Confederate general John Bell Hood
        in Tennessee, including the battles of Franklin and Nash-
        ville.

1824 Prebble, John. Buffalo Soldiers. Harcourt, 1960. y.
        Near the Texas border during the last months of the war,
        Lieutenant Byrne's troop of Union Blacks escort a band of

Commanche Indians on a buffalo hunt and seek the renegade
Quasia.

1825 Prescott, John. Valley of Wrath. Fawcett, 1961. y. P.
A handful of Yankee soldiers battle Indians and rebels in
the Southwest.

1826 Reeder, Red. Whispering Wind. Duell, Sloan, 1956. y.
Depicts the infamous 1864 Sand Creek massacre in Colorado.

1827 Rhodes, James A., and Jauchins Dean. Johnny Shiloh.
Bobbs-Merrill, 1960. y.
The Governor of Ohio and his co-author tell an adventure
based on true service experiences of John Clem.

1828 Richardson, Norval. The Heart of Hope. Dodd, Mead, 1905.
y.
Depicts Grant's siege of Vicksburg.

1829 Roark, Garland. Outlaw Banner. Doubleday, 1956. y.
A tale of divided military allegiance.

1830 Roberts, Walter A. Brave Mardi Gras: A New Orleans Novel of the '60's. Bobbs-Merrill, 1946. y.
The exploits of Confederate soldier Blaise Lamotte, at
Bull Run in 1861 and with General Richard Taylor in the
1864 Red River operation in Texas.

1831 Robertson, Constance. Salute to the Hero. Farrar, Straus,
1942. y.
A clever, calculating general convinces everyone he is a
hero.

1832 Robertson, Don. By Antietam Creek. Prentice-Hall, 1961.
y.
A look at the April 17, 1862 battle in western Maryland.

1833 _____. The River and the Wilderness. Doubleday, 1962.
y.
Burnside's failure at Fredericksburg and Hooker's wilderness campaign.

1834 _____. The Three Days. Prentice-Hall, 1959. y.
Depicts the 1863 Battle of Gettysburg.

1835 Rowell, Adelaide. On Jordan's Stormy Banks. Bobbs-Merrill, 1948. y.
A tale about a Confederate scout.

1836 Sage, William. The Claybornes. Houghton Mifflin, 1902. y.
General Grant's campaigns against Vicksburg and Richmond, 1863-1865.

1837 Saturday Evening Post (periodical). The Post Reader of Civil
      War Stories. Ed. by Gordon Carroll. Doubleday, 1959.
      y.
      Nineteen stories that originally appeared in the magazine
      between 1930 and 1959.

1838 Seifert, Shirley. Farewell, My General. Lippincott, 1954.
      y.
      The exploits of J. E. B. Stuart, the Confederate horse gen-
      eral who was killed defending against Custer in 1864.

1839 Shaara, Michael. The Killer Angels. David McKay, 1974.
      y.
      Focuses on Confederate generals Lee and Longstreet,
      Union general John Buford, and Colonel Joshua Chamber-
      lain in the Battle of Gettysburg.

1840 Sherburne, James. The Way to Fort Pillow. Harcourt, 1972.
      y.
      A young Union sympathizer in Kentucky joins one of Thom-
      as W. Higginson's all-black units and survives the Con-
      federate massacre at Fort Pillow.

1841 Shirreffs, Gordon D. The Border Guidon. New American
      Library, 1962. y.
      A Union soldier rides through Apache-held Arizona to res-
      cue his captain's daughter and to prevent arms reaching
      the Confederates.

1842 Sinclair, Harold. The Cavalryman. Harper, 1958. y.
      General Jack Marlowe leads 2000 untried Union troopers
      against the Sioux in the Dakota Badlands in 1864; sequel
      to the next title.

1843 _____. Horse Soldiers. Harper, 1956. y.
      Colonel Jack Marlowe leads an 1863 raid from La Grange
      to Baton Rouge; a fictionalized account of the exploit led
      by Benjamin Grierson.

1844 Sinclair, Upton. Manassas. Macmillan, 1904. y.
      A classic account of the First Battle of Bull Run, 1861.

1845 Singmaster, Elsie. A Boy at Gettysburg. Houghton Mifflin,
      1924. y.
      A youth aids Union soldiers in the 1863 Battle.

1846 _____. Emmeline. Houghton Mifflin, 1916. y.
      A Yankee girl is caught in the Battle of Gettybsurg.

1847 _____. Gettysburg: Stories of the Red Harvest and After-
      math. Houghton Mifflin, 1913. y.
      Examines the fight from different perspectives.

1848   _____ . Swords of Steel. Houghton Mifflin, 1933. y.
            Another yarn about a girl caught up in the Battle of Get-
            tysburg.

1849   Slaughter, Frank G. In a Dark Garden. Doubleday, 1946.
            Rpr. 1976. y.
            A southern surgeon treats both Union and Confederate
            wounded.

1850   _____ . Lorena. Doubleday, 1959. Rpr. 1977. y.
            A doctor becomes involved with Sherman's march to the
            sea.

1851   _____ . The Stonewall Brigade. Doubleday, 1975. Rpr.
            1976. y.
            A surgeon accompanies Stonewall Jackson in the latter's
            campaigns in the Shenandoah Valley.

1852   Solomon, Eric, ed. The Faded Banners: A Treasury of
            Nineteenth Century Civil War Fiction. Yoseloff, 1960.
            y.
            An important anthology of contemporary or near-contem-
            porary tales, most of which are not cited here.

1853   Steele, W. O. The Perilous Road. Harcourt, 1958. y.
            The exploits of Confederate general Joseph Wheeler.

1854   Steelman, Robert J. The Galvanized Rebel. Doubleday, 1977.
            y.
            Pictures a Confederate attempt to inflame the Plains Indi-
            ans against the Union and create a second front to worry
            the hard-pressed Yankee military.

1855   Stern, Philip V. D. Drums of Morning. By Peter Storme,
            pseud. Doubleday, 1942. y.
            The adventures of Illinois soldier Jonathan Bradford.

1856   Sterne, Emma. No Surrender. Dodd, Mead, 1932. y.
            People on an Alabama plantation face Yankee raiders and
            other problems during the last year of the war.

       Storme, Peter, pseud. See Stern, Philip V. D.

1857   Stover, Herbert E. Copperhead Moon. Dodd, Mead, 1952.
            y.
            Union Army deserters turn to pro-southern sabotage.

1858   Straight, Michael. A Very Small Remnant. Knopf, 1963. y.
            The militia under John Chivington massacres Cheyenne
            women and children at Sand Creek, Colorado, in 1864.

1859   Stratemeyer, Edward. Defending His Flag. Lothrop, 1907. y.
            The First Battle of Bull Run or Manassas in 1861.

1860 Street, James. Captain Little Axe. Lippincott, 1956. y.
      A company of boys fights for the Confederates, with all
      but one killed during the Battle of Chickamauga.

1861 Syers, William E. The Devil Guns. Putnam, 1976. y.
      After losing the Battle of Val Verde, Confederate survi-
      vors embark on a 1000-mile retreat from New Mexico.

1862 Thomason, John W. Gone to Texas. Scribner's, 1937. y.
      A handsome Yankee officer wins a Rebel hellcat after
      thrilling gunplay on both sides of the Rio Grande.

1863 _____. Lone Star Preacher. Scribner's, 1941. y.
      Eight short stories detailing the spiritual-military career
      of the Reverend Praxiteles Swan, fire-eating chaplain to
      Texas soldiers in the Army of Northern Virginia and dar-
      ing captain of infantry.

1864 Thomsen, Robert. Carriage Trade. Simon & Schuster, 1972.
      y.
      A doctor, a dance-hall girl, and an actor treat wounded
      soldiers in a saloon during the Battle of Gettysburg.

1865 Toepfer, Ray G. Scarlet Guidon. Coward-McCann, 1958. y.
      Experiences of members of the 43rd Alabama Infantry dur-
      ing the war, including the battles of Gettysburg, Fisher's
      Hill, Cold Harbor, and in the Shenandoah Valley.

1866 _____. The Second Face of Valor. Chilton, 1966. y.
      A youth enlists in the Confederate army in Virginia to
      fight Yankees and comes of age as a guerrilla in the Shen-
      andoah Valley.

1867 Tompkins, Jane. Cornelia, the Story of a Civil War Nurse.
           Crowell, 1959. y.
      A biographical novel about Cornelia Hancock.

1868 Travers, Libbie M. The Honor of a Lee. Cochrane, 1908.
      y.
      General Braxton Bragg's campaigns in Tennessee.

1869 Van Zandt, Edmund. The Seventh Girl. By Tom Pendleton,
           pseud. McGraw-Hill, 1970. y.
      A Confederate soldier from west Texas does not enjoy his
      duty.

1870 Vaughan, Mathew. Major Stepton's War. Doubleday, 1978.
      y.
      A Confederate officer escapes a Union P.O.W. camp and
      leads a rebel raid on a federal bullion depot in Massa-
      chusetts.

1871 Von Kreisler, Max. Stand in the Sun. Doubleday, 1978. y.

Colonel Kurt Marlin is sent to the Central Plains in late
1864 to halt a Confederate-inspired Indian uprising.

1872 Ward, Larry. Thy Brother's Blood. Cowman, 1961. y.
Two brothers fight on opposite sides.

1873 Warren, Robert Penn. Wilderness. Random House, 1961.
y.
Rejected from the Union Army due to lameness, a Bavari-
an exile finds a place in the supply train during the Battle
of the Wilderness.

Weaver, Ward, pseud. See Mason, Francis Van Wyck.

1874 Weekley, Robert S. The House in Ruins. Random House,
1958. y.
Rebels refusing to accept the Appomattox surrender attack
Union Army units.

1875 Wellman, Manly W. Appomattox Road: The Final Adventures
of the Iron Scouts. Washburn, 1960. y.
Cavalry action in 1865 Virginia.

1876 Wheelwright, Jere H. The Gray Captain. Scribner's, 1954.
y.
I Company of the 2nd Maryland Infantry fights for the Army of Northern Virginia in the summer of 1864.

1877 Whitney, Phyllis A. Step to the Music. Crowell, 1953.
Rpr. 1974. y.
Includes a vivid picture of the 1863 Draft Riot in New
York City.

1878 Williams, Ben A. House Divided. Houghton Mifflin, 1947.
y.
A friend of the Virginia Currain family, General James
Longstreet's battles, especially Gettysburg, are followed
closely.

1879 Williams, Churchill. The Captain. Lothrop, 1903. y.
The leadership of General Grant.

1880 Willsie, Honoré M. Benefits Forgot. Stokes, 1917. y.
The mother of a Union Army surgeon, not having heard
from her son, asks President Lincoln for information; the
President has the young man's brother to Washington,
where they compare notes on motherly love.

1881 Wilson, William E. The Raiders. Rinehart, 1955. y.
Morgan and his men invade Indiana and Ohio in 1863.

1882 Wolford, Nelson. The Southern Blade. Morrow, 1961. y.
When seven Confederate soldiers escape a P. O. W. camp,
they are relentlessly pursued by a Yankee captain.

1883 Zara, Louis. Rebel Run. Crown, 1951. y.
         Captain James Andrews and the 1862 "Great Locomotive
         Chase" in Georgia and Tennessee.

NORTH AMERICA: 1866 TO 1900

The stories in this section cover the United States and Canada from
the end of the Civil War to the turn of the century. Most of them
concern fighting between the U.S. cavalry and the Indians in the
west. Readers wishing to find stories on American involvement
elsewhere during these years, including the Spanish-American War,
will find them in our section on Latin America.

1884 Aldrich, Bess S. The Lieutenant's Lady. Appleton, 1942.
         Rpr. 1975. y.
         Depicts the experiences of an officer's young wife at an
         Army outpost on the Missouri River; based on an actual
         diary.

1885 Allen, Henry. Chirichua. By Will Henry, pseud. Lippin-
         cott, 1972. y.
         In the 1880's cavalry troopers engage the Apache in Ari-
         zona Territory.

1886 _____. Custer's Last Stand. By Will Henry, pseud. Chil-
         ton, 1966. y.
         Follows the "Yellow Hair" from the 1868 fight at Washi-
         taw to the Indian revenge of 1876 at Little Big Horn.

1887 _____. The Day Fort Larking Fell. By Will Henry, pseud.
         Chilton, 1968. y.
         Indians take a fort from the U.S. Army.

1888 _____. From Where the Sun Now Stands. By Will Henry,
         pseud. Random House, 1960. Rpr. 1978. y.
         Pictures of the 113-day retreat of Chief Joseph from White
         Bird Canyon of Idaho to the Bear Paws in Montana in the
         summer of 1877 as recalled by an aging Nez Percé Indian.

1889 _____. The Last Warpath. By Will Henry, pseud. Ran-
         dom House, 1966. y.
         Depicts the 40-year struggle of the Cheyenne against the
         whites, including the Sand Creek Massacre and the battles
         of the Washita, Rosebud, Little Big Horn, Powder River,
         and Wounded Knee.

1890 _____. No Survivors. By Will Henry, pseud. Random
         House, 1950. Rpr. 1977. y.
         Custer and his men are liquidated at Little Big Horn.

1891 _____. Yellowstone Kelly. By Clay Fisher, pseud.
        Houghton Mifflin, 1957. y.
    The activities of an Indian scout in the 1870's.

1892 Altsheler, Joseph A. Horsemen of the Plains. Macmillan,
        1910. y.
    A boy's adventures with fur traders and Cheyenne in the
    late 1860's, including the 1868 fight at the Washita.

1893 _____. The Last of the Chiefs. Appleton, 1909. y.
    Custer at Little Big Horn.

1894 Arnold, Elliott. Blood Brother. Duell, Sloan, 1950. y.
    Cochise, chief of the Chirichuas Apache, and white man
    Tom Jefferies help keep the Arizona peace, except for the
    breakaway of Geronimo. A version for young people was
    published by the same firm in 1954 as Broken Arrow.

1895 _____. The Camp Grant Massacre. Simon & Schuster,
        1976. y.
    Agreeing to surrender his tribe to U.S. 3rd Cavalry
    troopers outside Tucson in 1871, Chief Eskiminzin is
    powerless to stop a slaughter of his unarmed braves by a
    bloodthirsty civilian posse.

1896 Arthur, Herbert. Freedom Run. By Arthur Herbert, pseud.
        Rinehart, 1951. y.
    Californians repel a Russian invasion shortly after the
    U.S. purchase of Alaska in 1869.

1897 Barry, Jane. A Time in the Sun. Doubleday, 1962. y.
    Apaches capture a colonel's daughter in Arizona in the
    1870's.

1898 Bellah, James W. Reveille. Fawcett, 1962. y. P.
    Fictional reminiscences of Indian-fighting cavalrymen, as
    recalled during their final days at Fort Starke.

1899 _____. Sergeant Rutledge. Bantam, 1960. y. P.
    An epic tale about a horse-soldier the Apaches called
    "Captain Buffalo."

1900 _____. A Thunder of Drums. Bantam, 1961. y. P.
    Indians versus cavalrymen on the southwest frontier.

1901 Benchley, Nathaniel. Only Earth and Sky Last Forever.
        Harper, 1972. y.
    A Sioux-adopted Cheyenne warrior participates in the Bat-
    tle of Little Big Horn.

1902 Berger, Thomas. Little Big Man. Dial, 1964. Rpr. 1970.
        y.
    Ancient mountain man Jack Crabb becomes Custer's con-
    fidant before Little Big Horn.

1903 Birney, Hoffman. The Dice of God. Holt, 1956. y.
      Custer and his 7th Cavalry at Little Big Horn.

1904 Blackburn, Thomas W. A Good Day to Die. David McKay,
          1967. y.
      U. S. soldiers "defeat" the Sioux in the so-called Battle of
      Wounded Knee in 1890.

1905 Brady, Cyrus T. Britton of the Seventh. McClurg, 1914.
          y.
      Adventures of a 7th Cavalry trooper with Custer before
      Little Big Horn and in the pursuit of Chief Joseph in
      1877.

1906 Brarco, Edgar John. Boots and Saddles. Berkeley, 1959.
          y. P.
      Captain Shank Adams and his U. S. 5th Cavalry soldiers
      protect the settlers from Geronimo in 1880's Arizona.

1907 Brown, Dee. Action at Beecher Island. Modern Library,
          1970. y. P.
      A fictional recreation of the nine-day siege of Forsyth's
      Scouts by Plains Indians in western Kansas, September
      1868.

1908 _____. Yellowhorse. Houghton Mifflin, 1956. y.
      The western cavalry employs a balloon against the Sioux.

1909 Burnett, William R. Adobe Walls: A Novel of the Last
          Apache Rising. Knopf, 1953. y.
      Scout Walter Grein and cavalry troops pursue Geronimo.

1910-19 No entries.

1920 Burroughs, Edgar Rice. Apache Devil. Private printing,
          1934. Rpr. 1976. y.
      A young white serves with Geronimo; the author, creator
      of Tarzan, served with the U. S. cavalry on the frontier
      at the turn of the century.

1921 Byrd, Sigman, and John Sutherland. The Valiant. Jason,
          1955. y.
      Chief Joseph and the Nez Percé War of 1877.

1922 Cameron, William B. The War Trial of Big Bear. Duck-
          worth, 1927. y.
      Depicts the Cree Indian rebellion of 1885 in Canada and
      the Frog Lake Massacre.

1923 Carter, Forrest. Watch for Me on the Mountain. Delacorte,
          1978. y.
      Geronimo versus generals Crook and Howard.

1924 Castor, Henry. <u>Year of the Spaniard</u>. Doubleday, 1950. y.
       The year 1898 in American military history, as reflected
       in the lives of a young woman and her two suitors.

1925 Chadwick, Joseph. <u>The Apache Wars</u>. By John Conway,
       pseud. Monarch Books, 1961. y. P.
       White settlers and the cavalry battle Indians in the South-
       west.

1926 _____. <u>The Sioux Indian Wars</u>. By John Conway, pseud.
       Monarch, 1962. y. P.
       A fictionalized account of Custer's Last Stand.

1927 Champion, John C. <u>The Hawks of Noon</u>. McKay, 1965. y.
       Soldiers versus Apaches in 1870's Arizona.

1928 Cheshire, Gifford P. <u>Thunder on the Mountain</u>. Doubleday,
       1960. y.
       Chief Joseph and the Nez Percé War of 1877.

1929 Comfort, Will L. <u>Apache</u>. Dutton, 1931. Rpr. 1976. y.
       The unsuccessful effort of Mangus Colorado (Don-Ha) to
       drive the whites from Santa Rita.

1930 _____. <u>Trooper Tales: A Series of Sketches of the Real
       American Private Soldier</u>. Street & Smith, 1899. Rpr.
       1976. y.
       Seventeen "boots and saddles" stories of the Indian-fighting
       cavalry.

1931 Constantin-Weyer, Maurice. <u>Half-Breed</u>. Macaulay, 1930.
       y.
       Louis Riel's 1869 and 1885 revolts against the Canadian
       government.

       Conway, John, pseud. <u>See</u> Chadwick, John.

1932 Cook, Will. <u>The Peacemakers</u>. Bantam, 1961. y. P.
       A regimental cavalry commander fights for peace with the
       Indians.

1933 Cooke, David C. <u>Post of Honor</u>. Putnam, 1958. y.
       An isolated frontier fort is besieged by Indians in the
       1870's.

1934 Cooper, Courtney R. <u>The Last Frontier</u>. Little, Brown,
       1923. y.
       Buffalo Bill and General Custer in the opening of the fron-
       tier Indian lands after the Civil War.

1935 Culp, John H. <u>The Restless Land</u>. Sloane, 1961. y.
       The Commanches raid a northwest Texas community in
       the 1870's.

1936 _____. A Whistle in the Wind. Holt, 1968. y.
Renegade Indians and whites form a Comanchero camp in
Texas from which to raid peaceful homesteads.

1937 Drago, Harry S. Montana Road. Morrow, 1935. y.
The Indian attempt to halt white incursion into the Dakotas,
including a temporary victory in the Battle of Little Big
Horn.

1938 Evarts, Hal. The Shaggy Legion. Little, Brown, 1930. y.
The whites cause the disappearance of the buffalo, bringing
on the Indian wars; generals Custer and Sheridan take part.

1939 Everett, Wade. Cavalry Recruit. Ballantine, 1965. y. P.
A young cavalry soldier gains a reputation as a great Indian fighter in 1867 Arizona.

1940 _____. Temporary Duty. Ballantine, 1961. Rpr. 1975.
y. P.
A young lieutenant is sent to a post in Apache country to
help rebuild a fort.

1941 Fast, Howard. The Last Frontier. Duell, Sloan, 1941. Rpr.
1971. y.
Poorly treated on their Oklahoma reservation in 1878, 300
Cheyenne defy the U.S. cavalry and make for their homeland in Montana's Powder River country.

1942 Ferber, Richard. The Hostiles. Dell, 1958. y. P.
The Sioux and Little Big Horn.

Fisher, Clay, pseud. See Allen, Henry.

1943 Fisher, Richard. Judgment in July. Doubleday, 1962. y.
Conflict between gold miners and Indians in the Dakotas
brings on the Battle of Little Big Horn in 1876.

1944 Foreman, Leonard L. Renegade. Dutton, 1942. y.
Raised by the Sioux, a white brave has conflicting loyalties
in the Battle of Little Big Horn.

1945 Forman, James. People of the Dream. Farrar, Straus,
1972. Rpr. 1974. y.
Chief Joseph and the Nez Percé War of 1877.

1946 Fox, Norman A. Rope the Wind. Dodd, Mead, 1958. Rpr.
1973. y.
Chief Joseph's migration and its cavalry opposition.

1947 Garland, Bennett. Seven Brave Men. Monarch, 1962. y.
P.
Seven whites hold off 300 Indians.

Garland, George, pseud. See Roark, Garland.

1948 Goble, Paul and Dorothy. Brave Eagle's Own Account of the
        Fetterman Fight. Pantheon, 1972. y.
        Fictional reminiscences of an Indian victory over white
        pony-soldiers.

1949 _____. Red Hawk's Account of Custer's Last Battle. Pan-
        theon, 1969. y.
        Fictional reminiscences of the Battle of Little Big Horn
        from one Indian's viewpoint.

1950 Goshe, Frederick and Frank. The Dauntless and the Dreamers.
        Yoseloff, 1963. y.
        Views of the Indian wars of 1876 through the eyes of Chey-
        enne and Sioux warriors.

1951 Gruber, Frank. Bugles West. Rinehart, 1954. y.
        The Battle of Little Big Horn in 1876.

     Gulick, Bill, pseud. See Gulick, Grover C.

1952 Gulick, Grover C. The Hallelujah Trail. By Bill Gulick,
        pseud. Doubleday, 1965. Rpr. 1976. y.
        Colonel Gearheart must protect a wagon train of whiskey
        from Indians, women temperance crusaders, and a thirsty
        Denver citizens' militia; based on the actual misadventures
        of the Walsingham train and the "Battle of Whiskey Hills."

1953 _____. The Moon-Eyed Appaloosa. By Bill Gullick, pseud.
        Doubleday, 1962. y.
        Cavalry troops borrow some tricks from the Indians in
        order to outmaneuver them.

1954 Haines, William W. The Winter War. Little, Brown, 1961.
        y.
        Based on the Indian campaigns in Montana Territory dur-
        ing the summer and winter of 1876 after Custer's defeat.

1955 Hanes, Frank B. The Fleet Rabble. Farrar, Straus, 1961.
        y.
        Centers on the courage and fortitude of one of Chief Jo-
        seph's sub-chiefs in the 1877 war.

1956 Harris, Margaret and John. Medicine Whip. Morrow, 1953.
        y.
        Pictures Indian attacks on wagon trains.

1957 Haycox, Ernest. Bugles in the Afternoon. Little, Brown,
        1944. y.
        Wounded, Private Kern Shafter survives the Battle of Lit-
        tle Big Horn.

1958 Heckelmann, Charles N. Trumpets in the Dawn. Doubleday,
        1958. y.
      The Sioux Indian wars.

1959 _____ ed. See Western Writers of America.

1960 Heinzman, George. Only the Earth and the Mountains. Mac-
        millan, 1964. y.
      An Army scout describes the white destruction of the Chey-
      enne from the Sand Creek Massacre through the final blow
      at Wounded Knee in 1890.

      Henry, Will, pseud. See Allen, Henry.

      Herbert, Arthur, pseud. See Arthur, Herbert.

1961 Hooker, Forrestine. When Geronimo Rode. Doubleday, 1924.
        y.
      A frontier post is caught up in the 1880's uprising.

1962 Horgan, Paul. A Distant Trumpet. Farrar, Straus, 1960.
        y.
      Centers on the interaction between Lieutenant Matt Hazard
      and White Horn, an Apache scout, during Geronimo's in-
      surrection.

1963 Jones, Douglas C. Arrest Sitting Bull. Scribner's, 1977.
        Rpr. 1978. y.
      Washington orders the arrest of the Sioux chief in a move
      to quell possible ghost-dance rebellions.

1964 _____. The Court Martial of George Armstrong Custer.
        Scribner's, 1976. Rpr. 1977. y.
      Lone survivor of Little Big Horn, Custer is tried for
      "dangerously exposing the lives of his troops."

1965 _____. A Creek Called Wounded Knee. Scribner's, 1978.
        y.
      Fictionally recreates the Sioux-Army hostilities, which
      ended in the 1890 massacre.

1966 Kaler, James O. Across the Range and Other Stories. By
        James Otis, pseud. Harper, 1914. y.
      Eight tales of the frontier Indian wars of the 1870's and
      1880's.

1967 Kantor, MacKinley. Warwhoop. Random House, 1952. y.
      Two novelettes; the first, "Behold the Brown-Faced Men,"
      concerns Sioux warfare in Nebraska.

1968 Keene, Day. Guns Along the Brazos. Signet, 1967. y. P.
      A young woman tries to carve a state out of 1870's Texas,
      but is challenged by an ex-Confederate major.

1969   King, Charles.   An Apache Princess, a Tale of the Indian
                Frontier.   Hobart, 1903.   y.
        Depicts the Apache wars of 1872-1873; King, a former In-
        dian-fighting U. S. cavalry officer, left the service to be-
        come a very successful novelist.   Almost all of his tales,
        with the exception of the few in our earlier North America
        sections, deal with Indians and the cavalry after the Civil
        War and are based on his experiences.

1970   _____.   An Army Wife.   F. T. Neely, 1896.   y.
        Life on a frontier military post in the 1870's and 1880's.

1971   _____.   Captain Blake.   Lippincott, 1896.   y.
        The adventures of an Indian-fighting cavalry officer in the
        1880's.

1972   _____.   Captain Close and Sergeant Croesus, Two Novels.
                Lippincott, 1895.   y.
        Tales of the U. S. 5th Cavalry in the Sioux wars; originally
        published in Lippincott's Magazine.

1973   _____.   The Colonel's Daughter; or, Winning His Spurs.
                Lippincott, 1883.   y.
        A young cavalry officer's exploits in the post-Civil War
        Indian campaigns.

1974   _____.   The Conquering Corps Badge and Other Stories of
                the Philippines.   L. A. Rhoades, 1902.   Rpr. 1972.   y.
        Ten tales about the U. S. Army troops involved in the sup-
        presion of the Philippine Insurrection.

1975   _____.   A Daughter of the Sioux, a Tale of the Indian
                Frontier.   Hobart, 1903.   y.
        An Indian princess's involvement in the Dakota Indian wars.

1976   _____.   Foes in Ambush.   Lippincott, 1893.   y.
        Apaches attack U. S. cavalry units.

1977   _____.   Fort Frayne.   Hobart, 1901.   y.
        Hostile Indians attack an Army outpost; based on the au-
        thor's script for a drama.

1978   _____.   The Further Story of Lieutenant Sandy Ray.   R. F.
                Fenno, 1906.   y.
        A young officer's involvement in the Indian wars; sequel
        to Lieutenant Sandy Ray, entered below.

1979   _____.   A Garrison Tangle.   F. T. Neely, 1896.   y.
        Romance at a frontier army post, with a sprinkling of In-
        dian fighting.

1980   _____.   In Spite of Foes; or, Ten Years' Trial.   Lippin-
                cott, 1901.   y.
        The problems of a cavalry officer on the frontier.

1981 _____ . Kitty's Conquest. Lippincott, 1912. y.
First published in 1884; a tale of love and combat in and
around a frontier army post.

1982 _____ . Lanier of the Cavalry. Lippincott, 1909. y.
An Army officer is unjustly arrested for failure in an Indian campaign.

1983 _____ . "Laramie"; or, The Queen of Bedlam. Lippincott,
1909. y.
A tale of the 1876 Indian wars.

1984 _____ . Lieutenant Sandy Ray. R. F. Fenno, 1906. y.
A young cavalry officer is initiated into the problems of
frontier Indian fighting.

1985 _____ . Ray's Daughter, a Story of Manila. Lippincott,
1901. y.
Sandy Ray's daughter becomes involved in the Philippine
Insurrection of 1898-1901.

1986 _____ . Ray's Recruit. Lippincott, 1898. y.
The exploits of a man recruited into the frontier cavalry
by Sandy Ray.

1987 _____ . A Soldier's Secret. Lippincott, 1904. y.
A tale of the Sioux "war" of 1890; not overly sympathetic
to the Indians.

1988 _____ . Starlight Ranch and Other Stories of Army Life on
the Frontier. Lippincott, 1905. Rpr. 1973. y.
Five tales first published in 1890.

1989 _____ . Sunset Pass; or, Running the Gauntlet Through
Apache Land. Street & Smith, 1900. y.
First published in 1890; this tale concerns a small unit
action with the Apache during the 1872-1873 conflict.

1990 _____ . A Tame Surrender. Lippincott, 1896. y.
A tale about Army troops involved in the Chicago Pullman
Strike.

1991 _____ . To the Front. Harper, 1908. y.
A newly commissioned officer is sent to fight in the Indian wars.

1992 _____ . Tonio, Son of the Sierras. G. W. Dillingham,
1906. y.
A young Indian fights the whites in the Apache wars of
the 1880's.

1993 _____ . A Trooper Galahad. Lippincott, 1899. y.
Pictures a young soldier's exploits in the Indian wars.

1994 _____. Trooper Ross and Signal Butte. Lippincott, 1908.
        y.
        Pictures a young soldier's exploits in the Indian wars.

1995 _____. Trumpeter Fred. F. T. Neely, 1896. y.
        An Army bugler becomes involved in the Indian wars.

1996 _____. Two Soldiers and Dunraven Ranch. Lippincott,
        1907. y.
        Two tales of combat in the Indian wars.

1997 _____. Under Fire. Lippincott, 1895. y.
        Combat between cavalry troopers and Indians on the fron-
        tier.

1998 _____. Warrior Gap. F. T. Neely, 1897. y.
        A tale of the Indian rising of 1865-1869 and the Battle of
        the Washita.

1999 _____. A Wounded Name. F. T. Neely, 1898. y.
        A frontier army officer is falsely accused.

2000 _____., ed. Captain Dreams and Other Stories. Lippin-
        cott, 1899. y.
        Contents. --Captain Dreams, by Capt. C. King. --The Ebb-
        Tide, by Lt. A. H. Sydenham. --White Lilies, by A. H.
        Hamilton. --A Strange Wound, by Lt. W. H. Hamilton. --
        The Story of Alcatraz, by Lt. A. H. Sydenham. --The
        Other Fellow, by R. Monckton-Dene. --Buttons, by Capt.
        J. G. Leefe.

2001 _____. An Initial Experience and Other Stories. Lippin-
        cott, 1894. y.
        Twelve stories about Army life on the post-Civil War
        frontier.

2002 Kjelgaard, Jim. Wolf Brother. Holiday, 1957. y.
        An Apache boy joins Chief Cross Face's renegades in war-
        ring on white settlers in Arizona.

2003 La Farge, Oliver. Cochise of Arizona. Dutton, 1953. y.
        A biographical novel about the Apache leader who held the
        U.S. Army at bay for a decade.

2004 Lee, Wayne C. Skirmish at Fort Phil Kearney. Avalon,
        1977. y. P.
        Indians attempt to capture a cavalry post.

2005 LeMay, Alan. The Searchers. Harper, 1954. y.
        The Commanches oppose white encroachment into Texas
        in the late 1860's and 1870's.

2006 _____. The Unforgiven. Harper, 1957. y.
        Kiowa Indians attack whites in Texas in the 1870's.

2007   Leonard, Elmore. <u>Bounty Hunters.</u> Houghton Mifflin, 1954.
       y.
       A green cavalry officer and an experienced scout track an
       escaped Apache chief in the 1880's.

2008   Lott, Milton. <u>Dance Back the Buffalo.</u> Houghton Mifflin,
       1959.   y.
       The rise of Ghost Dancing in 1889, leading to the Battle
       of Wounded Knee the following year.

2009   Lugar, Harriet M. <u>The Last Stronghold.</u> Young Scott, 1973.
       y.
       Story of the crossing of paths between a young Indian,
       young soldier, and a young settler during the 1872-1873
       Modoc Indian War.

2010   Lutz, Giles A. <u>The Magnificent Failure.</u> Doubleday, 1967.
       y.
       The 1885 Riel Rebellion in Canada.

2011   Miller, Mark. <u>White Captive of the Sioux.</u> Winston, 1953.
       y.
       Sioux attack a wagon train and capture the survivors.

2012   Neihardt, John G. <u>When the Tree Flowered.</u> Macmillan,
       1951.   y.
       Fictional autobiography of a Sioux warrior of the 1870's.

2013   Newsome, Ed. <u>Wagons to Tucson.</u> Little, Brown, 1954. y.
       Whites versus Apaches in Arizona.

       Otis, James, pseud. <u>See</u> Kaler, James O.

2014   Overholser, Wayne D. <u>Standoff at the River.</u> Bantam, 1961.
       y.   P.
       An untrained and crippled cavalry company fights the Chey-
       enne.

2015   Parkhill, Forbes. <u>Troopers West.</u> Rinehart, 1945. y.
       In 1879 Lieutenant Starr McArthur and the men of the U.S.
       Cavalry are sent to save a beleaguered Indian agent and
       put down a Ute Indian uprising in Wyoming.

2016   Parrish, Randall. <u>Bob Hampton of Placer.</u> McClurg, 1906.
       y.
       Focuses on Custer's 1876 Last Stand.

2017   Patten, Lewis B. <u>Ambush at Soda Creek.</u> Doubleday, 1976.
       y.
       Apaches attack three troops of the U.S. 10th Cavalry out
       seeking a colonel's kidnapped wife.

2018   _____. <u>Cheyenne Captives.</u> Doubleday, 1978. y.

Two men chase wife-stealing Indians and participate in
Custer's massacre at the Washita.

2019 _____. Proudly They Die. Doubleday, 1964. y.
An Indian brought up as a white must choose sides when
war breaks out and Custer approaches Little Big Horn.

2020 _____. The Red Sabbath. Doubleday, 1968. y.
An Army scout sympathetic to the Sioux and Cheyenne describes the Battle of Little Big Horn and events leading
up to the fight.

2021 Patton, Oliver. My Heart Turns Back. Popular Library,
1978. y. P.
Irish troopers participate in the chase of Chief Joseph.

2022 Payne, Pierre S. R. The Chieftain. Prentice-Hall, 1953.
y.
Chief Joseph tries to get his Nez Percé to Canada, but
cannot.

2023 Prebble, John. Spanish Stirrup. Harcourt, 1953. y.
Commanches attack John A. Ferguson's cowboys during
the first great cattle drive from Texas to Kansas.

2024 Roark, Garland. Bugles and Brass. By George Garland,
pseud. Doubleday, 1964. y.
A discredited cavalry captain is ordered to keep watch on
the San Carlos Apache Reservation.

2025 Rush, William. Red Fox of the Kinapoo. Longmans, Green,
1949. y.
Chief Joseph and the Nez Percé War of 1877, as recalled
by that great leader's interpreter.

2026 Schaefer, Jack W. Company of Cowards. Houghton Mifflin,
1957. y.
Jared Heath is ordered to lead a small group of Union
soldiers, regarded as renegades, against the Apaches of
the Southwest.

2027 Shelly, John L. Cavalry Sergeant. Ballantine, 1960. y. P.
A cavalry noncom fights the Utes in Wyoming Territory.

2028 Shiflet, Kenneth E. The Convenient Coward. Stackpole, 1961.
y.
A fictionalized biography of Major Marcus Reno, who was
tried for not helping Custer at Little Big Horn.

2029 Shirreffs, Gordon D. The Lone Rifle. New American Library, 1965. Rpr. 1978. y.
Depicts the war between cattlemen and the Montana Sioux.

2030 _____ . Son of Thunder People. Westminster, 1957. y.
     The exploits of Geronimo.

2031 _____ . The Valiant Bugles. New American Library, 1962.
          y.
     A cavalry captain is driven by an obsession to kill the In-
     dian chief responsible for his brother's death.

2032 Shrake, Edwin. Blood Reckoning. Bantam, 1962. y. P.
     The U. S. Cavalry versus the Commanches in Texas.

2033 Steelman, Robert. Lord Apache. Doubleday, 1977. y.
     An English noble and Major George Dunaway's 6th Cavalry
     troopers take on the Apaches in the 1880's.

2034 Straight, Michael W. Carrington. Knopf, 1961. y.
     Cavalry colonel Henry Carrington is held responsible for
     the Sioux destruction of the 81 men of L. T. C. Fetterman's
     patrol in northern Wyoming, December 21, 1866.

     Sutherland, John, jt. author. See Byrd, Sigman.

2035 Tassin, Ray. Red Men in Blue. Bouregy, 1962. y.
     Captain Jim Murie is assigned to lead an experimental
     Pawnee Indian battalion on the 1867 frontier.

2036 Thomason, John. Gone to Texas. Scribner's, 1937. y.
     Danger and excitement at an Army post on the Rio Grande.

2037 Turner, William O. War Country. Houghton Mifflin, 1957.
          Rpr. 1978. y.
     Indians battle settlers for land in 1885 Washington Terri-
     tory.

2038 Ulyatt, Kenneth. North Against the Sioux. Prentice-Hall,
          1967. Rpr. 1978. y.
     Chief Red Cloud and the siege of Fort Philip Kearney and
     the Fetterman massacre.

2039 Van de Water, Frederic F. Thunder Shield. Bobbs-Merrill,
          1934. y.
     A white boy adopted by the Cheyenne participates in the
     Battle of Little Big Horn.

2040 Vane, Norman T. The Caves. Major, 1977. y. P.
     The desperate men of Major Emmett Pitcher's 4th U. S.
     Cavalry and a horde of Apache warriors are trapped to-
     gether in the caves of Arizona's Huachuca Mountains.

2041 Van Every, Dale. The Day the Sun Died. Little, Brown,
          1971. y.
     Sioux "ghost dancing" brings on the Battle of Wounded

Knee in December 1890, when troops of the U.S. 7th Cavalry avenge the Little Big Horn with a massacre of Indians.

2042   Warren, Charles M. Only the Valiant. Macmillan, 1943. y.
A U.S. cavalry commander and a handful of troopers ride
into a hopeless 1870's engagement with the Apache.

2043   . Valley of the Shadow. Doubleday, 1948. y.
A U.S. cavalry unit tackles Deesokay and his Apache warriors.

2044   Wellman, Paul I. Broncho Apache. Doubleday, 1950. y.
Massai, one of Geronimo's subchiefs, returns to Arizona
from his Florida exile and becomes a ruthless marauder.

2045   . The Commancheros. Doubleday, 1952. y.
Texas Rangers take on a dread band of white renegades
who are leading Indians in devastating raids on white set-
tlements along the Texas border in the 1870's.

2046   Western Writers of America. With Guidons Flying: Tales of
the US Cavalry in the Old West. Ed. by Charles N.
Heckelmann. Doubleday, 1970. y.
Twelve stories of "boots and saddles."

2047   Whitman, S. E. Captain Apache. Berkeley, 1965. y. P.
Adventures of an Indian officer in the U.S. Cavalry.

2048   . Change of Command. Berkeley, 1966. y. P.
A new officer leads a troop into battle with the Indians.

2049   Whittington, Harry. Vengeance Is the Spur. Abelard-Schuman, 1960. y.
Cavalry versus the Apache in 1880's Arizona.

2050   Wister, Owen. Red Man and White. Harper, 1896. Rpr.
1972. y.
Recreates the campaigns of Indian fighter General George
Crook.

2051   Worcester, Donald. Lone Hunter and the Cheyennes. Oxford
University Press, 1959. y.
The war with the Oglala.

2052   Young, Carter T. Winter of the Coup. Doubleday, 1972. y.
Chief White Wolf takes on the U.S. Cavalry in Wyoming
Territory.

LATIN AMERICA: TO 1800

The stories in this section concern Central and South America from ancient times to the nineteenth century. Subjects touched upon include Aztec warfare, the Spanish conquest, early Latin American revolts, Haiti's 1791 independence movement, and the Spanish-American War.

2054 Allen, Dexter. Coil of the Serpent. Coward-McCann, 1956. y.
Sequel to the next entry; Nezahual of Tezcuco repels an invasion of his realm.

2055 _____ . Jaguar and the Golden Stag. Coward-McCann, 1954. y.
Prince Nezahual seeks to win the throne of Anahuoc in fifteenth-century Mexico.

2056 _____ . Valley of Eagles. Coward-McCann, 1957. y.
Nezahual, the Aztec lord of Tezcuco, faces the Spanish three years after Cortez's landing.

2057 Anderson, John L. Night of the Silent Drums. Fawcett, 1978. P.
Centers around the 1773 slave rebellion in the Virgin Islands.

2058 Baggett, Samuel G. Gods on Horseback. McBride, 1953. y.
Cortez invades Mexico.

2059 Baker, Betty. The Blood of the Brave. Harper, 1966. y.
A blacksmith joins Cortez's invasion of Mexico.

2060 Baron, Alexander. The Golden Princess. Washburn, 1954. y.
Princess Marina helps Cortez against Montezuma.

2061 Batchelor, D. O. The Unstrung Bow. Sherman, French, 1910. y.
Exploits of an Englishman in Peru at the time of Pizarro's conquest.

2062 Beals, Carleton. Taste of Glory. Crown, 1956. y.

Bernardo O'Higgins and the eighteenth-century liberation of Chile.

2063 Blacker, Irwin R. Taos. World, 1959. y.
Depicts the Pueblo Indian revolt against the Spanish in the New Mexico of the 1680's.

2064 Blasco-Ibáñez, Vincente. Knight of the Virgin. Trans. from the Spanish. Dutton, 1930. y.
A Spanish don, veteran of Columbus's second voyage, faces problems of settling in the New World, including hostile Indians.

2065 Bontemps, Anna. Drums at Dusk. Macmillan, 1939. y.
The slave revolt in Haiti of 1791.

Bourne, Peter, pseud. See Jeffries, Graham M.

2066 Brereton, Frederic S. Roger the Bold. Blackie, 1906. y.
A young man participates in Cortez's conquest of Mexico.

2067 Bronson, W. S. Slooping Hawk and Stranded Whale. Harcourt, 1942. y.
The Seri Indians resist the invading Spanish Army, 1541-1550.

2068 Burton, John Blundelle. Fortune's My Foe. Appleton, 1899. y.
English troops tackle Cartagena in 1758.

2069 Calin, Hal. Kings of the Sun. Lancer, 1963. y. P.
Pictures the struggle of the Mayan people to keep their empire.

2070 Carpentier, Alezo. Explosion in a Cathedral. Trans. from the Spanish. Little, Brown, 1963. Rpr. 1978. y.
French ex-shopkeeper Victor Hugues captures Guadeloupe from the British in the time of the French Revolution.

2071 _____. Kingdom of This World. Trans. from the Spanish. Knopf, 1957. Rpr. 1971. y.
Slave Ti Noel tells the story of the 1791 Haitian revolt.

2072 Craine. Edith J. The Victors. Duffield, 1934. y.
A Spanish captain recalls the Conquistador capture of Peru.

2073 Delmar, Vina. A Time for Titans. Harcourt, 1974.
Toussaint and the liberation of San Domingo from French forces.

2074 DeMadariaga, Salvador. Heart of Jade. Creative Age, 1944. y.
Montezuma of Mexico versus Cortez's Spaniards.

175 Dixon

2075 Dixon, Thomas. The Sun Virgin. Liveright, 1929. y.
       Fighting and romance during Pizarro's conquest of Peru.

2076 Duguid, Julian. Cloak of Monkey Fur. Appleton-Century,
       1936. y.
       Indians defeat the army of Don Pedro de Mendoza near
       Buenos Aires in 1535.

2077 Duncombe, Frances R. The Quetzel Feather. Lothrop, 1967.
       y.
       A young Spaniard joins in Alvarado's 1523 conquest of
       Guatemala.

2078 Friedenthal, Richard. White Gods. Trans. from the German.
       Harper, 1931. y.
       Cortez and the conquest of Mexico.

2079 Green, Gerald. The Sword and the Sun. Scribner's, 1954.
       y.
       Diego de Almagro and the conquest of Peru.

2080 Griffith, George. The Virgin of the Sun. C. A. Pearson,
       1898. y.
       Pizarro and the Spanish conquest of Peru.

2081 Haggard, H. Rider. Montezuma's Daughter. Longmans,
       Green, 1894. Rpr. 1976. y.
       Romance, adventure, and combat during the Spanish con-
       quest of Mexico.

2082 Henty, George A. By Right of Conquest. Scribner's, 1891.
       y.
       A pro-Spanish view of Cortez and his conquerors.

2083 _____. A Roving Commission. Scribner's, 1900. y.
       Toussaint L'Ouverture and the Haitian revolt of 1791.

2084 Hudson, Charles B. The Crimson Conquest. McClure, 1908.
       y.
       Depicts Pizarro's subjugation of Peru.

2085 Hughes, Rupert. War of the Mayan King. Winston, 1952.
       y.
       Twelfth-century conflict in Yucatan.

2086 Jeffries, Graham M. Drums of Destiny. By Peter Bourne,
       pseud. Putnam, 1947. y.
       A Scotsman is involved in L'Ouverture's 1791 revolt in
       Haiti.

2087 Jennings, John E. Golden Eagle. Putnam, 1959. y.
       DeSoto in Peru and Florida.

2088 Kidwell, Carl. Arrow in the Sun. Viking, 1961. y.

The ancient pre-Aztec Indians of Mexico fight one another for supremacy.

2089 Lauritzen, Jonreed. The Rose and the Flame. Doubleday, 1951. y.
Spaniards versus Navajos in the New Mexico of the 1680's.

2090 Lee, Albert. The Inca's Ransom. Harper, 1898. y.
Pizarro's conquest of Peru.

2091 Leonard, Phyllis. A Warrior's Woman. Coward-McCann, 1971.
A Scotswoman joins in the Spanish conquest of Mexico.

2092 Locke, Charles O. Last Princess. Norton, 1954. y.
The Spanish conquest of Peru from the Inca viewpoint.

2093 Lytle, Andrew N. At the Moon's Inn. Bobbs-Merrill, 1941. y.
Hernando de Soto in the American Southwest.

2094 Maass, Edgard. Don Pedro and the Devil. Bobbs-Merrill, 1942. y.
Don Pedro accompanies Pizarro to Peru.

2095 MacLeod, R. P. Daring Destiny. Playboy, 1978.
Love and warfare in Mexico at the time of Cortez.

2096 Marshall, Edison. Cortez and Marina. Doubleday, 1963. y.
An Indian princess aids the Spanish conquerors.

2097 May, Stella B. The Conqueror's Lady. Farrar & Rinehart, 1930. y.
Pedro de Valdivia conquers Chile for Spain.

2098 Munroe, Kirk. The White Conquerors. Blackie, 1893. y.
Cortez takes Mexico.

2099 Nevins, Albert J. The Young Conquistador. Dodd, Mead, 1960. y.
Diego de Molina joins Cortez in the Mexican conquest.

2100 Niles, Blair. Day of Immense Sun. Bobbs-Merrill, 1936. y.
Pizarro conquers the Incas of Peru.

2101 O'Dell, Scott. The King's Fifth. Houghton Mifflin, 1966. y.
A young cartographer recalls Spanish excesses in the conquest of Central and South America.

2102 Ryan, J. Clyde. Revolt Along the Rio Grande. Naylor, 1964. y.
The Pueblo Indians revolt against the Spanish in 1539.

2103 Shedd, Margaret. Malinche and Cortez. Doubleday,
        1971.
      Romance and combat in the Spanish conquest of Mexico.

2104 Shellabarger, Samuel. The Captain from Castile. Little,
        Brown, 1945. Rpr. 1973. y.
      Spanish noble Pedro de Vargas escapes the Inquisition to
      participate with Cortez in the conquest of Mexico.

2105 Small, Sidney H. Sword and Candle. Bobbs-Merrill, 1927.
        y.
      The 1781 Spanish military expedition from Mexico to Cali-
      fornia.

2106 Smith, Arthur D. H. Conqueror. Lippincott, 1937. y.
      Cortez versus Montezuma.

2107 Stacton, David. A Signal Victory. Pantheon, 1962. y.
      Aztecs under Guerro, a former Spanish seaman, resist
      Cortez's invasion of Mexico.

2108 Stevens, Sheppard. The Sword of Justice. Little, Brown,
        1899. y.
      Pictures the French-Spanish conquest of Florida in
      1565.

2109 Stuchen, Eduard. The Great White Gods. Trans. from the
        German. Farrar & Rinehart, 1934. y.
      Cortez conquers Mexico.

2110 Taylor, James G., Jr. Dark Dawn. Mohawk, 1932. y.
      Centers on the Haitian revolution of 1791.

2111 Thorpe, Francis N. The Spoils of Empire. Little, Brown,
        1903. y.
      The Spanish conquest of Mexico.

2112 Wallace, Lew. The Fair God. Houghton Mifflin, 1873.
        y.
      Cortez and the Spanish conquest of Mexico.

2113 Wellman, Paul I. Ride the Red Earth. Doubleday, 1958.
        y.
      The Chevalier de St. Denis and the Franco-Spanish strug-
      gle for Texas in the early 1700's.

LATIN AMERICAN: 1800 TO 1900

The stories in this section cover the various rebellions, independence movements, and wars fought during the nineteenth century. Here one will find tales of American involvement in Mexico and elsewhere, as well as tales built around nations struggling against Spanish domination.

2114 Allen, Henry. San Juan Hill. By Will Henry, pseud. Random House, 1962. y.
A fictional account of the Rough Riders in Cuba in 1898.

2115 Baker, A. A. Border War. Avalon, 1976. y. P.
Cole Shacker and his band of ex-Confederate guerrillas depart Missouri after the Civil War for Arizona to join Maximilian's French Army in Mexico.

2116 Baker, Nina B. Juárez, Hero of Mexico. Vanguard, 1942. y.
A fictional biography of Maximilian's chief opponent.

2117 Barrett, William E. Woman on Horseback. Doubleday, 1952. y.
Francisco López and Paraguay, 1865-1870.

2118 Barry, Jane. Maximilian's Gold. Doubleday, 1966. y.
Six Southerners journey to Mexico after the Civil War and become involved in the ill-fated French expedition.

2119 Beebe, Elswyth T. Ever After. By Elswyth Thane, pseud. Duell, Sloan, 1943. y.
Journalist Bracken Murray records the 1898 American campaign in Cuba.

2120 Bellah, James W. The Journal of Colonel De Lancey. Chilton, 1967. y.
An Irish mercenary fights in the various Latin American wars of independence.

Bourne, Peter, pseud. See Jeffries, Graham M.

2121 Braddy, Haldeen. Cock of the Walk. New Mexico Press, 1955. y.
The rise and exploits of Pancho Villa.

2122 Brand, Charles N. Mexican Masquerade. By Charles Lorne, pseud. Dodge, 1938. y.
Napoleon III sets up Maximilian as emperor of Mexico and then abandons him to the forces of Juárez.

2123 Burney, Hoffman. Eagle in the Sun. Putnam, 1935. y.
Juárez versus Maximilian, 1860-1870.

2124 Burrnell, Basil. Our Brother the Sun. Hermitage, 1954. y.
      Tale of a Latin American Indian revolt in 1869.

      Collingwood, Harry, pseud. See Lancaster, William J. C.

2125 Conrad, Joseph. Nostrome. Harper, 1904. Rpr. 1976.
      Revolutions in South America, 1860-1870.

2126 Cook, G. Oram. Roderick Taliaferro. Macmillan, 1903. y.
      Fighting between the forces of Juárez and Maximilian.

2127 Crane, Stephen. Wounds in the Rain: A Collection of Stories
      Relating to the Spanish-American War of 1898. Schol-
      arly, 1977. y.
      Reprinted from various newspaper and periodical sources.

2128 Davis, Richard H. Soldiers of Fortune. Scribner's, 1899.
      Rpr. 1971. y.
      Pictures various Latin American revolutions, especially in
      Venezuela, between 1870 and 1890.

2129 Duguid, Julian. Father Coldstream. Appleton-Century, 1938.
      y.
      Jesuits, outlaws, Indians, and settlers fight one another in
      Paraguay.

2130 Duncan, Hailey. West of Appomattox. Appleton, 1961. y.
      Rather than surrender, Confederate general Joe O. Shelby
      takes his army to Mexico.

2131 Emerson, Peter H. Caoba, the Guerrilla Chief. Scribner's,
      1897. y.
      A sympathetic view of Cuban nationals fighting the Spanish
      in the 1890's.

2132 Faust, Irvin. Willy Remembers. Arbor House, 1971. y.
      The fictional reminiscences of a Spanish-American War
      veteran.

2133 Fuller, Roger. The Timeless Serpent. Simon & Schuster,
      1964. y.
      Depicts the struggle for power following the death of the
      Paraguayan dictator Carlos Antonio López in 1870.

2134 Garfield, Brian W. The Vanquished. Doubleday, 1964. y.
      Experiences of an American Expeditionary Force sent to
      Mexico in 1857 to assist native rebels in overthrowing a
      dictatorship.

2135 Gavin, Catherine. The Cactus and the Crown. Doubleday,
      1962. y.
      Dr. Andrew Lorimer and French Army soldier Pierre
      Franchet participate in Maximilian's ill-fated Mexican
      empire scheme.

2136 Gerould, Gordon H. Filibuster. Appleton-Century, 1924. y.
A young American fights with the Insurrectos in Spanish
Cuba during the mid-1890's.

Goode, Ruth, jt. author. See Pollock, Alyce.

2137 Gorman, Herbert S. Breast of the Dove. Rinehart, 1950.
y.
Experiences of a young French officer in Maximilian's
army.

2138 _____. Cry of Dolores. Rinehart, 1948. y.
Pictures the 1810-1820 Mexican revolution against the
Spanish.

2139 Grey, Zane. Desert Gold. Harper, 1913. Rpr. 1976. y.
Concerns U. S. -Mexican border clashes.

2140 Hagedorn, Hermann. Rough Riders. Harper, 1928. y.
A fictional recreation of Theodore Roosevelt's charge up
San Juan Hill in the Spanish-American War.

2141 Harding, Bertita. Phantom Crown. Bobbs-Merrill, 1934. y.
Maximilian versus Juárez.

2142 Haynes, Herbert. At the Point of the Sword. Nelson, 1903.
y.
Simon Bolívar and the war of liberation in Peru.

2143 _____. A Captain of Irregulars. Nelson, 1900. y.
The Chilean war of independence from Spain, 1816 to 1818.

2144 _____. An Emperor's Doom. Nelson, 1898. y.
Depicts the end of Maximilian's empire.

2145 _____. In the Grip of the Spaniard. Nelson, 1890. y.
Bolívar in Venezuela, 1818-1821.

2146 _____. The President's Scouts. Collins, 1891. y.
Combat during the Chilean revolution of 1816-1818.

2147 _____. Under the Lone Star. Nelson, 1901. y.
Depicts the 1854-1857 revolution in Nicaragua led by American filibuster William Walker.

2148 _____. A Vanished Nation. Nelson, 1899. y.
Francisco López and Paraguay, 1866-1868.

2149 Henderson, Daniel M. A Crown for Carlotta. Stokes. 1929.
y.
The tragic misadventures of Maximilian in Mexico during
the 1860's.

Henry, Will, pseud. <u>See</u> Allen, Henry.

2150 Hudson, W. H. <u>El Ombu</u>. Duckworth, 1902. y.
      The 1807 English incursion into Argentina.

2151 Jeffries, Graham M. <u>Flames of Empire</u>. By Peter Bourne,
          pseud. Putnam, 1949. y.
      Maximilian's ill-fated attempt to set up a Mexican empire.

2152 Lancaster, William J. C. <u>Under the Chilean Flag</u>. By Harry
          Collingwood, pseud. Blackie, 1908. y.
      The 1879-1881 war between Chile and Peru, including the
      Battle of Angamos.

Lorne, Charles, pseud. <u>See</u> Brand, Charles N.

2153 Lyle, Eugene P. <u>The Missourian</u>. Doubleday, Page, 1905.
          y.
      Former Confederate soldiers fight for Maximilian in Mexi-
      co.

2154 McElroy, Lee. <u>A Long Way to Texas</u>. Doubleday, 1976. y.
      Headed off in New Mexico by Union troops, Confederate
      cavalry officer Davey Buckalew leads his men into Mexico.

2155 McLaughlin, Fred. <u>Blade of Picardy</u>. Bobbs-Merrill, 1928.
          y.
      A tale about a French swordsman in the service of Maxi-
      milian.

2156 Maxwell, Patricia. <u>The Notorious Angel</u>. Fawcett, 1977. P.
      A woman's adventures in William Walker's Nicaraguan war
      of the mid-1850's.

2157 Nicole, Christopher. <u>Ratoon</u>. St. Martin's, 1962. y.
      Whites are caught in the turmoil of the 1823 slave insur-
      rection in British Guiana.

2158 Niles, Balir. <u>Passengers to Mexico</u>. Farrar & Rinehart,
          1943. y.
      The failure of Maximilian's plans for Mexico.

2159 Pearsall, Robert B. <u>Young Vargas Lewis</u>. Houghton Mifflin,
          1968. y.
      A young American engineer becomes involved in the nine-
      teenth-century War of the Triple Alliance in South America.

2160 Polley, Judith. <u>Val Verde</u>. Delacorte, 1974.
      A French girl becomes involved in the Juarista movement
      against Maximilian.

2161 Pollock, Alyce, and Ruth Goode. <u>Don Gaucho</u>. McGraw-Hill,
          1950. y.

Don Miguel and his gauchos save Buenos Aires from a
British invasion in the 1820's and later participate in several revolutions.

2162 Raine, Alice. The Eagle of Guatemala. Harcourt, 1947. y.
A biographical novel about Barrios, 1820-1830.

2163 Reid, Victor S. The New Day. Knopf, 1949. y.
Depicts the 1865 rebellion on Jamaica.

2164 Reynolds, Robert. Paquita. Putnam, 1947. y.
A tale of the 1810-1820 Mexican revolution.

2165 Roberts, Walter A. Single Star. Bobbs-Merrill, 1949. y.
The Cuban insurrection of the 1890's.

2166 Rundell, E. Ralph. The Color of Blood. Crowell, 1948. y.
Juan Manuel de Rosas comes to power in the Argentina of
the 1820's.

2167 Stanton, Maura. Molly Companion. Bobbs-Merrill, 1977.
Centers on the Paraguayan war with Brazil, 1865 to 1870.

2168 Strabel, Thelma. Storm to the South. Doubleday, 1944. y.
Peru's war of independence.

2169 Street, James. Mingo Dabney. Dial, 1950. y.
Cuba's insurrection against Spain, 1895 to 1898.

2170 Teilhet, Darwin. The Lion's Skin. Sloane, 1955. y.
William Walker attempts to take over Nicaragua in the
1850's.

2171 _____. Retreat from the Dolphin. Little, Brown, 1943.
y.
The 1815 revolution in Chile.

Thane, Elswyth, pseud. See Beebe, Elswyth T.

2172 Uslar Pietri, Arturo. The Red Lances. Trans. from the
Spanish. Knopf, 1963. y.
A tale of the Venezuelan war of independence, 1811-1821.

2173 Von Dombrowski, Katharina. Land of Woman. Little, Brown,
1935. y.
Love and war in López's Paraguay of 1868-1870.

2174 Wellman, Paul I. Angels with Spurs. Lippincott, 1942. y.
In 1865 a young Confederate goes to Mexico with Joe Shelby's cavalry to join Maximilian; compare with Hailey Duncan's West of Appomattox, above.

2175 _____. Death in the Desert. Macmillan, 1934. y.
A tale of the 1822 to 1886 war for the great Southwest.

2176   White, Edward L.   El Supremo: A Romance of the Great
            Dictator of Paraguay.   Dutton, 1916.   y.
       An American soldier-of-fortune attempts to overthrow Rod-
       ríguez de Francia, 1813-1840.

2177   Williams, J. R.   Mission to Mexico.   Prentice-Hall, 1959.
            y.
       Conditions in Mexico during Maximilian's "empire."

2178   Williams, Joel.   Coasts of Folly.   Reynal, 1942.   y.
       A filibustering expedition sets out from New York to lib-
       erate Venezuela in the 1820's.

2179   Wilson, Carter.   A Green Tree and a Dry Tree.   Macmillan,
            1972.   y.
       In the 1870's Pedro Díaz Cuscat leads an Indian rebellion
       in the Mexican province of Chiapas.

AFRICA, ASIA, AND THE PACIFIC: TO A.D. 1000

The tales in this section come from or are about Africa, Asia, and the Pacific nations in ancient times. Here one will find stories about the Egyptians, Jews, Persians, Alexander the Great, the Assyrians, the Trojans, and many other peoples and heroes. Readers should note that there is often some spill-over between these accounts and those in our section on Europe: To A.D. 400.

2180 Asch, Sholem. The Prophet. Trans. from the Yiddish. Putnam, 1955. y.
Deutero-Isaiah and the fifth-century B.C. conquest of Babylon by Cyrus of Persia.

2181 Baker, George E. Paris of Troy. Ziff-Davis, 1947. y.
The siege and fall of Troy by the Greeks.

2182 Baron, Alexander. Queen of the East. Washburn, 1956. y.
Pictures the conflict between Zenoba, Queen of Palmyra, and the Roman emperor Aurelian.

2183 Bible. Old Testament. Various publishers and dates.
One of the oldest sources of war stories.

2184 Bothwell, Jean. Flame in the Sky. Vanguard, 1954. y.
The prophet Elijah in Palestine, 875 B.C.

2185 Brady, Cyrus T. When the Sun Stood Still. Revell, 1917. y.
Joshua and Jericho.

2185a Butcher, Charles H. Armeuosa in Egypt. Blackwoods, 1897. y.
Pictures the Moorish conquest of Egypt in the seventh century.

2186 Carling, John R. The Doomed City. Ward, Lock, 1910. y.
The Roman siege and destruction of Jerusalem in A.D. 70.

2187 Challans, Mary. Fire from Heaven. By Mary Renault, pseud. Pantheon, 1969. Rpr. 1977. y.

2188 _____. The Persian Boy. By Mary Renault, pseud. Pan-
          theon, 1972. Rpr. 1974.
          The Persian eunuch Bagoas tells of the Asian conquests of
          Alexander the Great; homosexual implications.

2189 Chinn, Laurene. The Unannointed. Crown, 1959. y.
          The exploits and problems of Joab, military commander
          for King David of Israel.

2190 Church, Alfred J. Lords of the World. Scribner's, 1899.
          y.
          The fall of Carthage and Corinth to Roman troops.

2191 _____. A Young Macedonian. Putnam, 1890. y.
          The military campaigns of Alexander the Great.

2192 _____, and Robert Seeley. The Hammer. Putnam, 1890.
          y.
          The wars of the Maccabees.

2193 Clark, Alfred. Lemuel of the Left Hand. Low, 1909. y.
          Syria versus Israel at the time of Ahab and Obadiah.

2194 Coolidge, Olivia. Egyptian Adventures. Houghton Mifflin,
          1954. y.
          Exploits, some military, in the land of the Pharaohs.

2195 _____. The King of Men. Houghton Mifflin, 1966. y.
          Agamemnon and his Greek warriors besiege Troy.

2196 _____. The Trojan War. Houghton Mifflin, 1952. y.
          Tales rewritten from Homer's Iliad (q. v.)

2197 Crawford, F. Marion. Zoroaster. Macmillan, 1935. Rpr.
          1970. y.
          Love and war in 550 B. C. Persia, including the conquest
          of Babylon by Cyrus. Originally published in 1885.

2198 Daugherty, Sonia. Wings of Glory. Oxford University Press,
          1940. y.
          The exploits of David as youth and king.

2199 Davenport, Arnold. By the Ramparts of Jezreel. Longmans,
          Green, 1903. y.
          The Syrian invasion of Judea at the time of Ahab.

2200 Davis, William S. Belshazzar. Macmillan, 1925. y.
          Babylon is destroyed by Cyrus and his Persians.

2201 DeRopp, Robert S. If I Forget Thee. St. Martin's, 1956.
          Pictures the A. D. 66 Jewish revolt against Rome.

2202 DeWohl, Louis. David of Jerusalem. Putnam, 1963. y.

Includes a look at Goliath and other military problems of the shepherd king of Israel.

2203 _____ . Imperial Renegade. Lippincott, 1950. y.
Julian the Apostate, a fourth-century Roman emperor, is killed in combat with the Persians.

Druon, Maurice, pseud. See Kessel, Maurice.

2204 Duggan, Alfred L. Besieger of Cities. Pantheon, 1963. y.
How Demetrius of Macedonia attempted to revive the empire of Alexander the Great.

2204a Dumke, Glenn S. Tyrant of Bagdad. Little, Brown, 1956.
y.
Eric, Count of the Norman Shore and one of Charlemagne's nobles, battles the tyrant Harun al-Rashid.

2205 Ebers, Georg. The Bride of the Nile. Trans. from the German. Gottsberger, 1887. y.
Depicts the Moslem conquest of Egypt.

2205a _____ . Cleopatra. Trans. from the German. Appleton, 1894. y.
The later years of the Egyptian queen, including her military campaigns with Mark Antony.

2206 _____ . Uarda. Trans. from the German. Caldwell, 1877.
y.
Rameses II as Pharaoh and military chief of Egypt.

2207 Eiker, Karl V. Star of Macedon. Putnam, 1957. y.
Slave Gyges of Trapezus traces the military career of Alexander the Great.

2208 Fast, Howard. Agrippa's Daughter. Doubleday, 1964. y.
Herod the Great is caught between warring Jewish factions in Jerusalem and Titus's troops preparing to assault the city from without.

2209 _____ . My Glorious Brothers. Little, Brown, 1948.
Rpr. 1977. y.
The five Maccabeean brothers free Israel from its Syrian-Greek overlords.

2210 Feuchtwanger, Lion. Josephus. Trans. from the German. Viking, 1932. y.
The Jewish historian Flavius Josephus and the A.D. 70 fall of Jerusalem.

2211 Fisher, Vardis. Island of the Innocent. Abelard, 1952. y.
The Maccabees and their followers struggle for independence from the Syrian-Greeks in 200 B.C.

2212 Flaubert, Gustave. Salammbô. Trans. from the French.
Putnam, 1862. Rpr. 1977.
Hamilcar, Carthage, and their mercenaries.

2213 French, Henry W. Lance of Kanana. Lothrop, 1932. y.
A Bedouin boy rescues Arabians from their enemies at the
time of the Roman invasion of Arabia in the fourth century
A. D.

2214 Fuller, Robert H. The Golden Hope. Macmillan, 1905. y.
Alexander the Great conquers Egypt and the East.

2215 Gann, Ernest K. The Antagonists. Simon & Schuster, 1970.
Roman general Flavius Silva versus Jewish leader Eleazar
ben Yair at Masada in A. D. 73.

2216 Gardiner, G. S. Rusten, Son of Zal. Greening, 1911. y.
A legendary soldier of ancient Iran unknowingly kills his
son in battle.

2217 Gerson, Noel B. The Golden Lyre. Doubleday, 1963. y.
A tale of Ptolemy, one of Alexander's captains.

2218 _____. The Hittite. Doubleday, 1961. y.
Lord Marduck is a capable commander of the Hittite Army
at the time of Joshua.

2219 _____. That Egyptian Woman. Doubleday, 1956. y.
Cleopatra, Julius Caesar, and Mark Antony.

2220 _____. The Trojan. Doubleday, 1962. y.
Tells of the capture of Troy by the Greeks and the city's
later recovery by Loyalists, aided by Arabs and Israelites.

2221 Graves, Robert. The Siege and Fall of Troy. Doubleday,
1963. y.
A modern reworking of Homer's Iliad (q. v.).

2222 Haggard, H. Rider. Moon of Israel. Longmans, Green,
1918. y.
The Jewish Exodus from Egypt and Egyptian countermeas-
ures.

2223 _____. Pearl Maiden. Longmans, Green, 1903. Rpr.
1978. y.
The Roman destruction of Jerusalem in A. D. 70.

2224 _____, and Andrew Lang. The World's Desire. Longmans,
Green, 1891. Rpr. 1977. y.
Helen of Troy after the Trojan War.

2225 Harris, Clare W. Persephone of Eleusis. Stratford, 1923.
y.
The Persian invasion of Greece.

2225a Harrison, Frederic. Theophano. Chapman & Hall, 1903. y.
      The Byzantine Empire versus the Saracens in the mid
      tenth century.

2226 Haugaard, Erik C. The Rider and His Horse. Houghton Mif-
      flin, 1968. y.
      A boy's role in the Roman siege of Masada in A. D. 73.

2227 Henty, George A. For the Temple. Scribner's, 1888. y.
      The siege and fall of Jerusalem in A. D. 70.

2228 Hillman, George S. Persian Conqueror. Dodd, Mead, 1935.
      y.
      A fictional biography of Cyrus the Great.

2229 Homer. The Iliad. Trans. from the Greek. Doubleday,
      1975. y.
      Although originally an oral poem, this work is cited here
      as one of history's oldest war stories, the saga of the
      Trojan War.

2230 Hubler, Richard G. The Soldier and the Sage. Crown, 1966.
      y.
      A Roman soldier recalls his experiences during the Jewish
      revolt against Hadrian in A. D. 132.

2231 Hurley, Victor. The Parthian. Fleet, 1960. y.
      Battles and trials of a Roman soldier in Parthia and the
      East from 50 B. C. to A. D. 17.

2232 Hyman, Frieda C. Jubal and the Prophet. Farrar, Straus,
      1958. y.
      Jerusalem under siege by the Babylonians.

2233 Israel, Charles E. Rizpah. Simon & Schuster, 1961. y.
      Saul's army defeats the Philistines.

2234 Jenkins, Guyn. King David. Doubleday, 1961. y.
      Includes a look at his military difficulties.

2235 Jenkins, R. Wade. "O King, Live Forever. " Watts, 1911.
      y.
      Cyrus the Great conquers Babylon.

2236 Johnson, Gillard. Raphael of the Olive. Appleton-Century,
      1913. y.
      The Maccabees attempt to recover Jerusalem.

2237 Jones, Juanita N. David, Warrior of God. Association,
      1954. y.
      Reworks the Old Testament account.

2238 Kessel, Maurice. Alexander the God. By Maurice Druon,
      pseud. Scribner's, 1960. y.

The military and political victories of Alexander the Great.

2239 King, Marian. Young King David. Lippincott, 1948. y.
The slaying of Goliath and rout of the Philistines.

2240 Kirkman, Marshall M. Alexander and Roxana. Cropley &
Philips, 1909. y.

2241 _____. Alexander the King. Cropley & Philips, 1909. y.

2242 _____. Alexander the Prince. Cropley & Philips, 1909.
y.
A trilogy that traces the career of Alexander the Great.

2243 Kossoff, David. The Voices of Masada. St. Martin's, 1973.
Portrays the Jewish defense against the Roman siege in
A. D. 73.

Lang, Andrew, jt. author. See Haggard, H. Rider.

2244 Lang, Theodore. The Word and the Sword. Delacorte, 1974.
y.
Pontius Pilate sees himself trapped between the power
plays of Rome and rebellion in Palestine during the last
days of Christ.

2245 Lau, Josephine S. Slave Boy in Judea. Abingdon-Cokesbury,
1954. y.
Roman military operations in Palestine during the first
century A. D.

2246 Malvern, Gladys. Behold Your Queen. Longmans, Green,
1951. y.
Queen Esther saves her people from King Ahasuerus of
Persia in 150 B. C.

2247 _____. Saul's Daughter. Longmans, Green, 1956. y.
David, Goliath, and the Jewish-Philistine war.

2248 Marshall, Edison. Conqueror. Doubleday, 1962. y.
A fictional autobiography of Alexander the Great, dwelling
to a large extent on his military successes.

2249 Meisels, Andrew. Son of a Star. Putnam, 1969. y.
Jewish revolt against Rome in A. D. 132-135.

2250 Melville, G. J. Whyte. The Gladiators. Longmans, Green,
1863. y.
Centers around the Roman capture of Jerusalem in A. D.
70.

2251 _____. Sarchedon. Longmans, Green, 1871. y.
Ancient Babylon and the Assyrians.

2252 Miller, Elizabeth. The City of Delight. Bobbs-Merrill, 1908.
     y.
     The Roman siege and capture of Jerusalem in A.D. 70.

2253 Moray, Ann. Dawn Falcon. Morrow, 1974. y.
     Two brothers team up to oust Hyksos usurpers from Egypt
     in the sixteenth century B.C.

2254 More, E. Anson. A Captain of Men. Page, 1905. y.
     A biographical novel about Hiram, King of Tyre.

2255 Morgan, Barbara E. Hand of the King. Random House, 1963.
     y.
     Rebellion flares against an Assyrian king in 1750 B.C.

2256 Mundy, Talbot. The Purple Pirate. Appleton, 1935. Rpr.
     1978. y.
     After the death of Caesar, Tros of Samothrace becomes
     involved with Cleopatra and Mark Antony.

2257 Noller, Ella M. Ahira, Prince of Naphstali. Eerdmans,
     1947. y.
     The Hebrews fight their way into the land of Canaan.

2258 Norton, Alice M. Shadow Hawk. By Andre Norton, pseud.
     Harcourt, 1960. y.
     Pharaoh Kamose battles the Hyksos in Egypt in the six-
     teenth century B.C.

     Norton, Andre, pseud. See Norton, Alice M.

2259 Parker, Gilbert. The Promised Land. Stokes, 1928. y.
     The exploits of David in Israel.

2260 Payne, Robert. Alexander the God. Wyn, 1954. y.
     Alexander the Great, from his conquest of Thaissa to his
     death.

2261 Pendleton, Louis. In Assyrian Tents. Jewish Publications
     Society, 1948. y.
     David fights Goliath.

2262 Powell, Richard. Whom the Gods Would Destroy. Scribner's,
     1970. y.
     Captured by the Achaeans, a Trojan youth relates both
     sides of the Trojan War--without the intercessions of the
     gods.

2263 Rayner, William. The Last Days. Morrow, 1969. y.
     A young Zealot recounts the Masada story, A.D. 66-73.

     Renault, Mary, pseud. See Challans, Mary.

2264 Sackler, Harry. Festival at Meron. Covici, 1935. y.
      Simeon ben Yokai leads a Jewish revolt against Rome.

2265 Sallaska, Gladys. Priam's Daughter. Doubleday, 1970. y.
      A pro-Trojan view of the Trojan War.

2266 Schmitt, Gladys. David, the King. Dial, 1946. y.
      Includes a look at his military problems.

      Seeley, Robert, jt. author. See Church, Alfred J.

2267 Shamir, Moshe. David's Stranger. Trans. from the Yiddish.
      Abelard, 1965. y.
      Uriah the Hittite is sent out to die in battle by King David,
      who covets Uriah's wife, Bathsheba.

2268 _____. The King of Flesh and Blood. Trans. from the
      Yiddish. Vanguard, 1958. Rpr. 1978. y.
      The problems of Alexander Jannaeus, a descendant of Si-
      mon Maccabaeus, through the Roman conquest of Palestine.

2269 Siegel, Benjamin. The Sword and the Promise. Harcourt,
      1960. y.
      The slave Bias describes the A.D. 132 Bar Kochba up-
      rising in Palestine against Hadrian's Roman government.

2269a Simon, Edith. Twelve Pictures. Putnam, 1955. y.
      Twelve tales about people involved with Attila the Hun.

2270 Slaughter, Frank G. The Curse of Jezebel. Doubleday, 1961.
      y.
      The evil Queen Jezebel, her husband King Ahab, and the
      conflict between the Canaanite kings.

2271 _____. The Scarlet Cord. Doubleday, 1956. Rpr. 1972.
      y.
      Rahab of Jericho and Joshua during the famous siege.

2272 _____. The Song of Ruth. Doubleday, 1954. Rpr. 1977.
      y.
      A retelling of the Book of Ruth and of the war between
      Israel and Moab.

2273 Stuart, Frank S. Caravan to China. Doubleday, 1941. y.
      A Roman trading expedition of ancient times meets all
      kinds of problems, some of a military nature.

2274 Tapsell, A. F. The Year of the Horsetails. Knopf, 1967.
      y.
      Attila the Hun in Central Asia.

2274a Tietjens, Eunice S. Romance of Antar. Coward-McCann,
      1930. y.

Battles and loves of a great pre-Mohammedan Arab chief,
based on old folk tales.

2275 Treece, Henry. <u>The Amber Princess</u>. Random House, 1963.
      y.
      In her old age, Electra recalls the Trojan War.

2276 _____. <u>The Windswept City</u>. Meredith, 1968. y.
      One of Helen's slaves recounts the Greek siege of Troy.

2277 Watkins, Shirley. <u>The Prophet and the King</u>. Doubleday,
      1956. y.
      The ancient Israelites battle the Philistines.

2278 Weinreb, N. N. <u>The Babylonians</u>. Doubleday, 1953. y.
      Dwells on the exploits of Nebuchadnezzar.

2279 _____. <u>The Sorceress</u>. Doubleday, 1954. y.
      The Israelites conquer Canaan.

2280 Wilchek, Stella. <u>Judith</u>. Harper, 1969. y.
      How the Jewish heroine slew the Babylonian general Holo-
      fernes.

2281 Williams, Jay. <u>The Counterfeit African</u>. Oxford University
      Press, 1944. y.
      A tale of Marius's North African campaign of 186-156 B.C.

2282 Williams, Wirt. <u>The Trojans</u>. Bantam, 1967. y. P.
      An account of the Trojan War.

2283 Yonge, Charlotte M. <u>The Patriots of Palestine</u>. Whittaker,
      1889. y.
      Jerusalem and the Maccabean Revolt of 174 B.C.

AFRICA, ASIA, AND THE PACIFIC: 1000 TO 1600

The stories in this section are set in the Middle Ages and Renaissance. Here the reader will find citations to tales primarily of the
Crusades and the Asian hordes. You should note that there is in
this part, as in the last, certain spill-over between these accounts
and those in our section on Europe: 400 to 1500 (especially with
regards to the exploits of Richard the Lion Hearted).

2284 Arnold, Michael. <u>Against the Fall of Night</u>. Doubleday,
      1975.
      The Crusades and Emperor Andronikus Commenus of
      Byzantium.

2285 Baumann, Hans. Sons of the Steppe. Walck, 1958. y.
      Depicts the conflict between Kublai and Arik-Buka, grand-
      son of the great Genghis Khan.

2286 Bengtsson, Frans G. The Long Ships. Knopf, 1954. y.
      The adventures of Viking Red Orm in Arabia.

2287 Bennetts, Pamela. Richard and the Knights of God. St. Mar-
            tin's, 1973. y.
      Simon Fitzalan accompanies King Richard on the Third
      Crusade.

2288 Bothwell, Jean. Promise of the Rose. Harcourt, 1958. y.
      Akbar and the Mongols in India, 1483-1707.

      Bourne, Peter, pseud. See Jeffries, Graham M.

2289/90 Brooke, Teresa. Under the Winter Moon. Doubleday,
            1958. y.
      A tale of France and the First Crusade.

2291 Butcher, Charles H. The Oriflamme in Egypt. Dent, 1905.
            y.
      St. Louis' Eighth Crusade, 1249-1250.

2292 Byrne, Donn. Crusade. Little, Brown, 1928. y.
      An Irish soldier of fortune fights the Saracens in the Holy
      Land in the 1229 Sixth Crusade led by Frederick II.

2293 Cahun, Leon. The Blue Banner. Trans. Lippincott, 1877.
            y.
      The Crusades and Mongol Conquest, 1194 to 1254.

2294 Caldwell, Janet T. The Earth Is the Lord's. By Taylor
            Caldwell, pseud. Scribner's, 1941. Rpr. 1976. y.
      Genghis Khan unites the Mongols for conquest, 1206-1220.

      Caldwell, Taylor, pseud. See Caldwell, Janet T.

2295 Carse, Robert. The Wicked Blade. Popular Library, 1958.
            y. P.
      Jean Barqnault travels to the Mongol court of Il Khan seek-
      ing an alliance to save the Holy Land from the Moslems
      during the last Crusade.

2296 Charques, Dorothy. Men Like Shadows. Coward-McCann,
            1953. y.
      John of Oversley tells how he and two friends joined Rich-
      ard I in the Holy Land for the Third Crusade.

2297 Clift, Chaimain. Big Chariot. Bobbs-Merrill, 1953. y.
      The Manchus sweep over China, 1559-1626.

2298   Clou, John.   Caravan to Camul.   Bobbs-Merrill, 1954.   y.
       A tale of Kisil, a soldier in the entourage of Genghis
       Khan.

2299   _____ .   The Golden Blade.   Graphic Publishers, 1954.   y.
       The exploits of Genghis Khan's captain of horse.

2300/01 Coe, F. L.   Knight of the Cross.   Sloane, 1951.   y.
       Bohemond and the French in the Crusades.

       Colyton, Henry John, pseud.   See Zimmermann, Sarah.

2302   Coolidge, Olivia.   Tales of the Crusades.   Houghton Mifflin,
             1970.   y.
       A collection of short stories about the 1095 to 1291 expe-
       ditions from Europe to the Holy Land.

2303   Costain, Thomas B.   The Black Rose.   Doubleday, 1945.   y.
       A young English noble fights his way to the center of the
       Mongol empire in 1220.

2304   Crawford, F. Marion.   Via Crucis.   Macmillan, 1898.   y.
       War and romance during the 1147 Second Crusade.

2305   Creswick, Paul.   With Richard the Fearless.   Dutton, 1904.
       y.
       Richard I fights the Third Crusade.

2306   Cronyn, George.   Fool of Venus.   Covici, 1935.   y.
       Minstrel Peire Vidal of Provence records the Fourth Cru-
       sade, during which the Crusaders captured not Jerusalem
       but Constantinople.

2307   Daringer, Helen F.   A Flower of Araby.   Harcourt, 1958.   y.
       Life in a thirteenth-century Crusader castle in Syria.

2308   Davis, William S.   "God Wills It."   Macmillan, 1901.
       Norman knight Richard Longsword participates in the
       storming of Jerusalem in the 1095 to 1099 First Crusade.

2309   Duggan, Alfred.   Count Bohemond.   Pantheon, 1965.   y.
       A knight becomes Prince of Antioch during the First Cru-
       sade.

2310/11 _____ .   Knight with Armour.   Coward-McCann, 1950.
       y.
       Sir Roger, a son of William the Conqueror, joins the
       First Crusade, but is killed in the 1090 siege of Jerusalem.

2312/13 Duncan, David.   The Trumpet of God.   Doubleday, 1956.
       y.
       Knightly combat with the Moors during the First Crusade.

2314   Everard, William.   Sir Walter's Ward.   Blackie, 1888.   y.
       A squire and his master join Frederick II in the Sixth
       Crusade.

2315   Fenton, Ronald O.   Knight Crusader.   By Ronald Welch,
              pseud.   Oxford University Press, 1954.   y.
       A young knight joins Richard I on the Third Crusade.

2316   Gartner, Chloe.   The Infidels.   Doubleday, 1961.   y.
       The exploits of Sir Justin Le Noir during the First Cru-
       sade.

2317   Gay, Leverne.   Wine of Satan.   Scribner's, 1949.   y.
       Follows the exploits of Bohemond, the Norman Prince of ·
       Antioch, during the First Crusade.

       Grant, Allan, pseud.   See Smith, Arthur D. H.

2318   Haggard, H. Rider.   The Brethren.   McClure, 1904.   y.
       Richard I versus Saladin during the Third Crusade.

2319/20   Harrison, F. Blayford.   Brothers-In-Arms.   Blackie,
              1885.
       The siege of Acre during the Third Crusade.

2321   Haycraft, Molly C.   My Lord Brother the Lion Heart.   Lip-
              pincott, 1968.   y.
       Richard I asks Queen Joan of Sicily to accompany him on
       the Third Crusade.

2322   Henty, George A.   Winning His Spurs.   Sampson, Low, 1882.
              y.
       A youth joins King Richard I in fighting Saladin.

2323   Hewes, A. D.   A Boy of the Lost Crusade.   Houghton Mif-
              flin, 1923.   y.
       A youth participates in the ill-fated 1212 Children's Cru-
       sade.

2324   Holberg, Ruth L.   Marching to Jerusalem.   Crowell, 1943.
              y.
       A young knight participates in the First Crusade.

2325   Holland, Cecelia.   Antichrist.   Atheneum, 1970.   y.
       The military and religious problems of Frederick II, in-
       cluding his Sixth Crusade.

2326   _____ .   Until the Sun Falls.   Atheneum.   1969.   y.
       Two generals lead the army of the Mongol Khan into east-
       ern Europe during the thirteenth century.

2327   Holland, Rosemary.   Antichrist.   Lippincott, 1968.   y.
       How the Holy Roman Emperor Frederick II became King
       of Jerusalem in 1229.

2328 Hollis, Gertrude. Between Two Crusades. Gorham, 1908.
         y.
         Saladin and the fall of the Latin Kingdom at Jerusalem in
         1187.

2329 _____ . A Slave of the Saracen. Nelson, 1905. y.
         A tale of St. Louis and the Eighth Crusade.

2330 _____ . Two Dover Boys. Blackie, 1910. y.
         Our heroes become involved in the 1534-1535 capture of
         Tunis by Emperor Charles V.

      Hunter, Hall, pseud. See Marshall, Edison.

2331 Jefferies, Barbara. Time of the Unicorn. Morrow, 1974.
         y.
         Shipwrecked en route to the Crusades, English and Norman
         knights must survive a 40-day ordeal.

2332 Jeffries, Graham M. When God Slept. By Peter Bourne,
         pseud. Putnam, 1951. y.
         A pair of Englishmen are captured by the Saracens during
         the First Crusade.

      John, Evan, pseud. See Simpson, Evan J.

2333 Knight, R. A. The Land Beyond. Whittlesey House, 1954.
         y.
         The ill-fated Children's Crusade.

2334 Knox, Ester M. Swift Flies the Falcon. Winston, 1939. y.
         A tale of the First Crusade.

2335 Kossak-Szczucka, Zofja. Angels in the Dust. Roy, 1947. y.
         Three Silesian knights exiled from Poland fight in the
         First Crusade.

2336 _____ . The Leper King. Roy, 1945. y.
         Baldwin IV cannot hold his twelfth-century kingdom of
         Jerusalem, which is captured by Saladin.

2337 Lamb, Harold. Durandel. Doubleday, 1932. y.
         The adventures of Sir Hugh in the Crusades; betrayed by
         the Greek emperor, he is able to escape the Arabs, aided
         by Durandel, the famous sword of Roland.

2338 Ludlow, James M. Sir Raoul. Revell, 1905. y.
         Venice, Acre, and Constantinople during the Fourth Cru-
         sade.

2339 MacKaye, Loring. Silver Disk. Longmans, Green, 1955.
         y.
         Frederick II leads his Sixth Crusade.

2340 Marshall, Edison. Caravan to Xanadu. By Hall Hunter,
          pseud. Farrar, Straus, 1954. Rpr. 1977. y.
      Marco Polo travels to the East and the court of Kublai
      Khan.

2341 Mason, Francis Van Wyck. Silver Leopard. Doubleday,
          1955. y.
      A knight and his twin sister during the First Crusade.

2342 Mather, Berkely. Genghis Khan. Dell, 1965. y. P.
      A fictional biography of the barbarian conqueror.

2343/4 Meakin, Nevill M. The Assassins. Holt, 1902. y.
      Richard I and the 1191 siege of Acre.

2345 Motley, Annette. My Lady's Crusade. Bantam, 1978. P.
      Richard I and the romance and warfare of his Third Cru-
      sade.

2346 Myers, L. H. Pool of Vishnu. Harcourt, 1940. y.
      Akbar in India, 1542-1606.

2347 Oldenbourg, Zoe. The Heirs of the Kingdom. Trans. from
          the French. Pantheon, 1971. Rpr. 1976. y.
      Peter the Hermit, the weavers of Arras, and the storming
      of Jerusalem during the First Crusade.

2348 _____ . The World Is Not Enough. Trans. from the French.
          Pantheon, 1948. y.
      The Second and Third Crusades, as viewed by a French
      knight and his family of Champagne, France.

2349 O'Meara, Walter. The Devil's Cross. Knopf, 1957. y.
      The ill-fated Children's Crusade.

2350 O'Neal, Cothburn. Master of the World. Crown, 1953. y.
      Recreates the military exploits of Timur the Great, also
      known as Tamerlane, during the fourteenth century.

2351 Oz, Amos. "Crusade." In his collection Unto Death. Har-
          court, 1975. p. 1-81.
      A novella detailing the fate of a band of Christian soldiers
      bound for Jerusalem during the First Crusade.

2352 Potter, Margaret H. The Flame-Gatherers. Macmillan,
          1904. y.
      The Mohammedan conquest of India in 1250.

2353 Prescott, H. F. M. The Lost Fight. Dodd, Mead, 1956.
          y.
      Sir Adam de Morteigne and the Sixth Crusade.

2354 Price, Olive. Valley of the Dragon. Bobbs-Merrill, 1951. y.
      Kublai Khan's Chinese exploits.

2355 Proud, Franklin. The Tartar. Pocket Books, 1978. y. P.
      The story of Hsu Yung--half-Mongol, half-Chinese war-
      rior--of the twelfth century.

2356 Quinn, Vernon. The March of the Iron Men. Stokes, 1930.
      y.
      A tale of soldiers during the First Crusade.

2357 Raynolds, Robert. Quality of Quiros. Bobbs-Merrill, 1955.
      y.
      The 1595 voyage of Alvaro de Mendana to the Philippines.

2358 Rhodes, Evan H. An Army of Children. Dial, 1978. y.
      Depicts the disastrous Children's Crusade of 1212.

2359 Ritchie, Rita. Golden Hawks of Genghis Khan. Dutton, 1958.
      y.
      The power of the Mongol horde.

2360 _____. Year of the Horse. Dutton, 1957. y.
      Genghis Khan and his conquering Mongols.

2361 Sawyer, Philip. Minstrel Knight. Merrill, 1956. y.
      A European visits Mongolia in the time of Genghis Khan.

2362 Scarfolgio, Carlo. The True Cross. Trans. from the Italian.
      Pantheon, 1956. y.
      The Latin Kingdom and the disintegration of the Second
      Crusade, 1177 to 1192.

2363 Schoonover, Lawrence L. Golden Exile. Macmillan, 1951.
      y.
      A tale of the last Crusade and its aftereffects.

2364 Scott, Walter. Anne of Geierstein; or, The Maiden of the
      Mist. Dutton, 1927. y.
      First published in 1829, this tale tells of Count Robert of
      Paris during the First Crusade.

2365 _____. The Betrothed, a Tale of the Crusaders. Estes &
      Lauriat, 1894. y.
      Romance and combat during the 1189 to 1192 Third Cru-
      sade.

2366 _____. Count Robert of Paris. Bazin & Ellsworth, 1833.
      y.
      A tale of romance and dissention in the knightly ranks
      during the First Crusade.

2367 _____. The Talisman. Estes, 1825. Rpr. 1972. y.
      A disguised Sir Kenneth, Prince Royal of Scotland, fights
      with Richard I against Saladin in the Third Crusade.

2368   Shelby, Graham. The Knights of Dark Renown. Weybright &
            Talley, 1971. y.
        After Reynald of Chatillon causes Saladin to break his
        truce in the Holy Land, Baldwin and his nobles attempt to
        hold Jerusalem for Christianity.

2369/70   . The Knights of Vain Intent. Weybright & Tal-
            ley, 1970. y.
        With Saladin in control of Jerusalem, Richard I and Philip
        of France take their armies to the Holy Land to do battle;
        sequel to the previous title, although published earlier.

2371   Simpson, Evan J. Ride Home Tomorrow. By Evan John,
            pseud. Putnam, 1951. y.
        The last years of the Latin Kingdom of Jerusalem and the
        coming of the Third Crusade.

2372   Smith, Arthur D. H. Spears of Destiny. By Allan Grant,
            pseud. Doran, 1917. y.
        English knight Hugh de Chesby participates in the Fourth
        Crusade and the sack of Constantinople.

2373   Steel, Flora A. King Errant. Stokes, 1912. y.
        Baber founds the Mongol empire in India.

2374   Stein, Evaleen. Our Little Crusader Cousin of Long Ago.
            Page, 1921. y.
        A youth fights in the Third Crusade for Richard I against
        Saladin.

2375   Stratton, Clarence. Paul of France. Macmillan, 1927. y.
        How the Crusaders sacked Constantinople during the Fourth
        Crusade.

2376/7 Thomas, Cenethe. Michel's Singing Sword. Holt, 1937.
            y.
        Combat in France during the First and Second Crusades.

2378   Tolosko, Edward. Sakuran. Farrar, Straus, 1978. y.
        Pictures battles between rival Samurai in medieval Japan.

2379   Treece, Henry. Perilous Pilgrimage. Criterion, 1959. y.
        The disastrous 1212 Children's Crusade.

2380   Walsh, R. J. Adventures and Discoveries of Marco Polo.
            Random House, 1953. y.
        Based on the Italian's own memoirs.

        Welch, Ronald, pseud. See Fenton, Ronald O.

2381   White, L. T. Winged Sword. Morrow, 1955. y.
        Combat in France during the First Crusade.

2382 Williams, Jay. Tomorrow's Fire. Atheneum, 1965. y.
          A poet recalls the role of Richard I in the Third Crusade.

2383 Wingate, Lititia B. A Servant of the Mightiest. Lockwood,
          1927. y.
          Depicts the conquest of China by Genghis Khan.

2384 Yonge, Charlotte. The Prince and the Page. Macmillan,
          1866. y.
          A tale of the Eighth Crusade led by St. Louis.

2385 Yoshikawa, Eiji. Heiké Story. Trans. from the Japanese.
          Knopf, 1956. y.
          Combat of a warrior clan in twelfth-century Japan.

2386 Zimmermann, Sarah. Sir Pagan. By Henry John Colyton,
          pseud. Creative Age, 1947. y.
          A tale of the end of the Latin Kingdom of Jerusalem and
          the Third Crusade.

AFRICA, ASIA, AND THE PACIFIC: 1600 TO 1800

The stories in this section detail military exploits in our region
during the seventeenth and eighteenth centuries. Here you will find
fictional recreations of Napoleon's campaign in Egypt, military affairs in Japan and at Tunis, and Tippo Sahib's war with the English
in India. With regard to the Napoleon stories especially, there is
limited spill-over between this section and Europe: 1700-1800.

2387 Austin, F. Britten. Forty Centuries Look Down. Stokes,
          1937. y.
          A recreation of Napoleon's campaign in Egypt.

2388 Beddoe, David. The Last Mameluke. Dutton, 1913. y.
          Napoleon's Egyptian campaign.

       Casgoe, Richard, pseud. See Payne, Pierre S. R.

2389 Clavell, James. Shogun. Atheneum, 1975. Rpr. 1976. y.
          An Englishman helps a Japanese warlord win military con-
          trol of seventeenth-century Japan.

2390 Compton, Herbert. A Free Lance in a Free Land. Cassell,
          1895. y.
          A young English soldier participates in the British cam-
          paigns in India, 1798-1804.

2391 Durand, Henry M. Nadir Shah. Dutton, 1908. y.

Traces the Persian conqueror's eighteenth-century military exploits.

2392 Fitchett, William H. A Pawn in the Game. Eaton & Mains, 1908. y.
Follows Napoleon's campaigns in Egypt and Syria.

2393 Grant, James. The Royal Highlanders; or, The Black Watch in Egypt. Munro, 1885. y.
Fictional tale of a British regiment that battles Napoleon's troops in Egypt.

2394 Griffiths, Arthur. A Royal Rascal. Fisher, Unwin, 1905. y.
Tippo Sahib versus the English in India, 1790-1799.

2395 Henty, George A. At Aboukir and Acre. Scribner's, 1899. y.
Details the failure of Napoleon's campaigns in Egypt and Syria.

2396 _____. The Tiger of Mysore. Scribner's, 1896. y.
English troops battle Tippo Sahib in southern India, 1790-1799.

2397 _____. With Clive in India. Scribner's, 1884. y.
Robert Clive's mid eighteenth-century military campaigns in India.

2398 Inchbold, A. C. Phantasma. Blackwoods, 1906. y.
Napoleon in Egypt and Syria.

2399 McKenney, Ruth. Mirage. Farrar, Straus, 1956. y.
The problems of Napoleon's soldiers in Syria.

2400 Macmillan, Michael. In Wild Mahratha Battle. Blackie, 1906. y.
Sivaji and the founding of the Mahratha Empire in India during the seventeenth century.

2401 _____. The Princess of Balkh. Macmillan, 1905. y.
A Scotsman is involved in the seventeenth-century Indian wars of Aurungzebe, the Mogul emperor.

2402 Masters, John. Coromandel. Viking, 1955. y.
Jason Savage's adventures in India during the early years of the seventeenth century.

2403 Partington, Norman. Master of Bengal. St. Martin's, 1975. y.
A fictional biography of Robert Clive and his eighteenth-century campaigns in India.

2404 Payne, Pierre S. R. Young Emperor. By Richard Cargoe,
        pseud. Macmillan, 1950. y.
      The exploits of Shahzahan, Mogul emperor of India during
      the early seventeenth century.

2405 Percy-Graves, J. The Duke's Own. Dutton, 1887. y.
      Tippo Sahib and the 1798-1799 siege of Seringapatam in
      India.

2406 Pollard, Eliza F. The Silver Hand. Blackie, 1908. y.
      Warren Hastings versus Hyder Ali in India during the
      1770's.

2407 Rabie, Jan. A Man Apart. Trans. from the Afrikaans.
        Macmillan, 1969. y.
      Depicts the 1799 war between the Dutch and the black Af-
      rican Kaffirs in the area now known as South Africa.

2408 Scott, Walter. The Surgeon's Daughter. A. & C. Black,
        1897. y.
      First published in 1827, this story tells of a young doctor
      in India who witnesses the conflict between Hyder Ali and
      the British East India Company.

2409 Sell, Frank R. Bhim Singh. Macmillan, 1926. y.
      Indian emperor Aurungzebe and the seventeenth-century
      Rajput War.

2410 Stace, Henry. The Adventures of Count O'Connor. Alston
        Rivers, 1907. y.
      Imaginary memoirs of an Irish mercenary who fought for
      the Mogul emperor Aurungzebe in seventeenth-century In-
      dia.

2411 Strang, Herbert. One of Clive's Heroes. Bobbs-Merrill,
        1906. y.
      Robert Clive's soldiers win the Battle of Plassey in India
      during the 1750's.

2412 Taylor, Philip Meadows. Ralph Darnell. Scribner's, 1865.
        y.
      Clive's victory at Plassey.

2413 _____ . Tara. Paul, 1863. y.
      Pictures the 1657 uprising of the Mahrattes against the
      Mohammedans in India.

2414 _____ . Tippo Sultaun. Paul, 1840. y.
      Tippo Sahib and the 1798-1799 war against the English in
      India.

2415 Taylor, Winchcombe. Ram. St. Martin's, 1960. y.

The military adventures of an English soldier in eighteenth-
century India.

AFRICA, ASIA, AND THE PACIFIC: 1800 TO 1900

The nineteenth century witnessed a large number of imperial wars
by Europeans throughout Asia, Africa, and the Pacific. The tales
in this section reflect those conflicts. Here readers will find accounts of the Sepoy Revolt in India, the English-Boer wars in South
Africa, the English-Zulu war in Africa, the Afghan contests, Gordon
at Khartoum, French battles in North Africa, the Maori War in New
Zealand, and fighting in Burma and China. Many of these tales de-
pict a sort of "imperialistic glory" that in the years since the end
of the Second World War has largely died out.

2416 Anderson, Flavia. Rebel Emperor. Doubleday, 1959. y.
      The 1851-1865 Taiping Revolt in China.

2417 Blanch, Lesley. The Nine Tiger Man. Atheneum, 1965. y.
      A maharajah's son aids a forward English woman through
      the 1857 Sepoy Revolt in India.

      Boldrewood, Rolf, pseud. See Browne, Thomas A.

2418 Brereton, Frederic S. A Hero of Lucknow. Blackie, 1905.
      y.
      Cawnpore, Lucknow, and Delhi during the Sepoy Revolt.

2419   . Jones of the 64th. Blackie, 1907. y.
      Sir Arthur Wellesley and the 1803 battles of Assaye and
      Laswari in India.

2420   . With Roberts to Candahar. Blackie, 1907. y.
      A tale of the Third Afghan War of 1878-1880, with empha-
      sis on the siege of Kabul and the relief of Kandahar.

2421   . With Shield and Assegal. Blackie, 1900. y.
      Pictures the Zulu War of 1879, with emphasis on Isandula,
      Rorke's Drift, and Ulundi.

2422 Browne, Thomas A. War to the Knife. By Rolf Boldrewood,
      pseud. Macmillan, 1899. y.
      Fierce combat during the Maori War of the 1860's in New
      Zealand.

2423 Case, Josephine. Written in Sand. Houghton Mifflin, 1945.
      y.
      General William Eaton and Lieutenant O'Bannon lead their
      U.S. Marines to Tripoli in 1805.

2424 Chesney, George T. The Dilemma. Harper, 1876. y.
      The English battle rebels during the Sepoy Revolt.

2425 Clive, William. The Tune That They Play. Simon & Schus-
            ter, 1973. Rpr. 1975. y.
      Zulu chief Atskwayo defeats a small British force at the
      battle of Isandhiwana in 1879.

2426 Cloete, Stuart. The Hill of Doves. Houghton Mifflin, 1941.
      y.
      The South African Transvaal during the war of 1881.

2427 _____. The Mask. Houghton Mifflin, 1957. y.
      The Boers versus the Kaffirs in South Africa, 1852 to
      1854.

2428 _____. Rags of Glory. Doubleday, 1963. Rpr. 1973. y.
      The paramount novel of military action in the Boer War.

2429 _____. The Turning Wheels. Houghton Mifflin, 1937. y.
      The Boers fight Kaffirs and Zulus in 1837 to found the
      Orange Free State.

2430 _____. Watch for the Dawn. Houghton Mifflin, 1939. y.
      Free Boers battle the English in South Africa, c. 1816.

2431 Cobban, J. McLaren. Cease Fire! Methuen, 1900. y.
      Pictures the Transvaal War of 1881.

2432 Cullum, Ridgwell. The Compact. Doubleday, Doran, 1909.
      y.
      Another look at the Transvaal War of 1881.

2433 De la Ramée, Louise. Under Two Flags. By Ouida, pseud.
            Stein & Day, 1967. y.
      First published in 1867, this tale concerns a British of-
      ficer, accused of forgery, who joins the French Foreign
      Legion to fight the Kabyles in Algeria.

2434 Diver, Maud. The Great Amulet. Lane, 1908. y.
      British soldiers versus rebels on the Indian border.

2435 _____. The Judgment of the Sword. Putnam, 1913. y.
      Pictures the Afghan Wars of the 1830's and 1840's.

2436 DuBois, Theodora M. Tiger Burning Bright. Farrar, Straus,
            1964. y.
      A tale of the Sepoy Revolt of 1857.

2437 Eden, Dorothy. Siege in the Sun. By Mary Paradise, pseud.
            Coward-McCann, 1967. y.
      Demonstrates the siege of Mafeking in South Africa.

2438 _____ . Sleep in the Woods. Coward-McCann, 1961. Rpr.
            1978. y.
            English settlers battle the Maori in New Zealand during
            the 1860's.

2439 Eldridge, Nigel. The Colonel's Son. Peter Davies, 1962.
            y.
            A young man's father becomes commander of Bengal Lan-
            cers in India.

2440 Farrell, J. G. The Siege of Krishnapur. Harcourt, 1974.
            y.
            An English civil servant finds himself organizing and lead-
            ing a town's defense during the Sepoy Revolt.

2441 Forrest, R. E. Eight Days. Smith & Elder, 1891. y.
            The rebel victories early in the Sepoy Revolt.

2442 _____ . The Sword of Azrael. Methuen, 1903. y.
            An English soldier escapes the Sepoy mutineers.

2443 Fraser, George M. Flashman: From the Flashman Papers,
            1839-1842. World, 1969. Rpr. 1971.
            Expelled from school, an English cad receives a commis-
            sion in the 11th Light Dragoons, is sent to India, and
            through cowardice and lack of principle becomes a mili-
            tary hero. Mature.

2444 _____ . Flashman in the Great Game. Knopf, 1975. Rpr.
            1977.
            Harry Flashman is sent to India to investigate the causes
            of native unrest and ends up helpless to interfere in the
            Sepoy massacres of Jhansi and Cawnpore; nevertheless,
            he manages to win the Victoria Cross and a knighthood.

2445 _____ . Flashman's Lady. Knopf, 1978.
            Colonel Flashman and the heathen queen of Madagascar.

2446 Gardner, Mona. Hong Kong. Doubleday, 1958. y.
            A tale of the 1830's Opium War in China.

2447 Gartner, Chloe. Drums of Khartoum. Morrow, 1967. y.
            "Chinese" Gordon and the defense of Khartoum against the
            Madi in 1884 to 1885.

2448 Gibbon, Frederick P. The Disputed V. C. Blackie, 1903.
            y.
            Delhi and Lucknow during the Sepoy Revolt.

2449 Grant, James. Playing with Fire. 3 vols. Ward & Downey,
            1887. y.
            Gordon versus the Madi in the Sudan; an almost-contem-
            porary tale.

Gray, Maxwell, pseud. See Tuttiett, Mary G.

2450 Griffiths, Arthur. Before the British Raj. Everett, 1903.
         y.
      A British soldier's adventures in 1800 India.

2451 Haggard, H. Rider. Allan Quatermain. Longmans, Green,
         1914. Rpr. 1978. y.
      First published in 1887, this account tells of a young Eng-
      lish explorer's conflict with the Zulus.

2452 _____ . Finished. Longmans, Green, 1917. y.
      A tale of the 1879 Zulu War.

2453 _____ . Nada the Lily. Longmans, Green, 1892. y.
      Conflict in Zululand.

2454 Haines, D. H. Fighting Blood. Houghton Mifflin, 1927. y.
      Kitchener's campaign in the Sudan in the late 1880's.

2455 Harcourt, A. F. P. Jenetha's 'Venture. Cassell, 1899. y.
      Pictures the siege of Delhi during the Sepoy Revolt.

2456 _____ . The Peril of the Sword. Sheffington, 1903. y.
      The siege and relief of Lucknow during the Sepoy Revolt.

2457 Haynes, Herbert. Cleverly Sahib. Nelson, 1897. y.
      The First Afghan War of 1838-1842, ending with the mas-
      sacre of British troops at Khoord-Kabul Pass.

2458 _____ . A Fighter in Green. Nelson, 1906. y.
      An Englishman fights with the French against the Kabyles
      in 1857 Algeria.

2459 Henty, George A. At the Point of the Bayonet. Scribner's,
         1902. y.
      The Mahrattas under Holkar and Scindia battle the English
      in the 1803 battles of Assaye and Laswari.

2460 _____ . By Sheer Pluck. Scribner's, 1884. y.
      Shows the Ashanti War in Africa, up to the capture of
      Coomassie in 1874.

2461 _____ . For Name and Fame. Blackie, 1899. y.
      Afghanistan, 1878-1880, including scenes at the Khyber
      Pass, the advance to Kabul, and General Robert's march
      to Kandahar.

2462 _____ . Maori and Settler. Scribner's, 1897. y.
      Pictures the Maori War in New Zealand during the 1860's,
      including the massacre at Poverty Bay.

2463 _____ . On the Irrawaddy. Scribner's, 1897. y.

Sir Archibald Campbell and the Burmese War of 1822 to 1826.

2464 _____ . Through the Sikh War. Scribner's, 1894. y.
British troops conquer the Punjab area of India in 1845-1849.

2465 _____ . To Herat and Cabul. Scribner's, 1902. y.
A tale of the Afghan War of 1878.

2466 _____ . With Buller in Natal. Scribner's, 1900. y.
English conquest in northern India.

Hofland, Mrs., pseud. See Hoole, Barbara.

2467 Hoole, Barbara. The Young Cadet; or, Henry Delamere's
Voyage to India. By Mrs. Hofland, pseud. O. A.
Roorback, 1828. y.
A nearly contemporary tale of one young Englishman's
participation in the 1824-1826 Burmese War.

2468 Horback, Michael. The Lioness. Trans. from the German.
Lippincott, 1978. y.
A tale of the 1879 Zulu War in Africa.

2469 Horsley, Reginald. In the Grip of the Hawk. T. C. & E. C.
Jack, 1907. y.
Maoris versus settlers in New Zealand during the 1860's.

2470 Howarth, Anna. Sword and Assegai. Smith & Elder, 1899.
y.
The Kaffir rising of 1846-1847 in South Africa.

Iron, Ralph, pseud. See Schreiner, Olive.

2471 Irwin, H. C. With Sword and Pen. Fisher, Unwin, 1904.
y.
Combat in India during the Sepoy Revolt.

2472 Kaye, Mary M. The Far Pavilions. St. Martin's, 1978.
Closes with a look at the massacre of the British military
mission in Kabul during the Second Afghan War.

2473 _____ . Shadow of the Moon. Messner, 1957. y.
Combat in India during the Sepoy Revolt.

2474 Kipling, Rudyard. Soldier Stories. Doubleday, 1899. Rpr.
1970. y.
Contents. --With the Main Guard. --Drums of the Fore and
Aft. --The Man Who Was. --Courting of Dinah Shadd. --In-
carnation of Krishna Mulvaney. --The Taking of Lungtung-
pen. --The Madness of Private Ortheris.

Knight, Brigid, pseud. See Sinclair, Kathleen H.

2475 Krepps, Robert W. Courts of the Lion. McGraw-Hill, 1950.
         y.
      The 1821-1840 wars of the Zulu under King Tchaka.

2476 _____ . Earthshaker. Macmillan, 1959. y.
      Tells of the late nineteenth-century revolt of King Loben-
      gula's Matabele against the South African Boers.

2477 Leasor, James. Follow the Drum. Morrow, 1973. Rpr.
         1975. y.
      Young British officers Hodson and Nicholson displace their
      superiors and attempt to save India for the Crown during
      the Sepoy Revolt.

2478 _____ . Mandarin Gold. Morrow, 1974. Rpr. 1975. y.
      A British surgeon witnesses the Opium War in China.

2479 Macmillan, Michael. The Last of the Peshwas. Blackie,
         1906. y.
      Follows military operations in the Third Mahratta War in
      India, 1817-1818.

2480 MacMunn, George F. A Freelance in Kashmir. Dutton,
         1914. y.
      A British soldier's adventures in 1804 India.

2481 MacNeil, Duncan. By Command of the Viceroy. St. Mar-
         tin's, 1976. Rpr. 1977. y.
      Captain James Ogilvie must escort the Grand Dutchess of
      Russia and a Cossack regiment to Nepal ostensibly to ob-
      tain trade agreements.

2482 _____ . Charge of Cowardice. St. Martin's, 1978. y.
      With the British Raj in desperate straits, Captain Ogil-
      vie's regiment is dispatched to battle the rebels, but our
      hero must first contend with the egotism of his command-
      ing officer.

2483 _____ . Drums Along the Khyber. St. Martin's, 1973. y.
      Lieutenant Ogilvie is assigned to the crack 114th High-
      landers in India and is taken when the rebel Ahmed Khan
      seizes the fort at Jalalabad.

2484 _____ . The Gates of Kunarja. St. Martin's, 1974. y.
      Captain Ogilvie crosses a wintry Khyber Pass to deliver
      ransom terms for his regimental commander, who is be-
      ing held hostage by rebels.

2485 _____ . Lieutenant of the Line. St. Martin's, 1973. y.
      The young lieutenant of the 114th Highlanders goes against

orders and saves the day, by using artillery to break up
a rebel Pathan attack on a besieged fortress.

2486 _____. The Red Daniel. St. Martin's, 1974. Rpr. 1977.
          y.
The activities of Captain James Ogilvie of the Queen's Own
Royal Strathspeys in the Boer War.

2487 _____. Sadhu on the Mountain Peak. St. Martin's, 1974.
          y.
Captain Ogilvie attempts to prevent a holy man from rous-
ing rebel forces against the British in India.

2488 _____. The Subaltern's Choice. St. Martin's, 1974. Rpr.
       1977. y.
The problems of Captain Ogilvie with the British Raj.

2489 _____. Wolf in the Field. St. Martin's, 1977. y.
On London leave, Captain Ogilvie discovers a conspiracy,
which sends him back to India to halt a native mutiny before it can begin.

2490 Mason, Alfred E. W. Four Feathers. Macmillan, 1902. y.
In the Sudan a hero shows himself a coward through his
morbid fear of cowardice.

2491 Masters, John. Nightrunners of Bengal. Viking, 1951. y.
An epic tale of the Indian mutiny of 1857.

2492 Maugham, Robin. The Last Encounter. McGraw-Hill, 1973.
          y.
A fictional last diary of General Gordon of Khartoum,
1884-1886.

2493 Mitford, Bertram. The Gun Runner. Fenno, 1893. y.

2494 _____. The King's Assegai. Fenno, 1894. y.

2495 _____. The Luck of General Ridgeley. Chatto & Windus,
       1893. y.

2496 _____. A Romance of the Cape Frontier. Heinemann,
       1891. y.

2497 _____. The Sign of the Spider. Dodd, Mead, 1896. y.

2498 _____. 'Tween Snow and Fire. Cassell, 1892. y.

2499 _____. The Word of the Sorceress. Hutchinson, 1902.
          y.
Seven tales of the Kaffir uprising in South Africa during
the 1870's.

2500 Montupet, Jeanne. The Red Fountain. Trans. from the
         French. St. Martin's, 1961. y.
      Fighting between the French and Arabs in Algeria in 1837.

2501 Moore, William. Bayonets in the Sun. St. Martin's, 1978.
         y.
      An English lieutenant and private fight in the Sikh uprising
      of 1848, which results in the subjugation of the Punjab
      Plain to British India.

2502 Mundy, Talbot. Cock O' the North. Bobbs-Merrill, 1930.
         y.
      A Scotsman is drawn into romance and conflict on the Af-
      ghan border.

2503 _____. Rung Ho! Scribner's, 1914. y.
      A British officer is introduced to the political and military
      difficulties of upholding the empire in India.

2504 Mutswairo, Solomon M. Mapondera: Soldier of Zimbabive.
         Three Continents, 1978. y.
      Depicts the British takeover of what became Rhodesia
      from the viewpoint of the native defenders.

2505 Nicholson, Christopher. The Savage Sands. Fawcett, 1978.
         P.
      Love and warfare during the French expedition to Algeria
      in 1837.

2506 O'Connor, Richard. Officers and Ladies. Doubleday, 1959.
         y.
      U.S. Army officer Douglas Warriner participates in the
      Philippine Insurrection of 1898 to 1901.

2507 Ollivant, Alfred. Old Forever. Doubleday, Page, 1923. y.
      Combat during the Afghan War of the 1840's.

      Ouida, pseud. See De la Ramée, Louise.

      Paradise, Mary, pseud. See Eden, Dorothy.

2508 Parker, Gilbert. The Judgment House. Harper, 1923. y.
      First published in 1913, this tale tells about a Rhodes-ish
      character and the Boer War, with emphasis on the Jameson
      Raid.

2509 Pearce, Charles E. Love Besieged. Kegan, Paul, 1909. y.
      The siege of Lucknow during the Sepoy Revolt.

2510 _____. Red Revenge. Kegan, Paul, 1911. y.
      The siege and capture of Cawnpore in 1857.

2511 _____. A Star of the East. Kegan, Paul, 1912. y.
      Miscellaneous military actions of the Sepoy Revolt.

2512 Pollard, Eliza F. The White Dove of Amritzer. Partridge,
          1897. y.
          General John Nicholson in the 1857 siege of Delhi.

2513 _____. With Gordon at Khartoum. Blackie, 1906. y.
          How Chinese Gordon fought a losing defense.

2514 Ralli, Constantine S. The Strange Story of Falconer Thring.
          Hurst & Blackett, 1907. y.
          A tale of the Zulu War of 1879.

2515 Rooke, Daphne. Wizard's Country. Houghton Mifflin, 1957.
          y.
          A tale of the Zulu War of 1879-1880.

2516 Scholefield, Alan. The Hammer of God. Morrow, 1973. y.
          A British force must rescue diplomats and civilians incar-
          cerated by the mad King Theodore II of Abyssinia.

2517 Schreiner, Olive. Peter Halkett of Mashonaland. By Ralph
          Iron, pseud. Roberts, 1897. y.
          A tale of the Boers and their war with natives and the
          British.

2518 Shipway, George. Free Lance. Harcourt, 1975. y.
          Adventures of a British cavalry officer in early nineteenth-
          century India.

2519 Sinclair, Kathleen H. Westward the Sun. By Brigid Knight,
          pseud. Cassell, 1942. y.
          Details the 1895 Jameson Raid in South Africa.

2520 Skelton, C. L. The Maclarens: The First Volume in the
          Regiment Quartet. Dial, 1978. y.
          First of a projected series; concerns the nineteenth-cen-
          tury battles in China and India of the Scottish 148th Regi-
          ment of Foot.

2521 Sladen, Douglas. The Curse of the Nile. Kegan, Paul, 1913.
          y.
          The military problems of Gordon at Khartoum in the mid-
          1880's.

2522 Smith, Archibald W. The Sword and the Rose. Davies,
          1938. y.
          Shows events during a two-year stint of a British regiment
          on the Indian frontier.

2523 Smith, Wilbur A. When the Lion Feeds. Viking, 1964. y.
          Combat during the Zulu War of 1879-1880.

2524 Steel, Flora A. On the Face of the Waters. Macmillan,
          1896. y.

The rebel siege and capture of Delhi during the Sepoy Revolt.

2525 Strang, Herbert. Barclay of the Guards. Hodder & Stoughton,
         1908. y.
      A young British soldier's involvement in the siege of Delhi.

2526 Sutherland, Joan. The Edge of Empire. Mills & Boon, 1916.
         y.
      The 1895 British military expedition to Chitral.

2527 Taylor, Philip Meadows. Seeta. Kegan, Paul, 1873.
      Love and combat during the Sepoy Revolt.

2528 Tomkyns-Chesney, George. The Dilema. Abbatt, 1908. y.
      First published in 1876, this tale tells of combat during
      the Sepoy Revolt.

2529 Tracy, Louis. The Red Year. Clode, 1908. y.
      Rebel successes in India in 1857 at the outbreak of the
      Sepoy Revolt.

2530 Tuttiett, Mary G. In the Heart of the Storm. By Maxwell
         Gray, pseud. Appleton, 1891. y.
      Combat in India during the Sepoy Revolt.

2531 Watson, H. B. Marriott. Web of the Spider. Hutchinson,
         1891. y.
      Settlers battle Maoris in New Zealand during the 1860's.

2532 Wentworth, Patricia. The Devil's Wind. Putnam, 1912. y.
      Rebel successes at the beginning of the Sepoy Revolt.

2533 Yerby, Frank. The Dahomean. Dial, 1971. Rpr. 1976. y.
      Follows the exploits of Chief Nyassanu of Dahomey, an
      African native, during the early part of the nineteenth
      century.

2534 Young, Francis B. They Seek a Country. Heinemann, 1937.
         y.
      John Oakley, a condemned criminal, makes the Great Trek
      with the Boers and battles the Zulus.

PART II

THE TWENTIETH CENTURY

THE LAST YEARS OF INNOCENCE, 1900 TO 1914

The first fourteen years of the new century were marked by a mis-
cellany of military operations around the world. Revolutions took
place in the Americas, rebels continued to be active in India, the
Boxer Rebellion took place in China, and combat continued in Africa.
The stories in this section recall these little fights, some as mere
prelude to the opening of the Great War.

2535 Armandy, André. Renegade. Trans. from the French.
        Brentano's, 1930. y.
        A private deserts the French Foreign Legion to become
        an outlaw king over an African tribe.

2536 Azuela, Mariano. The Under Dogs. Trans. from the Spanish.
        Coward-McCann, 1929. y.
        Low-caste guerrilla bands carry on the Mexican Revolution
        begun in 1910.

2537 Baring, Maurice. Tinker's Leave. Doubleday, 1928. y.
        Fighting in Manchuria during the Russo-Japanese War.

2538 Beck, Lily. Treasure Ho! Dodd, Mead, 1924. y.
        A tale of the Boxer Rebellion.

      Bourne, Peter, pseud. See Jeffries, Graham M.

2539 Bozer, Johan. The King's Men. Trans. from the Norwegian.
        Appleton-Century, 1940. y.
        Army life in Norway to 1905, when troubles with Sweden
        ended.

2540 Bruckner, Karl. Vive Mexico! Trans. from the German.
        Roy, 1960. y.
        Francisco Madero is involved in the Mexican Revolution
        of 1911-1913.

2541 Buck, Pearl S. God's Men. Day, 1951. y.
        A tale of the Boxer Rebellion.

2542 _____. The Imperial Woman. Stein & Day, 1956. y.
        The role of the Dowager Empress Tzu-hsi in the 1900
        Boxer Rebellion.

2543 Burke, John. Those Magnificent Men in Their Flying Ma-
       chines. Pocket Books, 1965. y. P.
       Early civilian and military aviators compete in an air
       meet; adapted from the movie script.

       Caillou, Alan, pseud. See Lyle-Smythe, Alan.

2544 Castle, Frank. Guns to Sonora. Berkley, 1962. y. P.
       An ex-Army major becomes a gunrunner for Mexican revo-
       lutionaries, 1910-1913.

2545 Christowe, Stoyan. Mara. Crowell, 1937. y.
       Depicts the Macedonian uprising against the Turks, 1912-
       1913.

2546 Comfort, Will L. Routledge Rides Alone. Lippincott, 1910.
       y.
       A war correspondent becomes involved in the 1905 Russo-
       Japanese War.

2547 Coolidge, Dave. Yaqui Drums. Dutton, 1940. y.
       An American mercenary leads the Mexican Yaqui in a re-
       volt against Dictator Huerta.

2548 Davis, Richard H. Captain Macklin: His Memoirs. Scrib-
       ner's, 1902. y.
       A dismissed West Point cadet wins glory in a revolution
       in Honduras.

2549 _____. White Mice. Scribner's, 1909. y.
       A Yank is involved in a revolution in Venezuela.

2550 Eden, Dorothy. The Time of the Dragon. Coward-McCann,
       1975. y.
       A British merchant family is caught in Peking during the
       Boxer Rebellion.

       Edwards, Samuel, pseud. See Gerson, Noel B.

2551 Esler, Anthony. Forbidden City. Morrow, 1977. y.
       A girl and her father witness the Boxer Rebellion in Pe-
       king.

2552 Fagyas, M. The Devil's Lieutenant. Putnam, 1970. y.
       In 1909 a young Austrian officer attempts to poison the
       General Staff.

2553 Faust, Irvin. Foreign Devils. Arbor House, 1973. y.
       An American reporter covers the 1900 Boxer Rebellion in
       China.

2554 Gerson, Noel B. 55 Days at Peking. By Samuel Edwards,
       pseud. Bantam, 1963. y. P.

A U. S. Marine officer leads the defense of the legations
in Peking during the Boxer Rebellion; adapted from the
movie script.

2555 Jeffries, Graham M. Twilight of the Dragon. By Peter
          Bourne, pseud. Putnam, 1954. y.
      The military defense of the legations at Peking during the
      Boxer Rebellion.

2556 Le Poer, John. A Modern Legionary. Methuen, 1904. y.
      A French Foreign Legion soldier's combats in Algiers
      early in the twentieth century.

2557 Le Queux, William. The Invasion of 1910, With a Full Ac-
          count of the Siege of London. Nash, 1906. y.
      A tale about a fictional invasion of Britain by "unfriendly"
      forces.

2558 Li, Chin-Yang. Madame Goldenflower. Farrar, Straus,
          1961. y.
      The former lover of a German officer later persuades
      him to forego the complete destruction of Peking when he
      arrives in charge of the international force sent to put
      down the Boxer Rebellion.

2559 Lyle-Smythe, Alan. The Walls of Jolo. By Alan Caillou,
          pseud. Appleton, 1961. y.
      During the Philippine insurrection of 1901, U. S. Army
      officer Shay Sullivan is captured and ordered to teach the
      guerrillas American tactics.

2560 Miln, Louise. It Happened in Peking. Stokes, 1926. y.
      A tale of the Boxer Rebellion.

2561 Morgan, Michaela. Madelaina. Pinnacle, 1977. P.
      A girl is caught up in the 1910 Mexican Revolution.

2562 Mundy, Talbot. King of the Khyber Rifles. Burt, 1916. y.
      English Lancers versus Indian rebels on the frontier at
      the outbreak of World War I.

2563 Patten, Lewis. Villa's Guns. Doubleday, 1977. y.
      Seeking weapons, Pancho Villa's cutthroats raid an Ameri-
      can town.

2564 Tickell, Jerrard. Hussar Honeymoon. Doubleday, 1963. y.
      Two officers seek the hand of the colonel's daughter and
      a military position in 1903 Budapest.

2565 Traven, B. General from the Jungle. Trans. from the
          German. Hill & Wang, 1973. y.
      First published in 1940, this tale provides a masterful
      look at good guerrilla generalship projected into the Mexi-
      can revolution against Dictator Porfirio Diaz.

2566 Trevino, Elizabeth. The Fourth Gift. Doubleday, 1966. y.
        Guerrillas fight in Mexico to bring about the downfall of
        Diaz.

2567 Villareal, José A. The Fifth Horseman. Doubleday, 1974.
           y.
        A young American cowboy joins Pancho Villa in the Mexi-
        can Revolution of 1910.

2568 Wells, H. G. The War in the Air. Collins, 1921.
        A fictional prophecy; first appeared serially in Pall Mall
        Magazine during 1908.

2568a Wren, Percival C. Good Gestes. Stokes, 1920. y.
        Stories about Beau Geste, his brothers, and comrades, in
        the French Foreign Legion in North Africa.

WORLD WAR I, 1914 TO 1918

The tales in this section cover military action on the various world
fronts (mostly Europe) during the war that was supposed to make the
world "safe for Democracy." For the first time this conflict saw
much use of the new weapon known as the "aeroplane," and many
stories were and have been written around the glories of Red Baron-
type aerial combat. On the whole, however, this war must be
ranked as perhaps the most unglamourous of any, save Vietnam,
covered in this bibliography. Readers of the combat yarns herein
will soon sense the frustration--if not the pain--of those condemned
to fight that dirty trench conflict.

2569   Acland, Peregrine. All Else Is Folly. Coward-McCann,
          1929. y.
          A Canadian officer is desperately wounded in the French
          trenches.

2570   Aldington, Richard. Death of a Hero. Chatto & Windus,
          1929. Rpr. 1972. y.
          Crazed by the sight of death and destruction, an English
          captain springs into the path of German machine-gun fire
          and is killed; this tale treats, by flashback, his background
          and friends.

2571   _____. Roads to Glory. Doubleday, 1931. y.
          Thirteen stories of combat in France based on the author's
          personal experiences or reflections.

2572   Aldrich, Mildred A. A Hilltop on the Marne. Houghton Mif-
          flin, 1915. y.
          The victory of French soldiers in the 1914 First Battle of
          the Marne.

2573   Allain, Marcel. Yellow Document; or, "Fantomas of Berlin."
          Brentano's, 1920. y.
          A French colonel must protect a secret from agents of the
          German Army.

2574   Allen, Hervey. It Was Like This: Two Stories of the Great
          War. Farrar, Straus, 1940. y.
          "Report to Major Roberts" tells of a young Yank lieutenant

who comes to enjoy killing and whose only hold on reality
during combat is his title; "Blood Lust" sees the transfor-
mation of a simple youth into a professional soldier via a
heavy-handed introduction to the horrors of combat.

2575   Altsheler, Joseph A.   The Forest of Swords.   Appleton, 1915.
       y.
       A fictional recreation of the 1914 First Battle of the Marne.

2576   _____.   The Guns of Europe.   Appleton, 1915.   y.
       Pictures of combat in various areas along the Western
       Front.

2577   _____.   The Hosts of the Air.   Appleton, 1915.   y.
       Depicts early Great War aerial operations from an Allied
       viewpoint.

2578   Alverdes, Paul.   Whistler's Room.   Trans. from the German.
       Covici, 1930.   y.
       Four soldiers, three German and one English, recover
       from throat wounds in a German hospital and become
       friends.

2579   Ames, Franklin T.   Between the Lines on the American Front:
       a Boy's Story of the Great European War.   Dodd, Mead,
       1919.   y.
       Follows Tom Maillard and his cousins, the Dorrs, through
       military training and into the great battles at Chateau
       Thierry and St. Mihiel.

2580   Anderson, Robert G.   Cross of Fire.   Houghton Mifflin, 1919.
       y.
       A wounded veteran of Army service is drawn into recruit-
       ing service and romance in New York City.

2581   Andreiff, Leonid N.   Confessions of a Little Man During Great
       Days.   Trans. from the Russian.   Knopf, 1917.   y.
       A Russian clerk avoids military service until his conscience
       forces him to become an ambulance driver on the Eastern
       Front; presented in diary form.

2582   Andrews, Mary S.   His Soul Goes Marching On.   Scribner's,
       1922.   y.
       A young 42nd Rainbow Division soldier in France is in-
       spired by the spirit of Teddy Roosevelt.

2583   Angarsky, Andrew.   Eighty-Seven Days.   Knopf, 1964.   y.
       The April-July 1918 anti-Bolshevik uprising in Russia,
       which ended with the White defeat at Yaroslavi on the
       Volga.

2584   Arnall, Philip.   Portrait of an Airman.   Lane, 1932.   y.
       The exploits of Royal Flying Corps pilot Stephen Sloan.

2585 Aspen, Don. Mike of Company D. Scribner's, 1939. y.
      Tale of an American dog and his owner on the Western
      Front.

2586 Atkinson, Eleanor. "Poilu, " A Dog of Roublaix. Harper,
          1919. y.
      How Madame Daulac's dog was drafted to pull a machine
      gun for the French.

2587 Austin, Frederick B. According to Orders. Doran, 1919.
          y.
      Ten short stories showing German soldiers acting poorly,
      "zu befehl. "

2588 Ayres, Ruby M. Richard Chatterton, V. C. Watt, 1920. y.
      A young English noble enlists as a "Tommy" to fight in
      France and becomes a hero while fighting as a common
      man.

2589 Bahnold, Enid. Happy Foreigner. Century, 1921. y.
      The life and loves of Fanny, an English driver for the
      French near the end of the war.

2590 Ballinger, W. A. The Men That God Made Mad. Putnam,
          1969. y.
      Declan O'Donovan and the 1916 Irish Easter Rebellion.

2591 Balmer, Edwin. Ruth of the U. S. A. McClurg, 1919. y.
      Ruth Alden helps U. S. flyer Gerry Hull in France.

2592 Barbusse, Henri. Light. Trans. from the French. Dutton,
          1920. y.
      French soldier Simon Paulin, wounded in trench warfare,
      returns home wondering about the madness of war.

2593 _____ . Under Fire: The Story of a Squad. Trans. from
          the French. Dutton, 1917. Rpr. 1955. y.
      Pictures the dull misery of trench warfare on the Western
      Front.

2594 Barretto, Larry. Horses in the Sky. Day, 1930. y.
      The reactions of four American ambulance drivers to com-
      bat in the Great War.

2595 Bazin, Rene. F. N. M. Pierre and Joseph. Trans. from
          the French. Harper, 1920. y.
      Two Alsatian brothers join opposing sides.

2596 Bellah, James W. The Gods of Yesterday. Appleton, 1928.
          y.
      Stories of the U. S. Air Service in France first serialized
      in the Saturday Evening Post.

2597   Bennet, Robert A.   The Blond Beast.   Reilly, 1918.   y.
       Allan Thorpe and his girl friend enter the Red Cross am-
       bulance service on the Western Front in 1916.

2598   Benstead, Charles K.   Retreat.   Methuen, 1930.   y.
       An English chaplain breaks down during the Allied retreat
       occasioned by the Ludendorf offensive in the spring of
       1918.

2599   Berger, Marcel.   Ordeal by Fire.   Trans. from the French.
       Putnam, 1917.   y.
       In 1914 a French sergeant is transformed from a half-
       hearted soldier into a dedicated patriot.

2600   _____, and Maude Berger.   Secret of the Marne: How
       Sergeant Fritsch Saved France.   Trans. from the
       French.   Putnam, 1918.   y.
       How a French noncom supposedly tricked the German Ar-
       my in September 1914, thereby saving Paris from capture.

2601   Bertrand, Adrian.   Call of the Soil.   Lane, 1919.   y.
       Three French soldiers on the march and in battle during
       the early months of the war; all are killed in battle--as
       was the author in 1916.

2602   The Best Short Stories of the War: An Anthology.   Intro.
       by Henry M. Tomlinson.   Harper, 1931.   y.
       Contents. --Defeat, by J. Galsworthy. --Raid Night, by H.
       M. Tomlinson. --Them Others, by S. Aumonjer. --Coming
       Home, by E. Wharton. --Indomitable Tweedy, by A. P.
       Herbert. --Marie-Luise, by K. Wilke. --Lafreysse's Battle,
       by A. Arnoux. --Aube, by G. Van der Vring. --When Our
       Flag Come to Paris, by A. D. Turnbull. --Retreat, by W.
       Beumelburg. --Introduction to the Trenches, by R. Alding-
       ton. --Trench Fett, by A. Maurois. --Last Kindness, by
       F. Harris. --Man in the Next Bed, by P. Alverdes. --
       Touch of Irony, by A. Maurois. --Souvenirs, by W. F.
       Morris. --Misapplied Energy, by W. T. Scanlon. --"The
       Kaiser Has Abdicated," by J. and J. Tharaud. --Friends,
       by C. Dawson. --Red Light of Morning, by J. M. Wehner.
       --Sacrifice, by J. Bernier. --"Good Morning Major," by
       J. P. Marquand. --In the Interests of Discipline, by A.
       Arnoux. --End of the Epoch, by F. B. Austin. --Sixth
       Drunk, by "Sapper" (Herman C. McNeile). --On Patrol,
       by M. Armstrong. --Wingult, by R. J. Binding. --Last
       Squad, by J. B. Wharton. --Over the Top, by L. Tugel. --
       Among the Trumpets, by L. Nason. --No Quarter, by W.
       Townend. --Square Egg, by "Saki."--Cabaret De La Belle
       Femme, by R. Dorgeles. --Sequel to a Battle, by C. Mac-
       Arthur. --Traitor, by S. Maugham. --Devil's Own, by R.
       H. Mottram. --Two Masters, by A. Wheen. --Reconnais-
       sance in the Desert, by K. Federn. --Cain's Atonement,
       by A. Blackwood. --Alien Skull, by L. O'Flaherty. --Death

of a Cat, by A. Eggebrecht. --Miracle, by W. Duranty. --
Phantom Major, by L. Barretto. --Carnival, 1915, by G.
Britling. --War Dog, by J. W. Thomason. --On Leave, by
H. Barbusse. --Strange Home, by E. M. Remarque. --Fed
Up, by E. W. Springs. --Fear, by J. W. Bellah. --Flying
School, 1914, by R. Euringer. --Tale, by J. Conrad. --
Story of Jonathan Rust, by "Taffrail" (H. Dorling). --Port
Lookout, by "Bartimeus."--SOS Off Libau, by G. Von Gott-
berg, Honours Easy, by C. E. Montague. --Discipline, by
G. Duhamel. --Dead Alive, by H. Barbusse. --Champien,
by F. Von Unruh. --In Another Country, by E. Hemingway.
--Rechoussat's Christmas, by G. Duhamel. --"Esprit de
Corps, " by L. Stallings. --Armistice, by H. M. Tomlin-
son. --"The Watch on the Rhine, " by A. White. --Prentice,
by G. Bullett. --Blind Lieutenant, by G. Grabenhorst. --
One Hundred Per Cent, by L. V. Jacks.

2603 Bishop, Giles. Captain Comstock, U. S. M. C. Penn, 1923.
        y.
      Sequel to the next title; the hero serves with the 4th Ma-
      rines from Belleau Wood to the Meuse-Argonne.

2604 _____. Lieutenant Comstock, U. S. Marine. Penn, 1922.
        y.
      A young officer participates in early U. S. M. C. combat in
      France.

2605 _____. The Marines Have Landed. Penn, 1921. y.
      Adventures of enlisted Marine "Bill" and his companions
      during the Vera Cruz expedition of 1914.

2606 Blake, George. Path of Glory. Harper, 1929. y.
      First published in England the previous year; a colonel
      and his friend from a Highland regiment fight and die at
      Gallipoli in 1915.

2607 Blaker, Richard. Medal Without Bar. Hodder & Stoughton,
        1930. y.
      Experiences of a British subaltern of artillery on the
      Western Front.

2608 Blankfort, Michael. Behold the Fire. New American Library,
        1965. y. P.
      Jewish residents in Palestine cooperate with the British
      and attempt to overthrow Turkish rule in 1916.

2609 _____. I Met a Man. Bobbs-Merrill, 1965. y.
      A tale of friendship between two men in the 1915 German
      Army.

2610 Blasco-Ibáñez, Vincente. The Four Horsemen of the Apoca-
        lypse. Trans. from the Spanish. Dutton, 1918. y.
      Returning to France from Argentina, a young man who was

unsuccessful in love enters the Army and is killed; an important war story due to its vivid battle descriptions.

2611   Bonner, Charles. Legacy. Knopf, 1940. y.
       Five motherless boys see service in the trenches of the
       Western Front.

2612   Bourjaily, Vance. The End of My Life. Scribner's, 1947.
       y.
       A cynical American drives an ambulance for the British
       in Italy and the Levant.

2613   Boyd, Martin. Outbreak of Love. Reynal, 1957. y.
       A tale about Australian soldiers.

2614   Boyd, Thomas A. Points of Honor. Scribner's, 1925. y.
       Eleven stories about American soldiers in France, each
       showing how the ideal of honor guided the individual's ac-
       tions.

2615   _____. Through the Wheat. Scribner's, 1927. Rpr. 1978.
       y.
       Private Hicks, U.S.M.C., adjusts to the dangers of com-
       bat.

2616   Brereton, Frederic S. On the Road to Bagdad. Blackie,
       1917. y.
       A young British subaltern finds adventure with the Expe-
       ditionary Force in Mesopotamia.

2617   Brooks, Alden. Fighting Men. Scribner's, 1917. y.
       A war correspondent's psychological tales of men in com-
       bat. Contents. --The Parisian. --The Belgian. --The Odys-
       sey of Three Slavs. --The Man from America. --The Prus-
       sian. --The Englishman.

2618   Bryant, Will. Escape from Sonora. Random House, 1973.
       Rpr. 1974. y.
       Employing a 1907 Thomas Flyer, ten Americans escape
       from a band of Pancho Villa's raiders on the Mexican
       border in 1916.

2619   Buchan, John. Greenmantle. Doran, 1917. y.
       Major Richard Hannay, British Army, travels to Constan-
       tinople to find out about and halt a "jehad" or holy war
       being organized in the Near East.

2620   Burtis, Thomson. Russ Farrell, Airman. Doubleday, Page,
       1924. y.
       The adventures of a young pilot with the U.S. Air Service
       in France.

2621   Cable, Boyd. Front Lines. Dutton, 1918. y.
       A tale of trench warfare on the Western Front.

2622   _____ .   Grapes of Wrath.   Dutton, 1917.   y.
        Three Englishmen and an American participate in the 1916
        Battle of the Somme.

2623   Cameron, Lou.   Iron Men with Wooden Wings.   Belmont,
           1967.   y.   P.
        A tale of Great War aerial combat.

2624   Campbell, William E. M.   Company K.   By William March,
           pseud.   Peter Smith, 1960.   y.
        First published in 1933, this tale vividly depicts Yank
        soldiers in the trench warfare of the Western Front.

2625   Cather, Willa S.   One of Ours.   Knopf, 1922.   Rpr. 1971.
           y.
        A young American soldier in France finds the youth he
        missed in Nebraska and is "lucky" enough to be killed be-
        fore he becomes disillusioned with an extremely dirty kind
        of combat.

2626   Chambers, Robert W.   Barbarians.   Appleton, 1917.   y.
        Four Americans in English service are followed until their
        deaths in the Battle of the Somme.

2627   Chartres, Annie.   Outrage.   Knopf, 1918.   y.
        Published in Britain as Vae Victis, this is a tale of three
        women caught up in the barbarities of the 1914 German
        invasion of Belgium; the volume is usually cited as a
        prime example of Allied propaganda.

2628   Chase, Borden.   Viva Gringo!   Bantam, 1961.   y.   P.
        An American outlaw joins Pancho Villa's rebels in Mexico.

2629   Clote, Stuart.   How Young They Die.   Trident, 1970.   y.
        Follows a South African soldier through the infantry
        slaughters on the Western Front.

2630   Cobb, Humphrey.   Paths of Glory.   Viking, 1935.   Rpr. 1973.
           y.
        When a French general's plans for an advance go awry,
        members of a unit are executed for cowardice and to
        serve as examples; Kirk Douglas starred in an extremely
        powerful antiwar movie based on this title.

2631   Cocteau, Jean.   The Impoctec.   Trans. from the French.
           Appleton, 1925.   Rpr. 1957.   y.
        First published as Thomas the Imposter, this tale con-
        cerns an underage French youth who joins a nursing unit
        and is subsequently adopted by a regular squad; in the
        end, the boy dies a hero.

2632   Cogswell, A. M.   Ermytage and the Curate.   Longmans,
           Green, 1923.   y.
        A schoolmaster and his curate recover from shellshock

in a French hospital, reflecting on the stupidities of conflict and their military service.

Connor, Ralph, pseud. See Gorden, Charles.

2633 Conscript 2989. Dodd, Mead, 1915. y.
      An anonymous autobiographical tale detailing the difficulties
      of American Army training.

2634 Cookson, Catherine. The Cinder Path. Morrow, 1978.
      Charlie MacFell moves toward his destiny--the trenches
      of the Western Front.

2635 Cosíc, Dobrica. A Time of Death. Trans. from the Yugo-
          slav. Harcourt, 1977.
      General Mišic rallies the Serbian First Army, which is
      facing defeat by the forces of Austria-Hungary in 1914.

2636 Darling, Esther B. Navarre of the North. Sun Dial, 1930.
          y.
      A tale about the Army of the Vosges.

2637 Daugherty, Sonia. The Broken Song. Nelson, 1935. y.
      Russia before and during the Revolution of 1917.

2638 Davignon, Henri. Two Crossings of Madge Swalue. Lane,
          1919. y.
      A Belgian couple retreats to England, but returns to Eu-
      rope, where the husband is killed in combat in Flanders.

2639 Davis, Clyde B. Follow the Leader. Farrar & Rinehart,
          1942. y.
      An ordinary American doughboy becomes a hero on the
      Western Front.

2640 Dawson, Conigsby W. Carry On. Lane, 1917. y.
      Fictional letters from the Western Front.

2641 _____. Test of Scarlet. Lane, 1919. y.
      Follows the activities of an A. E. F. battery at the front.

2642 Dawson, Warrington. The Gift of Paul Clermont. Doubleday,
          1921. y.
      Depicts a young Frenchman's life and emotions on the
      Western Front until he is killed in action.

2643 Deeping, Warwick. Valour. McBride, 1934. y.
      A sensitive British officer is caught up in the slaughter-
      house Gallipoli campaign of 1915.

2644 Dent, W. Redvers. Show Me Death! Harper, 1930. y.
      A fictional autobiography of a gunner in the Canadian "Sui-
      cide Corps" on the Western Front.

2645 Divine, Charles. Cognac Hill. Payson & Clarke, 1927. y.
       Marjorie Lothrop, a war worker in a French military
       camp, romantically juggles two contrasting American dough-
       boys.

2646 Djilas, Milovan. Montenegro. Trans. from the Yugoslav.
          Harcourt, 1963. y.
       How outnumbered Montenegrins were defeated by the Aus-
       tro-Hungarians in the January 1916 Battle of Mojkovac.

2647 Dodd, Martha E. Sowing the Wind. Harcourt, 1945. y.
       Eric Landt wins fame as a German aviator, but is later
       corrupted by the Nazis; shades of Hermann Göring.

2648 Dos Passos, John R., Jr. First Encounter. Philosophical
          Library, 1945. y.
       The lives and loves of 1917 front-line soldiers as recorded
       by an ambulance driver; first published in Britain in 1920
       as One Man's Initiation--1917.

2649 _____. Three Soldiers. Doran, 1921. Rpr. 1964. y.
       An American war classic that traces the experiences of
       three doughboys through the Great War, showing how all
       are broken by the pressures of conflict and the "system";
       a bitter attack on what the author conceived as the misery,
       tyranny, and degredation found in Pershing's American
       Expeditionary Force.

2650 Driggs, Laurence L. T. The Adventures of Arnold Adair,
          American Ace. Little, Brown, 1918. y.
       A tale about an American volunteer pilot with the French
       during the period before the U.S. entry into the war; our
       hero becomes an "ace" (five victories), sinks a German
       U-boat, and escapes a German P.O.W. camp after sur-
       viving his own crash landing.

2651 _____. On Secret Air Service. Little, Brown, 1930. y.
       Major Adair tells of the exploits of a group of young avi-
       ators who pledged themselves to the doing of "special air
       service" for the Allies. Readers should note that quite a
       few tales of aerial combat were published in the various
       pulp aviation magazines of the 1920's and 1930's, some of
       which is being republished in the periodical Air Trails.

       DuBois, Gaylord, jt. author. See Lebeck, Oskar.

2652 Dunbar, Ruth. Swallow. Boni & Liveright, 1919. y.
       A young Texan's actions and romances as a volunteer pilot
       with the French air service before the entry of America
       into the conflict.

2653 Dunsany, Lord (Edward J. M. D. Plunkett). Tales of War.
          Boni & Liveright, 1918. y.

Exploits of the fictitious British Inniskilling Battalion on
the Western Front.

2654 Dunton, James G., ed. C'est La Guerre: The Best Stories
     of the World War. Stratford, 1928. y.
     A compilation of 16 stories drawn from various periodicals.

2655 Duranty, Walter. One Life, One Kopeck. Simon & Schuster,
     1937. y.
     A young Bolshevist fights for the Reds during the Russian
     Civil War.

2656 Dwinger, Edwin R. Between Red and White. Trans. from
     the German. Scribner's, 1932. y.
     Fictionalized reminiscences of a German officer caught up
     in the Russian Civil War of 1918-1921.

2657 Dyer, Walter A. Ben, the Battle Horse. Holt, 1919. y.
     Paul Brigham and his steed serve with the U.S. Marines
     in France.

2658 Elliot, Robert. The Eagle's Height. Aero, 1962. y. P.
     American fighter pilots battle the Germans.

2659 Empey, Arthur G. A Helluva War. Appleton, 1927. y.
     The trials and scrapes of happy Irish-American doughboy,
     Private Terrence X. O'Leary in France.

2660 _____. Tales from a Dugout. Century, 1918. Rpr.
     1978. y.
     Combat experiences of seven British machine-gunners on
     the Western Front.

2661 Erskine, Laurie Y. Comrades of the Clouds. Appleton,
     1930. y.
     Incidents of daily danger for a U.S. fighter squadron over
     France.

2662 _____. Fine Fellows. Appleton, 1929. y.
     Eleven stories of brave combat deeds on land and in the
     air.

2663 Faulkner, William. Soldier's Pay. Liveright, 1926. Rpr.
     1970. y.
     Donald Mahon is wounded in the American Air Service and
     returns to his home in Georgia.

2664 Fenner, Phyllis K., comp. Over There!: Stories of World
     War I. Morrow, 1961. y.
     Ten stories of combat, drawn from various sources.

2665 Fenton, Ronald O. Tank Commander. By Ronald Welch,
     pseud. Nelson, 1974. y.

A young British officer finds himself leading the newfangled
armored vehicles in the 1917 Battle of Cambrai.

2666 Findley, Timothy. The Wars. Delacorte, 1978. y.
      A young Canadian officer experiences the horrors of trench
      warfare on the Western Front.

2667 FitzGibbon, Constantine. High Heroic. Norton, 1970. y.
      Michael Collins participates in the 1916 Irish Easter Re-
      bellion.

2668 Ford, Ford Maddox. No More Parades. Grosset, 1926. y.
      A tale about a crowded American base camp in 1918
      France.

2669 Fox, Edward L. New Gethsemane. McBride, 1917. y.
      Anhalt, the cobbler of Oberammergau, refuses to answer
      the German call to arms on pacifist grounds--and is shot.

2670 Fredenburgh, Theodore. Soldiers March. Harcourt, 1930.
      y.
      Examines 18 months in the life on an American noncom
      with the A.E.F. in France in 1917-1918.

2671 French, Allen. At Plattsburg. Scribner's, 1917. y.
      Pictures the daily life of a young U.S. Army recruit just
      before the American entry into the war.

2672 Frey, Alexander M. Cross Bearers. Trans. from the Ger-
      man. Viking, 1931. y.
      Follows four years with a German medical unit on the
      Western Front.

2673 Gann, Ernest K. In the Company of Eagles. Simon & Schus-
      ter, 1967. y.
      French pilot Chamay battles German ace Kupper over Ver-
      dun in 1916.

2674 Gavin, Catherine. Give Me the Daggers. Morrow, 1972.
      Rpr. 1977. y.
      A Canadian war hero becomes involved in the Finnish War
      of Independence.

2675 _____. The Snow Mountain. Pantheon, 1974. Rpr. 1977.
      y.
      A tale of the Russian Revolution and the Red-White Civil
      War.

2676 Geraldy, Paul. The War, Madame. . . . Trans. from the
      French. Scribner's, 1917. y.
      Pictures one day in the life of a French soldier who re-
      turns on leave to Paris after 13 months of service on the
      line.

2677 Gibbs, George F. Splendid Outcast. Appleton, 1920. y.
      Two brothers exchange identification during the midst of a
      great battle.

2678 Gorden, Charles. The Major. By Ralph Connor, pseud.
         Doran, 1918. y.
      A deeply religious young Canadian officer discovers the
      necessary evil of killing Germans during the war.

2679 _____. Sky Pilot in No Man's Land. By Ralph Connor,
         pseud. Doran, 1919. y.
      Barry Dunbar's career, from ineffective missionary to in-
      spired battalion chaplain on the Western Front.

2680 Grabenhorst, Georg. Zero Hour. Trans. from the German.
         Little, Brown, 1929. y.
      The fictional autobiography of the author, a German soldier,
      who upon seeing the misery around him adopts a fatalistic
      philosophy.

2681 Guthrie, Ramon. Parachute. Harcourt, 1928. y.
      Lieutenant Richey, wounded while serving with the U. S.
      Air Service over France, is returned to an American hos-
      pital; interesting flying scenes.

2682 Haines, D. H. The Dragon-Flies. Houghton Mifflin, 1919.
         y.
      A tale of aerial combat over the Western Front.

2683 Hall, James Norman. Kitchener's Mob. Atlantic Monthly,
         1916. y.
      An American soldier serves with the British Army in
      Flanders.

      _____, jt. author. See Nordhoff, Charles B.

2684 Hamilton, Robert W. Belinda of the Red Cross. Sully &
         Kleinteich, 1917. y.
      An American nurse and an aviator romance and fight be-
      hind the Western Front.

2685 Harris, Credo F. Where the Souls of Men Are Calling.
         Britton, 1918. y.
      A fearful U. S. recruit becomes a battlefield hero in France,
      1918.

2686 Harris, John. Covenant with Death. Sloane, 1962. y.
      Mark Fenner and his English battalion are sent into slaugh-
      ter during the great July 1, 1916 Battle of the Somme.

2687 Harrison, Charles Y. Generals Die in Bed. Morrow, 1930.
         y.
      Incidents in the lives of Canadian soldiers who made up the
      "shock troops" of the British army on the Western Front.

2688 Hasek, Jaroslav. Good Soldier Schweik. Trans. from the
Yugoslav. Doubleday, Doran, 1930. Rpr. 1974. y.
A Prague dogcatcher is drafted into the Serbian Army and
is sent to the Russian front, where as a rearguard private
he serves meticulously and ridiculously the various fools
who are in command over him.

2689 Hay, David. No Through Road. Norman Adlard (Ipswich),
1966. y.
Subtitle. --"A Story of the Last Assyrian Campaign in
Kurdistan, the Nation Which Defied the Turkish Empire
and Became Britain's Smallest Ally of the 1914-18 War."

2690 Heinz, Max. Loretto: Sketches of a German War Volunteer.
Trans. from the German. Liveright, 1930. y.
A bloody tale of the horrors of trench combat.

2691 Hemingway, Ernest. A Farewell to Arms. Scribner's, 1929.
Rpr. 1967. y.
An American lieutenant wounded in Italy has a love affair
with an English nurse while convalescing.

2692 Herbert, Alan P. Secret Battle. Knopf, 1920. y.
How a British hero of Gallipoli and France was eventually
shot for cowardice.

2693 Hill, Susan. Strange Meeting. Saturday Review, 1972.
A tale about the friendship of two British officers on the
Western Front.

2694 Hodson, James L. Grey Dawn--Red Night. Gollancz, 1930.
y.
The experiences of a young English soldier on the Western
Front, who is killed just before he is due to return home
on leave.

2695 _____. Return to the Wood. Morrow, 1955. y.
A doughboy veteran returns to France many years later to
relive his combat experiences.

2696 Hogan, Ray. Ace of the White Death. Berkley, 1970. y.
P.

2697 _____. The Bad Staffel. Berkley, 1971. y. P.

2698 _____. Bombs from the Murder Wolves. Berkley, 1971.
y. P.

2699 _____. Flight from the Grave. Berkley, 1971. y. P.

2700 _____. The Mast of the Vulture. Berkley, 1971. y. P.

2701 _____. Purple Aces. Berkley, 1961. y. P.
Six tales of aerial combat featuring the exploits of Allied

pilot "G-8" and his super squadron, "The Battle Aces"; these tales were first published by Popular Publications in the mid-1930's.

2702 Holmes, Roy J., and Arward Starbuck, eds. War Stories. Crowell, 1919. y.
Twenty-one tales of Great War combat by various authors.

2703 Howath, Ferdinand H. Captured. Dodd, Mead, 1930. y.
A young Hungarian officer and several of his soldiers are captured by the Russians in 1915 and sent to a P.O.W. camp.

2704 Huard, Frances W. Lilies, White and Red. Doran, 1919. y.
A French orphan's bravery and how he won the Croix de Guerre for his actions under fire.

2705 Hunt, E. E. Tales from a Famished Land. Doubleday, Page, 1918. y.
Stories about the Allied effort at Gallipoli in 1915.

2706 Hunt, Frazier. Blown In by the Draft. Doubleday, 1918. y.
Character sketches of doughboy life in training camps.

2707 Hunter, Jack D. The Blue Max. Dutton, 1964. y.
Follows the megalomaniacal yearnings of German pilot Stackel to win Germany's highest honor, the Pour le Merite.

2708 Hutchinson, Graham S. The W Plan. By Graham Seaton, pseud. Cosmopolitan, 1930. y.
A Scottish colonel is dropped behind German lines in Flanders to obtain the plan for an attack on British positions.

2709 Hutchinson, Roy C. Testament. Farrar & Rinehart, 1938. y.
The friendship and reminiscences of two Russian officers captured by the Austrians early in the war.

2710 Iogolevitch, Paul. The Young Russian Corporal. Harper, 1919. y.
A tale about a Russian soldier in combat on the Eastern Front.

2711 Jack, Donald. The Bandy Papers. 2 vols. Doubleday, 1973. y.
The full saga of Canadian officer Bart Bandy in the trenches of the Western Front and in the Royal Flying Corps.

2712 _____. Three Cheers for Me: The Journals of Bartholomew Bandy, R.F.C. Macmillan, 1962. y.

235   Jenkins

Escaping trench service, Captain Bandy becomes a 30-victory British ace and wins the Croix de Guerre; expanded and continued in the previous volume. Readers should compare this title with Hunter's The Blue Max (above) and Whitehouse's Hero Without Honor (below).

2713   Jenkins, Burris A. It Happened Over There. Revell, 1919.
y.
Lady Mary Shoreham and an American ace pilot on leave are caught up in the German air raids on London in 1917-1918.

2714   Johannsen, Ernst. Four Infantrymen. Trans. from the German. Methuen, 1930. y.
German soldiers fight on on the Western Front in the summer of 1918 knowing that the war is lost.

2715   Johnson, David. Promenade in Champagne. Sloane, 1961.
y.
Examines the 1917 Battle of the Aisne from the viewpoint of the French Angevin Regiment of Infantry.

2716   Johnson, Owen M. Wasted Generation. Little, Brown, 1921.
y.
A young American soldier records the horrors of combat in diary form.

2717   Kauffman, Reginald W. Victorious. Bobbs-Merrill, 1919.
y.
A small-town American reporter is killed on the Western Front after winning the Distinguished Service Cross.

2718   Keable, Robert. Simon Called Peter. Dutton, 1922. y.
Activities of a U.S. Army chaplain on the Western Front.

2719   Kelly, Thomas H. What Outfit, Buddy? Harper, 1920. y.
The adventures of A.E.F. Private Jimmy McGee on the Western Front.

2720   Keneally, Thomas. Gossip from the Forest. Harcourt, 1976.
y.
Marshal Foch and the surrender of the Germans at Compiegne in November 1918.

2721   Kennedy, William A. The Invader's Son. Sully, 1920. y.
The first part of this story concerns the union of a French woman and a German soldier.

2722   Knipe, E.B. and A.A. Vive La France. Century, 1918. y.
General Joffre and the spirit of Joan of Arc.

2723   Koppen, Edlef. Higher Command. Faber & Faber, 1931.
y.

The disintegration of Adolf Reisiger in trench warfare is
followed from August 2, 1914 to September 2, 1918.

2724 Krasnov, Petr N. From Double Eagle to Red Flag. Trans.
from the Russian. Duffield, 1926.
Russia, the 1917 Revolution, and the 1918-1921 Civil War.

2725 Kreutz, Rudolp J. Captain Zillner. Trans. from the German. Doran, 1919. y.
After the first few months of conflict, an Austrian officer
finds the war a waste.

2726 Kueller, Jo V. A. Young Lion of Flanders. Trans. from the
French. Stokes, 1918. y.
Young motorcyclist Leon Casimur distinguishes himself at
Marbehe, winning the praise of Belgain King Albert.

2727 Kyne, Peter B. They Also Serve. Cosmopolitan, 1927. y.
A "Mr. Ed" type story in which a horse tells his owner
of action in France with the A. E. F.; despite the ridicu-
lous gimmick, the tale contains much information.

2728 Lardner, Ring. Treat 'Em Rough. Bobbs-Merrill, 1918. y.
An illiterate Chicago baseball player relates his war experiences.

2729 Latzko, Adolf A. Men in War. Boni & Liveright, 1918. y.
Sketches of Austrian soldiers grown tired of the war.

2730 Lebeck, Oskar, and Gaylord DuBois. Stratosphere Jim and
His Flying Fortress. Whitman, 1941. y.
A pair of young American flyers battle the evil Syndicate
(Germans).

2731 Lebedeff, Ivan. Legion of Dishonor. Liveright, 1940. y.
A group of German and Russian deserters inhabit a castle
in No Man's Land for several weeks.

2732 Lee, Mary. "It's a Great War." Houghton Mifflin, 1929.
y.
Anne Wentworth is bewildered by the misery she sees
while serving as a nurse in France.

2733 Le Queux, William. Behind the German Lines. London Mail,
1917. y.
Fictional "confessions" of Otto von Heynitz of the 16th
German Uhlans; a sequel to the next title.

2734 _____. Hushed Up at German Headquarters. London
Mail, 1917. y.
More "confessions" by von Heynitz.

2735 Lernet-Holenia, Alexander M. Glory Is Departed. Trans.
from the German. Harper, 1937. y.

An Austrian cavalry officer relates his adventures in the
Balkans during the last weeks of the war and the near an-
nihilation of his regiment during a mutiny; published in
Britain as The Standard.

2736 Levin, Meyer. The Settlers. Simon & Schuster, 1972. Rpr.
         1978. y.
         A Jewish refugee family is caught up in the British-Turkish
         war in Palestine.

2737 Lewis, Herbert C. Spring Offensive. Viking, 1940. y.
         Reflections on life by a fictional Hoosier doughboy who is
         caught in No Man's Land during a German push.

2738 Locke, William J. Rough Road. Lane, 1918. y.
         A rich British youth, cashiered as an officer, enlists as
         a "Tommy" to fight on the Western Front.

2739 Lohrke, Eugene. Overshadowed. Cape, 1929. y.
         The disintegration of a sensitive young doughboy serving
         with an American artillery unit in France.

      "The Londoner, " pseud. See Machen, Arthur.

2740 Love of an Unknown Soldier. Lane, 1918. y.
         The war letters of an unknown British Tommy supposedly
         discovered in an abandoned dug-out on the Western Front.

2741 Lowndes, Marie A. Red Cross Barge. Doran, 1918. y.
         A German Army surgeon stays behind to treat French
         wounded during his force's pullback after the First Battle
         of the Marne in 1914.

2742 Lussu, Emilio. Sardinian Brigade. Trans. from the Italian.
         Giniger, 1968. y.
         First published in 1939, this tale follows the Italian Sas-
         sari brigade into combat with the Austrians.

2743 Lutes, Della T. My Boy in Khaki. Harper, 1918. y.
         A mother's emotional story of her son's doughboy experi-
         ences.

2744 MacArthur, Charles G. War Bugs. Doubleday, Doran, 1929.
         y.
         The lusty and rowdy lives of several privates serving in
         the U. S. 42nd Rainbow Division in France.

2745 McClure, Robert E. Some Found Adventure. Doubleday,
         Doran, 1926. y.
         The life, love, and combat of an A. E. F. private in France.

2746 MacGill, Patrick. Dough Boys. Doran, 1918. y.
         After months of training, three A. E. F. comrades finally

get into combat in France and each experiences it differ-
ently.

2747 Machen, Arthur. The Angels of Mons. By "The Londoner,"
pseud. Books for Libraries, 1972. y.
Five tales of early combat first published in 1915.

2748 Mack, Charles E. Two Black Crows in the A. E. F. Bobbs-
Merrill, 1928. y.
The supposed reminiscences of two black doughboys in
France.

2749 McKay, Helen G. Chill Hours. Duffield, 1920. y.
Sketches about wounded men in hospital.

2750 MacNeile, Herman C. Human Torch. By "Sapper," pseud.
Doran, 1919. y.
Eight short stories showing the humor and experiences of
British soldiers on the Western Front.

2751 _____. "Sapper's" War Stories Collected in One Volume.
By "Sapper," pseud. Hodder & Stoughton, 1932. y.
Forty-five of the author's tales drawn from various
sources.

2752 Malone, Paul B. Barbed Wire Entanglements. Stackpole,
1940. y.
Lieutenant Douglas Atwell is an officer fighting with the
A. E. F. in France; written as part of the propaganda
movement designed to keep America out of World War II.

2753 Manning, Frederic. Her Private We. By Private 19022,
pseud. Putnam, 1930. y.
Details Private Bourne's last days as a member of a
British infantry battalion on the Somme front in 1916.

2754 Marbo, Camille. The Man Who Survived. Trans. from the
French. Harper, 1918. y.
Reminiscences of a wounded French soldier in hospital
after the war.

March, William, pseud. See Campbell, William E. M.

2755 Masters, John. The Ravi Lancers. Doubleday, 1972. y.
Pictures an Indian regiment from training to the horrors
of the trenches on the Western Front.

2756 Maurois, André. General Bramble. Trans. from the French.
Lane, 1922. y.
Sequel to the next citation; provides additional messroom
sketches of the men in a Scotch division.

2757 _____. The Silence of Colonel Bramble. Trans. from
the French. Lane, 1920. Rpr. 1965. y.

A series of messroom conversations among Scottish soldiers.

2758 Maxwell, William B. Life Can Never Be the Same. Bobbs-
         Merrill, 1920. y.
      Published in Britain as Great Interruption; 12 short stories
      paint the brutalities of German soldiery.

2759 Mayran, Camille. The Story of Gotton Conixloo. Trans.
         from the French. Dutton, 1921. y.
      Two tales concerning the German invasion of Flanders.

2760 Miller, Patrick. Natural Man. Brentano's, 1925. y.
      Bleven, a young British artillery officer, prefers life in
      the trenches to leave in Paris.

2761 Montague, Margaret P. England to America. Doubleday,
         Page, 1920. y.
      Reprinting of a short story from the September 1919 issue
      of Atlantic Monthly that won the O. Henry prize; an Amer-
      ican soldier on leave in Devonshire learns his hosts are
      concealing tragic news.

2762   . Of Water and the Spirit. Dutton, 1916. y.
      Belgium is overrun by German troops in 1914.

2763 Morgan, John H. Gentlemen at Arms. Doubleday, 1918. y.
      A number of short stories dealing with the battles of Mons,
      the Marne, the Aisne, Ypres, and the Somme.

2764 Morris, Walter F. The Strange Case of Gunner Rawley.
         Dodd, Mead, 1931. y.
      Lieutenant Rawley, having accidentally killed a superior
      officer, hides in various artillery units.

2765 Mottram, Ralph H. Armistice, and Other Memories. Dial,
         1929. y.
      Published in Britain as Ten Years Ago; 16 short stories
      of combat on the Western Front.

2766   . The Spanish Farm. Dial, 1924. y.
      Picture of a British unit billeted at a farm in Flanders
      and the love of a young lieutenant for a French girl.

2767 Mundy, Talbot. Hira Singh. Bobbs-Merrill, 1918. y.
      A story about an Indian Sikh fighting for the British in
      Flanders.

2768 Murdoch, Iris. The Red and the Green. Viking, 1966.
      The problems of a Dublin family during the Easter Rebel-
      lion of 1916.

2769 Myrivilis, Stratis. Life in the Tomb. Trans. from the
         Greek. University Press of New England, 1977. y.

Fictional tale of a Greek soldier fighting in Macedonia.

2770 Nadaud, Marcel. Birds of a Feather. Trans. from the
French. Doubleday, Page, 1919. y.
Four tales of French ace "Chignole, the Flying Poilu."

2771 _____. Flying Poilu. Trans. from the French. Doran,
1918. y.
French youth Chignole joins the air service and earns
glory in combat with German warplanes.

2772 Nason, Leonard H. Among the Trumpets. Houghton Mifflin,
1930. y.
Eight stories based on the experiences of one troop of the
U.S. 2nd Cavalry in France.

2773 _____. Chevrons. Doran, 1926. y.
Two U.S. doughboys participate in the battles of Mont Sec
and Montfaucon.

2774 _____. Corporal Once. Doubleday, 1930. y.
An Irish-American soldier fresh from Pershing's Mexican
expedition is sent into combat in France in 1917.

2775 _____. The Fighting Livingstones. Doubleday, 1931. y.
Rupert, commissioned an officer and anxious for war is
sent to run a training camp; his brother, John, who joins
the militia as a private to avoid the war, is sent immedi-
ately to the trenches.

2776 _____. The Man in the White Slicker. Doubleday, Doran,
1929. y.
An officer orders a doughboy machine-gun unit to turn its
guns on advancing American troops.

2777 _____. Sergeant Eddie. Doubleday, Doran, 1928. y.
Details the experiences of a noncom in the A.E.F.

2778 _____. Three Lights from a Match. Doubleday, Doran,
1927. y.
Three stories illustrating the hopes and fears of American
doughboys in France.

2779 _____. Top Kick. Doubleday, Doran, 1928. y.
Contents.--Sergeant of Cavalry.--The Roofs of Verdillot.--
A Matter of Business.

2780 Newberry, Perry. Forward Ho. Stokes, 1927. y.
A young man escapes the Germans to aid American doughboys fighting in the Meuse-Argonne in 1918.

2781 Newbolt, Henry. Tales of the Great War. Longmans, Green,
1918. y.

The British Expeditionary Force, the battle of Ypres, and aerial combat predominate.

2782   Newman, Bernard. The Cavalry Went Through. Gollancz,
            1930. y.
         A British Napoleon is transferred to the Western Front
         from North Africa and wins the Great War before the Amer-
         ican entry in 1917.

2783   Nordhoff, Charles B. and James Norman Hall. Falcons of
            France: A Tale of Youth in the Air. Little, Brown,
            1929. y.
         Two U.S. air veterans tell how Charlie Soldon served with
         the Lafayette Escadrille in France before America came
         into the war.

2784   O'Flaherty, Liam. Insurrection. Little, Brown, 1951. y.
         Bartley Madden becomes involved in the 1916 Easter Up-
         rising in Ireland.

2785   Olden, Balder. On Virgin Soil. Trans. from the German.
            Macauley, 1930. y.
         Lieutenant Huessen, a German officer in East Africa, is
         driven mad by his disreputable band of men.

2786   O'Rourke, Frank. A Mule for the Marquesa. Morrow, 1964.
            y.
         A beautiful young woman captured by Pancho Villa's Mexi-
         can bandits in 1916 is saved by a band of American mer-
         cenaries; this title was made into the Lee Marvin movie
         "The Professionals."

2787   _____. The Professionals. Avon, 1966. y. P.
         The movie-script version of the above citation.

2788   Palmer, J. L. The King's Men. Putnam, 1916. y.
         England's 1914-1916 appeal for soldiers to fight in Flan-
         ders.

2789   Paul, Elliott, H. The Amazon. Liveright, 1930. y.
         A girl in the American Signal Corps fights with the dough-
         boys in the trenches of France.

2790   Pertivee, Roland. Pursuit. Houghton Mifflin, 1930. y.
         Harley Trevelyan pursues the evil Major Fawth from the
         trenches of France to North Africa.

2791/2 Plowman, Stephanie. My Kingdom for a Grave. Houghton
            Mifflin, 1970. y.
         A tale of the Russian invasion of East Prussia, its defeat
         by the Germans, and the Revolution, 1914-1917.

Private 19022, pseud. See Manning, Frederic.

2793 Quirk, L. W. <u>Jimmy Goes to War</u>. Little, Brown, 1931.
      y.
      The adventures of a young American truck driver in
      France.

2794 Raymond, Ernst. <u>The Jesting Army</u>. Cassell, 1931. y.
      The British Legion at Gallipoli in 1915 and on the Western
      Front a year later.

2795 _____ . <u>Tell England</u>. Cassell, 1922. y.
      Follows three schoolboy "Tommies" who serve at Gallipoli
      and who are all later killed in France.

2796 Rebreanu, Liviu. <u>The Forest of the Hanged</u>. Trans. from
      the Rumanian. Duffield, 1930. Rpr. 1967. y.
      A Rumanian officer with the Austrians must decide which
      side to join when Rumania goes with the Allies; the title
      is taken from his unpleasant duty of executing Rumanian
      deserters from the Austrian army.

2797 Redman, Ben R. <u>Down in Flames</u>. Breiver, 1930. y.
      Ten stories of fighting pilots of the Royal Flying Corps.

2798 Remarque, Erich M. <u>All Quiet on the Western Front</u>. Trans.
      from the German. Little, Brown, 1929. Rpr. 1978.
      y.
      Of three young Germans plucked from school and sent to
      serve in the trenches, only one survives, his spirit de-
      stroyed; considered the greatest combat novel of the war,
      the book focuses on the lives of common soldiers.

2799 Renn, Ludwig. <u>War</u>. Trans. from the German. Dodd,
      Mead, 1929. y.
      A German corporal remembers the fighting, misery, dis-
      ease, and death in the trenches of the Western Front.

2800 Robinson, Derek. <u>Goshawk Squadron</u>. Viking, 1972. y.
      Major Woolley, a tough new commander, takes over an
      R. F. C. squadron on the Western Front and whips it into
      shape for the air war against the Red Baron's Flying Cir-
      cus.

2801 Rolt-Wheeler, Francis. <u>The Wonder of War in the Air</u>.
      Lothrop, 1917. y.
      Adventures of British and French flyers 1914-1916.

2802 _____ . <u>The Wonder of War in the Holy Land</u>. Lothrop,
      1919. y.
      Stories of the British campaigns in Palestine and Mesopo-
      tamia.

2803 _____ . <u>The Wonder of War on Land</u>. Lothrop, 1918. y.
      A tale of the Battle of the Marne.

2804   Romains, Jules. <u>Verdun.</u> Trans. from the French. Knopf,
        1939. y.
        Originally published in France the previous year, this
        story concerns a number of young French poilus caught
        up in the slaughter of the great 1916 battle.

        "Sapper," pseud. <u>See</u> McNeile, Herman C.

2805   Sassoon, Siegfried L. <u>Memoirs of an Infantry Officer.</u> Cow-
        ard-McCann, 1930. Rpr. 1966. y.
        The fictional reminiscences of a German officer concerning
        the war on the Western Front.

2806   Scanlon, William T. <u>God Have Mercy on Us: A Story of</u>
        <u>1918.</u> Houghton Mifflin, 1929. y.
        Fictional memoirs of U.S. Marines in combat at Belleau
        Wood and Blanc Mont.

2807   Schindel, Bayard. <u>The Golden Pilgrimage.</u> Doubleday, Doran,
        1929. y.
        A professional U.S. Army officer comes to despise the
        new war of machines and hysteria; based on the author's
        own experiences.

2808   Scholefield, Alan. <u>Lion in the Evening.</u> Morrow, 1974. y.
        In East Africa during 1916, an American railroad engineer
        is faced with pressures from the German Army.

        Seaton, Graham, pseud. <u>See</u> Hutchinson, Graham S.

2809   Serge, Victor. <u>Conquered City.</u> Trans. from the French.
        Doubleday, 1975. y.
        A semi-documentary study of the 1919-1920 siege of St.
        Petersburg; first published in France in 1932.

2810   Shepherd, William G. <u>The Scar That Tripled.</u> Harper, 1918.
        y.
        A young American volunteer in the British Army in Salo-
        nika, wounded while saving a friend under difficult condi-
        tions, leaves his unit and is branded a coward.

2811   Sholokhov, Mikhail. <u>And Quiet Flows the Don.</u> Trans. from
        the Russian. <u>Knopf, 1934.</u> Rpr. 1965. y.
        The role of the Don Cossacks in the Russian Revolution.

2812   Sidgwick, Cecily U. <u>Salt of the Earth.</u> Watt, 1917. y.
        Sent to London to direct Zeppelin raids, German pilot Lo-
        thar Erdmann is caught and executed.

2813   Singer, Isaac J. <u>Steel and Iron.</u> Trans. from the Yiddish.
        Funk & Wagnalls, 1970. y.
        Benjamin Lerner serves as an infantryman in the Czar's
        Imperial Army in 1915 despite the fact that he is a Jew.

2814 Slade, Gurney. <u>Lawrence in the Blue</u>. Stokes, 1936. y.
      A biographical novel about Lawrence of Arabia.

2815 Sleath, Frederick. <u>Sniper Jackson</u>. Houghton Mifflin, 1919.
            y.
      English lieutenant Ronald Jackson's activities as a sharp-
      shooter in Flanders.

2816 Smith, Bertha W. <u>Only a Dog</u>. Dutton, 1917. y.
      A French dog finds a home with a British regiment in the
      trenches; much information on daily living under fire.

2817 Smith, Frederick E. <u>A Killing for the Hawks</u>. David McKay,
            1968. y.
      American volunteer McConnell joins the Royal Flying Corps
      squadron headed by the daring and sadistic ace John Sey-
      mour.

2818 Smith, Helen Z. <u>Stepdaughters of War</u>. Dutton, 1930. y.
      Published in Britain as <u>Not So Quiet</u>; a tale of woman am-
      bulance drivers for the British Expeditionary Force in
      Flanders.

2819 Smith, Paul. <u>Esther's Altar</u>. Abelard-Schuman, 1960. y.
      A young Irish girl is caught up in the 1916 Easter Rebel-
      lion.

2820 Snaith, John C. <u>Undefeated</u>. Appleton, 1919. y.
      An ineffectual fellow becomes a hero in the trenches.

2821 Solzhenitsyn, Alexandre. <u>August 1914</u>. Trans. from the Rus-
            sian. Farrar, Straus, 1972. Rpr. 1974. y.
      Explores the responsibility for the Russian defeat in the
      battle of Tannenburg.

2822 Sommi-Picenardi, Girolamo. <u>Snow and Steel</u>. Trans. from
            the Italian. Appleton, 1926. y.
      Eleven short stories based on actual incidents from the
      campaigns on the Italian Alpine front.

2823 Springs, Elliott W. <u>Contact: A Romance of the Air</u>. Sears,
            1930. y.
      An American ace writes in fictional terms of a flying
      man's experiences in the war--fear, death, loss of friends,
      and the futility of fighting.

2824 _____. <u>Nocturne Militaire</u>. Doubleday, Doran, 1927. y.
      Examines the life of an American aviator in France and
      England, with special attention to his lighter moments.

2825 _____. <u>The Rise and Fall of Carol Banks</u>. Doubleday,
            Doran, 1931. y.
      Martial and amatory tales concerning U.S. pilot Banks.

2826 Stallings, Laurence. Plumes. Harcourt, 1924. y.
Wounded in France, Lieutenant Richard Plume, son of a
long line of military men, comes to hate war.

Starbuck, Arward, jt. editor. See Holmes, Roy J.

2827 Steele, Dan. Snow Trenches. McClurg, 1932. y.
Fictional reminiscences of an American soldier with the
A. E. F. in Russia in 1919.

2828 Sterrett, Frances R. Jimmie the Sixth. Appleton, 1918. y.
A young Virginia costume designer joins the French Foreign Legion and wins the Croix de Guerre for his work in
camouflage.

2829 Stevens, James. Mattock. Knopf, 1927. y.
The experiences of one Kansas doughboy from training
camp through the battles in France and back to America.

2830 Stowell, Gordon. The History of Button Hill. Gollancz, 1930.
y.
Reflects on the services of the young men of an average
English town in the trenches along the Western Front.

2831 Strong, Charles. The Spectre of Masuria. Caxton, 1933. y.
Recreates a decisive battle in East Prussia when Von
Hindenburg crushed the Russians at the Masurian Lakes;
compare with August 1914 by Solzhenitsyn, above.

2832 Swarthout, Glendon. They Came to Cordura. Random House,
1958. y.
An Army major leads civilians to safety during the period
of Pancho Villa's 1916 Texas border raids; the movie version starred Gary Cooper.

2833 _____. The Tin Lizzie Troop. Doubleday, 1972. y.
Mounted in two Model T Fords, six Philadelphia Light
Horse members pursue raiding Mexican guerrillas across
the border in 1916.

2834 Taboureau, Jean. Borru, Soldier of France. Trans. from
the French. Dutton, 1930. y.
A year of heroism by a young poilu in the fighting around
Verdun, 1915-1916.

2835 Tales of Wartime France. Trans. from the French. Dodd,
Mead, 1918. y.
Fourteen short stories by contemporary writers designed
to illustrate "the spirit of the French people at war."

2836 Tenenbaum, Joseph. Mad Heroes. Knopf, 1931. y.
Fifteen tales of combat on the Eastern Front.

2837   Thomason, John W. , Jr.   Fix Bayonets.   Scribner's, 1925.
          y.
          Five short stories built around the actions of the 49th
          Company, 1st Battalion, 5th Marine Regiment at Belleau
          Wood, Soissons, and Blanc Mont.

2838   _____. Red Pants and Other Stories.   Scribner's, 1927.
          y.
          Short stories about American doughboys in France; first
          serialized in Scribner's Magazine.

2839   Thompson, Edward J.   Damascus Lies North.   Knopf, 1933.
          y.
          Two English officers and two American nurses in the clos-
          ing days of General Allenby's 1916 Palestine campaign.

2840   Tomlinson, E. T.   Scouting with General Pershing.   Double-
          day, Page, 1918.   y.
          A young doughboy's reconnaissance missions.

2841   Trevor, Elliston.   Bury Him Among Kings.   Doubleday, 1970.
          y.
          Two brothers from the English aristocracy serve in the
          trenches.

2842   Upson, William H.   Me and Henry and the Artillery.   Double-
          day, Doran, 1928.   y.
          Short humorous stories about U. S. artillerymen in France.

2843   Van Dyke, Henry.   The Broken Soldier and the Maid of
          France.   Harper, 1919.   y.
          A dispirited French soldier is inspired to return to his
          unit by the memory of Joan of Arc; reprinted from the
          December 1918 issue of Harper's Magazine.

2844   Von der Vring, Georg.   Private Suhren.   Trans. from the
          German.   Harper, 1929.   y.
          Believing in his cause despite defeats, a German rifleman
          doggedly serves on both the Western and Eastern fronts.

2845   Von Rhau, Henry.   To the Victor. . . .   Longmans, Green,
          1931.   y.
          Having killed a prince in a duel, Rudolph von Ulm is
          forced to enter the French Foreign Legion.

2846   Von Unruh, Fritz.   Way of Sacrifice.   Trans. from the Ger-
          man.   Knopf, 1928.   y.
          Depicts the advance of German shock troops in the 1916
          Battle of Verdun.

2847   Wallace, Edgar.   Tam O' the Scoots.   Small, 1919.   y.
          Ten short stories concerning Scottish ace Tam in the
          R. F. C.

2848 Walpole, Hugh. Dark Forest. Doubleday, 1916. y.
      Combat on the Russian Galacian front.

2849 _____. The Secret City. Doran, 1919. y.
      Petrograd in the Russian Revolution.

      Welch, Ronald, pseud. See Fenton, Ronald O.

2850 Werfel, Franz V. The Forty Days of Musa Dagh. Trans.
          from the German. Viking, 1935. y.
      Pictures the 1915 Turkish siege of the Armenian town of
      Musa Dagh and Bagradian's defense until the French ar-
      rive to break the siege.

2851 Wharton, Edith N. Marne. Appleton, 1919. y.
      Troy Belknap at 18 becomes an ambulance driver and par-
      ticipates in the Second Battle of the Marne.

2852 _____. Son at the Front. Scribner's, 1923. y.
      The son of an American painter who opposes the war is
      wounded in France, forcing the father to realize that the
      conflict is necessary for world freedom.

2853 Wharton, James B. Squad. Coward-McCann, 1928. y.
      Eight soldiers making up an A. E. F. unit in France in
      1918 are examined for their feelings and reactions.

      Whitehouse, Arch, pseud. See Whitehouse, Arthur G. J.

2854 Whitehouse, Arthur G. J. The Casket Crew. Doubleday,
          1971. y.
      During the last year of the war, an R. A. F. bomber is
      sent behind the German lines to rescue Allied P. O. W.'s.

2855 _____. Hero Without Honor. Doubleday, 1972. y.
      American Max Kenyon becomes an unbeloved ace with the
      R. F. C.

2856 _____. The Laughing Falcon. Putnam, 1969. y.
      Whenever Yank airmen of the Lafayette Escadrille are
      threatened by German flyers, a mysterious pilot comes to
      the rescue.

2857 _____. Playboy Squadron. Doubleday, 1970. y.
      Lost in the shuffle, a group of American pilots are invited
      to join an R. F. C. squadron equipped with Sopwith Camels
      and rack up an excellent combat record.

2858 _____. Squadron 44. Doubleday, 1965. y.
      Pictures the efforts of seasoned R. F. C. officer to keep an
      adventurous young pilot from getting himself shot down
      over the Western Front.

2859 _____ . Squadron Shilling. Doubleday, 1968. y.
Yank Bartley Crispin "takes the shilling" when he enlists
in the R. F. C. and ends up in mortal combat with a renegade American in the German air service.

2860 _____ . Wings for the Chariots. Doubleday, 1973. y.
R. F. C. biplanes and new Royal Armoured Corps tanks
make their combined tactical debute in the Cambrai-Arras
area in the summer of 1917.

2861 _____ . The Zeppelin Fighters. Doubleday, 1966. y.
Pictures the contest between R. F. C. fighters and German
airships over England in 1915-1916.

2862 Williamson, C. E. Everyman's Land. Doubleday, Page, 1918.
y.
German forces attack France and Belgium in 1914.

2863 Williamson, Henry. Patriot's Progress. Bles, 1930. y.
The fictional reminiscences of British private John Billah,
from his enlistment to the Armistice.

2864 _____ . A Test to Destruction. MacDonald, 1960. y.
Follows the combat experiences of a group of English soldiers in the fields of Flanders.

2865 Wise, Jennings C. The Great Crusade. Dial, 1930. y.
The fictional memoirs of a Virginia officer fighting with
the A. E. F. in France.

2866 Wittlin, Jozef. Salt of the East. Trans. from the German.
Sheridan, 1941. y.
Peter Neviadomski, a peasant, is called to serve in the
Austrian Army during the first six weeks of the war.

2867 Witwer, Harry C. From Baseball to Boches. Somall, 1918.
y.
U. S. baseball star Ed Harmon records his adventures as
a doughboy.

2868 Wolpert, Stanley. An Error in Judgement. Little, Brown,
1970.
On April 3, 1919 men of the Gurka Rifles kill hundreds of
civilians at Jallianwala Bagb, India, on the orders of a
British general.

2869 Wylie, Ida A. R. Towards Morning. Lane, 1918. y.
After three years in the German Army, the fine nature
of a man is brutalized.

2870 Yeates, Victor M. Winged Victory. Cape, 1934. y.
Tom Cundall and his Sopwith Camel fight with the R. A. F.
during the last six months of the war.

2871   Yeo.   Soldier Men.   Lane, 1918.   y.
       Stories of Gallipoli, Egypt, and Arabia as reprinted from
       Punch and London Outlook magazines.

2872   Zweig, Arnold.   The Case of Sergeant Grischa.   Trans. from
       the German.   Viking, 1928.   Rpr. 1970.
       Erroneously condemned to death as a spy, a German sol-
       dier, found at the last moment to be innocent, is never-
       theless executed "for the good of discipline."

2873   _____ .   Education Before Verdun.   Trans. from the Ger-
       man.   Viking, 1936.   y.
       A German private is befriended by two officers during the
       great 1916 battle.

THE YEARS OF CIVIL WAR AND AGGRESSION, 1918 TO 1939

The years between the World Wars were marked by a series of
sharp local conflicts, several of which were very intense. The stories in this section deal with these, especially the civil wars in
Spain, Ireland, and Russia; Italian aggression; the Latin American
banana fights; and unrest in China and Africa. Note that a few tales
concerning the Russian Civil War, an outgrowth of the 1917 Revolution, are cited in our previous section on World War I.

2874 Acland, Baldwyn D. Filibuster. McBride, 1930. y.
        A pair of Americans are involved in fighting in the South
        American republic of Unaboa during the 1920's.

2875 Alington, Argentine F. Gentlemen--The Regiment! By Hugh
        Talbot, pseud. Harper, 1933. y.
        Competition in love and war of two British professional
        military families bound up with the 137th and 138th Regi-
        ments.

2876 Allan, Ted. This Time a Better Earth. Morrow, 1939. y.
        Six members of the International Brigade during the first
        eight months of the Spanish Civil War.

2877 Appell, George C. Tin Trumpet in China. Duell, Sloan,
        1950. y.
        When a Russian-inspired Nationalist attack on Japanese
        positions fails in the winter of 1938, a corrupt Chinese
        general seeks out company commander Captain Liang as
        a scapegoat.

2878 Babel, Isaak E. Red Cavalry. Trans. from the Russian.
        Knopf, 1929. y.
        Follows the Cossacks in the Polish campaign of 1920.

2879 Balmer, Edwin. Flying Death. Dodd, Mead, 1927. y.
        A woman ace and a mad scientist attack U. S. Navy air-
        craft in an effort to prove the possibility of conquest
        through the air.

2880 Binns, Archie. The Laurels Are Cut Down. Reynal, 1937.
        y.

Two American soldier brothers take part in the Siberian
intervention of 1919.

2881   Blankfort, Michael.   The Brave and the Blind.   Bobbs-Mer-
          rill, 1940.   y.
       The siege and defense of Alcazar during the Spanish Civil
       War.

2882   Bridge, Ann.   Dark Moment.   Macmillan, 1952.   y.
       Mustafa Kemel and the Turkish Revolution and war with
       Greece.

2883   _____.   Frontier Passage.   Little, Brown, 1942.   y.
       Intrigue in the Spanish Civil War.

2884   Buchan, John.   Courts of the Morning.   Houghton Mifflin,
          1929.   y.
       A group of young Americans seek to overthrow the evil
       Castor, dictator of a South American state.

2885   Buck, Pearl S.   Young Revolutionist.   Day, 1932.   y.
       A tale of the Chinese Revolution of 1918-1921.

2886   Charlton, Lionel E. O.   The Next War.   Longmans, Green,
          1937.   y.
       A fictional account of the defeat of England in a weekend
       air war.

2887   Chaves-Nogales, Manuel.   Heroes and Beasts of Spain.   Trans.
          from the Spanish.   Doubleday, 1938.   y.
       Nine stories of military action during the Spanish Civil
       War.

2888   Clifford, Francis.   A Wild Justice.   Coward-McCann, 1972.
          y.
       Three Irish Republican Army rebels are caught up in the
       post-war rebellion against Britain.

2889   Conner, Rearden.   Shake Hands with the Devil.   Morrow,
          1934.   y.
       A young Irish-English medical student is tragically drawn
       into the Irish Civil War of 1918-1922.

2890   Cordell, Alexander.   The Dream and the Destiny.   Doubleday,
          1975.   y.
       Recreates the time in 1934 when Mao's army broke out of
       a Nationalist siege and made in the Long March from
       southern China to the northwest.

2891   Davis, Robert.   Pepperfoot of Thursday Market.   Holiday
          House, 1941.   y.
       A story of Berbers in the interior of Africa.

2892 Del Castillo, Michel. The Disinherited. Trans. from the
           French. Knopf, 1960. y.
           A young Communist is disillusioned by the bloodshed of the
           Spanish Civil War.

2893 Dohrman, Richard. The Cross of Baron Samedi. Houghton
           Mifflin, 1958. y.
           Follows the adventures of a U.S. Marine Corps officer in
           Haiti.

2894 Doone, Radko. Red Bears of the Yellow River. Macrae
           Smith, 1939. y.
           A tale of bandits and warlords in China, 1918-1927.

2894a Eden, Matthew. The Murder of Lawrence of Arabia. Cro-
           well, 1979.
           Was the legendary guerrilla leader accidentally killed?

2895 Farrell, Michael. Thy Tears Might Cease. Knopf, 1964.
           y.
           A young man comes of age during the Irish Civil War of
           the 1920's.

2896 Flewelling, W. Endell. Bad Hombre. Meador, 1931. y.
           The activities of U.S. Marines in Santo Domingo during
           the 1920's.

2897 Forbes, Rosita. Cavaliers of Death. Macaulay, 1930. y.
           Describes the struggle between a sect of Syrian devil wor-
           shippers and the Cavaliers of Death, a secret organization
           of Europeans.

2898 Frances, Stephen D. La Guerra: A Spanish Saga. Dela-
           corte, 1970. y.
           Residents of the village of Escoleras describe the horrors
           of the Spanish Civil War.

2899 Franklyn, Irwin R. Knights of the Cockpit. Dial, 1931. y.
           U.S. Marine aviators versus rebel troops in Haiti.

2900 Gallo, Max. With the Victors. Doubleday, 1974. y.
           Traces the rise of Mussolini in Italy as seen by a member
           of his entourage.

2900a Garfield, Brian. Kolchak's Gold. David McKay, 1973. y.
           The first part of this spy story details the saga of Admi-
           ral Kolchak's White Russian Army, which was destroyed
           in combat with the Reds, but not before it had secreted
           away 500 tons of the late Czar's gold.

2901 Gibbs, Philip H. This Nettle Danger. Doubleday, 1939. y.
           A tale built around the Munich Crisis of 1938.

2902 Gilman, La Selle. The Golden Horde. Smith & Durrell,
         1942. y.
         Escaping from the U. S. S. R., a White Russian officer and
         his guerrilla followers come upon a plot by the descendants
         of Genghis Khan to take over China.

2903 Gironella, José M. One Million Dead. Trans. from the
         Spanish. Doubleday, 1964. y.
         A tale of the Spanish city of Gerona and the Alvear family
         in the 1936-1939 Civil War.

2904 Halidé, Edib. Shirt of Flame. Trans. from the Turkish.
         Duffield, 1925. y.
         Ayesha, a young woman of Smyrna, leads a revolt during
         the post-war Greco-Turkish conflict in Asia Minor.

2905 Hannay, James O. Adventures of the Night. Doubleday, 1921.
         y.
         "Black and Tans" versus the I. R. A. in Ireland after the
         war.

2906 Hardman, Ric. Fifteen Flags. Little, Brown, 1968. y.
         Admiral Kolchak, the Cossack Citamans, and the A. E. F.
         in Siberia, 1919-1921.

2907 Harris, John. The Jade Wind. Doubleday, 1969. y.
         In the 1920's, Chinese general Tsu-hi hires American pi-
         lot Ira Penaluma and his mechanic to build him an air
         force with which to oppose Chiang Kai-shek.

2908 _____. Light Cavalry Action. Morrow, 1967. y.
         Just before World War II, a retired officer in Britain sues
         a serving officer, ruining the latter's efforts to secure a
         high command.

2909 Hemingway, Ernest. The Fifth Column and Four Stories of
         the Spanish Civil War. Scribner's, 1969. y.
         Contents. --The Fifth Column. --The Denunciation. --The
         Butterfly and the Tank. --Night Before Battle. --Under the
         Ridge.

2910 _____. For Whom the Bells Toll. Scribner's, 1940. y.
         Robert Jordan, an American professor fighting for the
         Royalists in the Spanish Civil War, is dispatched to help
         some guerrillas blow a bridge; hurt, he awaits the arrival
         of Franco's troops.

2911 Henriques, Robert D. Q. No Arms, No Armour. Nicholson,
         1940. y.
         A look at British Army life on Salisbury Plain and in the
         Sudan from 1928 to 1930.

2912 Herrick, William. Hermanos. Simon & Schuster, 1969. y.

Jake Starr and the men and women of the International
Brigade fight a losing war against Franco's troops in
Spain.

2913   Hurst, John S.   Then Gilded Dust.   Bobbs-Merrill, 1943.   y.
       An American pilot and a Russian flyer fight the Japanese
       Army Air Force on behalf of the defense of Shanghai and
       Nanking.

2914   Hutchinson, James.   Operation Rebel.   T. Gaus, 1967.   y.
       A tale of the I. R. A. in the Irish Civil War.

2915   Kesten, Hermann.   Children of Guernica.   Routledge, 1939.
       y.
       Pictures a raid by the German Condor Legion on a Basque
       town during the Spanish Civil War.

2915a Kirst, Hans H.   The Affairs of the Generals.   Trans. from
       the German.   Coward-McCann, 1979.   y.
       Hitler trumps up false evidence against two patriotic Ger-
       man generals.

2916   Lambert, Derek.   For Infamous Conduct.   Coward-McCann,
       1970.   y.
       Traces the unhappy careers of a British Army doctor
       with the Indian Medical Service and a subaltern with the
       Gurkha Rifles near the Khyber Pass.

2917   Lappin, Peter.   Land of Cain.   Doubleday, 1958.   y.
       Three Belfast I. R. A. members participate in the Irish
       Civil War.

2918   Litten, Frederic N.   Rhodes of the Leathernecks.   Dodd,
       Mead, 1935.   y.
       Exploits of a U. S. Marine Corps aviator in Haiti.

2919   Lynam, Shevawn.   The Spirit and the Clay.   Little, Brown,
       1954.   y.
       Portrays Basque resistance to Franco during the Spanish
       Civil War and German air raids by the Condor Legion on
       their towns, especially Guernica.

2920   Macken, Walter.   The Scorching Winds.   Macmillan, 1965.
       y.
       Two brothers in Galway are caught up in the Irish Civil
       War.

2921   Malraux, André.   Man's Fate.   Trans. from the French.
       Smith & Hass, 1934.   Rpr. 1969.   y.
       Occidental problems amidst the Shanghai Insurrection of
       1927.

2922   .   Man's Hope.   Trans. from the French.   Random
       House, 1938.   y.

A look at the aerial aspects of the first eight months of
the Spanish Civil War; the author served as the commander
of the Royalist government's international air force.

2923 Mather, Berkeley. The White Dacoit. Scribner's, 1974. y.
      A British Army officer becomes involved with brigands on
      India's northwest frontier during the 1920's.

2924 Morgulas, Jerrold. The Siege. Holt, 1972. y.
      Centers around the July-August 1936 siege by Republican
      forces of 1800 people barricaded in the Alcazar of Toledo
      in Spain.

2925 Mundy, Talbot. Hundred Days, and the Woman Ayisha. Cen-
          tury, 1931. y.
      Tales of adventure in India and Arabia centering around
      the exploits of British major James Grim.

2926 Murciaux, Christian. The Unforsaken. Trans. from the
          French. Pantheon, 1964. y.
      The exploits of Republican officer Juanito Sanchez in the
      Spanish Civil War.

2927 Nason, Leonard H. Corporal Once. Doubleday, 1930. y.
      A horsetender corporal is demoted in France, but cheer-
      fully cares for his officers' steeds as a private.

2928 Newsom, J. D. Garde à Vous! (On Guard!) Doubleday,
          Doran, 1928. y.
      Tale of an American in the French Foreign Legion; ro-
      mance and the Arab siege of a town.

2929 Paine, Ralph D. The Wall Between. Scribner's, 1924. y.
      A U.S. Marine quartermaster sergeant sees action in
      Nicaragua.

2930 Palmer, Bruce. They Shall Not Pass. Doubleday, 1971. y.
      Follows a number of heroes into the cauldron of the Spanish
      Civil War, from which most do not emerge alive.

2931 Pozner, Vladimir. Bloody Baron. Trans. from the French.
          Random House, 1938. y.
      White general Ungern-Sternberg fights the Communists in
      Siberia during the Russian Civil War of 1919-1921.

2932 Reinhardt, Richard. The Ashes of Smyrna. Harper, 1971.
          y.
      The Greco-Turkish war of 1919-1922, in which Smyrna is
      first occupied by the Greeks and later retaken by the
      Turks.

2933 Ripley, Clements. Devil Drums. Brewer, 1930. y.
      Con Scott, ex-U.S. cavalry officer, joins a troop of wild

Mongols in an attack on the evil Chinese High Commissioner
at Ta Kure.

2934 _____. Dust and Sun. Brewer, 1929. y.
Escaping from jail, a young American executive joins a
soldier of fortune in a Mexican revolution during the
1920's.

2935 Roberts, Cecil. Sagusto. Doubleday, Doran, 1928. y.
An English major helps an Italian woman recapture her
private island and daughter from an evil enemy.

2936 Sandys, Michael. Cruel Easter. Pantheon, 1958. y.
Focuses on I. R. A. fighter Desmond Farquahar and a raid
on an English camp in 1920.

2937 Sender, Ramon J. Pro Patria. Trans. from the Spanish.
Houghton Mifflin, 1935. y.
The 1921 Moroccan Rif revolt against the Spaniards led by
abd-el-Krim is recalled by a Spanish private.

2938 Sholokhov, Mikhail. The Don Flows Home to the Sea. Trans.
from the Russian. Knopf, 1959. Rpr. 1965. y.
The Don Cossacks fluctuate back and forth between Reds
and Whites during the Russian Civil War.

2939 Smith, Wilbur. Cry Wolf. Doubleday, 1977. y.
Some Americans ferry armored cars to Ethiopian defenders
during Mussolini's 1935 invasion.

2940 Snaith, John C. Surrender. Appleton, 1928. y.
Two young men desert the French Foreign Legion and
make their way across the Arabian desert to sanctuary.

2941 Surdez, Georges. Demon Caravan. Dial, 1928. y.
Captain Paul Lartal and a handful of French Foreign Le-
gionnaires seek to capture a band of Arab raiders.

Talbot, Hugh, pseud. See Alington, Argentine F.

2942 Tasaki, Hanama. Long the Imperial Way. Trans. from the
Japanese. Houghton Mifflin, 1950. y.
Private Takeo Hanimura records the events of the Sino-
Japanese War of 1931-1941.

2943 Thomason, John W., Jr. Marines and Others. Scribner's,
1929. y.
Stories about U. S. Marines in China, Texas, and Central
America in the 1920's.

2944 _____. Salt Winds and Gobi Dust. Scribner's, 1934. y.
Stories about U. S. Marines in action in China and Nicaragua.

2945   Toynbee, Philip. Barricades. Doubleday, 1944. y.
       An English schoolmaster fights with the International Bri-
       gade in the Spanish Civil War.

2946   Tracy, Louis. Sirdar's Sabre. Clode, 1920. y.
       Bengal Lancer Reginald Wayne tells ten stories concerning
       the exploits of Sirdir Banadur Mohammedan Khan, a "fire-
       eating" native officer in 1920's India.

2947   Treynor, Albert M. Flaming Sands. Dodd, Mead, 1930. y.
       Escaping the chieftain Ras Tager, a young American sci-
       entist returns to the Sahara two years later.

2948   Uhse, Bodo. Lieutenant Bertram. Trans. from the German.
           Simon & Schuster, 1944. y.
       Follows a German squadron in training and in the Spanish
       Civil War.

2949   Wren, Percival C. Beau Geste. Stokes, 1925. y.
       In the most famous tale of the French Foreign Legion,
       our hero takes the blame for the loss of a priceless gem,
       joins the legion with two friends, and faces action in North
       Africa.

2950   _____. Beau Ideal. Stokes, 1928. y.
       For the love of John Geste's wife, Otis Vanburgh joins the
       Legion to search for him in North Africa.

2951   _____. Beau Sabreur. Stokes, 1926. y.
       A French officer hero, a young American woman, and
       troopers of the Foreign Legion face unruly Arabs in North
       Africa.

2952   _____. Flawed Blades. Stokes, 1934. y.
       Sixteen short stories record death and courage in the For-
       eign Legion.

2953   _____. Fort in the Jungle. Houghton Mifflin, 1936. y.
       Sinbad Dysart and the Foreign Legion battle pirates in the
       woods of northern Annam.

2954   _____. The Man the Devil Didn't Want. Macrae Smith, 1940.
           y.
       Twin brothers and members of the French Foreign Legion
       love the same woman and battle the Arabs.

2955   _____. The Port of Missing Men. Macrae Smith, 1943.
           y.
       Twenty tales of death and courage in the French Foreign
       Legion.

2956   _____. Sowing Glory. Stokes, 1931. y.
       The fictional reminiscences of Mary Ambree, who, after

driving an ambulance on the Western Front in World War
I, enlisted in the French Foreign Legion disguised as a
man and served in Morocco for five years.

2957 _____ . Valiant Dust. Stokes, 1932. y.
The adventures of Legionnaire Otho Belleme in combat
with Arabs in North Africa.

2958 Yourcenar, Marguerite. Coup de Grace. Trans. from the
French. Farrar, Straus, 1957. y.
An East Prussian officer begins his military career by
fighting for the Whites against the Reds in the Russian
Civil War.

WORLD WAR II, 1939 TO 1945

The tales in this section cover military action on the various world fronts during the conflict that many Americans have called "the last good war." The Second World War was the most widespread fight in history, with combat recorded almost everywhere. Survivors of the fighting presently recall the war with something like fondness, even though the battles were often nasty. Readers should keep in mind that this section is limited to military-air action; we do not cover concentration-camp, home-front, or sea stories here.

Albrand, Martha, pseud. See Loewengard, Heidi H.

2959 Aldiss, Brian W. A Soldier Erect. Coward-McCann, 1971.
Young Horatio Stubbs of the British Army in India is sent to battle the Japanese in Burma.

2960 Aldridge, James. I Wish He Would Not Die. Doubleday, 1958.
An R. A. F. pilot in Egypt has his life altered by an obsessive hate for one of his superior officers.

2961 _____. Sea Eagle. Little, Brown, 1944. y.
An Australian soldier left behind when the British evacuate Crete in 1941 hides and escapes from the Germans.

2962 _____. Signed with His Honour. Little, Brown, 1942. y.
John Quayle and the men of R. A. F. No. 80 Squadron fly their antiquated Gladiator biplane fighters from Libya to Greece in a vain attempt to halt the Axis assault; first published serially in Collier's as Flight to the Sun.

2963 Allen, James. We Always Come Back. Paul, 1945. y.
A U. S. 8th Air Force B-24 Liberator fights her way back to Britain after a raid on Hamburg.

2964 Allen, Ralph. The High White Forest. Doubleday, 1964. y.
American soldiers battle the Germans in the 1944 Battle of the Bulge.

2965 Ambler, Eric. State of Siege. Knopf, 1956. y.

A military coup d'état in Southeast Asia during the war.

2966 Andersch, Alfred. Winterspelt. Trans. from the German.
         Doubleday, 1978. y.
         A German major elects to surrender his battalion to the
         Americans before the war is officially over; combat be-
         tween the U. S. 106th and German 416th Divisions at a
         German village on the Belgian border in late 1944.

2967 Andrews, Laurie W. Deadly Patrol. David McKay, 1957. y.
         An 11-member British patrol is sent to plot the position
         of a Japanese artillery unit in Burma.

2968 Andric, Ivo. Bridge on the Drina. Trans. from the Yugo-
         slav. Macmillan, 1959. Rpr. 1977. y.
         A tale of combat in Yugoslavia.

2969 Appel, Benjamin. Fortress in the Rice. Bobbs-Merrill,
         1952. y.
         David McVay fights as a guerrilla in the Philippines after
         the fall of Bataan in 1942.

2970 Archer, Charles S. Hankow Return. Houghton Mifflin, 1941. y.
         Disgusted with the Chinese war, a U. S. aerial mercenary,
         who is also a veteran of the air wars over Spain and
         China, is on his way home when events force him to re-
         turn to the fight.

2971 Arnold, Elliott. The Commandos. Duell, Sloan, 1942. Rpr.
         1979. y.
         British Combined Service raids on Norway in 1941.

2972 _____ . Proving Ground. Scribner's, 1973. y.
         While ferrying wounded Yugoslavian partisans to Italy, a
         U. S. C-47 is downed over Albania, where the survivors
         must elude capture by the Germans.

2973 _____ . Tomorrow Will Sing. Duell, Sloan, 1945. y.
         Italian-American relations at a U. S. bomber base in 1944
         Italy.

2974 _____ . Walk with the Devil. Knopf, 1950. y.
         A story built around the advance of the U. S. 5th Army in
         1944 Italy.

2975 Ashmead, John. The Mountain and the Feather. Houghton
         Mifflin, 1961. y.
         Wartime Hawaii and the 1943-1944 American drive in the
         Central Pacific.

2976 Astrup, Helen, and B. L. Jacot. Oslo Intrigue. McGraw-
         Hill, 1954. y.
         The Norwegian Resistance battles the Nazis.

2977   Atwell, Lester. Private. Simon & Schuster, 1958. y.
       The adventures of a middle-aged U. S. soldier in Europe
       from Normandy through the Battle of the Bulge.

2978   Baillie, Peter. Dropping Zone. Associated Booksellers,
              1960. y. P.
       A tale of Anglo-American paratroopers in northern Europe.

2979   Baker, Ivon. Grave Doubt. David McKay, 1972. y.
       The salvage of a German Heinkel bomber from a British
       swamp raises all sorts of questions relative to the war.

2980   Baker, Richard M. The Revolt of Zengo Takakuwa. Farrar,
              Straus, 1962. y.
       The perils faced by a Japanese Army officer who deserts
       during the campaign in the South Pacific.

2981   Baklanov, Grigorii I. The Foothold. Trans. from the Rus-
              sian. Dufour, 1965. y.
       A group of Soviet soldiers establish a bridgehead on the
       west bank of the Dniester River in the summer of 1944.

2982   _____. South of the Main Offensive. Trans. from the
       Russian. Dufour, 1963. y.
       Soviet soldiers battle the Germans in a small-unit action
       south of the main battlefield.

2983   Ball, John. Phase Three Alert. Little, Brown, 1977. y.
       Examines the loss of an American B-17 carrying a special
       cargo over Labrador in March 1943.

2984   Barak, Michael. The Enigma. Morrow, 1978. y.
       An adventurer known as the Baron enters wartime Paris
       to capture an "Ultra Secret" encoding machine.

2985   Barley, Rex. Cross to Bear Proudly. New American Li-
              brary, 1963. y. P.
       Pictures the exploits of a heroine of the French Resist-
       ance or Marquis.

2986   Baron, Alexander. From the City, from the Plough. Wash-
              burn, 1949. y.
       A compassionate colonel trains an English brigade and
       leads it during the invasion of Normandy.

2987   _____. Human Kind. Washburn, 1953. y.
       Short tales about English soldiers during the war.

2988   Barr, George. Epitaph for an Enemy. Harper, 1958. y.
       While herding French evacuees to the Normandy beachhead,
       an American sergeant comes to understand the enemy as a
       result of the humane activities of a German officer.

Bartlett, Sy, jt. author. See Lay, Beirne.

2989   Bartov, Hanokh. The Brigade. Trans. from the Yiddish.
         Holt, 1968. y.
       A Jewish brigade serves with the British Army in Italy.

2990   Bates, Herbert E. Fair Stood the Wind for France. By
         "Flying Officer X, " pseud. Little, Brown, 1944. Rpr.
         1977. y.
       A French girl helps a downed British bomber crew escape
       to safety.

2991   _____. The Jacaranda Tree. Little, Brown, 1949. Rpr.
         1977. y.
       Civilians attempt to escape from the Japanese drive into
       Burma early in 1942.

2992   _____. A Moment in Time. Farrar, Straus, 1964. y.
       A girl and her grandmother view the Battle of Britain
       from their R. A. F. -requisitioned manor house near the
       English Channel.

2993   _____. The Purple Plain. Little, Brown, 1947. Rpr.
         1977. y.
       An injured R. A. F. officer in Burma fights to survive with
       the aid of a Burmese girl.

2994   _____. There's Something in the Air. By "Flying Officer
         X, " pseud. Knopf, 1943.
       Twenty-one short stories concerning the pilots of the
       R. A. F.

2995   Baxter, Walter. Look Down in Mercy. Putnam, 1952. y.
       Chronicles the brutalizing of Tony Kent, an officer and
       company commander in the China-Burma-India Theater.

2996   Beals, Carleton. Dawn Over the Amazon. Duell, Sloan,
         1943. y.
       When the Axis invades Chile and Brazil in 1940, an Amer-
       ican engineer leads the effort to prevent their rendezvous
       on the Amazon.

2997   Beaty, David. The Donnington Legend. Morrow, 1949. y.
       On a far northern R. A. F. base, Squadron Leader Donning-
       ton is viewed by his fellow airmen as either a god or a
       ruthless machine.

2998   Beck, Howard. The Hero Machine. New American Library,
         1967. y. P.
       Life at a U. S. air base in the China-Burma-India Theater.

2999   Becker, Jurek. Jacob the Liar. Harcourt, 1975.
       During the 1944 Warsaw Uprising against the Nazis, an

aged Jewish man employing a hidden radio reports on an imminent Soviet advance that will relieve the defenders.

3000   Bek, Aleksandr A.   On the Forward Fringe.   Trans. from the Russian.   Hutchinson, 1945.   y.
A story about Soviet General Panfilov's division.

3001   Bergamini, David.   The Fleet in the Window.   Simon & Schuster, 1961.   y.
A young Filipino boy becomes a guerrilla fighter after the Japanese invade his homeland.

3002   Bernhardsen, Christian.   The Fight in the Mountains.   Trans. from the Danish.   Harcourt, 1968.   y.
Two brothers escape the Gestapo and join the Norwegian resistance in battling the Nazis.

3003   Berto, Giuseppe.   Works of God.   Trans. from the Italian.   New Directions, 1950.   y.
Four stories showing the effect of the Italian campaign on U. S. 5th Army soldiers and anti-Nazi Italian partisans.

3004   Beste, R. Vernon.   The Moonbeams.   Harper, 1961.   y.
A British Army captain is detailed to find a traitor in a French Marquis group; published in Britain as Faith Has No Country.

3005   Beverley-Giddings, Arthur R.   Broad Margin.   Morrow, 1945. y.
Wounded in action with the R. A. F., an American volunteer airman is sent back home to Virginia to recover.

3006   Beylen, Robert.   The Way to the Sun.   Trans. from the French.   Little, Brown, 1972.
A British Army lieutenant, an American woman, and a French ex-boxer flee the Axis advance in the 1941 Western Desert.

3007   Bickers, Richard.   The Guns Boom Far.   Hutchinson, 1960. y.
Action with a British artillery unit.

3008   _____.   Italian Episode: Hard Action with Italian Skymen Against the Germans.   Associated Booksellers, 1959. y. P.
The adventures of a British liaison officer with pro-Allied Italian paratroopers over northern Italy in early 1945.

3009   _____.   Jungle Pilot.   Associated Booksellers, 1960.   y. P.
R. A. F. fighter pilots in combat over Burma and India.

3010 _____ . The Liberators. Associated Booksellers, 1960.
          y. P.
          Lives and loves of U. S. 8th Air Force B-24 crewmen
          during the strategic bombing campaign against Germany.

3011 _____ . Night Intruder. Associated Booksellers, 1960. y.
          P.
          Pictures R. A. F. night bombers in action over the Middle
          East.

3012 Blackstock, Josephine. Island on the Beam. Putnam, 1944.
          y.
          Malta struggles to survive the Axis aerial onslaught.

3013 Blagowidow, George. Last Train from Berlin. Doubleday,
          1977. y.
          Adam Leski survives execution at the hands of the Nazis
          and, seeking vengeance, is used by the Himmler faction of
          the Gestapo to kill Hitler.

3014 Blankenship, William. Tiger Ten. Putnam, 1976. Rpr.
          1978. y.
          Riley Stone, roughest of General Chennault's Flying Tigers,
          accepts a British request to swipe a Zero fighter from a
          Japanese airfield behind the lines in Burma.

3015 Blunden, Godrey. Room on the Route. Lippincott, 1947. y.
          Yugoslavian partisans battle the German invaders in the
          mountains.

3016 _____ . Time of the Assassins. Lippincott, 1952. y.
          Life and death in Kharkov from its capture by the Germans
          in the late fall of 1941 to its recapture by Soviet forces
          16 months later.

3017 Böll, Heinrich. Absent Without Leave: Two Novellas. Trans.
          from the German. McGraw-Hill, 1965. y.
          Two narratives, "Absent Without Leave" and "Enter and
          Exit, " dealing with compassionate German soldiers in the
          war.

3018 _____ . Adam, Where Art Thou? Trans. from the Ger-
          man, Criterion, 1955. y.
          Depicts the retreat of a German unit along the Romanian-
          Hungarian border in 1944.

3019 _____ . And Where Were You, Adam? Trans. from the
          German. Secker & Warburg, 1974. y.
          A tale about a German soldier who avoids combat.

3020 Bonham, Frank. Burma Rifles. Berkley, 1960. y. P.
          A young Nisei fights with the U. S. 5307th Composite Unit
          (Provisional), known as Merrill's Marauders, in Asia in
          1944.

3021   _____. The Ghost Front. Dutton, 1968. y.
        Focuses on two young American soldiers of the 106th In-
        fantry Division who are caught up in the Battle of the
        Bulge.

3022   Booth, Fred W. Victory Also Ends. Rinehart, 1952. y.
        The exploits of Mike Andrews as a U.S. Army combat
        officer in Italy.

3023   Bost, Jacques L. Last Profession. Trans. from the French.
        Doubleday, 1948. y.
        Sketches depicting the experiences of a group of French
        soldiers early in the war.

3024   Boulle, Pierre. The Bridge Over the River Kwai. Trans.
        from the French. Vanguard, 1954. Rpr. 1970. y.
        Colonel Nicholson's British unit, captured at Singapore,
        constructs a bridge in Siam as P.O.W.'s of the Japanese;
        this tale was made into an Academy Award winning motion
        picture.

3025   _____. Garden on the Moon. Trans. from the French.
        Vanguard, 1964. y.
        Includes an interesting view of German rocket work at
        Peenemunde on the Baltic coast during the war.

3026   Bourjaily, Vance. The End of My Life. Scribner's, 1947.
        y.
        Four American ambulance drivers serve with the British
        Army in Syria and later in Italy.

3027   Bowman, Peter. Beach Red. Random House, 1945. y.
        How American Marines and G.I.'s established a beachhead
        on a Pacific island.

3028   Boyd, Dean. Lighter-Than-Air. Harcourt, 1962. y.
        A Queeg-like U.S. Navy blimp pilot battles his co-pilot
        from Massachusetts to Tunisia to South America.

3029   Boyington, Gregory "Pappy." Tonya. Bobbs-Merrill, 1960.
        The nymphomaniac wife of an American pilot becomes in-
        volved with a group of American aerial mercenaries,
        known as the "Flying Sharks" (doubtlessly modeled on the
        Flying Tigers), in Burma just before and after Pearl Har-
        bor.

3030   Boyle, Kay. His Human Majesty. McGraw-Hill, 1949. y.
        Focuses on the training of U.S. ski troops in 1944 Colo-
        rado.

3031   Braddon, Russell. The White Mouse. Norton, 1957. y.
        A tale about the French Marquis and its battles with the
        Germans in southern France.

3032 Brelis, Dean. The Drop. Random House, 1958. y.
      Airborne action with Wingate's Raiders in the 1944 Burma.

3033 _____ . The Mission. Random House, 1958. y.
      Americans organize the native Kachin Force to oppose the
      Japanese retreat from Myitkyina, Burma, in 1944.

3034 Brennan, Dan. Never So Young Again. Rinehart, 1946. y.
      Mark Norton is an American gunner in the R. A. F. who
      takes part in night bomber missions over the Reich.

3035 _____ . Suicide Squadron. Belmont-Tower, 1977. y. P.
      Losses in an R. A. F. Bomber Command unit during the
      war.

3036 _____ . The Third Time Down. Ace, 1962. y. P.
      An American volunteer serves with the R. A. F. during the
      Battle of Britain.

3037 _____ . Winged Victory. Belmont-Tower, 1978. y. P.
      U. S. air power in Europe.

3038 Bromfield, Louis. Mr. Smith. Harper, 1951. y.
      While fighting on a Pacific island, a U. S. Marine major
      reviews his life.

3039 Brophy, John. The Immortal Sergeant. Collins, 1942. y.
      On patrol in the Libyan desert in the spring of 1941, 12
      British soldiers are attacked by Italian dive bombers.

3040 _____ . Spearhead. Collins, 1943. y.
      A tale of two British commando raids, one on Norway and
      one on France.

3041 Brown, Ernest H. P. The Balloon. St. Martin's, 1954. y.
      The exploits of a handful of Allied soldiers during the
      1940 campaign in France and Belgium.

3042 Brown, Eugene. The Locust Fire. Doubleday, 1957. y.
      George Lewis is an unhappy radio operator on the "Hump"
      C-47 flights between India and China.

3043 Brown, Harry. A Walk in the Sun. Knopf, 1944. y.
      Following the loss of their officer and sergeant at Anzio,
      a corporal leads his platoon to the accomplishment of their
      mission.

3044 Brown, Joe D. Kings Go Forth. Morrow, 1956. y.
      Two American artillery officers see action against the
      Germans in Italy and southern France, with their service
      highlighted by a daring reconnaissance mission behind en-
      emy lines.

3045 Buck, Pearl S. The Promise. Day, 1943. y.
      A tale of the war in Burma, 1942-1943.

3046 Burgan, John. Two Per Cent Fear. Farrar, Straus, 1947.
           y.
      One soldier's exploits during the capture of a Pacific is-
      land.

3047 Burton, Anthony. The Coventry Option. Putnam, 1976. y.
      Nazi-recruited I. R. A. air guides are active in English
      cities, helping the Luftwaffe to bomb by radio signals;
      culminates in the 1941 destruction of Coventry.

3048 Bykov, Vasily. The Ordeal. Trans. from the Russian. Dut-
           ton, 1972. y.
      A character study of two Russian partisans operating be-
      hind German lines during the winter of 1942.

3049 Caidin, Martin. The Last Dogfight. Houghton Mifflin, 1974.
           y.
      An A. A. F. P-38 ace and his Japanese counterpart fight a
      gladiatorial air battle over a backwater island in the Pacific
      during the days just before Hiroshima.

3050 _____. Whip. Houghton Mifflin, 1976. Rpr. 1977. y.
      In 1942 Captain Whip Russell's B-25 equipped "Death's
      Head Brigade" is formed to hit the Japanese from a secret
      base in New Guinea; their exploits are capped by an attack
      on a strongly defended convoy.

3051 Caldwell, Erskine. All Night Long. Duell, Sloan, 1942. y.
      Soviet guerrillas battle the Germans in 1941 Russia.

3052 Calin, Harold. Combat. Lancer, 1963. y. P.
      Lieutenant Gil Hanley and Sergeant Chip Saunders lead their
      men on a slow, nerve-shattering crawl across a minefield
      in order to hit a German position; based on the TV series.

3053 _____. Dieppe. Belmont-Tower, 1978. y. P.
      A fictional recreation of the great 1942 commando raid on
      France.

3054 _____. Men, Not Heroes. Lancer, 1963. y. P.
      Hanley, Saunders, and their men fight to hold off a Ger-
      man advance.

3055 _____. Signal Red. Lancer, 1964. y. P.
      Hanley, Saunders, and their men participate in the libera-
      tion of Paris.

3056 Callison, Brian. Dawn Attack. Putnam, 1973. y.
      Pictures a British commando raid on Norway in 1941.

3057   Calmer, Ned. The Strange Land. Scribner's, 1950. y.
       American G. I. 's participate in "Operation Uppercut, " a
       small-unit offensive against the Siegfried Line in November
       1944.

3058   Camerer, David M. The Damned Wear Wings. Doubleday,
              1958. y.
       An A. A. F. B-24 Liberator group is ordered to hit the oil
       fields at Ploesti, Romania; based on an actual operation.

3059   Cameron, Lou. The Big Red Ball. Fawcett, 1963. y. P.
       The exploits of the men of the U. S. Army Transportation
       Service in Europe after D-Day.

3060   _____. The Black Camp. Fawcett, 1963. y. P.
       A look at U. S. soldier-prisoners in a stockade in England.

3061   _____. The Dirty War of Sergeant Slade. Fawcett, 1966.
              y. P.
       An American noncom battles Germans in the Battle of the
       Bulge.

3062   _____. Drop Into Hell. Fawcett, 1976. y. P.
       A group of American paratroops are air-dropped into bat-
       tle in Europe.

3063   _____. The Green Fields of Hell. Fawcett, 1964. y.
       American soldiers land at Normandy on June 6, 1944.

3064   Camp, William M. Retreat, Hell! Appleton-Century, 1943.
              y.
       The exploits of three U. S. Marines in the Philippines
       from the 7th of December 1941 to the fall of Cavite to ad-
       vancing Japanese troops.

3065   Campbell, David. Flame and Shadow: Selected Stories. Uni-
              versity of Queensland Press, 1977. y.
       Tales of Australian fighting men and pilots in the war.

3066   Caniff, Milton. April Kane and the Dragon Lady. Whitman,
              1942. y.
       Terry (of "Terry and the Pirates") journeys to China with
       his friends, where they meet the Dragon Lady and her
       guerrilla army fighting a death's struggle with the Japa-
       nese invaders.

3067   Carrington, John W. Bombardier. Putnam, 1970. y.
       An A. A. F. colonel selects a group of psychological mis-
       fits to form an elite corps of bombardiers for the air cam-
       paign against Germany.

3068   Carse, Robert. Unconquered. McBride, 1943. y.
       Stories of resistance and partisan operations in nine oc-
       cupied European countries.

3069 Castle, John. The Seventh Fury. Walker, 1964. y.
A joint Anglo-American team is sent to destroy a chemical warfare agent in an R. A. F. plane that has crashed in
neutral Turkey near the Russian border.

3070 Chamales, Tom T. Never So Few. Scribner's, 1957. y.
Con Reynolds leads the Kachin guerrillas in Burma in
1944.

3071 Chamberlain, William. The Mountain. Stein & Day, 1968.
y.
The problems of a young officer with his superiors during
the Monte Cassino operation in Italy.

3072 _____., ed. Combat Stories of World War II and Korea.
John Day, 1962. y.
Action on the ground and in the air.

3073 _____. Hellbent for Glory. Paperback Library, 1966. y.
P.
Adventures of fighting G. I. 's from North Africa to New
Guinea.

3074 _____. More Combat Stories of World War II and Korea.
John Day, 1964. y.
Additional tales of G. I. combat around the world.

3075 Chambers, Whitman. Invasion! Dutton, 1943. y.
A group of southern Californians escape a Japanese in-
vasion of the U. S. West Coast and hide until A. A. F.
B-17's can dislodge the enemy.

3076 Charles, Mark. Here Come the Marines! Associated Booksellers, 1960. y. P.
U. S. Marine Corps action in the South Pacific.

3077 Charlwood, D. E. No Moon Tonight. Angus & Robertson,
1956. y.
Traces the fate of 18 Canadian airmen in action with the
R. A. F. Bomber Command over Europe.

3078 Chin, Kee O. Silent Army. Longmans, Green, 1954. y.
A Malayan-Chinese teacher tells of the 1941-1942 Japanese invasion of Malaya and the fall of Singapore.

3079 Chukovskii, Nikolai K. Baltic Skies. Trans. from the Russian. Foreign Languages Publishing House, 1967. y.
Soviet fighter pilots battle the Luftwaffe in the far north.

3080 Cikalo, Walter. Doomed in Russia. Pageant, 1960. y.
The fate of German soldiers fighting in the Soviet Union.

3081 Cittafino, Ricardo. Conscript. Trans. from the Italian.
Associated Booksellers, 1960. y. P.

An Italian conscript serves first with Mussolini's Army
and then with the partisans.

3082 Clarke, Arthur C. Glide Path. Harcourt, 1963. Rpr. 1973.
      y.
      The early development and use of radar as recalled by
      British and American scientists and technicians working at
      a Cornish air base.

3083 Clavell, James. King Rat. Little, Brown, 1962. Rpr. 1974.
      A "straight" R. A. F. flight lieutenant and a wheeling-dealing
      American corporal become friends in the Japanese P O W
      camp at Changi, outside Singapore.

3084 Claymore, Rod. Flare Path. Morrow, 1942. y.
      Pictures the R. A. F. bomber patrol over the North Atlantic
      in the spring of 1941.

3085 Cleary, John. The Long Pursuit. Morrow, 1967. y.
      A group of Singapore survivors reach Sumatra only to see
      the last rescue plane leave before they can get on; the cri-
      sis forces them to join native guerrillas against the in-
      vading Japanese.

3086 Clebert, Jean Paul. The Blockhouse. Trans. from the
      French. Coward-McCann, 1958. y.
      Six German Army laborers are trapped in a bombed-out
      building and must survive until rescue.

      Clifford, Francis, pseud. See Thompson, Arthur L. B.

      Clive, John, jt. author. See Gilman, J. D.

3087 Cockrell, Boyd. The Barren Beaches of Hell. Holt, 1959.
      y.
      U. S. Marine Andrew Willy battles his way with his com-
      rades from Tarawa to Okinawa.

3088 Collison, Thomas, ed. This Winged World: An Anthology of
      Aviation Fiction. Coward-McCann, 1943. y.
      Includes the war stories "Bombardier," by Paul Gallico,
      and "A Bomber Goes Back Home," by Guy Gilpatrick.

3089 Connell, Evan S. The Patriot. Viking, 1961. y.
      Exploits of U.S. naval aviator Melvin Isaacs in Pacific
      combat.

3090 Coppel, Alfred. Order of Battle. Harcourt, 1968. y.
      U. S. P-38's in the air war over Europe and North Africa.

3091 Cosić, Dobrica. Far Away Is the Sun. Trans. from the
      Yugoslav. "Jugoslavija" (Belgrade), 1963. y.
      A tale of guerrilla warfare in the mountains of Yugoslavia.

3092 Cotler, Gordon. <u>Bottletop Affair</u>. Simon & Schuster, 1957.
      y.
      U. S. Army troops seek a harmless, but supposedly dan-
      gerous, Japanese soldier-guerrilla on a Pacific atoll.

3093 Cozzens, James G. <u>Guard of Honor</u>. Harcourt, 1948. y.
      Authority and racial unrest among troops at a Florida
      A. A. F. base in 1943.

3094 Cranston, Edward. <u>A Matter of Duty</u>. Longmans, Green,
      1943. y.
      Short stories of combat, three of which are aerial.

3095 Creasey, John. <u>Legion of the Lost</u>. Daye, 1944. y.
      Allied agents led by Dr. Palfrey rescue scientists in Nor-
      way, Germany, and Denmark who are being liquidated by
      the Nazis.

3096 Crichton, Robert. <u>The Secret of Santa Vittoria</u>. Simon &
      Schuster, 1966.
      The populace of an Italian town rallies to confront German
      occupation by refusing to tell where the town's wine supply
      is.

3097 Crockett, Lucy H. <u>Magnificent Bastards</u>. Farrar, Straus,
      1954. y.
      The work of Red Cross women in a canteen on a Pacific
      island base.

3098 Croft-Cooke, Rupert. <u>Seven Thunders</u>. St. Martin's, 1956.
      y.
      The German destruction of the port of Marseilles in Janu-
      ary 1943.

3099 Crowley, Robert T. <u>Not Soldiers All</u>. Doubleday, 1967. y.
      A story of U. S. Army medics under fire in Italy.

3100 Cunningham, Andrew. <u>Tumult in the Clouds</u>. Davies, 1954.
      y.
      R. A. F. night fighter operations against the Luftwaffe, based
      partly on the author's wartime experiences.

3101 Dahl, Roald. <u>Over to You</u>. Reynal, 1946. y.
      Ten short stories concerning aerial operations during the
      war.

3102 Daniels, Norman. <u>Battalion</u>. Pyramid, 1965. y. P.
      While attempting to break through Nazi lines, a general
      finds that his son is a traitor.

3103 _____. <u>Moments of Glory</u>. Paperback Library, 1965. y.
      P.
      A G. I. machine-gun squad slashes its way across north-
      west Europe.

3104 _____ . Strike Force. Lancer, 1965. y. P.
A special U. S. Army force operates against the Germans
in 1944 France.

3105 Davis, Franklin M. , Jr. Combat: The Counterattack. Whit-
man, 1964. y.
Sergeant Chip Saunders leads his men on a raid against
German positions; a tale based on the TV series.

3106 Davis, Paxton. Two Soldiers. Simon & Schuster, 1956. y.
Two tales of American fighting men in Burma.

3107 Dawson, Robert P. All My Laurels. Exposition, 1964. y.
Follows the exploits of an airborne unit in Europe.

3108 Dean, G. M. Wings Over the Desert. Viking, 1945. y.
A story about the U. S. Civil Air Patrol, A. A. F. auxiliary.

3109 Dedmon, Emmett. Duty to Love. Houghton Mifflin, 1946. y.
A composite picture of the lives of an R. A. F. bomber
crew ending with the final fatal bomb run over a German
target.

3110 De Gramont, Sanche. Lives to Give. Trans. from the
French. Putnam, 1971.
French Marquis irregulars battle the Germans in Paris.

3111 Deighton, Len. Bomber. Harper, 1970. y.
A Luftwaffe night fighter battles an R. A. F. Lancaster
bomber during a 1943 British raid on the Ruhr.

3111a _____ . SS-GB: Nazi-Occupied Britain, 1941. Knopf, 1979.
Murder and resistance in a Britain captured by the Germans.

3112 Delderfield, Robert F. Stop at a Winner. Simon & Schuster,
1978.
The M*A*S*H-like antics of two R. A. F. recruits.

3113 Den Doolaard, A. The Land Behind God's Back. Trans.
from the Dutch. Simon & Schuster, 1958. y.
An engineer blows up a bridge to keep the Italians out of
Montenegro in the fall of 1940.

3114 _____ . Roll Back the Sea. Trans. from the Dutch. Simon & Schuster, 1948. y.
Dutch patriots attempt to halt the 1940 German invasion of
their country by destroying the dikes holding back the sea.

3115 Denham, Elizabeth. I Looked Right. Doubleday, 1956. y.
A girl rescues stranded British soldiers in Occupied
France.

3116 Devilliers, Catherine. Lieutenant Katia. Trans. from the
        French. Constable, 1964. y.
        A woman officer with the French Marquis.

3117 Divine, Arthur D. The Sun Shall Greet Them. By David
        Rame, pseud. Macmillan, 1941. y.
        An English idealist works in the evacuation of Dunkirk.

3118 Duncan, Robert L. The Day the Sun Fell. By James A.
        Robertson, pseud. Morrow, 1970. y.
        Just before the A-bombing of Nagasaki, three U.S. sol-
        diers disguised as priests, are dropped in to persuade a
        bishop to evacuate the city.

3119 Dunmore, Spencer. Bomb Run. Morrow, 1971. Rpr. 1972.
        y.
        A tale about an R.A.F. Bomber Command raid on Berlin.

3120 _____ . The Last Hill. Morrow, 1973. y.
        What happens to a British battalion that is cut off by the
        Japanese outside Singapore in early 1942.

3120a _____ . Means of Escape. Coward-McCann, 1979. y.
        A downed English flyer and a disillusioned Wehrmacht of-
        ficer escape the German lines only to end up fighting in
        the Battle of the Bulge.

3121 Dunsany, Lord (Edward J.M.D. Plunkett). Guerrilla. Bobbs-
        Merrill, 1941. y.
        When his family is wiped out, a Balkan youth joins the
        Yugoslav partisans in their war on the Germans.

3122 Eastlake, William. Castle Keep. Simon & Schuster, 1965.
        y.
        Depicts the conflict between a Wehrmacht major who wants
        a tenth-century castle held against the advancing Americans
        and a captain who wants to surrender it to prevent its de-
        struction.

3123 Eddy, Roger. Best by Far. Doubleday, 1966.
        Fictional reminiscences of U.S. Army veterans at a re-
        union on the site of a bloody Italian battleground.

3124 Egleton, Clive. The Bormann Brief. Coward-McCann, 1974.
        Rpr. 1975. y.
        Late in the war a group of Allied commandos are sent in-
        to Germany to assassinate Martin Bormann.

3125 Elstob, Peter. Warriors for the Working Days. Coward-
        McCann, 1962. y.
        A newly trained British tank regiment is sent to France
        just after the D-Day invasion of June 1944.

3126   Facos, James.   The Silver Lady.   Atheneum, 1972.   y.
       A pair of U.S. 8th Air Force B-17 crewmen become close
       friends as the result of shared danger during repeated air
       raids on Germany.

3127   Falstein, Louis.   Face of a Hero.   Harcourt, 1950.   y.
       Tail-gunner Ben Isaacs reveals the experiences of a U.S.
       bomber crew that flew 50 missions from an Italian base in
       late 1943.

3128   Fast, Howard.   The Winston Affair.   Crown, 1959.
       Depicts the trial of a U.S. soldier accused of killing a
       British Tommy in the China-Burma-India Theater.

3129   Felsen, Gregor.   Struggle Is Our Brother.   Trans. from the
       Russian.   Dutton, 1943.   y.
       To keep it from the advancing Germans, a group of Cos-
       sacks blow up the great Amsov Dam.

3130   Fenner, Phyllis, comp.   No Time for Glory: Stories of World
       War II.   Morrow, 1962.   y.
       An anthology of tales by various authors.

3131   Fenton, Charles A., ed.   The Best Stories of World War II:
       An American Anthology.   Viking, 1957.   y.
       Twenty G.I. tales with military-air emphasis.

3132   Fields, Alan.   V-J Day.   Dell, 1978.   P.
       What August 14, 1945 meant to various people, including
       some in military uniform.

3133   Fields, Arthur C.   World Without Heroes.   McGraw-Hill,
       1950.   y.
       A U.S. Army rifle squad takes part in mopping up last-
       ditch German resistance in April 1945.

3134   Flavin, Martin.   Corporal Cat.   Harper, 1941.   y.
       A Nazi paratrooper comes down in Germany in 1940 be-
       lieving himself to be in Holland.

       "Flying Officer X, " pseud.   See Bates, Herbert E.

3135   Flynn, Robert.   The Sounds of Rescue, the Signs of Hope.
       Knopf, 1970.   y.
       When a U.S. Navy flyer is downed and saved from the
       surf, the flyer and his rescuer prepare to wait for a res-
       cue that never comes.

3136   Follett, Ken.   Eye of the Needle.   Dutton, 1978.   y.
       A German attempts to alert Berlin that the Allied Normandy
       invasion will come where it did and not at Calais as was
       expected.

Forbes, Colin, pseud. See Sawkins, Raymond H.

3137 Forester, Cecil S. Gold from Crete. Little, Brown, 1970.
          Rpr. 1976. y.
          Ten short stories that include a look at two R. A. F. fighter
          pilots, a British tank major, and the speculative tale, "If
          Hitler Had Invaded England. "

3138 Forman, James. Horses of Anger. Farrar, Straus, 1967.
          y.
          Reveals the experiences of a German youth in an A. A.
          battery near Munich.

3139 _____. The Skies of Crete. Farrar, Straus, 1963. y.
          Pictures the German air and airborne attacks on Crete in
          May 1941.

3140 Forsythe, Rose. That Morning at Dawn. Exposition, 1965.
          y.
          Commandos attack a town in Occupied Europe.

3141 Fosburgh, Hugh. View from the Air. Scribner's, 1953. y.
          The story of a U.S. bomber group in combat over the
          South Pacific.

3142 Frankau, Gilbert. Air Ministry Room 28. Dutton, 1942. y.
          A love story unfolds amidst the bustle of the headquarters
          of the British Air Ministry during the Battle of Britain.

3143 Frankau, Pamela. Over the Mountain. Random House, 1967.
          y.
          Captured at Dunkirk in 1940, an English soldier escapes
          across France to Spain, where he is interned for the du-
          ration of the war.

3144 Frizell, Bernard. The Grand Defiance. Morrow, 1972. y.
          A French general captured by the Germans in 1940 at-
          tempts to escape his fortress prison.

3145 _____. Ten Days in August. Simon & Schuster, 1957.
          y.
          French Marquis troops and irregulars in Paris battle the
          Germans just before the 1944 Liberation.

3146 Fullerton, Charles. If Chance a Stranger. Sloane, 1958. y.
          The Japanese conquer Hong Kong just after Pearl Harbor.

3147 Furman, Abraham L. Air Force Surgeon. Sheridan, 1944.
          y.
          An A. A. F. doctor aids a small group of Marines holding
          an island against the advancing Japanese in 1942.

3148 Gabriel, Gilbert W. I Got a Country. Doubleday, 1944. y.

The adventures of three American soldiers stationed in
Alaska.

3149   Gaiser, Gerd. <u>The Last Squadron.</u> Trans. from the Ger-
           man. Pantheon, 1956. y.
       The problems of a Luftwaffe fighter squadron attempting to
       down Allied bombers over the North Sea late in the war.

3150   Gallico, Paul W. <u>The Snow Goose.</u> Knopf, 1941. y.
       A great white Canadian bird flies over Dunkirk, providing
       inspiration to Allied soldiers during their 1940 evacuation.

3151   Gann, Ernest K. <u>Island in the Sky.</u> Viking, 1944. y.
       An A. A. F. transport crashes in the frozen Canadian wastes
       forcing its five-member crew to make do until it can be
       rescued.

3152   Garfield, Brian. <u>The Romanov Succession.</u> Evans, 1974. y.
       During the early days of the war, White Russians try to
       kill Stalin and install a constitutional monarchy in Russia.

3153   Garrett, James. <u>And Save Them for Pallbearers.</u> Messner,
           1958. y.
       Sergeant Peter Donatti serves at Normandy and in the Bat-
       tle of the Bulge.

3154   Garth, David. <u>Thunderbird.</u> Kinsey, 1942. y.
       Three people, including an escaped German pilot, find
       themselves involved in ground-sea-air combat on a small
       West Indies island.

3155   _____. Watch on the Bridge. Putnam, 1957. y.
       A Jewish girl and a demoralized American soldier-turned-
       hero figure in this tale of the U. S. Army's 1945 capture
       of the Rhine River bridge at Remagen.

3156   Gavin, Catherine. <u>None Dare Call It Treason.</u> St. Martin's,
           1978.
       Tells of the in-fighting between French Marquis leaders on
       the eve of an important battle.

3157   Gellhorn, Martha E. <u>Wine of Astonishment.</u> Scribner's,
           1948. y.
       Pictures American G. I. 's in the Battle of the Bulge and
       the push on Munich.

3158   Gerlach, Heinrich. <u>The Forgotten Army.</u> Trans. from the
           German. Harper, 1959. y.
       Stories of the German 6th Army's losing fight at Stalingrad.

3159   Gibbs, Philip H. <u>Amazing Summer.</u> Doubleday, 1941. y.
       Guy, a member of England's Norton family, crashes in
       France during the Battle of Britain and eludes capture.

3160 _____. Long Alert. Doubleday, 1942. y.
The strain on English pilots fighting in the Battle of Britain.

3161 _____. Sons of the Others. Doubleday, 1941. y.
Sons of English veterans of World War I are sent to France in 1939 and forced to evacuate at Dunkirk in 1940.

3162 Gilman, J. D., and John Clive. KG 200. Simon & Schuster, 1972. Rpr. 1977. y.
Employing captured Allied aircraft, a crack Luftwaffe unit attempts to mount a spectacular daylight raid on England.

3163 Gilroy, Frank D. Private. Harcourt, 1971.
A young draftee in Europe learns that the U.S. Army is not a democracy.

3164 Giovannitti, Len. The Prisoners of Combine D. Holt, 1957. y.
Six Allied aviators are downed over Hitler's Germany and suffer many hardships in a P.O.W. camp.

3165 Giovene, Andrea. The Dice of War. Trans. from the Italian. Houghton Mifflin, 1974. y.
Italian officer Sansevero participates in the occupation of the French Alps and Mussolini's comic-opera invasion of Greece.

3166 Goethals, Thomas. Chains of Command. Random House, 1955. y.
American rear command officers ignore warnings of a German push just before the opening of the 1944 Battle of the Bulge.

3167 Goodman, Mitchell. The End of It. Horizon, 1961. y.
A young U.S. Army officer faces the physical and emotional horrors of the Italian campaign.

3168 Gracq, Julian. Balcony in the Forest. Trans. from the French. Braziller, 1959. y.
French Marquis irregulars battle the Germans.

3169 Grady, James. A Game for Heroes. Doubleday, 1970. y.
Allied commandos take out a German fortress on the Channel island of St. Pierce in 1945.

3170 Graves, Charles. The Thin Blue Line. Hutchinson, 1941. y.
An account of the Battle of Britain, focusing on the gallant fighter pilots of the Royal Air Force.

3171 Green, Gerald. Holocaust. Bantam, 1978. y. P.
A tale about two German families, one Nazi and one

Jewish, in the war, including young Rudi Weiss's time
with a partisan band; based on the script for a TV mini-
series.

3172   Greenfield, George C. Desert Episode. Macmillan, 1945. y.
Thoughts of two British company commanders during the
1942 Battle of El Alamein.

3173   Griffin, Gwyn. The Occupying Power. Putnam, 1968. y.
When the British take over an Italian colony on the Mediterranean island of Baressa in 1940, a young major becomes its governor.

3174   Groom, A. J. Pelham. Mohune's Nine Lives. Liveright,
1944. y.
An R. A. F. pilot forced down in enemy territory escapes
with information on a forthcoming German invasion; English
title, What Are Your Angels Now?

3175   Gwaltney, Francis I. The Day the Century Ended. Rinehart,
1955. y.
U. S. G. I. 's battle the Japanese in the South Pacific.

3176   Hackett, Charles J. The Last Happy Hour. Doubleday, 1976.
y.
Removed to a backwater, three incompetent but genius-
level U. S. soldiers embark on singular adventures in support of the Allied war effort.

3177   Haggerty, Edward. Guerrilla Padre in Mindanao. Longmans,
Green, 1946. y.
An American padre fights with the Filipino guerrillas in
1942-1944.

3178   Hailslip, Harvey. Escape from Java. Doubleday, 1962. y.
Civilians and soldiers attempt to escape the advancing
Japanese in the Netherland East Indies in early 1942.

3179   Haines, William W. Command Decision. Little, Brown,
1947. y.
The difficult problems of Brigadier General Dennis, commander of an 8th Air Force air division.

3180   _____. Target. Little, Brown, 1964. y.
Major Hal Brett, A. A. F., and a beautiful British flight
lieutenant are sent out on a mission together.

Hall, James Norman, jt. author. See Nordhoff, Charles B.

3181   Hallstead, William F. The Missiles of Zajecar. Chilton,
1969. y.
A duel between an A. A. F. B-24 Liberator and a Luftwaffe
Me-109 Messerschmitt over Yugoslavia in 1944.

3182   Hammond-Innes, Ralph. Attack Alarm. By Hammond Innes,
         pseud. Macmillan, 1942. y.
       Action on and above an R. A. F. fighter station during the
       Battle of Britain.

3183   Hanley, Gerald. See You in Yasukuni. World, 1970. y.
       Focuses on the problems of a conscience-ridden Japanese
       soldier who helps a British soldier escape during the fall
       of Singapore.

3184   Hardy, René. Bitter Victory. Trans. from the French.
         Doubleday, 1957. y.
       A pair of British commandos in love with the same woman
       are sent on a dangerous patrol into the Sahara near Ben-
       ghazi in 1941.

3185   Harkins, Philip. Bomber Pilot. Harcourt, 1944. y.
       After training, an American bomber pilot is sent to Europe
       to participate in the strategic air campaign against Ger-
       many.

3186   Harris, John. The Sea Shall Not Have Them. Hurst, 1953.
         y.
       Pictures the wartime operations of the British air-sea res-
       cue service in picking up downed aviators in the English
       Channel.

3187   Harris, MacDonald. Yukiko. Farrar, Straus, 1977. y.
       A U. S. demolitions team is sent to blow up a heavy-water
       plant in Japan.

3188   Hartley, A. B. Unexploded Bomb. Norton, 1958. y.
       A tale of the British bomb disposal service.

3189   Hassel, Sven. Comrades in Arms. Trans. from the Danish.
         Corgi, 1968. y. P.
       A tale of the Danish underground in action against the
       Nazis.

3190   _____. Legion of the Damned. Trans. from the Danish.
         Farrar, Straus, 1957. y.
       A look at the exploits of the German penal battalion on the
       Eastern Front.

3191   _____. S. S. General. Trans. from the Danish. Corgi,
         1972. y. P.
       A story about a German officer in Belgium.

3192   Heinrich, Willi. The Crack of Doom. Trans. from the Ger-
         man. Farrar, Straus, 1958. y.
       Wehrmacht Sergeant Kolodzi and his unit battle Czech par-
       tisans in 1944.

3193 _____ . The Cross of Iron.   Trans. from the German.
         Bobbs-Merrill, 1956.   y.
         Cut off behind Russian lines, Corporal Steiner's platoon
         seeks to regain German positions near Krimskaya.

3194 _____ . The Crumbling Fortress.   Trans. from the Ger-
         man.   Dial, 1964.   y.
         A motley collection of Germans is trapped between French
         Marquis irregulars and advancing American troops in sum-
         mer 1944.

3195 Heller, Joseph.   Catch-22.   Simon & Schuster, 1962.   Rpr.
         1973.   y.
         Colonel Cathcart, fanatical leader of the 256th Bomb Squad-
         ron's B-25's, operating from the Mediterranean island of
         Pianosa in 1943, keeps increasing his men's quota of mis-
         sions; in impossible comic moments the unit's lead bom-
         bardier, Captain Yossarian, tries to beat the system be-
         fore finally deserting.

3196 Hemingway, Leicester.   The Sound of the Trumpet.   Holt,
         1953.   y.
         In this first novel by Ernest Hemingway's younger brother,
         G. I. cameraman Danforth Granham shoots his way across
         Europe from D-Day to V-E Day.

3197 Hendryx, Gene.   Semper Fi.   Pageant, 1959.   y.
         A fictional account of the U.S. 9th Marines in Pacific ac-
         tion.

3198 Henriques, Robert D. Q.   The Commander.   Viking, 1968.
         y.
         Pictures the constant training and waiting of a British
         Commando captain during 1940-1941 and quick, bloody
         raids.

3199 _____ . No Arms, No Armour.   Farrar, Straus, 1940.   y.
         A young British Army officer in Libya is influenced by
         two older men.

3200 _____ . Red Over Green.   Viking, 1956.   y.
         A fearful ex-London solicitor becomes a hero during a
         commando raid.

3201 _____ . The Voice of the Trumpet.   Farrar, 1943.   y.
         Exiting a Norwegian raid, a group of British Commandos
         are cut off by the Germans at the last moment and deci-
         mated.

3202 Herber, William.   Tomorrow to Love.   Coward-McCann,
         1958.   y.
         Lieutenant Mike Andreas and his company of 2nd Marine
         leathernecks battle the Japanese on Saipan in 1944.

3203 Hersey, John. A Bell for Adano. Knopf, 1944. Rpr. 1970.
         y.
         An American major helps to rebuild an occupied Italian
         town.

3204 _____ . The Wall. Knopf, 1950. Rpr. 1967. y.
         Follows the adventures of a group of Jews during the War-
         saw Uprising.

3205 _____ . The War Lover. Knopf, 1960. y.
         B-17 pilot Buzz Marrow grows too fond of action in the
         8th Air Force strategic bombing campaign against Germany.

3206 Hewes, J. V. The High Courts of Heaven: A Story of the
         R. A. F. Doubleday, 1943. y.
         Four British pilots join in the Battle of Britain on Au-
         gust 5, 1940; all are shot down and killed by September 16.

3207 Heydenau, Friedrich. Wrath of Eagles. Dutton, 1943. y.
         An American officer fights with the Chetnik guerrillas in
         Yugoslavia.

3208 Heym, Stefan. The Crusaders. Little, Brown, 1948. y.
         Follows the exploits of an American division from Nor-
         mandy through the liberation of Paris, across to Germany,
         in the Battle of the Bulge, and into the occupation of a
         Ruhr industrial city.

      Higgins, Jack, pseud. See Patterson, Henry.

3209 Hirschorn, Richard. Target Mayflower. Harcourt, 1977.
         Rpr. 1978. y.
         Nazi agents liberate a P. O. W. camp in America and lead
         the released soldiers on a raid against a secret train
         loaded with uranium for the U. S. atomic bomb project.

3210 Hoffman, William. The Trumpet Unblown. Doubleday, 1955.
         y.
         The experiences of a U. S. soldier in a field hospital during
         the Battle of the Bulge.

3211 _____ . Yancey's War. Doubleday, 1966.
         A stout, aging misfit Army enlistee rapidly becomes de-
         spised by his fellows for his boastful manner and shifty
         habits.

3212 Home, Michael. Attack in the Desert. Morrow, 1942. y.
         A British aviator helps Free French troops attack Italian
         outposts in 1940 Libya.

3213 Howard, Clark. The Doomsday Squad. Weybright & Talley,
         1970. y.
         Fugitive U. S. Army sergeant Stoner leads six volunteers

in a suicidal decoy mission in support of MacArthur's
on a Pacific island.

3214 Howe, George. Call It Treason. Viking, 1949. y.
      Three German P.O.W.'s in the pay of the U.S. Army are
      parachuted as saboteurs into the Third Reich.

3215 Hubler, Richard G. I've Got Mine. Putnam, 1946. y.
      Based on the U.S. Marine landing at Choiseul Island as a
      diversion to the 1943 invasion of Bougainville.

3216 _____. Man in the Sky. Duell, Sloan, 1957. y.
      The exploits of A.A.F. ace fighter pilot Gib Miller.

3217 Hughes, Paul. Challenge at Changsha. Macmillan, 1946. y.
      The 1941-1942 Japanese effort to take a town in China's
      Hunan Province and its impact on the invaders and defend-
      ers.

3218 _____. Retreat from Rostov. Random House, 1943. y.
      Pictures the lot of the soldiers involved in the November
      1941 Russo-German battle for the city.

3219 Huie, William B. The Hero of Iwo Jima and Other Stories.
      New American Library, 1962. y.
      The author's World War II yarns reprinted from Cavalier
      Magazine.

3220 Hunt, Howard. Limit of Darkness. Random House, 1944. y.
      The experiences of a group of Cactus Air Force flyers at
      Henderson Field, Guadalcanal, during one 24-hour period,
      including a raid on a Japanese port.

3221 Hurwood, B. J. Assault on Bordeaux. Belmont-Tower, 1978.
      y. P.
      American G.I.'s attack the German defenses of a French
      city.

3222 Ingersoll, Ralph M. Wine of Violence. Farrar, Straus,
      1951. y.
      An ex-staff officer becomes a combat soldier at Normandy
      and into the Ardennes.

      Innes, Hammond, pseud. See Hammond-Innes, Ralph.

      Jacot, B. L., jt. author. See Astrup, Helen.

3223 Jahn, Mike. Black Sheep Squadron: Devil in the Slot. Ban-
      tam, 1978. y. P.
      "Pappy" Boyington's Marine fighter squadron takes on a
      crack Japanese ace.

3224 Jameson, Storm. The Fort. Macmillan, 1941. y.

French soldiers attempt to defend their country during the
1940 Blitz.

3225 Jamieson, Leland S. Attack! Morrow, 1940. y.
U. S. carrier planes attack German vessels attempting to
establish a base in South America.

3226 Johnston, Jennifer. How Many Miles to Babylon. Doubleday,
1974. y.
Two Irish boys enlist in the British Army to fight in Normandy.

3227 Jonas, Carl. Beachhead on the Wind. Little, Brown, 1945.
y.
An American beach party is put ashore on Tartu in the
Aleutians and left to shift for itself against the Japanese.

3228 Jones, James. From Here to Eternity. Scribner's, 1951.
The joys and problems of Private Robert Prewitt and First
Sergeant Milton Warden of the American Army in Hawaii
until just after the Pearl Harbor attack; this volume was
called by the Saturday Review of Literature "the best picture of Army life ever written by an American. "

3229 _____. The Pistol. Scribner's, 1958. y.
Private Richard Mast obtains and wields a hand gun on
Pearl Harbor day in Hawaii, but refuses to surrender it
to his friends or superiors after the attack because it has
become a symbol of salvation to him.

3230 _____. The Thin Red Line. Scribner's, 1962. Rpr.
1975. y.
Company C-for-Charlie is examined in a many-leveled tale
of the bitter U. S. Marine battle for Guadalcanal.

3231 _____. Whistle. Delacorte, 1978.
Four wounded soldiers are sent from the Pacific to a hospital in Tennessee.

3232 Jordan, Roland K. Dawn Command. Belmont-Tower, 1978.
y. P.
A single U. S. bomber squadron must attack a heavily de-
fended Japanese convoy in early 1942.

3233 Julitte, Pierre. Block 26: Sabotage at Buchenwald. Trans.
from the French. Doubleday, 1971. y.
French Marquis P. O. W. 's blow up a German V-2 assembly
plant inside the infamous concentration camp.

3234 Kadish, M. R. Point of Honor. Random House, 1951. y.
A story about American artillerymen in the Italian campaign.

3235   Kapusta, Paul. Avenging Eagle: War in the Air Over Poland,
        France, and Great Britain. Associated Booksellers,
        1959. y. P.
        Polish flyers escape to join other Allied air forces.

3236   Kark, Leslie. Red Rain. Macmillan, 1946. y.
        In June 1944 an R. A. F. Lancaster bomber is downed over
        Munich; the lives of its seven-member crew are reviewed,
        as is the successful escape of the lone survivor.

3237   Karl, S. W. Tank Fighters. Manor, 1978. y. P.
        Joe Harmon's American company battles a German regi-
        ment at Monte Cassino.

3238   Karp, Marvin A. , ed. The Brave One. Popular Library,
        1965. y. P.
        Six tales of combat from such magazines as the Saturday
        Evening Post.

3239   Kata, Elizabeth. Someone Will Conquer Them. St. Martin's,
        1962. y.
        A native girl protects a U.S. flyer downed over Japan in
        late 1944.

3240   Kazakevich, Emmanuil G. Spring on the Oder. Trans. from
        the Russian. Foreign Languages Publishing House,
        1953. y.
        Soviet troops battle the Germans in Russia in the spring
        of 1944.

3241   Keefe, Frederick L. The Investigating Officer. Delacorte,
        1966. y.
        Why did a U.S. Army officer shoot two German S.S. of-
        ficers while escorting them to a P.O.W. camp?

3242   Keith, Agnes N. Beloved Exiles. Little, Brown, 1972.
        A British officer and his American wife are captured in
        Borneo by the Japanese.

3243   Kelly, John. The Unexpected Peace. Gambit, 1970.
        A U.S. Army company from Cebu is sent to Japan for oc-
        cupation duty on V-J Day.

3244   _____ . The Wooden Wolf. Dutton, 1976. y.
        Two R. A. F. Mosquitos are sent to destroy Hitler in his
        private train under cover of a Bomber Command raid on
        Berlin.

3245   Kelly, Michael. Assault. Harcourt, 1969. y.
        Four S. O. E. operatives are parachuted into Denmark to
        help the Resistance destroy a German factory near Copen-
        hagen.

3246 Keneally, Thomas. A Season in Purgatory. Harcourt, 1977.
An English surgeon is parachuted into Yugoslavia to treat the wounded of the 22nd Partisan Division.

3247 Kennedy, Byron. The Eagles Roar. Harper, 1942. y.
Exploits of American volunteers serving in the R. A. F. Eagle Squadrons, 1940-1941.

3248 Kent, Alexander. Winged Escort. By Douglas Reeman, pseud. Putnam, 1976. y.
Tim Rowan, Fleet Air Arm pilot, finds adventure and danger in combat from a Royal Navy escort carrier in the North Atlantic and later in the Pacific.

3249 Kersh, Gerald. Faces in a Dusty Picture. Heinemann, 1945. y.
Examines the thoughts and reactions of a group of British soldiers before and during a battle with the Italians in the Western Desert.

3250   . Sergeant Nelson of the Guards. Winston, 1945. y.
After losing an eye during the fall of France, a Coldstream Guard becomes a tough training officer.

3251   . They Die with Their Boots Clean. Heinemann, 1967. y.
Combat experiences of British soldiers in the Middle East.

3252 Kessel, Joseph. The Army of Shadows. Trans. from the French. Knopf, 1944. y.
The French Marquis battles the Nazis.

3253 Killens, John O. And Then We Heard the Thunder. Knopf, 1963. y.
A black American amphibious regiment is led by a white officer into South Pacific combat.

3254 King, David. The Brave and the Damned. Paperback Library, 1966. y. P.
Sergeant Bailey leads a unit of Merrill's Marauders on a dangerous mission deep into Burma.

3255 Kirschner, Fritz. SS. Associated Booksellers, 1959. y. P.
A German S. S. conscript joins the French Marquis out of revulsion to Nazi methods.

3256 Kirst, Hans H. The Adventures of Private Faust. Trans. from the German. Coward-McCann, 1971.
At a British P. O. W. camp near Cairo in 1945, two British sergeants must deal with a cunning subordinate.

3257   . The Affairs of the Generals. Trans. from the
German. Coward-McCann, 1978. y.
Hitler and Göring maltreat two generals who had prevented
them from taking control of the German Army in earlier
days.

3258   . Brothers-in-Arms. Trans. from the German.
Harper, 1967.
Explores the unhappy death of a Wehrmacht soldier who,
"killed in action," returns alive after the war.

3259   . Forward Gunner Asch. Trans. from the German.
Little, Brown, 1956. Rpr. 1976. y.
An overzealous officer wants Asch and his "mates" to show
more enthusiasm for the war on the Russian front; sequel
to The Revolt of Gunner Asch, below.

3260   . Gunner Asch Goes to War. Trans. from the German. Little, Brown, 1956. y.
In the winter of 1942, Asch and his comrades are too
comfortable on the Eastern Front to suit a new commander.

3261   . Hero in the Tower. Trans. from the German.
Coward-McCann, 1972. Rpr. 1973. y.
A crack Nazi artillery outfit in Occupied France is plagued
by a series of fatal and mysterious accidents.

3262   . Last Stop Camp Seven. Trans. from the German.
Coward-McCann, 1969. y.
An American P.O.W. camp commander works quick judgment on German prisoners, while his Jewish "exec" cau-
tions that guilt must be proved.

3263   . The Night of the Generals. Trans. from the German. Harper, 1963. Rpr. 1978.
Which of three Wehrmacht generals murdered a prostitute
in the wartime Warsaw of 1942?

3264   . The Night of the Long Knives. Trans. from the
German. Coward-McCann, 1976. Rpr. 1977. y.
When the body of a middle-aged man is found in Switzer-
land, investigators detail his involvement with the ultra-
secret S.S. Wesel Group during the war.

3265   . The Officer Factory. Trans. from the German.
Harper, 1963.
Pictures the corrupt goings on at a Wehrmacht O.C.S.
camp in early 1944.

3266   . The Return of Gunner Asch. Trans. from the
German. Little, Brown, 1957. Rpr. 1976. y.
Asch's company makes a doomed stand as the Russians
close in on Berlin in 1945; sequel to Forward Gunner Asch.

3267   _____. The Revolt of Gunner Asch. Trans. from the Ger-
        man. Little, Brown, 1955. Rpr. 1975. y.
        Private Asch takes on three sadistic noncoms who are
        causing trouble for his company.

3268   _____. Soldiers' Revolt. Trans. from the German. Har-
        per, 1966. y.
        The July 20, 1944 bomb plot against Hitler as seen by
        Captain von Brackwede.

3269   _____. The Wolves. Trans. from the German. Coward-
        McCann, 1968. y.
        A villager in East Prussia, who is outraged by the excesses
        of the local Nazis, engineers the garrison's destruction.

3270   Klaas, Joe. Maybe I'm Dead. Macmillan, 1955. y.
        A group of Americans are part of a large number of Allied
        airmen-P. O. W. 's who are evacuated by the Germans from
        Sagan (Silesia) in January 1945.

3271   Kluge, Alexander. The Battle. Trans. from the German.
        McGraw-Hill, 1967. y.
        Follows a group of German soldiers into Stalingrad.

3272   Koontz, Dean R. Hanging On. Evans, 1973.
        A company of G.I. misfits is parachuted into France by a
        crackpot general to carry out a demented mission.

3273   Kramer, Gerhard. We Shall March Again. Trans. from the
        German. Putnam, 1955.
        Traces the activities of one Wehrmacht civilian-soldier,
        Victor Velten, during the war.

3274   Kuby, Erich. The Sitzkrieg of Private Stefan. Trans. from
        the German. Farrar, Straus, 1962. y.
        A satire on German militarism; a misfit is conscripted in-
        to the German Army early in the war.

3275   Kuniczak, W. S. The Thousand Hour Day. Dial, 1967. y.
        Focuses on the first days of the German-Polish war of
        September 1939 with emphasis on the resistance of General
        Janusz Prus.

3276   Kuznetsov, Anatoly. Babi Yar: A Documentary. Trans. from
        the Russian. Dial, 1967.
        German soldiers execute 50,000 Jews in a ravine outside
        Kiev known as Babi Yar.

3277   Kyle, Duncan. Black Camelot. St. Martin's, 1978. y.
        A Nazi commando, set up as a pawn in a last-ditch effort
        against the Allies, eludes his betrayers and eventually dis-
        covers Himmler's castle, where devastating secrets of war
        remain hidden.

3278   Lakin, Richard. A Body Fell on Berlin. Putnam, 1943. y.
        A former detective and now an R.A.F. flight lieutenant in-
        vestigates a reconnaissance photo that shows a body drop-
        ping away from a bomber during a raid on Berlin; the plot
        thickens when it appears that no one is missing from the
        Lancaster in question.

3279   Lalic, Michailo. The Wailing Mountain. Trans. from the
            Yugoslav. Harcourt, 1965.
        The adventures of a Red partisan who is cut off from his
        band in wartime Montenegro.

3280   Lamott, Kenneth C. The Stockade. Little, Brown, 1952.
        American soldiers are ordered to guard 5,000 Okinawans
        and Koreans on an island in the Pacific at the time of
        V-J Day.

3281   Landon, Christopher. Ice Cold in Alexandria. Sloane, 1957.
            y.
        Two English soldiers and two nurses escape from Tobruck,
        encircled by Rommel's Afrika Korps in the 1942.

3282   Landon, Joseph. Angle of Attack. Doubleday, 1952. y.
        A U.S. bomber crew violates the rules of "civilized" war-
        fare and becomes a primary objective of enemy vengeance.

3283   Landsborough, Gordon. Battery from Hellfire. Cassell,
            1958. y.
        Focuses on a British artillery unit during the Western
        Desert campaign.

3284   Larsen, Milar. Runner. Pyramid, 1975. y. P.
        During the Battle of the Bulge, Sioux Indian sergeant Jay
        Runner helps a shell-shocked private escape the German
        onslaught.

3285   Larteguy, Jean. The Bronze Drums. Trans. from the
            French. Knopf, 1968. y.
        Francois Ricq is dropped into Laos in 1944 to form a re-
        sistance group for operations against the Japanese.

3286   Lay, Beirne, and Sy Bartlett. Twelve O'Clock High. Harper,
            1948. y.
        Brigadier General Frank Savage's trials as he tries to re-
        juvenate a demoralized 8th Air Force bomber group;
        based on an actual event; Savage was well portrayed by
        Gregory Peck in the movie version.

3287   Leckie, Robert. Marines! Bantam, 1960. y. P.
        Ten short stories about U.S. Marines in Pacific action.

3288   Ledig, Gert. Tortured Earth. Trans. from the German.
            Regnery, 1956. y.

Learning of his family's death, a German major orders
his unit to make a suicidal attack on the defenses of Len-
ingrad.

3289 Lee, John. The Ninth Man. Doubleday, 1976. Rpr. 1977.
          y.
      A White House liaison colonel tracks down a Nazi assassin
      sent to kill President Roosevelt.

3290 _____. The Thirteenth Hour. Doubleday, 1978. y.
      A U.S. Army intelligence officer, trapped in Berlin in late
      April 1945, learns the "truth" about Hitler's end when his
      Russian captors send him on a commando raid to get the
      Führer.

3291 Lefevre, Gui. We Were There. Associated Booksellers,
          1960. y. P.
      Three Belgian fighter pilots escape the fall of their nation
      in 1940 and flee to Britain to fight with the R. A. F.

3292 Leicester, Grant. Kamikaze. Associated Booksellers, 1960.
          y. P.
      Japanese suicide pilots harry the U. S. fleet off Okinawa.

3293 Leigh, Michael. Comrade Forest. McGraw-Hill, 1947. y.
      Russian partisans hit German weak points; based on the
      real-life story of the woman guerrilla leader Lija Ivanovna
      Chaikind.

3294 Lenz, Siegfried. The Survivor. Trans. from the German.
          Hill & Wang, 1965. y.
      The story of a Resistance leader in German-occupied Nor-
      way.

3295 Leonard, George. Shoulder the Sky. McDowell, 1961. y.
      The experiences of two R. A. F. flight instructors at an
      A. A. F. school in 1944 Georgia.

3296 Leonov, Leonid M. Chariot of Wrath. Trans. from the Rus-
          sian. L. B. Fischer, 1946. y.
      Out of touch, a lone Soviet tank makes a "dagger raid" on
      a German truck convoy.

3297 Leopold, Christopher. Blood and Guts Is Going Nuts. Double-
          day, 1977. How Patton laid plans for World War III
      with the Russians.

3298 Leslie, Peter. The Bastard Brigade. Pyramid, 1971. y.
          P.
      Malcontent U. S. G. I. 's battle the Germans in 1944 France.

3299 Lestienne, Voldemar. Furioso. Trans. from the French.
          St. Martin's, 1973. y.

Three French Marquis commandos seek to rescue a propaganda folio from Reinhardt Heydrich.

3300 Levitt, Saul. The Sun Is Silent. Harper, 1951. y.
Follows the crew of one U.S. 8th Air Force B-17 on 25 missions over Germany.

3301 Lewis, Cecil. Pathfinders. Davies, 1944. y.
Pictures the lives of six men comprising an R. A. F. bomber crew as flashbacked on the night their plane was shot down.

3302 Lewis, Elizabeth. When the Typhoon Blows. Winston, 1942.
y.
Depicts the Japanese push into China.

3303 Lewis, Warfield, ed. Fighting Words. Lippincott, 1944. y.
Subtitle. --Stories and Cartoons by Members of the Armed Forces of America.

3304 Linakis, Stephen. In the Spring the War Ended. Putnam,
1965. y.
Chronicles the artful dodging of military police by a U.S. Army deserter in Europe during the final days of the war.

3305 Lind, Jakov. Landscape in Concrete. Trans. from the German. Grove, 1966. P.
At the end of the war, reality and fantasy are indistinguishable to a German sergeant who travels across Europe in search of his sanity.

3306 Linklater, Eric. Private Angelo. Cape, 1947. y.
An unenthusiastic Italian soldier fights for Mussolini, Hitler, and later, the British.

3307 Linna, Vaino. The Unknown Soldier. Trans. from the Finnish. Putnam, 1957. y.
A Finnish battalion versus the Russians in the 1941-1944 "Continuation War. "

3308 Llewellyn, Richard. None but the Lonely Heart. Macmillan,
1969. y.
A London youth saves himself from a life of crime by enlisting.

3309 Lodwick, John. Aegean Adventure. Dodd, Mead, 1946. y.
British commandos raid a German-held island off the coast of Greece.

3310 Loewengard, Heidi H. Without Orders. By Martha Albrand,
pseud. Little, Brown, 1943. y.
An American soldier works with the Italian underground.

3311 Lolos, Kimon. Respite. Trans. from the Greek. Harper,
1961. y.

Exhibiting a hatred of war and a devotion to duty, a Greek
lieutenant fights to stem the Nazi invasion of his country
in 1941.

3312 Loomis, Edward. End of a War. Ballantine, 1957. y. P.
Follows a U.S. infantryman from boot camp to combat in
Belgium and Germany in 1944-1945.

3313 The Lost Legions. Trans. from the Italian. Knopf, 1968.
y.
Three tales, including Mario Tobino's "The Deserts of
Libya" and Mario R. Stern's "The Sergeant in the Snow,"
showing the disintegration of Italian army morale in North
Africa and central Russia.

3314 Ludlum, Robert. The Rhinemann Exchange. Dial, 1974.
Rpr. 1975. y.
A U.S. colonel is involved in the immoral swap of U.S.
diamonds for German gyroscopes; made into a TV mini-
series.

3315 Lull, Roderick. Call to Battle. Doubleday, 1943. y.
Home guard troops battle a Japanese paratroop force attempting to capture a town on a western American river.

3316 Lynds, Dennis. Combat Soldier. New American Library,
1962. y. P.
A young G.I. feels death is a greater enemy than the Germans he is fighting.

3317 Lyon, Allan. Toward an Unknown Station. Macmillan, 1948.
y.
The problems and sufferings of U.S. infantrymen fighting
in Europe; presented in the tradition of newsman Ernie
Pyle.

3318 McAlister, Ian. The Skylark Mission. Fawcett, 1973. y.
P.
A small group of British commandos and Singapore survivors must hold open the Vitiaz Straits, near New Guinea,
in early 1942 to allow other survivors to reach Australia.

3319 McClenaghan, Jack. Moving Target. Harcourt, 1966.
Depicts the difficulties of an army deserter in wartime
New Zealand.

3320 MacCuish, David. Do Not Go Gentle. Doubleday, 1960. y.
An immature U.S. Marine gradually learns to overcome
his fear of combat in the South Pacific.

3321 McDougall, Colin. Execution. St. Martin's, 1958. y.
During the ferocity of the Canadian Corps' Italian advance,
a soldier is shot for a crime he did not commit.

3321a McGivern, William P. Soldiers of '44. Arbor House, 1979.
        y.
        An American gun crew is cut off on a snowy hill during
        the Battle of the Bulge.

3322   MacKaye, David L. Twenty-Fifth Mission. Longmans, Green,
        1945. y.
        Returning from their 25th mission, an A. A. F. bomber
        crew is forced to bail out over Denmark where they join
        the local underground.

3323   McLaughlin, Robert. The Side of the Angels. Knopf, 1947.
        y.
        The reactions of two U. S. Army brothers to their Medi-
        terranean service.

3324   McLean, Alistair. Force 10 from Navarone. Doubleday,
        1968. Rpr. 1978. y.
        Three heroes from The Guns of Navarone are dropped into
        Yugoslavia to help the partisans mount a diversion to draw
        the Germans out of Italy; made into a movie.

3325   . The Guns of Navarone. Doubleday, 1957. Rpr.
        1977. y.
        A British Army sabotage team is sent to destroy a German
        coastal battery blocking the evacuation of a small island in
        the eastern Mediterranean; made into a movie.

3326   . Where Eagles Dare. Doubleday, 1967. Rpr. 1978.
        y.
        British commandos attempt to rescue an American general
        from a forbidding German mountain prison in Bavaria;
        made into a movie.

3327   McSwigan, Marie. Juan of Manila. Button, 1947. y.
        A Filipino youth fights as a guerrilla after the fall of Cor-
        regidor.

3328   Mailer, Norman. The Naked and the Dead. Rinehart, 1948.
        Rpr. 1977. y.
        Pictures the reactions of the members of an American
        platoon to their part in the invasion of a Japanese-held is-
        land.

3329   Majdalaux, Fred. Patrol. Houghton Mifflin, 1953. y.
        Demonstrates a futile 24-hour period in the life of a young
        U. S. officer in 1943 Tunisia.

3330   Maltz, Albert. The Cross and the Arrow. Little, Brown,
        1944. y.
        Why does an honored German factory worker fire dry hay
        to attract the attention of R. A. F. bombers to his facility?

3331 Mandel, George. The Wax Boom. Random House, 1962. y.
Demonstrates the psychological effects of bad leadership
and extreme stress on an American platoon serving on a
tough assignment in Holland late in 1944.

3332 Mann, Mendel. At the Gates of Moscow. Trans. from the
French. St. Martin's, 1964. y.
A biographical novel based on one year in the life of a
Polish Jew who served in the Soviet Army during the 1941
invasion of Russia.

3332a Manning, Olivia. The Battle Lost and Won. Atheneum, 1979.
Men from Cairo join the British for the Battle of El Alamein.

3333 March, Anthony. Quit for the Next. Scribner's, 1945. y.
An American cavalry troop retreats down Luzon to Bataan
in 1942.

3334 Margulies, Leo, ed. Flying Wildcats. Hampton, 1943. y.
Twelve tales of aerial combat by various authors.

3335 Marlowe, Stephen. The Valkyrie Encounter. Putnam, 1978.
y.
Anti-Nazi German officers conspire to assassinate Hitler.

3336 Masselink, Ben. The Deadliest Weapon. Little, Brown,
1965. y.
Explores the conflicting emotions of a young U. S. Marine
who is sent into battle on a Pacific atoll.

3337 Masters, John. The Field Marshal's Memoirs. Doubleday,
1975. y.
An old general matches his war recollections with the aide
assigned to help him write his memoirs.

3338 Masterson, Graham. The Devils of D-Day. Pinnacle, 1978.
y. P.
Focuses on an abandoned Allied tank lost on June 6, 1944.

3339 Mathai, K. Easo. Blood-Stained Footprints. Army Educational Stores (New Delhi), 1970. y.
Combat between Indian troops and the Japanese in 1943-
1944.

3340 Matheson, Richard. The Beardless Warriors. Little, Brown,
1960. y.
Young Everett Hackermeyer's experiences as a combat soldier in Europe.

3341 Meissner, Hans. Duel in the Snow. Trans. from the German. Morrow, 1942. y.
Japanese scouts battle American soldiers in the Aleutians.

3342   Melchoir, Ib. The Haigerlock Project. Harper, 1977. Rpr.
            1978. y.
        Two U.S. commandos are sent deep into Germany to de-
        stroy Nazi work on an A-bomb project late in the war.

3343   _____. Order of Battle. Harper, 1972.
        A crack German guerrilla unit known as the Werewolves
        attempt to kill General Eisenhower in the last days of the
        war.

3344   Merle, Robert. Weekend at Dunkirk. Trans. from the
            French. Knopf, 1952. y.
        The difficulties of a group of French soldiers stranded on
        the beaches during the 1940 evacuation.

3345   Merrick, Gordon. The Strumpet Wind. Morrow, 1947. y.
        An American officer aids the French Resistance.

3346   Meyer, Karl H. The Bloodiest Bivouac. Manor, 1978. y.
            P.
        When Patton's 3rd U.S. Army exhausts its fuel supply, the
        G.I.'s think they can catch their breath.

3347/8 Meyneng, Mayette. Broken Arc. Harper, 1944. y.
        Just after his marriage, a young French soldier goes off
        to help his comrades halt the 1940 German invasion and
        dies a hero.

3349   Middleton, Jan. Learn to Say Goodbye. Dodd, Mead, 1965.
            y.
        The adventures of a young American nurse serving in a
        forward combat area.

3350   Miller, E. F. The Third Battle. Manor, 1978. y. P.
        U.S. 8th Air Force B-17's, just 200 miles past their tar-
        get and heading for home, are met by Luftwaffe Focke-
        Wulfs in the third and fiercest German interception of this
        particular mission.

3351   Miller, Merle. Island 49. Crowell, 1945. y.
        Examines the thoughts of American G.I.'s about to land on
        a Japanese-held island.

3352   Monsarrat, Nicholas. The Kappillan of Malta. Morrow,
            1974. Rpr. 1975. y.
        Smartly aided by the R.A.F., the populace of Malta re-
        sists the Axis aerial onslaught of 1941-1942.

3353   Monsey, Derek. The Hero. Knopf, 1961. y.
        Having escaped a German P.O.W. camp, a young British
        Army officer faces a brutal winter in the snows of north-
        ern Italy.

3354 Montgomery, R. G.   Rough Riders Ho! David McKay, 1946.
          y.
          U. S. tanks drive into Germany in 1945.

3355 Moore, Donald.   Scramble Six Hurricanes.   Doubleday, 1958.
          y.
          R. A. F. pilots catapulted from merchant ships help a Brit-
          ish convoy survive an Atlantic crossing during the winter
          of 1943.

3356 Morriss, Mark.   The Proving Ground.   Duell, Sloan, 1951.
          y.
          Follows the adventures of a G. I. from training camp to
          combat in Europe.

3357 Moss, Sidney and Samuel.   Thy Men Shall Fall.   Ziff-Davis,
          1948.   y.
          U. S. soldier George Walburne fights in North Africa,
          France, Holland, and Germany.

3358 Mott, Michael.   Helmet and Wasps.   Houghton Mifflin, 1964.
          y.
          The fictional diary of a young German officer in Italy re-
          veals his change of attitude toward war and life.

3359 Mullally, Frederic.   Hitler Has Won.   Simon & Schuster,
          1975.   y.
          The Germans win the war in 1941 and commence building
          their Reich.

3360 Mullins, Richard.   Sound the Last Bugle.   Cape, 1960.   y.
          English soldiers in combat during the last month of the
          European war.

3361 Mulville, William.   Fire Mission.   Ballantine, 1957.   y.   P.
          Follows U. S. artillery battery "Alligator-Able" in the Bat-
          tle of the Bulge and the drive into Germany.

3362 Myrer, Anton O.   The Big War.   Appleton, 1957.   y.
          Follows a group of U. S. Marines from boot camp to action
          in the Pacific.

3363 Nablo, James B.   Long November.   Dutton, 1946.   y.
          Wounded and hiding in an Italian foxhole, a soldier must
          decide whether or not take out a nearby German machine
          gun post.

3364 Nathanson, E. M.   The Dirty Dozen.   Random House, 1965.
          Rpr. 1966.   y.
          "Project Amnesty" called for the commando training of a
          dozen condemned U. S. Army criminals and the dropping
          of the men behind the lines in France to take out a Ger-
          man headquarters on the eve of D-Day.

3365   Newhafer, Richard L.   The Last Tallyho.   Putnam, 1964.   y.
       Five U. S. Navy carrier pilots and their combat exploits
       in the Pacific.

3366   Nicole, Christopher.   The Thunder and the Shouting.   Double-
          day, 1969.
       Follows the fate of the Polish Janski family in the war
       from 1939-1944.

3367   Nolan, Frederick.   The Algonquin Project.   Morrow, 1974.
          Rpr. 1976.   y.
       U. S. Army officers plot to assassinate General George
       Patton.

3368   _____ .   The Mittenwald Syndicate.   Morrow, 1976.   Rpr.
          1977.   y.
       U. S. Army officers plot to escape Europe with millions in
       Nazi booty.

3369   _____ .   The Ritter Double Cross.   Morrow, 1975.   y.
       British commandos are parachuted into Germany in 1940
       to destroy a Nazi nerve gas factory.

3370   Nordhoff, Charles B., and James Norman Hall.   High Bar-
          baree.   Little, Brown, 1945.   y.
       Depicts a battle between a U. S. N. P. B. Y. patrol bomber
       and a Japanese submarine.

3371   Norton, Alice M.   The Sword Is Drawn.   By Andre Norton,
          pseud.   Houghton Mifflin, 1944.   y.
       A Dutch lad escapes the Japanese invasion of Java and re-
       turns to his own country, after training in the U. S., to
       fight with the underground against the Germans.

       Norton, Andre, pseud.   See Norton, Alice M.

3372   Norway, Nevil Shute.   Landfall, a Channel Story.   By Nevil
          Shute, pseud.   Morrow, 1940.   y.
       An R. A. F. Coastal Command pilot believes he has sunk a
       British submarine by mistake.

3373   _____ .   Pastoral.   By Nevil Shute, pseud.   Morrow, 1944.
          Rpr. 1973.   y.
       A W. A. A. F. officer finds her love for an R. A. F. bomber
       pilot is certain when his plane is reported missing during
       a raid over France.

3374   Ogilvie, Charlton, Jr.   The Marauders.   Fawcett, 1964.   y.
          P.
       Fictionalized exploits of Merrill's Marauders in Burma,
       1944.

3375   Ollis, Robert.   101 Nights.   Cassell, 1957.   y.

Pictures the work of an R. A. F. radio intercept and jam-
ming squadron, based on the author's experiences with
No. 107 Squadron.

3376 Olson, Alton M. Hell Bent for Blitzkrieg. Greenwhich, 1962.
         y. P.
      G. I. 's battle the Germans in France and Holland in 1944.

3377 Olson, Lloyd E. Skip Bomber. Ace, 1960. y. P.
      A U. S. B-17 Flying Fortress mounts daring attacks on the
      Japanese during the early days of the Pacific war.

3378 Ooka, Shokei. Fires on the Plain. Trans. from the Japa-
         nese. Knopf, 1957. y.
      Japanese soldier Tamura recalls the American invasion of
      Leyte in 1944.

3379 Opitz, Karlludwig. The General. Trans. from the German.
         Stein & Day, 1957. y.
      A batman or valet, Sergeant-Major Horlacker reveals his
      military relationship with his general from D-Day to V-E
      Day and the strain of constant reversals in fortune.

3380 O'Rourke, Frank. "E" Company. Simon & Schuster, 1945.
         y.
      A young U. S. Army officer forges a top infantry company
      and tests it in combat during and after the North African
      landings of 1942.

3381 Pashko, Stanley. Ross Duncan at Bataan. Messner, 1950.
         y.
      A young American soldier battles the Japanese in the
      Philippines in 1942.

3382 Patterson, Henry. The Eagle Has Landed. By Jack Higgins,
         pseud. Holt, 1975. Rpr. 1976. y.
      A crack group of specially-trained German airborne troops
      lands on the Norfolk coast in 1943 with orders to kidnap
      or kill British Prime Minister Winston Churchill.

3383 _____. The Valhalla Exchange. By Jack Higgins, pseud.
         Stein & Day, 1977. Rpr. 1978. y.
      Martin Bormann escapes Berlin in 1945 with an "insurance
      plan" involving U. S. Army war hero Hamilton Canning.

3384 Patterson, Sarah. The Distant Summer. Simon & Schuster,
         1976. y.
      In 1943 R. A. F. gunner Johnny Stewart falls in love and
      must pursue the woman in light of the dangers of his pro-
      fession as a night bomber crewman.

3385 Paul, Louis. This Is My Brother. Crown, 1943. y.
      Five captured U. S. soldiers await execution by the Japa-
      nese.

3386   Pease, Howard. Heart of Danger. Doubleday, 1946.   y.
       Troops of the French Marquis battle the Germans.

3387   Pepper, Dan. The Enemy General. Monarch, 1960. y. P.
       French underground troops battle the Nazis; based on the
       screenplay for a Van Johnson movie.

3388   Perna, Albert F. The Glider Gladiators. Pine Hill, 1970.
           y.
       British and American glider pilots in operation in Holland,
       1944.

3389   Piper, David. Trial by Battle. Chilmark, 1966.   y.
       A Cambridge University graduate is posted to the Indian
       Army and killed while resisting the 1941 Japanese invasion
       of Malaya.

3390   Pirro, Ugo. A Thousand Betrayals. Trans. from the Italian.
           Simon & Schuster, 1961.   y.
       An Italian soldier, steeped in Fascist philosophy, becomes
       disillusioned when Italy surrenders in 1943.

3391   Plantz, Donald J. Sweeney Squadron. Doubleday, 1961.   y.
       Pictures a major's efforts to unite his command and turn
       his Florida-based outfit into a first-rate fighting unit.

3392   Plievier, Theodor. Berlin. Trans. from the German.
           Doubleday, 1957.   y.
       Shows the weak German resistance to the Russian onslaught
       of April 1945.

3393   _____. Moscow. Trans. from the German. Doubleday,
           1954.   y.
       A fictional recreation of events on the Moscow front from
       June 1941 to the spring of 1942.

3394   _____. Stalingrad. Trans. from the German. Appleton,
           1948.   y.
       A fictional recreation of the great battle from the view-
       point of German 6th Army soldiers.

3395   Potter, Jeffrey. Elephant Bridge. Viking, 1957.   y.
       Allied troops battle the Japanese in Burma.

3396   Powell, Anthony. The Soldier's Art. Little, Brown, 1966.
           Rpr. 1976.   y.
       A story of army life in Great Britain during the war.

3397   _____. The Valley of Bones. Little, Brown, 1964. Rpr.
           1976.   y.
       Lieutenant Nicholas Jenkins and his company of Welsh in-
       fantry in training just before the 1940 Dunkirk debacle.

3398 Powell, Richard P. The Soldier. Scribner's, 1960. y.
        A look at G.I. combat and human behavior set in the Chi-
        na-Burma-India Theater.

3399 Pozner, Vladimir. The Edge of the Sword. Trans. from the
        French. Viking, 1942. y.
        Follows the disintegration of one French regiment during
        the German invasion of 1940.

3400 Pratt, Rex K. You Tell My Son. Random House, 1959. y.
        Following a bloody South Pacific patrol, four surviving U.S.
        Army soldiers are ordered to whip a raw National Guard
        unit into shape for a new campaign.

3401 Pratt, Theodore. Mr. Winkle Goes to War. Duell, Sloan,
        1943. y.
        A henpecked husband goes off to war and comes home a
        combat hero.

3402 Price, Anthony. The '44 Vintage. Doubleday, 1978. y.
        The adventures of Corporal Butler in the British Chandos
        Force, which is assigned to capture a castle from the
        Germans.

3403 Pump, Hans W. Before the Great Snow. Trans. from the
        German. Harcourt, 1959. y.
        Soviet partisans attack German troops in Russian swamps,
        October 1942.

3404 Pynchon, Thomas. Gravity's Rainbow. Viking, 1973.
        A U.S. Army lieutenant in Britain is physically able to
        sense when the Germans will launch their rocket bombs;
        much sex.

3405 Quayle, Anthony. Eight Hours from England. Heinemann,
        1946. y.
        A British officer is landed on the Albanian coast to insure
        delivery of an arms shipment to the partisans.

3406 Quigley, Martin. Tent on Corsica. Lippincott, 1949. y.
        Depicts the exploits of a group of flyers in a U.S. 12th
        Air Force B-26 squadron based on Corsica in 1943-1944.

        Rame, David, pseud. See Divine, Arthur D.

3407 Ramrus, Al, and John Shaner. The Ludendorff Pirates.
        Doubleday, 1978. y.
        Twelve British commandos and a neutral American playboy
        hijack a German battleship and employ it to destroy a
        submarine facility.

3408 Redding, John M., and Thor Smith. Wake of Glory. Bobbs-
        Merrill, 1945. y.

Doug Bruce takes over the A. A. F. 's 834th Bomb Group in England, formerly led by a popular officer; similar in thrust to 12 O'Clock High.

Reeman, Douglas, pseud. See Kent, Alexander.

3409 Remarque, Erich M. A Time to Love and a Time to Die. Trans. from the German. Harcourt, 1954. y.
At the end of the war a kindly German soldier releases four Russian P. O. W. 's, one of whom turns about and kills his former guard.

3410 Rhys, John L. England Is My Village. Faber & Faber, 1941. y.
A collection of short stories including some of the first wartime fictional accounts of R. A. F. service; Flight Lieutenant Rhys, the author, was shot down on August 5, 1940 during the Battle of Britain.

3411 Rice, Earl. Tiger Lien Hawk. Fearon-Pitman, 1977. y. P.
A slow-reader's book that describes the aerial duel between a Japanese ace and a U. S. Flying Tiger over Thailand in early 1942.

3412 Richards, David. Four Men. Associated Booksellers, 1960. y. P.
Four British commandos take part in a number of special operations and heroic combats.

3413 _____ . Hurricane Squadron. Associated Booksellers, 1960. y. P.
British fighters battle Axis warplanes over the Mediterranean.

3414 Rigby, Ray. The Hill. John Day, 1965.
Five soldiers in a British prison camp in North Africa pit their wills against the staff and against the methods used to break their resistance.

3415 _____ . Jackson's War. Lippincott, 1967. y.
A British Tommy battles the Germans in North Africa.

3416 Rimanelli, Giose. The Day of the Lion. Trans. from the Italian. Random House, 1955. y.
Marco remembers his service as a soldier in Mussolini's Army from 1940 to 1943.

3417 Roberts, Cecil. Eight for Eternity. Doubleday, 1948. y.
Traces the lives of eight soldiers killed at Monte Cassino.

3418 _____ . The Labyrinth. Doubleday, 1944. y.
A young English nurse and her brother, an archaeologist, take part in the 1941 Battle of Crete.

Robertson, James A. , pseud. See Duncan, Robert L.

3419 Robinson, Derek. Kramer's War. Viking, 1977. Rpr. 1978.
      y.
      A bailed-out U. S. airman wreaks havoc on German occu-
      pation forces on the Channel Island of Jersey.

3420 Robinson, Wayne. Barbara. Doubleday, 1962. y.
      U. S. tanks smash their way into Germany.

3421 Rosenhaupt, Hans W. True Deceivers. Dodd, Mead, 1955.
      y.
      The psychological warfare work of U. S. Army Lieutenant
      Charles Croft in interrogating German prisoners.

3422 Ross, James E. The Dead Are Mine. David McKay, 1964.
      y.
      Sergeant Terry Lewis is ordered to take his squad on a
      suicidal attack at Anzio in early 1944.

3423 Rowland, Donald S. The Battle Done. Associated Booksel-
      lers, 1960. y. P.
      Follows three brothers in a British infantry unit during
      the D-Day invasion of Normandy.

3424 Roy, Jules. The Navigator. Knopf, 1955. y.
      Depicts the inner conflicts of a navigator serving with a
      Free French component of R. A. F. Bomber Command.

3425 Royo, Rodrigo. The Sun and the Snow. Trans. from the
      Spanish. Regnery, 1956. y.
      A tale of the Spanish "Blue Division, " which fought for the
      Germans on the Eastern Front in 1941.

3426 Ruttle, Lee. The Private War of Dr. Yamada. Stein & Day,
      1978. y.
      A Japanese doctor is torn between the Hippocratic oath and
      the Samurai code during the closing stages of the 1944
      Battle of Peleliu.

3427 Ryan, Patrick. How I Won the War. Morrow, 1965. y.
      Humorous spoof on the war as seen through the eyes of
      one of the lowest forms of military life, an American 2nd
      lieutenant.

3428 Rydberg, Lou and Ernie. The Shadow Army. Nelson, 1976.
      y.
      When the Germans invade Crete in 1941, young Demetrios
      joins his comrades in the mountains vowing to help the
      underground.

3429 Saeki, Shoichi, comp. The Shadow of Sunrise: Selected Sto-
      ries of Japan and the War. Trans. from the Japanese.
      Kodansha International, 1966. y.

Contents. --The Catch, by K. Oe. --Sakurajima, by H. Ume-
zaki. --Summer Flower, by T. Hard. --Bones, by F. Haya-
shi. --The Far-Worshiping Commander, by M. Ibuse.

3430 St. George, Geoffrey. The Proteus Pact. Little, Brown,
1975.
A top-secret armaments project is formulated by the
Nazis early in the war.

3431 Samuels, Gertrude. Mottele. Harper, 1976. y.
Illuminates the life of a Jewish Resistance fighter and his
comrades in the forests of Poland.

3432 Sarlat, Noah. Danger Patrol. Paperback Library, 1963. y.
P.
Four G. I. 's are chosen for special missions due to their
size and intelligence.

3433 _____., ed. War Cry. Paperback Library, 1962. y. P.
Tales of U. S., British, French, Russian, and Italian com-
mandoes and partisans in warfare behind the German lines.

3434 Sawkins, Raymond H. The Heights of Zervos. By Colin
Forbes, pseud. Dutton, 1970. y. Rpr. 1972.
A four-man Allied attempt to prevent the German Alpen-
korps from capturing a monastery atop a Greek mountain
in 1941.

3435 _____. The Palermo Affair. By Colin Forbes, pseud.
Dutton, 1972. Rpr. 1973. y.
A British officer and an American captain are sent to Sicily on a daring raid with the help of local Mafiosi two days
before the 1943 Allied invasion.

3436 _____. Tramp in Armor. By Colin Forbes, pseud. Dut-
ton, 1970 Rpr. 1971. y.
A British tank crew is caught behind German lines in
France in May 1940.

3437 Scannal, Francis P. In Line of Duty. Harper, 1946. y.
A six-member American patrol on reconnaissance pene-
trates a Japanese-held jungle on a South Pacific island.

3438 Scarelli, W. E. The Brother. Associated Booksellers, 1960.
y. P.
Combat and family feuding in wartime Sicily.

3439 Schoendoerffer, Pierre. Farewell to the King. Trans. from
the French. Stein & Day, 1970.
British sergeant Learoyd is air dropped into the jungles
of Borneo in 1944 to lead the natives in fighting the Japanese.

3440 Scott, Paul. A Division of the Spoils. Morrow, 1975.
      Combat and politics in 1945 India.

3441 _____. March of the Warrior. Morrow, 1958. y.
      Japanese troops drive the British out of Burma in 1942.

3442 Sela, Owen. An Exchange of Eagles. Pantheon, 1977.
      Between August 1939 and December 1940 a U.S. Army in-
      telligence colonel and a German military intelligence colo-
      nel team up to prevent war between their two countries.

3443 Sentjurc, Igor. The Torrents of War. Trans. from the Ger-
           man. David McKay, 1962. y.
      A tale about three German soldiers on the Eastern Front
      just after the fall of Stalingrad.

3444 Seymour, Alta H. On the Edge of the Fjord. Presbyterian
           Board, 1944. y.
      Norwegian underground patriots battle the Nazis.

      Shaner, John, jt. author. See Ramrus, Al.

3445 Shann, Renée. Air Force Girl. Triangle, 1942. y.
      Focuses on the love affair between a W.A.A.F. member
      and famous ace "Tips" Poel-Sanders, R.A.F., at the time
      of the Battle of Britain.

3446 Shapiro, Lionel. The Sixth of June. Doubleday, 1955. Rpr.
           1975. y.
      A love story set against the involvement of U.S. para-
      troopers in the D-Day invasion of Normandy; Robert Taylor
      played the movie lead.

3447 Shaw, Charles. Heaven Knows, Mr. Allison. Crown, 1953.
           y.
      A U.S. Marine and a nun find themselves the sole Allied
      inhabitants of an island occupied by the Japanese; Robert
      Mitchum played the movie lead.

3448 Shaw, Irwin. The Young Lions. Random House, 1948. Rpr.
           1976. y.
      The lives of a Jew, an American G.I., and a German sol-
      dier are traced from 1938-1945, when only the latter sur-
      vives a combat in a Bavarian forest; made into a movie.

3449 Sheldon, Douglas. The Rainbow Man. Doubleday, 1975. y.
      Centers around the love- and military-lives of the crew of
      the U.S. 8th Air Force B-17 "Lady Bee."

      Shute, Nevil, pseud. See Norway, Nevil Shute.

3450 Silliphant, Stirling. Pearl. Dell, 1978. P.

Colonel Jason Forrest, his wife, and acquaintances in love
and combat in Hawaii, December 4-7, 1941; made into a
TV mini-series.

3451 Sillitoe, Alan. The General. Knopf, 1961. y.
When an entire orchestra is captured, a general is dis-
mayed when he is ordered to execute its noncombatant
members.

3452 Simonov, Konstantin M. Days and Nights. Trans. from the
Russian. Simon & Schuster, 1945. y.
A Soviet officer and a Red Army nurse share the perils
of the Battle of Stalingrad.

3453 _____. The Living and the Dead. Trans. from the Russian. Doubleday, 1963. y.
Vanya Sintsov relates the terrible Soviet defeats in the six-
month period following the German invasion of June 22,
1941.

3454 Sire, Glen. The Deathmakers. Simon & Schuster, 1961. y.
Captain Brandon and the push of Patton's 3rd U.S. Army
into Bavaria during the closing days of the war in Europe.

3455 Skidmore, Hobert D. Valley of the Sky. Houghton Mifflin,
1944. y.
Combat and rest for the crew of the U.S. bomber "Heart-
less Harpie" in the South Pacific during the early months
of the conflict.

3456 Skvorecky, Josef. The Cowards. Trans. from the Czech.
Grove, 1971.
Focuses on the May 1945 Soviet liberation of Czechoslo-
vakia.

3457 Slaughter, Frank G. Surgeon, U.S.A. Doubleday, 1966.
Rpr. 1976.
An American heart surgeon volunteers after Pearl Harbor
and serves throughout the war.

3458 Smith, Bradford. Arms Are Fair. Bobbs-Merrill, 1943. y.
Sickened by Japanese atrocities in China, an Imperial soldier joins the Chinese resistance.

3459 Smith, Frederick E. 633 Squadron. Hutchinson, 1956. y.
A crack R.A.F. Mosquito squadron is sent to bomb out a
difficult German secret installation in Norway.

3460 _____. 633 Squadron: "Operation Rhine Maiden." Cassell,
1976. y.
The unit's Mosquitos operate with U.S. Flying Fortresses
on a vital strike; sequel to the above title.

3461   Smith, Stan. Ten Against the Third Reich. Belmont, 1961.
           y. P.
       Ten tales of underground combat, based on fact.

       Smith, Thor, jt. author. See Redding, John M.

3462   Solon, Gregory. Let Us Find Heroes. Random House, 1958.
           y.
       Soviet Army hero Captain Andrei Kagorin is suspected of
       disloyalty.

3463   Sowers, Phyllis A. Sons of the Dragon. Whitman, 1942.   y.
       Chinese irregulars resist the Japanese invaders.

3464   Sperber, Manes. Journey Without End. Trans. Doubleday,
           1954.   y.
       Action in Yugoslavia and Poland toward the end of the war.

3465   Stagg, Delano. Bloody Beaches. Monarch, 1961.   y.   P.
       The influences of a U.S. Marine captain on his men during
       a Pacific island assault.

3466   _____ . The Glory Jumpers. Monarch, 1959.   y.   P.
       A group of U.S. paratroopers are sent on a dangerous
       mission behind German lines during the Normandy invasion.

3467   Stanton, Paul. The Gun Garden. Mill, 1965.   y.   P.
       Concentrates on an R.A.F. pilot's love affairs and battle
       experiences during the Axis aerial siege of Malta.

3468   Statham, Leon. Welcome, Darkness. Crowell, 1950.   y.
       Depicts guerrilla warfare in the Japanese-occupied Philip-
       pines.

3469   Stevens, William. The Gunner. Atheneum, 1968.   y.
       Deacon, gunner on an A.A.F. B-24, is the only member
       of his crew to survive a bombing mission over Vienna;
       returning to Italy, he goes A.W.O.L. as a result of com-
       bat fatigue.

3470   Strange, J. S. Catch the Golden Ring. Doubleday, 1955.   y.
       French Marquis irregulars battle the Germans.

3471   Strange, Stephen. Brave Journey. Associated Booksellers,
           1960.   y.   P.
       South African troops fight Rommel's Afrika Korps in the
       Western Desert.

3472   Strong, Anna L. Wild River. Little, Brown, 1943.   y.
       German advances force the Soviets to blow up their great
       dam on the Dnieper River.

3473   Suhl, Yuri. Uncle Misha's Partisans. Four Winds, 1974.   y.

A Jewish youth joins a Russian partisan band fighting the
Nazis.

3474 Tabor, Michael. The Battle of the Bulge. Popular Library,
           1965. y. P.
      An aggressive German colonel leads his panzers against
      the Americans in December 1944; based on the screenplay
      for a movie of the same title.

3475 Takeyama, Michio. The Harp of Burma. Trans. from the
           Japanese. Little, Brown, 1966. y.
      A company of Imperial soldiers survive the war in Burma
      because of the men's love of music.

3476 Tamas, Istvan. Sergeant Nikola. L. B. Fischer, 1942. y.
      The exploits of General Mihailovich's Chetnik guerrillas
      against the Germans in Yugoslavia is reported by a non-
      com.

3477 Tarrant, John. The Rommel Plot. Lippincott, 1977. Rpr.
           1978. y.
      French Marquis irregulars seek to kill the German field
      marshal on the eve of the Allied D-Day invasion of Nor-
      mandy.

3478 Taylor, Geoff. Court of Honor. Simon & Schuster, 1966.
           y.
      Pictures a German general's last-ditch attempts to change
      the course of the war.

3479 Taylor, Ward. Roll Back the Sky. Holt, 1956. y.
      Captain Richardson and his B-29 Superfortress crew par-
      ticipate in the first U. S. low-level fire bombing missions
      over Japan in 1945.

3480 Terlouw, Jan. Winter in Wartime. Trans. from the Dutch.
           McGraw-Hill, 1976. y.
      Michiel and his fellow villagers join the Dutch Resistance.

3481 Thayer, James S. The Hess Cross. Putnam, 1977. Rpr.
           1978. y.
      A German commando team is landed on the Maine coast
      with orders to proceed to Chicago and destroy the U. S.
      atomic experiment and capture scientist Enrico Fermi.

3482 Theiss, Lewis E. Flying with the Air-Sea Rescue Service.
           Wilde, 1946. y.
      Wartime adventures--saving downed U. S. flyers.

3483 The Third Flare: Three War Stories. Foreign Languages
           Publishing House, 1963. y.
      Contents. --Ivan, by V. Bogomolov. --The Third Flare, by
      V. Bykov. --The Perch, by V. Nekrasov.

3484 Thomas, Harlan C. A Yank in the R. A. F. Random House,
          1941. y.
          A young American mail pilot in England enlists in the
          Royal Air Force and sees action over Dunkirk; made into
          a popular movie.

3485 Thompson, Arthur L. B. A Battle Is Fought to Be Won. By
          Francis Clifford, pseud. Coward-McCann, 1961. y.
          In early 1942 Lieutenant Gilling and a small group of
          Burmese try to delay the advance of a superior Japanese
          force.

3486 Thompson, Brian. Buddy Boy. St. Martin's, 1978. y.
          Focuses on the abrupt maturing of a British schoolboy and
          the breakdown of a much-admired American pilot just be-
          fore D-Day.

3487 Tibbets, Albert B., comp. Salute to the Brave: Stories of
          World War II. Little, Brown, 1960. y.
          Ten short stories about American G. I. 's taken from popu-
          lar U. S. magazines (mostly the Saturday Evening Post) and
          designed to show gallantry and courage.

3488 Tobino, Mario. The Underground. Trans. from the Italian.
          Doubleday, 1966. y.
          Italian partisans battle the Nazis in 1944-1945.

3489 Tomlinson, Henry M. The Trumpet Shall Sound. Random
          House, 1957. y.
          Sir Anthony Gale's family in the Battle of Britain.

3490 Tregaskis, Richard W. Stronger Than Fear. Random House,
          1945. y.
          Captain Krieder's uncertainty shows itself during house-to-
          house combat in Germany in March 1945.

3491 Trevor, Elleston. The Big Pick Up. Macmillan, 1955. y.
          A fictional recreation of the 1940 evacuation of Dunkirk.

3492 _____. Killing Ground. Macmillan, 1958. y.
          Follows the adventures of a small British tank troop during
          the Normandy invasion and the Battle of Falaise.

3493 _____. Squadron Airborne. Macmillan, 1956. y.
          Pictures one R. A. F. squadron based near London in the
          Battle of Britain.

3494 Tripp, Niles. Faith in a Windsock. Davies, 1952. y.
          The night bombing exploits of one R. A. F. bomber crew.

3495 Tunis, John R. His Enemy, His Friend. Morrow, 1967.
          The psychological problems of a German sergeant detailed
          to execute prisoners.

3496 _____ . The Silence Over Dunkirk. Morrow, 1962. y.
Two English soldiers seek to escape France after the 1940
evacuation.

3497 Turner, George. Scobe. Simon & Schuster, 1959. y.
Allied troops battle the Japanese in New Guinea, 1942-
1943.

3498 Uris, Leon M. Angry Hills. Random House, 1955. Rpr.
1972. y.
American Mike Morrison is caught up with the Resistance
during the 1941 German invasion of Greece.

3499 _____ . Battle Cry. Putnam, 1953. Rpr. 1978. y.
Follows the radio squad of the 2nd Battalion, 6th U.S.
Marines, from Guadalcanal to Iwo Jima.

3500 _____ . Mila 18. Doubleday, 1961. Rpr. 1970. y.
Centers around the unsuccessful Jewish uprising against
the Nazis in Warsaw in 1944.

3501 Vailland, Roger. Playing for Keeps. Trans. from the French.
Houghton Mifflin, 1948. y.
Five French Marquis irregulars take part in 1944 Parisian
street fighting just before the Liberation.

3502 Van der Haas, Henrietta. Orange on Top. Trans. from the
Dutch. Harcourt, 1945. y.
Dutch guerrillas defeat a group of German soldiers.

3503 _____ . Victorious Island. Trans. from the Dutch. Har-
court, 1947. y.
The final success of the Dutch in the Netherlands East
Indies.

3504 Van Doren, Mark, ed. Night of the Summer Solstice and Other Stories of the Russian War. Holt, 1943. y.
Twenty stories of combat on the Eastern Front as told
from a Red Army point of view.

3505 Van Praag, Van. Day Without End. Sloane, 1949. y.
Depicts the 59th consecutive day spent by Lieutenant Paul
Roth and his men on the lines in Normandy and his unit's
action-filled patrols towards St. Lo.

3506 Vasillou, George. The Panama Story. Exposition, 1974.
The activities of American troops in the Canal Zone during
the war.

3507 Vonnegut, Kurt. Slaughterhouse Five. Delacorte, 1969. Rpr.
1971.
As a P.O.W., an American witnesses the 1945 fire-bomb-
ing of Dresden.

3508 Vrettos, Theodore. Hammer on the Sea. Little, Brown,
            1965. y.
      Depicts the Greek resistance to the German occupation.

3509 Wagner, Geoffrey. The Sands of Valour. Knopf, 1968. y.
      In North Africa a British tank regiment fights overwhelm-
      ing odds in combat with the Afrika Korps.

3510 Wallace, J. H. A Walk in the Forest. Associated Booksel-
            lers, 1960. y. P.
      A small group of British soldiers successfully opposed a
      large force of Japanese troops in Burma.

3511 Walsh, J. Paton. The Dolphin Crossing. Macmillan, 1967.
            y.
      Two English teenagers are involved in the 1940 Dunkirk
      evacuation.

3512 Waugh, Evelyn. The End of the Battle. Little, Brown, 1962.
            y.
      Guy Crouchback ends the war as a commando serving with
      the Yugoslav partisans.

3513   . Men-At-Arms. Little, Brown, 1952. y.
      Guy Crouchback serves in the Royal Halberdiers in 1939-
      1940.

3514   . Officers and Gentlemen. Little, Brown, 1955. y.
      Guy Crouchback, back from Dunkirk, is trained as a com-
      mando and participates in the 1941 Battle of Crete.

3515 Webber, Gordon. The Far Shore. Little, Brown, 1954. y.
      How Allied forces invaded Normandy on June 6, 1944.

3516 Wernick, Robert. The Freebooters. Scribner's, 1944. y.
      Exploits of American soldiers in North Africa and Italy.

3517 Westheimer, David. Lighter Than a Feather. Little, Brown,
            1971. y.
      Imagining that the A-bomb was not ready, the author ex-
      plores what might have happened in an Allied invasion of
      Kyushu in 1945.

3518   . Song of the Young Sentry. Little, Brown, 1969.
            y.
      After his B-24 Liberator crashes into the Mediterranean,
      unpopular navigator Steve Lang becomes a P. O. W. camp
      leader when his men are held by the Italians.

3519   . Von Ryan's Express. Doubleday, 1964. y.
      A group of Allied P. O. W. 's, led by U. S. martinet colonel
      Joseph Ryan, capture a German train and attempt to flee
      1943 Italy; the movie version starred Frank Sinatra and
      Trevor Howard.

3520 Wheatley, Dennis. Strange Conflict. Heron, 1972. y. P.
The use of secret weapons in Europe by Allied commandos.

3521 _____. They Used Dark Forces. Hutchinson, 1964. y.
The use of special electronic gear by the Allies.

3522 _____. V for Vengeance. Heron, 1972. y. P.
A tale about the effects of the German guided missile on-
slaught.

3523 White, Alan. Dark Finds the Day. Harcourt, 1965. y.
Probes the emotions and motivations of three soldiers who
volunteer for dangerous Allied missions.

3524 _____. The Long Drop. Harcourt, 1970. y.
Commando Unit 404 executes a daring raid into Belgium.

3525 _____. The Long Fuse. Harcourt, 1974. y.
British commandos must return a captured former British
citizen and Nazi sympathizer, who became a defector, back
to his role as a newscaster on a Strasburg radio station
so that the man might deliver an anti-Nazi diatribe.

3526 _____. The Long Midnight. Harcourt, 1974. y.
Two British commandos are dropped into Norway to destroy
a German titanium mine.

3527 _____. The Long Night's Walk. Harcourt, 1969. y.
Four British commandos are parachuted behind German
lines in Holland to destroy an important signals headquarters.

3528 _____. The Long Silence. Charter, 1977. y.
British commandos are dropped into France to destroy an
important railroad center.

3529 _____. The Long Summer. Harcourt, 1975. y.
The travels of a young British private during the D-Day
invasion.

3530 _____. The Long Watch. Harcourt, 1971. y.
In late 1943 a British commando team is parachuted into
France with orders to find a French scientist being held
captive by the Nazis.

3531 White, Leslie T. His Majesty's Highlanders. Macfadden,
1967. y. P.
Scotch soldiers in combat on various fronts.

3532 White, Robb. Flight Deck. Doubleday, 1961. y.
A tale about a U.S. Navy pilot on missions during the
Battle of Midway.

3533   _____. Surrender! Doubleday, 1966. y.
         Two young Americans elude the Japanese in the Philippines
         after the fall of Bataan.

3534   White, Theodore H. Mountain Road. Sloane, 1958. y.
         Major Philip Baldwin's demolition team is trapped while
         trying to blow a vital road during the Sino-American evacu-
         ation from Liuchow to Tushan, China, in 1944.

       Whitehouse, Arch, pseud. See Whitehouse, Arthur G. J.

3535   Whitehouse, Arthur G. J. Adventure in the Sky. Duell,
         Sloan, 1961. y.
         Ten tales of combat.

3536   _____. Bombers in the Sky. Duell, Sloan, 1960. y.
         Eleven short stories about bombing operations during the
         war.

3537   Williams, George. The Blind Bull. Abelard, 1952. y.
         An American major in a Saipan hospital recalls his com-
         bat experiences.

3538   Willock, Colin. The Fighters. St. Martin's, 1973. y.
         Two friends, one German and one British, oppose each
         other in the air during the Battle of Britain.

3539   Wilson, Guthrie. Brave Company. Putnam, 1950. y.
         A journalist records the thoughts and actions of New Zea-
         land infantrymen battling the Germans near Forli, on the
         eastern end of Italy's Gothic Line.

3540   Wilson, John. Court Martial. Associated Booksellers, 1959.
         y. P.
         Reveals the circumstances behind the trial of a British
         Army officer for cowardice.

3541   Wolff, Perry S. The Friend. Crown, 1950. y.
         U. S. Company K is ambushed by the Germans during the
         Battle of the Bulge.

3542   Woods, William H. The Edge of Darkness. Lippincott, 1942.
         y.
         Norwegian partisans battle the Nazis.

3543   Wormser, Richard. "Operation Crossbow." Dell, 1965. y.
         P.
         Three commandos are sent on a dangerous mission against
         a German V-weapons site.

3544   Wouk, Hermann. War and Remembrance. Little, Brown,
         1978.

Follows the exploits of members of the Henry family from Pearl Harbor to the defeat of the Axis; sequel to the next title.

3545   . The Winds of War. Little, Brown, 1971. Rpr. 1977.
A servant impersonates his boss, a colonel in the French Foreign Legion.
The outbreak of the war affects one American family, the Henrys.

3546 Wren, Percival C.   The Uniform of Glory.   Murray, 1941. y.
A servant impersonates his boss, a colonel in the French Foreign Legion.

3547 Wylie, James.   The Homstead Grays.   Putnam, 1978.
Led by L. T. C. Jonathan Fremont, an all-black U. S. P-51 fighter squadron tackles the Luftwaffe's best in the skies of Europe.

3548 Wyllie, John.   Johnny Purple.   Dutton, 1956.   y.
Pictures a conflict between Allied fighter pilots and ground administrators during the 1942 defense of Sumatra.

3549 Yates, Richard.   A Special Providence.   Knopf, 1969.   y.
A young American soldier matures during combat in Belgium in 1944.

3550 Yerby, Frank.   The Voyage Unplanned.   Dial, 1974.
Love and combat as experienced by two French Marquis irregulars.

3551 Zeno.   The Cauldron.   Stein & Day, 1967.   y.
A group of British paratroopers hold out in a Dutch village during the 1944 Battle of Arnhem.

3552   . The Four Sergeants.   Atheneum, 1977.   y.
Four British noncoms and a platoon of Jewish airborne soldiers are parachuted into 1943 Sicily to blow up a vital bridge.

THE YEARS OF COLD WAR AND HOT POLICE ACTIONS,
1945 TO 1978

The stories in this section concern four principal areas: the Korean
War, the Arab-Israeli conflicts, the war in Southeast Asia, and
mercenary-terrorist operations. Some of the actions described also
involve soldiers in training or on the homefronts, although for the
most part the tales are operational. The military and quasi-military
actions of our times do not fit any uniform pattern, and most are
less-than-glorious in their action or results.

3553 Abrahams, Peter. A Wreath for Udomo. Knopf, 1956. y.
        Depicts a black revolution in an imaginary African nation.

3554 Albert, Marvin H. All the Young Men. Pocket Books, 1960.
        y. P.
        Examines racial prejudice among U.S. Marines fighting in
        Korea.

3555 _____. The Gargoyle Conspiracy. Dell, 1976. P.
        Moroccan terrorists attempt to assassinate King Hussein
        of Jordan and then-Secretary of State Henry Kissinger.

3555a Aldiss, Brian W. A Rude Awakening. Random House, 1979.
        A British soldier sweats out his discharge in 1945 Sumatra
        fighting rebels.

3556 Aldridge, James. A Mockery in Arms. Little, Brown, 1975.
        Focuses on the 1968 revolt of Kurdish forces against the
        Iraqi Army.

3557 Allen, Ralph. Ask the Name of the Lion. Doubleday, 1962.
        y.
        Mercenaries participate in the Congolese civil war of 1960.

3558 Amis, Kingsley. The Anti-Death League. Harcourt, 1966.
        A British army captain searches for an intruder into his
        camp.

3559 Anders, Curtis. The Price of Courage. Sagamore, 1950. y.
        Follows the exploits of a company of U.S. G.I.'s and their
        commander during the Korean War.

3560   Anderson, Thomas.   Your Own Beloved Sons.   Random House,
            1956.   y.
            Surrounded by the enemy in Korea, a U. S. company com-
            mander calls for a volunteer patrol to find a way out.

3561   Anderson, William C.   The Gooney Bird.   Crown, 1968.
            The story of a U. S. helicopter crew, a reporter, and the
            Viet Cong during the Vietnamese War.

3562   Arvay, Harry.   Operation Kuwait.   Bantam, 1975.   P.
            Israeli commandos break up a terrorist skyjack training
            camp in the desert.

3563   Ash, William.   Ride a Paper Tiger.   Walker, 1969.
            Guerrillas attack the establishment in a small southern Af-
            rican nation.

3564   Bagley, Desmond.   High Citadel.   Doubleday, 1965.
            When Communist insurgents force down the plane of a South
            American president, the survivors must hold off guerrilla
            attacks with improvised weapons.

3565   Bahr, Jerome.   Holes in the Wall.   David McKay, 1970.
            Pictures an East-West tank confrontation at the Berlin
            wall.

        Bailey, Charles W. , 2nd. , jt. author.   See Knebel, Fletcher.

3566   Balka, M.   Outpost.   Trans. from the French.   Delacorte,
            1973.
            French soldiers hunt two renegades near an isolated out-
            post in central Africa.

3567   Ball, John D.   Rescue Mission.   Harper, 1966.   y.
            Two Civil Air Patrol pilots undertake a vital mission in
            an unfamiliar Lockheed Constellation.

3568   Ballinger, William S.   The Carrion Eaters.   Putnam, 1971.
            Depicts the bloody Moslem-Hindu war on India's northwest
            frontier.

3569   Barahat, Halim.   Days of Dust.   Trans. from the Arabic.
            Medina University Press, 1974.
            A series of fictional scenes depicting the Six Day War of
            1967 from the Arab viewpoint.

3570   Barak, Michael.   The Secret List of Heinrich Roehm.   Mor-
            row, 1976.   Rpr. 1977.
            Isreali commandos attack a neo-Nazi-controlled missile
            site in Egypt.

3571   Barbeau, Clayton C.   The Ikon.   Coward-McCann, 1961.
            A young American soldier searches for his identity during
            the fighting in Korea.

3572 Barber, Rowland. The Midnighters. Crown, 1970.
Based on the memoirs of Jewish hero Martin Allen Riba-
kof, this is a "nonfictional novel" showing how an "air
force" was smuggled into Israel in 1948.

3573 Barlow, James. This Side of the Sky. Simon & Schuster,
1964.
A love story mixed into the exploits of a peace-time U.S.
Strategic Air Command bomber pilot.

3574 Becker, Stephen W. The Chinese Bandit. Random House,
1975. Rpr. 1977.
Forced to desert, a U.S. Marine becomes a brigand in
China in the days just before Mao takes over the mainland.

3575 Beech, Webb. Warrior's Way. Fawcett, 1962. P.
Examines the life of one professional American soldier,
Captain Amos Carter.

3576 Bergee, L. K. Rendezvous with Hell. Marine Enterprises,
1963.
The experiences of a U.S. Marine platoon in the Korean
War.

3577 Bernstein, Kenneth. Intercept. Coward-McCann, 1971. y.
Two surviving crew members attempt to escape Russia
after their U.S. reconnaissance plane is downed near the
Crimean coast.

3578 Blacker, Irwin K. Search and Destroy. Random House,
1966.
U.S. Special Forces troops are sent on a secret mission
to destroy a North Vietnamese military installation at
Hanoi.

3579 Blakenship, William D. The Leavenworth Irregulars. Bobbs-
Merrill, 1974.
Three U.S. G.I.'s make off with their post's payroll and
are tracked down by a determined and evil sergeant.

3580 Blatty, William P. John Goldfarb, Please Come Home.
Doubleday, 1963.
An Israeli U-2 pilot crashes in Egypt.

3581 Boatman, Alan. Comrades-In-Arms. Harper, 1974.
Vietnam war reminiscences by wounded U.S. Marines re-
covering in a stateside hospital.

3582 Böll, Heinrich. End of a Mission. Trans. from the German.
McGraw-Hill, 1967. y.
A young West German soldier and his father destroy a
jeep near a Rhineland village; the pair are then arrested
and tried.

3583   Boulle, Pierre.   Ears of the Jungle.   Trans. from the French.
            Vanguard, 1972.
            A North Vietnamese attempts to devise countermeasures to
            the U. S. electronic sensors dropped on the Ho Chi Minh
            Trail that bring aerial attack on any movement detected.

3584   Breit, Harvey.   A Narrow Action.   World, 1964.   y.
            Felipe and his guerrillas take over a Caribbean island;
            modeled on Castro and Cuba.

3585   Briley, John.   The Traitors.   Putnam, 1969.
            The survivors of a U. S. patrol in Vietnam are taken in
            hand by the Viet Cong and interrogated by an American
            renegade who convinces two soldiers to change sides.

3586   Bryan, C. D. B.   P. S. Wilkinson.   Harper, 1965.
            A lieutenant is successful in Korean combat, but unsuccess-
            ful in his domestic life.

3587   Bryant, Peter.   Red Alert.   Ace, 1958,   y.   P.
            Failing to respond to their fail-safe system, American
            S. A. C. B-25's bomb Russia.

3588   Buchard, Robert.   Thirty Seconds Over New York.   Trans.
            from the French.   Morrow, 1970.
            A deranged Chinese colonel attempts to use a converted
            Boeing 707 to drop an A-bomb on New York City.

3589   Bunting, Josiah.   The Lionheads.   Braziller, 1972.
            U. S. 12th (Lionhead) Division boss General George Lem-
            ming orders a colonel to attack a Viet Cong stronghold in
            1968 Vietnam but refuses air support.

        Burdick, Eugene, jt. author.   See Lederer, William J.

3590   Burgess, Jackson.   The Atrocity.   Putnam, 1961.
            The effect of a brutal incident on an American G. I. serving
            with an ordnance company in post V-E Day Italy.

3591   Burmeister, Jon.   The Hard Men.   St. Martin's, 1978.
            American Steve Quayle's mercenary band fights in Angola
            in 1975 to avenge the death of their leader's sister at the
            hands of the Cubans.

3592   Caidin, Martin.   Almost Midnight.   Morrow, 1971.   y.
            U. S. Air Force personnel work to recover five A-bombs
            taken by terrorists and placed in major American cities.

3593   _____ .   Cyborg.   Arbor House, 1972.
            U. S. Air Force colonel Steve Austin is nearly killed in a
            plane crash; put back together with bionics, his new powers
            are first tested on an anti-terrorist raid.

3594 _____. Operation Nuke. Daivd McKay, 1973.
    Colonel Steve Austin foils an international black market in
    nuclear weapons.

Caillou, Alan, pseud. See Lyle-Smith, Alan.

3595 Calin, Harold. Genesis in the Desert. Belmont-Tower, 1978.
    P.
    A veteran of desert fighting becomes a forceful mercenary
    leader.

3596 _____. Mercenary. Nordon, 1977.
    A modern soldier of fortune fights in the Arabian desert.

3597 Cappelli, Mario. Scramble. Ace, 1962. y. P.
    Colonel Gormann's fighter-interceptor squadron plays real-
    istic war games with S. A. C. bombers.

3597a Carney, Daniel. The Wild Geese. Bantam, 1978. P.
    Mercenaries free a politician held in Africa.

3598 Carpentier, Alejo. Reasons of State. Trans. from the Span-
    ish. Knopf, 1976. y.
    After twenty years a people's revolt forces a South Ameri-
    can dictator to flee to Paris.

3599 Chandler, David. Captain Hollister. Macmillan, 1973.
    Reporting Vietnam casualties breaks the mind of an Ameri-
    can officer on his second tour of duty.

3600 Chesnof, Richard Z. If Israel Lost the War. Coward-Mc-
    Cann, 1971. y.
    What might have happened had the Arabs opened the Six
    Day War of 1967 instead of the Isrealis; written before the
    October War of 1973.

3601 Clare, John. The Passionate Invaders. Doubleday, 1967.
    Depicts the first armed invasion of the U. S. from Canada
    since the War of 1812.

3602 Clark, Alan. The Lion Heart. Morrow, 1969.
    What happens when a U. S. Special Forces soldier joins a
    regular Army infantry unit in Vietnam.

3603 Clark, Roger W. Ride the White Tiger. Little, Brown,
    1959. y.
    A Korean boy helps the U. S. Army in Korea and befriends
    a G. I.

3604 Cleary, Jon. Peter's Pence. Morrow, 1974.
    I. R. A. terrorists kidnap the Pope.

3605 Cohen, Stanley. 330 Park. Putnam, 1977. y.

Using tactics learned in Vietnam, a private platoon under Larry Devereau captures a New York City building and holds 600 hostages.

Collins, June, jt. author. <u>See</u> Moore, Robert L.

3606 Condon, Richard. <u>The Whisper of the Axe</u>. Dial, 1976. Rpr. 1978.
Twelve Americans trained as guerrilla fighters in China prepare to launch the Final American Revolution on July 4, 1976.

3607 Conroy, Pat. <u>The Great Santini</u>. Houghton Mifflin, 1976. Rpr. 1977.
The domestic problems of U.S. Marine fighter pilot Bull Meecham in present-day South Carolina.

3608 Coon, Gene. <u>Meanwhile Back at the Front</u>. Bantam, 1961. y. P.

3609   . <u>The Short End</u>. Dell, 1964. y. P.
Two tales of American soldiers fighting in the Korean War.

3610 Coppel, Alfred. <u>The Dragon</u>. Harcourt, 1977. Rpr. 1978.
What happens when the Chinese develop a laster anti-missile weapon.

3611   . <u>Thirty-Four East</u>. Harcourt, 1974. Rpr. 1975.
When the President is killed and the Vice-president is kidnapped, only the local Sanai co-operation between U.S. and Russian generals prevents a third world war.

3611a Corder, E.M. <u>The Deer Hunter</u>. Jove, 1979. P.
Follows an American into the hell of Vietnam, its battles, prison camps, and disillusionment; the movie version won the 1979 Oscar for "Best Picture of the Year."

3612 Corley, Edwin. <u>Siege</u>. Stein & Day, 1969.
Militants trick a black Marine general into leading an underground army attempting to gain control of Manhattan.

3613 Cox, Richard. <u>Sam-7</u>. Ballantine, 1978. P.
Terrorists bring down a jet liner in the heart of London.

3614 Craig, William. <u>The Tashkent Crisis</u>. Dutton, 1971.
The generals urge a U.S. President not to back down in the face of a Soviet surrender ultimatum.

3615 Crane, Robert. <u>Operation Vengeance</u>. Pyramid, 1965. P.
A Communist heroin ring corrupts U.S. troops in Korea.

3616   . <u>Sergeant Corbin's War</u>. Pyramid, 1963. P.
The personal conflicts of an American noncom fighting in Korea.

3617 Crawford, William. Give Me Tomorrow. Putnam, 1962.
     Traces the last Korean War patrol of Marine Lieutenant
     David R. Martin.

3618 Crosby, John. Dear Judgment. Stein & Day, 1978.
     Mafia chief Cosimo Belardi steals two Air Force jet fight-
     ers and their nuclear bombs and holds them for ransom.

3619 Crowther, John. Fire Base. St. Martin's, 1976.
     Racial problems between white and black troops manning
     an artillery outpost in Vietnam.

3620 Crumley, James. One to Count Cadence. Random House,
     1969.
     In 1962 a new company of enlistees arrives at an Air Force
     base in Vietnam, where Sergeant Stag Krummel learns the
     value of friendship and the horror of war.

3621 Cruttwell, Patrick. A Kind of Fighting. Macmillan, 1960.
     Lin Soe, a young revolutionary, leads his Far Eastern
     nation to independence and chaos.

3622 Cussler, Clive. Vixen 03. Viking, 1978.
     African terrorists plan a missile attack on Washington,
     D. C.

3623 Daniels, J. R. Fire Gold. Coward-McCann, 1975.
     Australian pilot and gunrunner Pete White crashes into
     Celebes mountains and is captured by insurgents who want
     to gain Sulawesi independence.

3624 Debray, Regis. Undesirable Alien. Trans. from the French.
     Viking, 1978.
     A European is drawn into a guerrilla revolution somewhere
     in Latin America.

3625 De Mille, Nelson. By The Rivers of Babylon. Harcourt,
     1978.
     A small group of Israeli officials enroute by Concorde to
     New York for peace talks are downed by Palestinian ter-
     rorists and battle for survival against almost impossible
     odds.

3626 De St. Jerre, John, and Brian Shakespeare. The Patriot
     Game. Houghton Mifflin, 1973.
     Pictures I. R. A. terrorists at work in Northern Ireland and
     Great Britain.

3627 Dixon, H. Vernor. Guerrilla. Monarch, 1963. P.
     An American soldier defends five civilians in a Communist-
     held jungle in Malaya.

3628 Doulis, Thomas. Path for Our Glory. Simon & Schuster,
     1963.

U. S. paratroopers in peacetime, especially the personal problems of one officer and two enlisted men.

3629 Downs, Hunton. The Compassionate Tiger. Putnam, 1960. American soldier of fortune Daniel King becomes involved in the struggle between the French and the Viet Minh in 1954 Indochina.

3630 Driscoll, Peter. The Barboza Credentials. Lippincott, 1976. Rpr. 1978. Black nationalists battle Portuguese troops in Mozambique.

3631 Drury, Allen. The Promise of Joy. Doubleday, 1975. Rpr. 1976. y. A U. S. President becomes involved in a nuclear war between China and Russia.

3632 Du Maurier, Daphne. Rule Britannia. Doubleday, 1973. Rpr. 1974. When the U. S. and U. K. merge into one country, U. S. Marines are sent to protect the citizens of Cornwall, who are protesting the American takeover.

3633 Durden, Charles. No Bugles, No Drums. Viking, 1976. y. U. S. Army Kilo Company's activities in Vietnam.

3634 Durrell, Laurence. White Eagles Over Serbia. Criterion, 1957. y. Pictures an abortive Royalist uprising against Tito in Yugoslavia.

3635 Eastlake, William. The Bamboo Bed. Simon & Schuster, 1970. The adventures of U. S. Army helicopter pilot Captain Knightbridge in Vietnam.

Eberhardt, Alfred F., jt. author. See Proud, Franklin M.

3636 Egleton, Clive. Last Post for a Partisan. Coward-McCann, 1971. When the Russians capture Britain, English partisans battle occupying Soviet troops.

3637 Ehrlich, Jack. Court Martial. Pyramid, 1959. P. A U. S. airman is tried for desertion and, indirectly, for running off with his general's daughter.

3638 Eunson, Robert. Mig Alley. Ace, 1961. y. P. A U. S. Air Force fighter pilot seeks glory in aerial combat over Korea.

3639 Fergusson, Bernard E. Rare Adventure. Rinehart, 1954. y.

Depicts a native uprising against the French administration
of an island off the North African coast.

3640 Field, Della. Vietnam Nurse.   Avon, 1966. P.
      A love story about a U.S. nurse in Vietnam; little combat.

3641 Flood, Charles B.   More Lives Than One.   Houghton Mifflin,
          1967. y.
      A Harvard senior is sent to Korea, is captured by the Chi-
      nese, and is held as a P.O.W. for three years.

3642 Fogg, Charles.   The Panic Button. Ace, 1960. y. P.
      A U.S. Army captain commands a company of misfits in
      Korea.

      Forbes, Colin, pseud. See Sawkins, Raymond H.

3643 Ford, Daniel.   Incident at Muc Wa.   Doubleday, 1967.
      A tale of Vietnam combat.

3644 Ford, Norman R.   The Black, the Gray, and the Gold.
          Doubleday, 1961. y.
      Focuses on the mass violation of the West Point honor
      code in 1951.

3645 Forman, James.   The Shield of Achilles.   Farrar, Straus,
          1966.
      Conflict between the Greek and Turkish populations on
      Cyprus.

3646 Forrest, William.   Stigma.   Crown, 1957.
      During the Korean War, an American soldier is ordered
      to obtain information on the Chinese by having himself
      captured and held as a P.O.W.

3647 Forsyth, Frederick.   The Dogs of War.   Viking, 1974. Rpr.
          1975. y.
      Top mercenary Cat Shannon, supported by a British multi-
      millionaire mining baron, recruits a gang of soldiers of
      fortune to overthrow the West African dictatorship of
      Zangaro, where a secret source of platinum lies waiting
      for exploitation.

3648 _____.   The Shepherd.   Viking, 1976. Rpr. 1977. y.
      A young R.A.F. pilot guides his damaged Vampire high
      over the North Sea and somehow survives to tell the tale
      of his last Christmas Eve.

3649 Fournier, Pierre.   Lambs of Fire.   Trans. from the French.
          Braziller, 1963.
      French terrorists attack the De Gaulle government during
      the Algerian conflict.

3650   Frank, Pat. Hold Back the Night. Lippincott, 1952. y.
       Dog Company, U.S. Marines, covers a Korean withdrawal.

3651   Frankel, Ernest. Band of Brothers. Macmillan, 1958. y.
       In Korea a U.S. Marine officer learns the difference be-
       tween command and leadership.

3652   Frankel, Sandor. The Aleph Solution. Stein & Day, 1978.
       P. L. O. terrorists take control of the U.N. General Assem-
       bly, demanding the dissolution of Israel.

3653   Frankel, Zygmunt. Short War, Short Lives. Abelard, 1971.
       An Israeli defense worker reviews the Six Day War of
       1967.

3654   Franklin, Edward H. It's Cold in Pongoni. Vanguard, 1965.
       y.
       A tale of fighting during the Korean War.

3655   _____. Man on a Wire. Crown, 1978.
       Two men, one American and one Chinese, stage a rematch
       of a Korean War battle in the D. M. Z.

3656   Fraser, George M. The General Danced at Dawn. Knopf,
          1973. Rpr. 1974. y.
       Nine short stories celebrating the post-war history of a
       kilted Scottish infantry regiment.

3657   _____. McAuslan in the Rough. Knopf, 1974.
       Seven more stories about the same Scottish regiment.

3658   Friedman, Philip. Rage. Atheneum, 1972.
       A father is bent on damaging a U.S. Air Force installation
       after the accidental death of his son; George C. Scott
       played the movie lead.

3659   Garfield, Brian. The Last Bridge. Dale, 1978.
       Pictures a challenging mission behind enemy lines in Viet-
       nam.

3660   Geer, Andrew C. Canton Barrier. Harper, 1956. y.
       A violent tale of commercial aviation in turbulent 1949
       China.

3661   George, Peter. Commander-1. Dial, 1965. y.
       The Chinese formulate a successful plan to force the U.S.
       and U.S.S.R. into a nuclear war.

3662   Giovannitti, Len. The Man Who Won the Medal of Honor.
          Random House, 1973.
       On trial, a soldier recalls the patrols and battles he took
       part in during his tour of duty in Vietnam.

3663 Godey, John. The Talisman. Putnam, 1976. Rpr. 1977.
      Disgruntled Vietnam veterans and radicals form a secret
      organization to kidnap the body of the Unknown Soldier and
      hold it for the release of a religious activist.

3664 Gordon, Donald. Flight of the Bat. Morrow, 1964. y.
      Faced with a Soviet nuclear ultimatum, a newly-developed
      R. A. F. bomber is dispatched to demonstrate Western weap-
      on equality.

3665 Gray, Anthony. The Penetrators. Putnam, 1965. y.
      When America replaces her manned bomber fleet with an
      all-I. C. B. M. force, a lone R. A. F. pilot is sent on a
      dummy mission to point out the fallacy of the policy.

3666 Green, William M. The Man Who Called Himself Devlin.
          Bobbs-Merrill, 1978.
      A soldier of fortune is hired by Petrolux Oil to infiltrate
      and destroy the group of terrorists who have taken over
      the firm's holdings on the oil-rich Persian Gulf island of
      Dhasai and who are holding 500 former commandos as
      prisoners.

3667 Greenfield, Irving. High Terror. Fawcett, 1978. P.
      A doctor investigates the doings of Francis Gary Powers'
      U-2.

3668 Groom, Winston. Better Times Than These. Simon & Schu-
          ster, 1978.
      A vivid look at the 1966-1967 battles and skirmishes of
      U. S. Bravo Company in Vietnam.

3669 Grossback, Robert. Easy and Hard Ways Out. Harper, 1975.
          y.
      A new, but flawed, U. S. Navy attack plane is tested in
      Vietnam combat.

3670 Haddah, C. A. The Moroccan. Trans. from the Yiddish.
          Harper, 1975.
      A bungling Israeli soldier marries his beautiful and de-
      manding sergeant before being sent on a commando raid
      into Syria.

3671 Halberstam, David. One Very Hot Day. Houghton Mifflin,
          1968. Rpr. 1973. y.
      Concentrates on the details of one combined U. S. -South
      Vietnamese raid from briefing to body-count, with emphasis
      on the carnage of war and the difference of methods be-
      tween westerner and oriental.

3672 Haldeman, Joe W. War Year. Holt, 1972. y.
      Describes the experiences of a 19-year-old U. S. soldier
      during his tour of duty in Vietnam.

Hall, Adam, pseud. See Trevor, Elleston.

3673 Hallstead, William. The Ghost Plane of Blackwater. Har-
      court, 1974. y.
      Two young men seek a bomber lost over a South Carolina
      swamp.

3674 Hammond-Innes, Ralph. Air Bridge. By Hammond Innes,
      pseud. Knopf, 1952. y.
      Ex-R. A. F. pilot Neil Fraser participates in the Berlin
      Airlift of 1948.

3675 Hardman, Richards L. The Chaplain's Raid. Coward-Mc-
      Cann, 1965. y.
      Three Marine chaplains try to guide a young recruit back
      onto the straight and narrow.

3676 Hardy, René. Sword of God. Trans. from the French.
      Doubleday, 1954. y.
      A former Spanish Republican soldier joins the French in
      their 1946 campaign against the Viet Minh in the jungles
      around Hanoi.

3677 Hardy, Ronald. Place of the Jackels. Doubleday, 1955. y.
      Depicts a chaplain's experiences with French troops in
      their fight with the Viet Minh in 1954 Indochina.

3678 Harris, Leonard. The Masada Plan. Popular Library, 1978.
      P.
      Tells of an ingenious Israeli plan to avoid defeat in a new
      Middle East war by the use of a secret atomic bomb.

3679 Harris, Thomas. Black Sunday. Putnam, 1975. Rpr. 1977.
      P. L. O. terrorists and a disgruntled American attempt to
      blow up the Super Bowl employing a TV blimp.

3680 Harrison, William. Africana. Morrow, 1977.
      Three men lead a clandestine mercenary army in central
      Africa during the 1960's.

3681 Hartmann, Michael. A Game for Vultures. Crowell, 1975.
      A Rhodesian government official seeks 50 U. S. helicopters
      and the means of containing black guerrillas.

3682 _____ . Leap for the Sun. St. Martin's, 1977.
      Before he can hunt treasure, an English mercenary must
      help depose General Toga Tambo, ruler of the Uganda-
      like African state of Kodanga.

3683 Harvey, Frank. Jet. Ballantine, 1958. y. P.
      Stories of the U.S. Air Force on guard during the Cold
      War.

3684 Hebden, Mark. The Mask of Violence. Harcourt, 1970.
      Two U. S. Army officers must safeguard the security of a
      missile base against thousands of demonstrators.

3685 Heinemann, Larry. Close Quarters. Farrar, Straus, 1974.
         Rpr. 1978.
      A tale of U. S. covert operations in Southeast Asia.

3686 Hempstone, Smith. In the Midst of Lions. Harper, 1968.
         y.
      The Arab-Israeli War of 1967 is examined from both view-
      points.

3687 _____. A Tract of Time. Houghton Mifflin, 1966. y.
      When Diem sends troops against the Viet Cong, an Ameri-
      can advisor's plans for holding Montagnard tribes together
      is betrayed.

3688 Heym, Stefan. Five Days in June. Prometheus, 1978. y.
      An hour-by-hour fictional recreation of the East German
      workers revolt of 1953.

      Higgins, Jack, pseud. See Patterson, Henry.

3689 Hoffenberg, Jack. 17 Ben Gurion. Berkley, 1978. P.
      Strategic oil deposits become targets for Arab terrorists
      attempting to destroy Israel.

3690 Hollands, Douglas J. Able Company. Houghton Mifflin, 1956.
         y.
      A look at the soldiers fighting in a British Army unit in
      Korea, 1950.

3691 Hooker, Richard. M*A*S*H. Morrow, 1968. Rpr. 1978.
      The misadventures of doctors and nurses of a mobile sur-
      gical hospital in Korea in 1951; made into a movie and
      popular TV series.

3692 Howe, Charles. Valley of Fire. Dell, 1964. y. P.
      The exploits of five men of an American platoon in the
      Korean War.

      Hudson, James, jt. author. See Rivers, Gayle.

3693 Huggett, William T. Body Count. Putnam, 1973. Rpr. 1974.
      Marine lieutenant Chris Hawkins leads his platoon on bloody
      patrols and against a hilltop North Vietnamese position.

3694 Hyman, Mac. No Time for Sergeants. Random House, 1954.
         y.
      The misadventures of Georgia cracker Will Stockade and
      his buddy Ben in the post-Korean War U. S. Air Force.

Innes, Hammond, pseud. See Hammond-Innes, Ralph.

3695   Iroh, Eddie. Forty-Eight Guns for the General. Heinemann,
           1976.
       Pictures combat in the 1967-1970 civil war in Nigeria.

3696   Jacks, Oliver. The Autumn Heroes. St. Martin's, 1978. y.
       A group of former World War II British soldiers is sent
       to rescue Princess Anne and her husband, who are being
       held prisoners by terrorists in the broiling Chalbi Desert.

3697   Johnston, Ronald. The Black Camels. Harcourt, 1970.
       A deposed leader of an Arab state plans a military opera-
       tion against the new order and its oil-alliance.

3698   Just, Ward. Stringer. Little, Brown, 1974.
       The last mission of a U.S. civilian guerrilla is to destroy
       a North Vietnamese convoy in the mountains.

3699   Kantor, MacKinley. Don't Touch Me. Random House, 1951.
           y.
       A U.S. Air Force major participates in a bombing mission
       during the Korean War.

3700   Karlin, Wayne, ed. Free Fire Zone: Short Stories by Viet-
           nam Veterans. McGraw-Hill, 1973. y. P.
       A series of tales describing the horrors of that conflict.

3701   Katcher, Leo. Hot Pursuit. Atheneum, 1971.
       Seven mercenaries attack a Communist rebel camp on the
       Greco-Albanian border during the Greek civil war of the
       late 1940's.

3702   Kazantzakis, Nikos. The Fratricides. Trans. from the
           Greek. Simon & Schuster, 1965.
       A priest tries to mediate between Loyalist and Insurgents
       during the Greek Civil War.

3703   Kempley, Walter. The Invaders. Saturday Review, 1976.
       A fanatical North Vietnamese Army colonel and a brain-
       washed American deserter with dreams of revenge set up
       rocket launchers in Harlem.

3704   Kennaway, James. Tunes of Glory. Harper, 1957. y.
       Colonel Jock Sinclair, leader of a Scottish Highland regi-
       ment, outrageously survives his more politically astute
       successor; made into a movie.

3704a Kenrick, Tony. The Nightime Guy. Morrow, 1979.
       The U.S. Army tests a new night-vision weapon.

3705   Keon, Michael. The Durian Tree. Simon & Schuster, 1960.
       Communist terrorists strike in Malaya in 1948.

3706 Kiefer, Warren. The Lingala Code. Random House, 1972.
      A Texan is caught up in the Congolese civil war of 1960.

3707 King, Harold. Four Days. Bobbs-Merrill, 1976.
      When Stalin dies certain military events occur: a Polish
      pilot defects to Denmark in a M. I. G. , a U. S. patrol plane
      violates Czech air space, the Russians down an R. A. F.
      Lancaster over East Germany, and the American S. A. C.
      holds full-scale drills over the eastern United States.

3708 Kirkwood, James. Some Kind of Hero. Crowell, 1975.
           Rpr. 1976.
      Eddie Kellar is captured in Vietnam, serves four years as
      a P. O. W. , and then is released to return to America,
      where he becomes a criminal.

3709 Kirst, Hans H. The Seventh Day. Trans. from the German.
           Doubleday, 1959. y.
      Conflict between the Germanys brings the U. S. and U. S. -
      S. R. into a nuclear war.

3710 _____ . What Became of Gunner Asch? Trans. from the
           German. Harper, 1964. y.
      As a post-war hotel owner, Asch becomes involved in a
      rivalry between a new Luftwaffe unit and a Bundeswehr
      regiment.

3711 Klose, Kevin. The Typhoon Shipments. Norton, 1974.
      Corrupt U. S. Army officers in Vietnam conspire to ship
      heroin into the states in the body bags of dead soldiers.

3712 Knebel, Fletcher, and Charles W. Bailey, 2nd. Seven Days
           in May. Harper, 1962. y.
      A military coup is planned against the U. S. government.

3713 Kolpacoff, Victor. The Prisoners of Quai Dong. New Ameri-
           can Library, 1967. P.
      A savage view of U. S. military stockades and interrogation
      methods in Vietnam.

3714 _____ . The Raid. Atheneum, 1971.
      Follows Al Fatah guerrilla leader Faisal and his people
      on an attack on an Israeli power station.

3715 Kruger, Carl. Wings of the Tiger. Fell, 1966. y.
      A fictionalized account of U. S. Air Force operations in
      Vietnam.

3715a Langley, Bob. The War of the Running Fox. Scribner's,
           1979.
      Six Rhodesian commandos attempt to steal plutonium in
      Britain.

3716 Larteguy, Jean. The Centurions. Trans. from the French.
         Dutton, 1962. y.
         Returning to France from a Viet Minh P. O. W. camp after
         the 1954 Battle of Dien Bien Phu, a unit of paratroopers
         is reformed and sent to battle terrorists in Algeria.

3717 _____. The Praetorians. Trans. from the French. Dut-
         ton, 1963. y.
         French paratroopers battle Algerian terrorists in the
         1950's; sequel to the above title.

3718 _____. Yellow Fever. Trans. from the French. Dutton,
         1966. y.
         Depicts the last days of the French effort against the Viet
         Minh.

3719 Lasly, Walter D. Turn the Tigers Loose. Ballantine, 1957.
         y. P.
         Colonel Tim Loring leads his squadron of U. S. Air Force
         B-26 night bombers into action during the Korean War.

3720 Lauer, Pierre. The Suns of Badarane. Trans. from the
         French. Morrow, 1972.
         Thirteen mercenaries are sent to capture and hold an out-
         post in the oil-rich kingdom of Ramador.

3721 Layne, McAvoy. How Audie Murphy Died in Vietnam. Double-
         day, 1973.
         An alienated Marine is captured by the Viet Cong after
         winning an undeserved Silver Cross.

3722 Lederer, William J., and Eugene Burdick. Sarkhan. Mc-
         Graw-Hill, 1965. Rpr. 1977.
         Depicts an American military response to Communist sub-
         version in a small Southeast Asian country.

3723 Lehrer, James. Viva Max. Duell, Sloan, 1966. y.
         A patriotic Mexican general attempts to seize the Alamo
         to restore glory to his nation.

3724 Levin, Meyer. The Harvest. Simon & Schuster, 1978.
         Jewish settlers battle the Arabs in 1948 Israel.

3725 Lewis, David D. The Mahogany Battleship. David McKay,
         1966.
         Civilians clash with military men in the Pentagon over the
         organization of the U. S. national defense.

3726 Lewis, Norman. A Small War Made to Order. Harcourt.
         1966.
         The U. S. military proposes the invasion of Castro's Cuba.

3727 Lilley, Tom. The Officer from Special Branch. Doubleday,
         1971.

Looks at a British counter-terrorist organization set up to
help quash the 1948 Communist insurgency in Malaya.

3728 Liston, Robert A. An Affair of State. Pinnacle, 1978. P.
A U. S. President plots a revolution that will allow him to
become America's first dictator.

3729 Little, Charles. The Bold and the Lonely. David McKay,
1966.
A Marine officer is sentenced to prison for a crime he did
not commit.

3730 Little, Lloyd. Parthian Shot. Viking, 1975.
Forgotten by bureaucrats in Saigon and Washington, a small
group of U. S. soldiers due to return home open a textile
factory on the Cambodian border, co-operating covertley
with both the Viet Cong and the South Vietnamese.

3730a Ludlum, Robert. The Matarese Circle. Richard Marek,
1979.
Top U. S. and Soviet agents battle the Matarese terrorists.

3731 Lundgren, William R. The Primary Cause. Morrow, 1963.
y.
A behind-the-scenes look at the lives of the airmen who
man S. A. C. bombers.

3732 Lyall, Gavin. Shooting Script. Scribner's, 1966.
Two former R. A. F. pilots find themselves on opposite
sides in a Caribbean island's revolution.

3733 Lyle-Smythe, Alan. Afghan Assault. By Alan Caillou, pseud.
Pinnacle, 1973. P.
Colonel Tobin's mercenaries versus Communist terrorists
in Afghanistan.

3734 _____. Assault to Kolchak. By Alan Caillou, pseud.
Avon, 1964. y. P.
Mercenaries battle terrorists in Africa.

3735 _____. Congo War Cry. By Alan Caillou, pseud. Pinnacle, 1972. P.
Colonel Tobin's soldiers of fortune battle Communist irregulars in the former Belgian Congo.

3736 _____. Death Charge. By Alan Caillou, pseud. Pinnacle,
1973. P.
Mexican terrorists in the Sierra Madres are hunted by
Tobin and his mercenaries.

3737 _____. Terror in Rio. By Alan Caillou, pseud. Pinnacle, 1973. P.
Colonel Tobin's mercenaries tackle terrorists in Argentina.

3738 Lynch, Michael. An American Soldier. Little, Brown, 1970.
      In the last months of the Korean War, Corporal Edward
      Condit, a patriotic G. I., begins to wonder why the police
      action was necessary.

3739 MacAlister, Ian. Strike Force Seven. Fawcett, 1974. P.
      A band of mercenaries led by a cynical ex-Army officer
      rescue two women from a terrorist stronghold.

3740 McCallister, David. Sabres Over Brandywine. Hesperian
          House, 1961. y.
      A U. S. Air Force F-86 pilot with domestic problems is
      recalled to active service during the Korean War.

3741 McCurtin, Peter. Ambush at Derali Wells. Belmont-Tower,
          1978. P.

3742 _____. Battle Pay. Belmont-Tower, 1978. P.

3743 _____. Body Count. Belmont-Tower, 1978. P.

3744 _____. The Guns of Palembang. Belmont-Tower, 1977.
          P.

3745 _____. Operation Hong Kong. Belmont-Tower, 1978. P.
      Five tales about a tough international mercenary force
      fighting in Asia and Africa.

3746 McDonald, Hugh C. Five Signs from Ruby. Pyramid, 1976.
          P.
      A madman plans to destroy five U. S. cities with A-bombs
      unless the American government approves of his plan for
      the destruction of Israel.

3747 Maclean, Alistair. Ice Station Zebra. Doubleday, 1974.
          Rpr. 1978.
      Russian paratroopers attempt to foil the Anglo-American
      rescue of the survivors of a meteorological station ex-
      plosion near the North Pole.

3748 Maggio, Joe. Company Man. Putnam, 1972. Rpr. 1978.
      C. I. A. mercenaries in action in Africa and Asia.

3749 Malgonkai, Manohar. The Distant Drum. Taplinger, 1964.
      Life in the British-oriented Indian Army before and after
      the 1948 partition.

3750 Malliol, William. A Sense of Dark. Atheneum, 1968.
      U. S. Marines train at Parris Island and fight in Korea.

3751 Mano, D. Keith. War Is Heaven. Doubleday, 1970.
      Pictures an imaginary conflict in Canaguay, a country not
      unlike Vietnam.

3752 Marquand, John P. Melville Goodwin, U. S. A. Little, Brown,
        1951. y.
        A general becomes a hero, but cannot handle his family
        problems.

3753 Mason, Colin. Hostage. Walker, 1973.
        Israeli right-wing terrorists steal some U. S. strategic
        A-bombs stockpiled in Tel Aviv.

3754 Masters, John. Thunder at Sunset. Doubleday, 1974.
        General David D. Jones and the Resident clash with guer-
        rillas and each other on the eve of Britain's granting of
        independence to the Southeast Asia country of Mingora.

3755 Mayer, Tom. The Weary Falcon. Houghton Mifflin, 1971.
        y.
        A collection of short stories concerning the war in South-
        east Asia.

3756 Meader, Stephen W. Sabre Pilot. Harcourt, 1956. y.
        Pictures the training and combat experiences of a young
        Air Force F-86 fighter pilot during the Korean War.

3757 Michener, James A. The Bridges at Toko-Ri. Random
        House, 1953. Rpr. 1978. y.
        U. S. Navy jets must destroy a Communist bridge in Korea.

3758 _____ . Sayonara. Random House, 1954. Rpr. 1978.
        An American Air Force major, engaged to his general's
        daughter, sets up housekeeping with the beautiful Japanese
        woman.

3758a Mirdrekvandi, Ali. No Heaven for Gunga Din: Consisting of
        the British and American Officers' Book. Dutton, 1965.
        A Persian peasant writes a fable for the amusement of
        Allied officers recounting how they will journey to heaven
        after World War III.

3759 Momaday, N. Scott. The House Made of Dawn. Harper,
        1968. y.
        Depicts a young American Indian's unsuccessful attempt to
        adjust himself to the white world during a seven-year hitch
        in the U. S. Army, 1945-1952.

3760 Monsarrat, Nicholas. The Tribe That Lost Its Head. Sloane,
        1956. y.
        Natives revolt against British rule on an imaginary island
        off the African coast.

3761 Moore, Gene D. The Killing at Ngo-Tho. Norton, 1967.
        Life and actions of a U. S. Army colonel-advisor to the
        South Vietnamese Army in 1964.

3762 Moore, Robert L. The Country Team. By Robin Moore,
         pseud. Crown, 1967.
         When the situation in a guerrilla-ridden but unnamed South-
         east Asian nation deteriorates, drastic measures are nec-
         essary.

3763 _____. The Green Berets. By Robin Moore, pseud.
         Crown, 1965.
         Short stories detailing the counterinsurgency operations of
         U.S. Special Forces troops in Vietnam during the early
         days of that war.

3764 _____, and June Collins. The Khaki Mafia. Crown, 1971.
         Based on facts involving corruption of U.S. troop support
         services in Vietnam.

3765 _____, and Henry Rothblatt. Court-Martial. Doubleday,
         1971.
         A semi-fictionalized account of U.S. Special Forces liqui-
         dators in Vietnam, five of whom are tried for the death
         of a local.

      Moore, Robin, pseud. See Moore, Robert L.

3766 Morris, Edita. Love to Vietnam. Monthly Review, 1968.
         A short story about a young girl with napalm burns in
         Vietnam.

3767 Murphy, John. The Long Reconnaissance. Doubleday, 1970.
         The involvement of a U.S. Air Force major in the Cuban
         Missile Crisis.

3768 Naipaul, V. S. Guerrillas. Knopf, 1976.
         Two English visitors are caught on a Caribbean island and
         become involved with a band of revolutionaries.

3769 Norway, Nevil Shute. On the Beach. By Nevil Shute, pseud.
         Morrow, 1957. y.
         The people of Melbourne, Australia, face termination as
         the result of a nuclear war which has destroyed the north-
         ern hemisphere.

3770 O'Brien, Tim. Going After Cacciato. Delacorte, 1978.
         U.S. soldiers pursue a deserter who has abandoned his
         Vietnam unit.

3771 Osmond, Andrew. Saladin. Doubleday, 1976. Rpr. 1977.
         A British mercenary leads a team assigned to destroy an
         Arab group planning to wipe out Shin Beth's new H.Q. in
         Jerusalem and establish an independent Palestinian state.

3772 Pace, Eric. Any War Will Do. Random House, 1973.
         An amoral organization supplies arms to anyone on the
         basis of the above title/motto.

3773   Patterson, Henry. Toll for the Brave. By Jack Higgins,
            pseud. Fawcett, 1976. P.
       Ellis Jackson, an English mercenary, escapes the Viet
       Cong and returns to Britain, only to find a Vietnamese
       agent on his tail.

3774   Payne, Pierre S. R. The Tortured and the Damned. Hori-
            zon, 1978.
       Depicts the military excesses of the 1971 revolution in
       Bangladesh--then East Pakistan.

3775   Peacock, Jere. Valhalla. Putnam, 1961.
       Returning to Japan just after the armistice, a group of
       U. S. Marine veterans of the Korean War find it difficult
       to adjust to peacetime.

3776   Pearl, Jack. Stockade. Trident, 1965. y.
       During the Korean War an American G. I. must decide if
       he has the right to take the law into his own hands.

3777   Pelfrey, William. The Big V. Liveright, 1972.
       Harry Winstead's fictional diary of how he and his buddies
       fought in 1968 Vietnam.

       Pendleton, Tom, pseud. See Van Zandt, Edmund.

3778   Perowne, Barry. Rogue's Island. Mill, 1950. y.
       An English soldier of fortune arrives on a Spanish island,
       where a girl's father is having shady dealings with neo-
       Fascists.

3779   Perry, Robin. Welcome for a Hero. Livingston, 1975.
       An Army map reader discovers Soviet missiles in Cuba in
       1962.

3780   Pollini, Francis. Night. Houghton Mifflin, 1961.
       How captive G. I.'s were brainwashed during the Korean
       War.

3781   Poyer, Joe. North Cape. Doubleday, 1969. Rpr. 1970.
       Soviet interceptors try to down a U. S. spy plane over the
       Russo-Chinese border.

3782   Prada, Renato. The Breach. Trans. from the Spanish.
            Doubleday, 1971.
       Two young men are caught up in guerrilla actions in the
       mountains of Bolivia.

3783   Pratt, John C. The Laotian Fragments. Viking, 1974.
       Silver Star winner Major William Blake serves as a "ci-
       vilian" forward air controller over Laos during the Viet-
       nam War.

3784 Proud, Franklin M., and Alfred F. Eberhardt. Tiger in the
          Mountain. St. Martin's, 1977.
      Vietnam veteran Courtney Palmer hijacks a U.S.A.F. C-
      141 to fly to North Vietnam and rescue his captured buddy
      and other downed U.S. pilots.

3785 Quirk, John. The Survivor. Avon, 1965. P.
      A mercenary battles a South American dictator.

3786 Ramati, Alexander. Rebel Against the Light. Page, 1961.
      Ex-Polish Army veteran Arthur Weiss fights for the Hag-
      anah during the 1948 Arab-Israeli war.

3787 Rhodes, Hari. A Chosen Few. Bantam, 1965. P.
      Depicts the experiences of a recruit at an all-black Marine
      Corps boot camp in the heart of the South.

3788 Richards, Guy. Two Rubles for Times Square. Duell, Sloan,
          1956. y.
      A Soviet general peacefully occupies New York City some-
      time in the future.

3789 Rivers, Gayle, and James Hudson. The Five Fingers.
          Doubleday, 1978.
      During the Indochina conflict U.S. Special Forces teams
      are sent into enemy country to kill 11 top Chinese and
      North Vietnamese leaders.

3790 Robbins, Harold. The Pirate. Simon & Schuster, 1974.
          Rpr. 1978.
      When his family is captured by Palestinian terrorists, an
      Arab financier is forced to turn to the Israelis for help
      in saving them; a TV mini-series.

3791 Roberts, Suzanne. Vietnam Nurse. Ace, 1966. y. P.
      Another tale of love and war in Southeast Asia; compare
      with Della Field's title cited above.

3792 Rosa, Joao G. The Devil to Pay in the Backlands. Trans.
          from the Portuguese. Knopf, 1963.
      A tale of savage guerrilla warfare in the jungles of Brazil.

3793 Ross, Glen. The Last Campaign. Harper, 1963. y.
      Corporal Hunter and his fellow musicians are sent to
      Korea from Japan as part of the all-out effort to turn
      back the invading Chinese.

3794 Rostand, Robert. Vipers Game. Delacorte, 1974.
      A guerrilla leader modeled on Che Guevara leads irregu-
      lars in an uprising against the colonial "oppressors" on a
      Pacific island.

3795 Rosten, Leo. Captain Newman, M.D. Harper, 1961.

The psychiatric chief of a U.S. Air Force hospital wages
war on the stupidity of the brass for the benefit of his
patients; made into a movie.

3796 Roth, Robert. Sand in the Wind. Little, Brown, 1973. Rpr.
          1977.
      The experiences of U.S. Marine officers and enlisted men
      in Vietnam are examined from their perspectives.

      Rothblatt, Henry, jt. author. See Moore, Robert L.

3797 Rowe, James N. The Judas Squad. Little, Brown, 1975.
          Rpr. 1977.
      Revolutionaries and U.S. ex-soldiers take over a Pennsyl-
      vania nuclear reactor and hold it for ransom.

3798 Ruark, Robert. Something of Value. Doubleday, 1955. Rpr.
          1977. y.
      Pictures the spread of the Mau Mau terror in 1950's
      Kenya.

3799 _____. Uhuru. McGraw-Hill, 1962. Rpr. 1977. y.
      A white hunter becomes involved in Kenya's Mau Mau up-
      rising.

3800 Rubin, Jonathan. The Barking Deer. Braziller, 1974.
      Contrasts a Montagnard legend with the arrival of twelve
      U.S. military personnel to protect a Central Highlands
      village from the Viet Cong.

3801 Runyan, Poke. Night Jump--Cuba. Pyramid, 1965. P.
      Four American paratroopers land in Cuba in an effort to
      prevent World War III.

3802 Salinger, Pierre. On Instructions of My Government. Double-
          day, 1971.
      A Chinese-led revolutionary army topples the South Ameri-
      can republic of Santa Clara.

3803 Salter, James. The Arm of Flesh. Harper, 1962. y.
      Examines the problems of men in a U.S. Air Force jet
      fighter squadron stationed in the German Rhineland in
      1955.

3804 _____. The Hunters. Harper, 1956. y.
      Cleve Saville's F-86 fighter group guards the skies near
      the Yalu River during the Korean War.

3805 Sanderson, James D. The Boy with a Gun. Holt, 1958. y.
      A Hungarian youth recalls the Budapest street combat of
      1956.

3806 Sawkins, Raymond H. Year of the Golden Ape. By Colin
          Forbes, pseud. Dutton, 1974. Rpr. 1975. y.

Two Arab leaders are killed as a prelude to the destruction
of Israel.

3807 Schoonover, Lawrence. Central Passage. Sloane, 1962. y.
      The Panama Canal is the target of an atomic attack.

3808 Scott, Paul. A Division of Spoils. Morrow, 1975.
      The difficulties faced by a British colonel and sergeant
      upon the approach of Indian independence in 1947.

3809 Scott, Robert L. Look of the Eagle. Dodd, Mead, 1956. y.
      A transport pilot and a former Flying Tigers ace conspire
      to steal a Russian jet out of North Korea; good scenes of
      jet combat in the skies over that peninsula during the
      Korean War.

3810 Seaman, Donald. The Bomb That Could Lip-Read. Stein &
         Day, 1974.
      The I. R. A. hires soldier of fortune Kelly to train its
      guerrillas and to plant a bomb in a British military head-
      quarters.

3811 Searls, Hank. Pentagon. Geis, 1971. Rpr. 1977.
      Public relations, security, and censorship affect the lives
      of some officers working there.

3812 Setlowe, Rick. The Brink. Arthur Field, 1976. y.
      Examines the men of a U. S. Navy fighter squadron aboard
      a carrier sent to the Quemoy-Matsu area off Taiwan in
      1960.

3813 Seymour, Gerald. Harry's Game. Random House, 1975.
         Rpr. 1977.
      A British Army officer is ordered to infiltrate and destroy
      the militant elements of the I. R. A. in Northern Ireland.

      Shakespeare, Brian, jt. author. See De St. Jerre, John.

3814 Shaw, Irwin. Evening in Byzantium. Delacorte, 1973. Rpr.
         1974.
      Film director Jesse Craig becomes involved in a terrorist
      plot to destroy three American cities; made into a TV
      mini-series.

3815 Shepherd, Michael. The Road to Gandolfo. Dial, 1975.
      U. S. Army general MacKenzie Hawkins plots an unusual
      crime.

3816 Sherlock, John. The Ordeal of Major Grigsby. Morrow,
         1964.
      A British major in 1948 Malaya must capture a former
      Chinese friend of World War II days who is now a Com-
      munist insurgent.

Shute, Nevil, pseud. See Norway, Nevil Shute.

3817   Sidney, George. For the Love of Dying. Morrow, 1969.
       Focuses on the last days of a U.S. Marine unit on the
       line in 1951 Korea.

3818   Simon, Pierre-Henri. An End to Glory. Trans. from the
       French. Harper, 1961.
       Disgusted with the brutality of fighting in Indochina and
       Algeria, a professional French soldier resigns from the
       service he loves.

3819   Simpson, Howard R. Assignment for a Mercenary. Harper,
       1965. y.
       U.S. soldier of fortune Michael Craig goes undercover to
       help overthrow an African dictatorship.

3820   _____. To a Silent Valley. Knopf, 1962. y.
       Under hardbitten General Cogolin, French paratroopers
       besiege the North Vietnamese valley of Lao Bang; the
       French position is in turn invested, shelled, and overrun
       by the Viet Minh.

3821   Slager, Nigel. Crossfire. Atheneum, 1978.
       Mercenaries tackle a military dictatorship in an African
       nation not unlike present-day Uganda.

3822   Slaughter, Frank G. Sword and Scalpel. Doubleday, 1957.
       Rpr. 1976. y.
       The combat and P.O.W. problems of a young U.S. Army
       doctor in the Korean War.

3823   Slimming, John. In Fear of Silence. Harper, 1959. y.
       On patrol in the 1948 Malayan jungle, British soldiers
       encounter Communist insurgents.

3824   Sloan, James P. War Games. Houghton Mifflin, 1971. Rpr.
       1973.
       Repelled by the behavior of his fellow Rangers on Vietnam
       sweeps, a U.S. soldier kills the entire patrol; returning
       to base, his actions are misconstrued and he is decorated.

3825   Smith, Steven P. American Boys. Putnam, 1975.
       Examines the one-year tours of four American G.I.'s who
       volunteer to go to Vietnam from garrison duty in Ger-
       many; three are killed in a firefight with the Viet Cong.

3826   Smith, Terence L. The Money War. Atheneum, 1978.
       In an effort to halt a U.S.-Israeli trade deal, a band of
       mercenaries sack St. Louis and kill 1,300 innocent people.

3827   Smith, Wilbur A. The Dark of the Sun. Dell, 1977. P.
       Mercenary activities in contemporary Africa.

3828 _____ . The Train from Katanga. Viking, 1965.
Four white mercenaries discover their individual destinies
as they take a native task force into the Congo interior in
1960.

3829 Southwell, Samuel. If All the Rebels Die. Doubleday, 1966.
y.
When the U. S. surrenders to Russia after the latter's first
strike, the people of the town of Travam band together to
resist the Soviet occupation.

3830 Spicehandler, Daniel. Burnt Offerings. Macmillan, 1961.
American explosives expert Trigve Connant agrees to
destroy an Arab-held monastery at Stella Montes, which
is blocking the Israeli advance to Jerusalem in 1948.

3831 Stanley, John. World War III. Avon, 1978. P.
Fought on the Chinese mainland in the future where the
Chinese forces are led by the legendary Ju-Chao, a sur-
vivor of Mao's Long March of the 1930's.

3832 Stanton, Paul. Village of Stars. Mill, 1961. y.
British troops battle Russian tanks in a Middle East country called Kanjistan.

3833 Stern, Richard M. High Hazard. Scribner's, 1962. y.
Revolution engulfs a West Indian island.

3834 Styron, William. The Long March. Random House, 1952.
Rpr. 1968. y.
The rigors of a 36-mile forced training march at a U. S.
Marine boot camp in the Carolinas.

3835 Sutton, Henry. Vector. Geis, 1970.
Pictures a 1968 error at the U. S. Army's Chemical and
Biological Warfare testing center.

3836 Tarr, Herbert. The Conversion of Chaplain Cohen. Geis,
1963. y.
Examines the problems of a young Jewish chaplain in the
U. S. Air Force.

3837 Taylor, Thomas. A-18. Crown, 1967.
A tale of combat in Vietnam.

3838 _____ . A Piece of This Country. Norton, 1970.
The military and domestic problems of black U. S. Army
advisor Roscoe Jackson before and during his tour of duty
in Vietnam.

3839 Thomas, Craig. Firefox. Holt, 1977. Rpr. 1978.
Veteran combat pilot Mitchell Grant seeks to steal a
brand-new Soviet M. I. G. -31 fighter, code-named "Firefox."

3840 Thomas, Leslie. The Virgin Soldiers. Little, Brown, 1966.
      Brigg and other young conscripts in the British Army bat-
      tle Communist insurgents in Malaya.

3841 Thorin, Duane. The Ride to Panmunjom. Regnery, 1957.
      y.
      Flashback stories about 12 U. S. servicemen aboard a Chi-
      nese truck enroute to repatriation after the Korean armi-
      stice.

3842 Tibbets, Albert B. , comp. Courage in Korea: Stores of the
      Korean War. Little, Brown, 1962. y.
      A reprinting of several short tales from various popular
      magazines.

3843 Tiede, Tom. The Coward. Trident, 1968.
      Convicted of cowardice for not wanting to fight in Vietnam,
      U. S. Army private Nathan Long is sent there anyway and
      dies in a firefight with the Viet Cong.

3844 Tinnin, David B. The Hit Team. Dell, 1977. P.
      An Israeli execution squad hunts down and liquidates Arab
      terrorists.

3845 Tippette, Giles. The Mercenaries. Delacorte, 1976. y.
      Looks at an elite mercenary force mission against Zambian
      camps housing Rhodesian terrorists.

3846 Topol, Allan. The Fourth of July War. Morrow, 1978. y.
      When the O. P. E. C. nations begin to cut back oil exports
      to the U. S. , Director of Energy George Morrow decides
      that normal procedures must be bypassed.

3847 Tregaskis, Richard. The Last Plane to Shanghai. Bobbs-
      Merrill, 1961. y.
      An American war correspondent is involved in covering
      the Chinese civil war of 1945-1949.

3848 Trevor, Elleston. The Freebooters. Doubleday, 1967.
      Eight men of the British 4th Royals battle the Vendettu
      guerrillas in a colonial African nation.

3849 _____. The Sinkiang Executive. By Adam Hall, pseud.
      Doubleday, 1978.
      Agent Quiller is ordered to fly a hijacked Soviet M. I. G.
      to Yelingrad, near the Chinese border; compare with
      Craig Thomas's Foxfire above.

3850 Trew, Antony. Ultimatum. St. Martin's, 1976.
      Pictures a raid on a P. L. O. group threatening to blow up
      London with an A-bomb.

3850a Truscott, Lucien K. Dress Gray. Doubleday, 1979.

Murder and cover-up at the U.S. Military Academy in the late 1960's.

3851   Tully, Andrew. A Race of Rebels. Simon & Schuster, 1960.
An American news reporter fights with Castro during the late 1950's.

3852   Uris, Leon. Armageddon. Doubleday, 1964.
An American Army captain's experiences in the civil government of Berlin from V-E Day to the end of the 1948 Airlift.

3853   _____. Exodus. Doubleday, 1959. Rpr. 1975. y.
Jewish refugees fight the Arabs to establish Israel, 1947-1948; made into a movie.

3854   Van Der Post, Laurens. A Far-Off Place. Morrow, 1974.
Rpr. 1978. y.
When Maoist guerrillas overrun a South African family's farm, the survivors must battle hostile natives and the elements in order to reach British troops then holding maneuvers on the African west coast.

3855   Van Greenaway, Peter. Take the War to Washington. St. Martin's, 1975.
Some 500 battle-weary Vietnam veterans take out their frustrations on the cities of New York and Washington, D. C.

3856   Van Zandt, Edmund. Husak. By Tom Pendleton, pseud.
McGraw-Hill, 1969.
A U.S. Marine and a Tulsa oil heiress become involved in a Latin American revolution.

3857   Vaughan, Robert. The Valkyrie Mandate. Simon & Schuster, 1974. Rpr. 1975.
Buddists, the U.S. Army, and Madame Nhu dominate this tale of the Vietnamese War, 1961-1963.

3858   Voorhees, Melvin B. Show Me a Hero. Simon & Schuster, 1954. y.
Three Americans--a general, a chaplain, and a journalist--are caught up in the Panmunjom impasse.

3859   Wager, Walter. Blue Leader. Arbor House, 1978.
Employing surplus B-17's and led by a woman agent, a group of former wartime American airmen attack a convoy of heroin in Burma.

3860   _____. Viper Three. Macmillan, 1971.
Five escaped murderers take over an American S.A.C. missile base.

3861 Wahlöö, Per. The Generals. Pantheon, 1974.
      How a revolution fails on a Caribbean island.

3862 Watkins, Leslie. The Killing of Idi Amin. Avon, 1977. P.
      A team of mercenaries and assassins attempt to kill the
      unpopular Ugandan leader.

3863 Webb, James H., Jr. Fields of Fire. Prentice-Hall, 1978.
      A platoon of Marines slogging its way through battles and
      skirmishes in the rice paddies and jungles of South Viet-
      nam evokes the ambiguous and gruesome character of that
      war and contrasts the realization of war's dangers with the
      attraction to combat as the ultimate test of survival.

3864 Webb, Lucas. Stribling. Doubleday, 1973. y.
      Problems of love, dope, and cruelty are faced by a young
      Indian man in the U.S. Army of the 1960's.

3865 West, John A. Osborne's Army. Morrow, 1967.
      Mercenaries fight a revolution on a West Indian island.

3866 West, Morris. The Salamander. Morrow, 1973. y.
      An Italian general leads a conspiracy against his govern-
      ment.

3867 Weston, John. Hail Hero. David McKay, 1968. y.
      Leaving an Arizona ranch for Vietnam, a young man won-
      ders about war and blames the older generation for the
      disillusionment of young people with the modern world;
      made into a movie.

3868 Whittington, Harry. Guerrilla Girls. Pyramid, 1961. P.
      Women guerrillas battle the French in Algeria.

3869 _____. Rebel Women. Avon, 1960. P.
      Castro's women guerrilla fighters in action in Cuba.

3870 Williams, Alan. Shah-Mak. Coward-McCann, 1976. Rpr.
      1977.
      A group of mercenaries are paid to kill the Shah of Iran.

3871 Williamson, Tony. The Doomsday Contract. Simon & Schu-
      ster, 1978.
      American soldiers of fortune tackle a terrorist group that
      threatens to employ a captured A-bomb.

3872 Wilson, William. The L.B.J. Brigade. Apocalypse Corp.,
      1967.
      A recent college graduate recalls the horror of his search-
      and-destroy mission in Vietnam.

3873 Wolfe, Michael. The Chinese Fire Drill. Harper, 1976.

A band of irregular Vietnamese rebels kidnap an important American Army officer.

3874 _____ . Man on a String. Harper, 1973.
A cameraman in Vietnam undertakes one last mission before returning home.

3875 _____ . Two-Star Pigeon. Harper, 1975.
By threatening to release secret U.S. plans, an American Army general in Vietnam attempts to return the monarchy to that country.

3876 Woods, William C. The Killing Zone. Harper, 1970.
The training ideals of an American Army officer and his sergeant come into conflict when real bullets are substituted for plastic ones during a mock battle.

3877 Wylie, Philip. Tomorrow. Rinehart, 1954. y.
Projects a Soviet nuclear attack on the United States.

PART III

CHRONICLES COVERING MORE THAN ONE PERIOD

The tales listed in this section, often family sagas, cover various
time periods, all of which overlap the artificial guidelines of our
chronology.   Readers might wish to compare the appropriate parts
of some of these with tales listed in other sections of this work.

3878   Allen, Henry.   The Last Warpath.   By Will Henry, pseud.
            Random House, 1966.   y.
            Traces the problems of the Cheyenne Indians with the
            whites in North America from 1680 to 1896.

3879   Austin, Frederick B.   Saga of the Sword.   Macmillan, 1929.
            y.
            Fictional recreations of famous battles from ancient times
            to World War I are used to illustrate advances in the mili-
            tary arts.

3880   Bellah, James W.   Fighting Men, U. S. A.   Regency, 1963.
            y.
            Eight stories about American men in war and its effect
            on them, physically and mentally, from the Revolution to
            World War II.

3881   Brick, John.   They Ran for Their Lives.   Doubleday, 1954.
            y.
            Three stories about escapees during the American Revo-
            lution and Civil War.

3882   Caldwell, Janet T.   Dynasty of Death.   By Taylor Caldwell,
            pseud.   Scribner's, 1938.   y.
            Examines a Pennsylvania family's armaments industry
            from the Civil War to World War I.

       Caldwell, Taylor, pseud.   See Caldwell, Janet T.

3883   Corley, Edwin.   The Jesus Factor.   Stein & Day, 1970.
            In Part I the narrator is the 1945 A. A. F. bombardier
            scheduled to drop the first A-bomb on Tokyo; in Part II
            he is a 1964 Presidential candidate involved in an inter-
            national crisis over American missiles in Japan.

3884   Davis, Paxton.   The Season of Heroes.   Morrow, 1967.
            Follows three generations of the Virginia Gibboney family:

Matt, who resigns from the U.S. Army to join the Confederacy; Robert, who rides in Colonel McNaught's 1864
foray into Pennsylvania; and Will, who serves in the peace-
time U.S. Army in 1914.

3885 Deighton, Len. Eleven Declarations of War. Harcourt, 1975.
        Rpr. 1977. y.
        Eleven short stories about dramatic confrontations in the
        lives of American soldiers and airmen.

3886 Dunmore, Spencer. Ashley Landing. Morrow, 1976. y.
        Traces the history of one British aerodrome and the flyers
        using it from 1911 to 1939.

3887 Eden, Dorothy. Salamanca Drum. Coward-McCann, 1977.
        Rpr. 1978. y.
        A right-wing English mother pushes her son into every
        Empire conflict between the Boer War and early World
        War II.

3888/9 Forester, Cecil S. The General. Little, Brown, 1936. y.
        Pictures the career of an English professional soldier
        from the Boer War through World War I.

3890 Frankau, Gilbert. World Without End. Dutton, 1943. y.
        A British soldier advances in experience and rank as he
        fights in every conflict from the Chaco War (Paraguay
        versus Bolivia) to World War II.

3891 Gilpatrick, Guy. Guy Gilpatrick's Flying Stories. Dutton,
        1946. y.
        Includes tales of military aviation in both World Wars.

Grant, Allen, pseud. See Smith, Arthur D. H.

3892 Hemingway, Ernest, ed. Men at War: The Best War Stories
        of All Time. Crown, 1942. y.
        A series of tales by various authors covering military
        events from the 1066 Battle of Hastings to the 1942 clash
        at Midway.

Henry, Will, pseud. See Allen, Henry.

3893 Hunter, Evan. Sons. Doubleday, 1970. Rpr. 1971.
        Follows three generations of the Tyler family in American
        wars: Bert serves as a World War I doughboy; Will is an
        A.A.F. crewman in World War II; and Wat is drafted to
        fight in the Vietnamese conflict.

3894 Jakes, John. The Kent Family Chronicles. Jove, 1976- .
        P.
        In one of the most popular of paperback series, conceived
        as a tribute to the American Bicentennial, the author

follows one American family's experiences in American
wars from 1775 onward; Titles available as of December
1978 include: The Bastard, The Rebels, The Seekers, The
Furies, The Titans, The Warriors, and The Lawless.

3895   Jennings, John E.   Call the New World.   Macmillan, 1941.
       y.
       Follows the military career of Peter Brooke from West
       Point, through the War of 1812, his court-martial on false
       charges, and his success as a leader in South American
       wars of independence fought during the 1820's.

3896   Johnson, Annabel and Edgar.   The Last Knife.   Simon &
       Schuster, 1971.   y.
       When a youth studies other incidents of conscientious ob-
       jection in American history, he comes to understand why
       his brother is a Vietnam war "draft-dodger."

3897   Jolly, Andrew.   A Time of Soldiers.   Dutton, 1976.   Rpr.
       1977.   y.
       Traces three generations of an American military family
       from the Mexican War to the conflict in Southeast Asia.

3898   Longstreet, Stephen.   The General.   Putnam, 1974.
       Follows the military career of Simon Bolivar Copperwood
       from the pre-World War I West Point through the war in
       Vietnam; toward the end, he begins to realize that his
       retirement, his "fifth star," and his life are in jeopardy
       from unknown sources.

3899   McHargue, Georgess, comp.   Little Victories, Big Defeats:
       War As the Ultimate Pollution.   Delacorte, 1974.
       A selection of short stories designed to demonstrate the
       wastefulness and tragedy of organized combat.

3900   Marshall, William L.   The Age of Death.   Viking, 1971.
       Examines the military experiences of the sons of two gen-
       erations in World War I, the Spanish Civil War, and World
       War II.

3901   Mason, Francis Van Wyck, ed.   Fighting Americans: A War-
       Chest of Stories of American Soldiers from the French
       and Indian Wars Through the First World War.   Reynal,
       1943.   y.
       A series of accounts taken from the fictional works of such
       writers as Cooper, Lancaster, Jennings, and Marquand.

3901a Masters, John.   The Rock.   Putnam, 1970.   y.
       Thirteen tales of Gibraltar in different military eras.

3902   Michelaard, B.   The Sudden Sky.   David McKay, 1974.
       Traces the lives of two German cousins from their first
       flying experiences for the Third Reich until they meet each
       other in combat in the skies over Korea in 1951.

3903 Michener, James A. The Source. Random House, 1965.
      Rpr. 1978. y.
      An archaeological mission digs up 100 centuries of Israeli
      history, including evidence of many wars and battles.

3904 Myrer, Anton. Once an Eagle. Holt, 1968. Rpr. 1977.
      Traces the interlocking careers of soldier-humanist Sam
      Damon and grasping Courtney Massingale, who looks for
      power and considers war a game, from World War I to
      the Korean conflict; a TV mini-series.

3905 Reynolds, Quentin J. Known but to God. Day, 1961. y.
      Pictures the last days of three American soldiers, one
      each in World War I, World War II, and the Korean con-
      flict, who may have been chosen as the Unknown Soldiers
      in Arlington National Cemetary.

3906 Scanlon, John. Davis. Doubleday, 1969.
      Follows a career officer's service from West Point to serv-
      ice with Wingate's Raiders in World War II Burma, his
      peacetime promotion, and death in the Korean War.

3907 Skelton, C. L. The Regiment: Vol. 2, the Imperial War.
      Dial, 1979. y.
      Follows the Scottish 148th regiment from the Sepoy Revolt
      to World War II; Colonel Andrew Maclaren retires, his
      command going to Willie Bruce.

3908 Smith, Arthur D. H. Grey Maiden. By Allen Grant, pseud.
      Longmans, Green, 1929. y.
      Like King Arthur's Excalibur, the legendary sword Grey
      Maiden is a tool of magic; its exploits are traced from
      ancient Athens through the Elizabethan Age.

3909 Thomason, John W., Jr. --And a Few Marines. Scribner's,
      1943. y.
      The author's various U. S. Marine Corps tales from works
      cited in the various parts of Section II above plus a few
      more reprinted from the pages of the Saturday Evening
      Post.

3910 _____. Marines and Others. Scribner's, 1929. y.
      Ten short stories about U. S. Marines in World War I and
      in aerial combat over Nicaragua in the 1920's.

3911 _____. Red Pants and Other Stories. Scribner's, 1927.
      y.
      Ten tales of U. S. Marines in World War I and the "Ba-
      nana Wars" of the 1920's.

3912 Tomlinson, Henry M. All Our Yesterdays. Heinemann,
      1930. y.

Presents a panorama of the British Empire from 1900 to
1918; begins with the Boer War and ends with the 1918
Armistice.

3913 Treece, Henry. The Invaders: Three Stories. Crowell, 1972.
Focuses on the futility of war in the Roman, Viking, and
Norman invasions of England.

3914 Wellman, Paul I. Magnificent Destiny. Doubleday, 1962.
The intertwining lives of Andrew Jackson and Sam Houston
from the War of 1812 through the Battle of San Jacinto.

Whitehouse, Arch, pseud. See Whitehouse, Arthur G. J.

3915 Whitehouse, Arthur G. J. Fighters in the Sky. By Arch
Whitehouse, pseud. Duell, Sloan, 1959. y.
Exploits of Allied fighter pilots in combat in World War I,
World War II, and the Korean conflict.

3916 Williams, John A. Captain Blackman. Doubleday, 1972. y.
A black U.S. Army officer, wounded in Vietnam combat,
undergoes surgery and dreams of his participation in all
of America's previous conflicts back to the War of 1812.

3917 Zara, Louis. This Land Is Ours. Houghton Mifflin, 1940.
y.
Pictures American frontier life from the Susquehanna to
the Mississippi River, 1755 to 1835, with wars and ap-
pearances by such leading characters as Chief Pontiac,
George Rogers Clark, and "Mad" Anthony Wayne.

INDEXES

INDEX TO PSEUDONYMS

A pseudonym is to an author what camouflage is to a soldier or cloud cover to an airman: protective covering designed to hide a true identity. A number of war-story writers have chosen, for different reasons, to make their contributions in disguise. In comparison to those who pen sea- or spy-fiction, however, their ranks are relatively thin.

For their assistance in the compilation on this and other indexes below, my special thanks goes to Salem College students Rebecca I. Schweigart and Binh T. Pham. Without their aid, this part of the book would still be in filing boxes.

Grier, Sidney C., pseud. see
Gregg, Hilda C.
Gulick, Bill, pseud. see Gul-
ick, Grover C.
Hall, Adam, pseud. see
Trevor, Elleston
Hazel, Harry, pseud. see
Jones, Justin
Henry, Will, pseud. see Al-
len, Henry
Herbert, Arthur, pseud. see
Arthur, Herbert
Heyer, Georgette, pseud see
Rougier, G. R.
Higgins, Jack, pseud. see
Patterson, Henry
Innes, Hammond, pseud. see
Hammond-Innes, Ralph
Iron, Ralph, pseud. see
Schreiner, Olive
J. S. of Dale, pseud. see
Stimson, Frederic J.
John, Evan, pseud. see
Simpson, Evan J.
Knight, Brigid, pseud. see
Sinclair, Kathleen
Lorne, Charles, pseud. see
Brand, Charles N.
McAuley, Allan, pseud. see
Stewart, Charlotte
Maclaren, Ian, pseud. see
Watson, John
March, William, pseud. see
Campbell, William E. M.
Merriman, H. Seton, pseud
see Scott, Hugh S.
Moore, Robin, pseud. see
Moore, Robert L.
Morris, Ira J., pseud. see
Jeffries, Ian
North, Anison, pseud. see
Wilson, May
Norton, Andre, pseud. see
Norton, Alice M.
Oliver, Jane, pseud. see
Rees, Helen C. E.
Otis, James, pseud. see
Kaler, James O.
Ouida, pseud. see De La
Ramee, Louise
Oxenham, John, pseud. see

Dunkerley, William A.
Paradise, Mary, pseud. see
Eden, Dorothy
Plaidy, Jean, pseud. see
Hibbert, Eleanor
Presland, John, pseud. see
Skelton, Gladys
Private 19022, pseud. see
Manning, Frederic
Rame, David, pseud. see
Divine, Arthur D.
Reeman, Douglas, pseud. see
Kent, Alexander
Renault, Mary, pseud. see
Challans, Mary
Robertson, James A., pseud.
see Duncan, Robert L.
Samarow, Gregor, pseud. see
Meding, Oskar
"Sapper," pseud. see McNeile,
Herman C.
Sarasin, J. G., pseud. see
Salmon, Geraldine G.
Seaton, Graham, pseud. see
Hutchinson, Graham S.
Sharp, Luke, pseud. see
Barr, Robert
Shute, Nevil, pseud. see
Norway, Nevil S.
Storme, Peter, pseud. see
Stern, Philip V. D.
Talbot, Hugh, pseud. see
Alington, Argentine F.
Thane, Elswyth, pseud. see
Beebe, Elswyth T.
Vaughan, Carter A., pseud.
see Gerson, Noel B.
Vestal, Stanley, pseud. see
Campbell, Walter S.
Weaver, Ward, pseud. see
Mason, Francis V. W.
Welch, Ronald, pseud. see
Felton, Ronald O.
Whittle, Tyler, pseud. see
Tyler-Whittle, Michael S.
Wilson, Charlotte, pseud. see
Baker, Keith
Wycliffe, John, pseud. see
Bedford-Jones, Henry
Wynne, May, pseud. see
Knowles, Mabel W.

Asch, Sholem, 2180
Ash, William, 3563
Ashley, Robert, 1637
Ashmead, John, 2975
Aspen, Don, 2585
Astrup, Helen, 2976
Atherton, Mrs. G. F., 4
Atkinson, Eleanor, 2586
Atwell, Lester, 2977
Austin, Frederick B., 772,
2387, 2587, 3879
Avery, Harold, 893-894
Ayres, Ruby M., 2588
Azuela, Mariano, 2536

Babcock, William H., 125
Babel, Isaak E., 2878
Bacheller, Irving, 1219, 1446
Baggett, Samuel G., 2058
Bagley, Desmond, 3564
Bagnold, Enid, 2589
Bahr, Jerome, 3565
Bailey, H. C., 127, 535, 773,
895-897
Bailey, Paul D., 1512
Baille, Peter, 2978
Baines, Annie M., 1120
Baker, A. A., 2115
Bakeless, John, 1220
Baker, Amy J., 128
Baker, Betty, 1513, 2059
Baker, George, 129, 2181
Baker, H. Barton, 536
Baker, James, 130-131
Baker, Keith, 1514
Baker, Nina B., 2116
Baker, Richard M., 2980
Baklanov, Grigorii I., 2981-
2982
Balchin, Nigel, 132
Balfour, Andrew, 774
Balka, M., 3566
Ball, John, 2983
Ball, John D., 3567
Ballantyne, R. M. 133
Ballard, Willis T., 1638
Ballinger, W. A., 2592
Ballinger, William S., 3568
Balmer, Edwin, 2591, 2879
Banks, Polan, 1447
Barahat, Halim, 3569
Barak, Michael, 2984, 3570
Barbeau, Clayton C., 3571

Barber, Rowland, 3574
Barbour, R. H. 1065
Barbusse, Henri, 2592-2593
Baring, Maurice, 2537
Barker, Shirley, 1221-1222
Barley, Rex, 2985
Barlow, James, 3573
Barnes, Margaret C., 134-136
Baron, Alexander, 2060, 2182,
2986-2987
Barr, Amelia E., 1515
Barr, George, 2988
Barr, Robert, 137
Barrett, Monte, 1516-1517
Barrett, William E., 2117
Barretto, Larry, 2594
Barrington, Michael, 537
Barroll, Clare, 136
Barry, Jane, 1223-1224, 1897,
2118
Barry, William 898
Bartos-Hoppner, B., 538-539,
899
Bartov, Hanokh, 2989
Batchelor, D. O., 2061
Bates, Herbert E., 2990-2994
Baumann, Hans, 6, 2285
Baxter, J. Dowling, 7
Baxter, Walter, 2995
Bazin, Rene F. N. M., 2595
Beals, Carleton, 2062, 2996
Bean, Amelia, 1518
Beatty, John and Patricia, 540
Beaty, David, 2797
Beaty, J. C., 139
Bechdolt, Frederick R., 1639
Beck, Howard, 2998
Beck, Lily, 2538
Becker, Jurek, 2999
Becker, Stephen, 1640, 3574
Beddoe, David, 2388
Bedford-Jones, Henry, 541-543
Beebe, Elswyth T., 1225, 2119
Beebe, Ralph, 1448
Beech, Webb, 3575
Beers, Lorna, 1226
Bek, Aleksandr A., 3000
Bell, John, 1641
Bell, Kensil, 1227-1228
Bellah, James W., 1642-1643,
1898- 1900, 2120, 2596,
3880
Bellamy, Edward, 1449

Belloc, Hilaire, 776
Benchley, Nathaniel, 1901
Bengtssom, Frans, 140, 2286
Benner, Judith A., 1644
Bennett, Louie, 777
Bennett, Robert A., 141, 2597
Bennetts, Pamela, 142-143,
    544, 2287
Benson, Blackwood K., 1650
Benson, Edward F., 900-901
Benstead, Charles K., 2598
Bentley, Phyllis, 8
Bergamini, David, 3001
Bergee, L. K., 3576
Berger, Marcel, 2599-2600
Berger, Thomas, 144, 1902
Bernhardsen, Christian, 3002
Bernstein, Kenneth, 3577
Berry, Erick, 145
Berto, Giuseppe, 3003
Bertrand, Adrian, 2601
Best, Allena C., 1229
Best, Herbert, 1121-1122
Beste, R. Vernon, 3004
Bevan, Tom, 9, 146-147, 545
Beverley-Giddings, Arthur R.,
    3005
Beylen, Robert, 3006
Bickers, Richard, 3007-3011
Bierce, Ambrose, 1649
Binns, Archie, 2880
Binns, Ottwell, 546
Bird, Robert M., 1450
Birney, Hoffman, 1903
Bishop, Farnham, 10
Bishop, Giles, 2603-2605
Blackburn, Thomas W., 1904
Blacker, Irwin R., 2063, 3578
Blackmore, Richard D., 547
Blackstock, Josephine, 3012
Blagowidow, George, 3013
Blake, Bass, 778
Blake, George, 2606
Blake, M. M., 148-149
Blake-Foster, Charles F.,
    548
Blaker, Richard, 2607
Blanch, Lesley, 2417
Blankenship, William, 3014,
    3579
Blankfort, Michael, 2608-
    2609, 2881
Blasco-Ibáñez, Vincente, 11,

2064, 2610
Blatty, William P., 3580
Blayney, Owen, 549
Bloem, Walter, 902
Bluden, Godrey, 3015-3016
Boatman, Alan, 3581
Bodkin, M. McDonnell, 779
Boll, Heinrich, 3017-3019,
    3582
Bolton, I. M., 150-152
Bonallack, Basil, 153
Bonham, Frank, 3020-3021
Bonner, Charles, 2611
Bontemps, Arna, 1451, 2065
Booth, Fred W., 3022
Borland, Hal G., 1650
Borowsky, Marvin, 154
Bost, Jacques L., 3023
Bothwell, Jean, 2184, 2288
Boulle, Pierre, 3024-3025,
    3583
Bourjaily, Vance, 2612, 3026
Bowers, Gwendolyn, 155
Bowher, Alfred, 156
Bowman, Peter, 3027
Boyce, Burke, 1230-1231
Boyd, Dean, 3028
Boyd, James, 1232, 1651
Boyd, Martin, 2613
Boyd, Thomas A., 1123, 1233,
    2614-2615
Boyington, Gregory "Pappy,"
    3029
Boyle, Kay, 3030
Bozer, Johan, 2539
Brackett, Leigh, 1519
Braddon, Russell, 3031
Braddy, Haldeen, 2121
Brady, Charles A., 157
Brady, Cyrus T., 903-904,
    1254, 1520, 1652-1654,
    1905, 2185
Braine, Sheila E., 158, 780
Bramston, M., 159
Brand, Anna, 1521
Brand, Charles N., 2122
Branson, H. C., 1655
Brarco, Edgar J., 1906
Bray, Anna E., 160
Brebner, Percy J., 550
Breem, Wallace, 161
Breit, Harvey, 3584
Brelis, Dean, 3032-3033

Carlisle, Henry, 1529
Carmichael, E. M., 791
Carney, David, 3597
Carpenter, E. Childs, 1530
Carpentier, Alezo, 2070-
    2071, 3598
Carrington, John W., 3067
Carse, Robert, 2295, 3069
Carter, Forrest, 1923
Carter, Jefferson, 1246
Carter, R. G., 170
Case, Josephine, 1455, 2423
Casey, Robert J., 171
Castle, Frank, 2544
Castle, John, 3069
Cather, Willa S., 2625
Catherwood, Mary H., 1067
Catton, Bruce, 1672
Chadwick, Joseph, 1925-1926
Challans, Mary, 16-18, 2187-
    2188
Chalmers, Harvey, 1131, 1247
Chalmers, Stephen, 557
Chamales, Tom T., 3070
Chamberlain, William, 3071-
    3074
Chambers, Robert W., 910-
    913, 1132, 1248-1250,
    1456, 1531, 1674, 2626
Chambers, Whitman, 3075
Champion, John C., 1927
Chandler, David, 3599
Chapman, A. Edward, 172
Chapman, Ann S., 1251
Chapman, Mary and Stanton,
    1252, 1457
Chapman, Vera, 173
Charles, Mark, 3076
Charlton, Lionel E. O., 2886
Charlwood, D. E. 3077
Charques, Dorothy, 558, 2296
Chartres, Annie, 2627
Chase, Borden, 2628
Chavadze, Paul, 914
Chaves-Nogales, Manuel, 2887
Cheshire, Giff, 1532, 1928
Chesney, George T., 2424
Chesnof, Richard Z., 3600
Chetwode, R. D., 174
Chidsey, Donald B., 175
Chin, Kee O., 3078
Chinn, Laurene, 2189
Choate, R. G., 1533

Christgau, John, 1677
Christowe, Stoyan, 2545
Chukovskii, Nikolai F., 3079
Church, Alfred J., 19-21, 559,
    2190-2192
Church, Samuel H., 560
Churchill, Winston, 1253
Cikalo, Walter, 3080
Cittafino, Ricardo, 3081
Clare, John, 3601
Clark, Alan, 3602
Clark, Alfred, 2193
Clark, Roger W., 3603
Clarke, Arthur C., 3082
Clarke, Henry, 561
Clavell, James, 2389, 3083
Claymore, Rod, 3084
Cleary, John, 3085, 3604
Clebert, Jean Paul, 3086
Clemens, Jeremiah, 1534
Clifford, Francis, 2888
Clift, Chaimain, 2297
Clive, William, 2425
Cloete, Stuart, 2426-2430,
    2629
Close, Hannah, 176
Clou, John, 2298-2299
Coatsworth, Elizabeth J.,
    1068, 1133
Cobb, Humphrey, 2630
Cobb, Sylvanus J., 1254
Cobban, J. McLaren, 2431
Cockrell, Boyd, 3087
Cocteau, Jean, 2631
Coe, F. L., 2300
Coffman, Virginia, 1255
Cogswell, A. M., 2632
Cohen, Stanley, 3605
Collingwood, W. G., 177
Collins, Wilkie, 178
Collison, Thomas, 3088
Comfort, Will L., 1929-1930,
    2546
Compton, Herbert, 2390
Comstock, Seth C., 562
Conan-Doyle, Arthur, 179-
    180, 563-564, 915-918
Condon, Richard, 3606
Connell, Evan S., 3089
Connor, Rearden, 2889
Conrad, Joseph, 2125
Conroy, Pat, 3607
Conscience, Hendrick, 181, 565

Grierson, Edward, 620
Griffin, Gerald, 621
Griffin, Gwyn, 3173
Griffis, William E. , 1296
Griffith, George, 2080
Griffiths, Arthur, 821, 2394, 2450
Gringhuis, Dirk, 1157
Grisley, L. , 619
Grogan, Walter E. , 622
Groom, A. J. Pelham, 3174
Groom, Winston, 3668
Grossback, Robert, 3669
Gruber, Frank, 1728-1729, 1951
Gudmundsson, Kristmann, 52
Gulick, Grover C. , 1952-1953
Gull, C. Ranger, 286
Gunter, A. C. , 967, 1562
Guthrie, Ramon, 2681
Gwaltney, Francis I. , 3175

Haas, Ben, 1730
Habeck, Fritz, 623
Hackett, Charles J. , 3176
Haddah, C. A. , 3670
Hagedorn, Hermann, 2140
Haggard, H. Rider, 287, 624, 2081, 2222-2224, 2318, 2351-2452
Haggerty, Edward, 3177
Hailslip, Harvey, 3178
Haines, D. H. , 2454, 2682
Haines, William W. , 1954, 3179-3180
Halberstam, David, 3671
Haldeman, Joe W. , 3672
Hale, Edward E. , 1474
Hales, A. G. , 625, 968
Halide, Edib, 2904
Hall, James N. , 2683
Hall, Marjory, 1297
Hall, Rubylea, 1563
Hallet, Richard, 1564
Hallstead, William F. , 3181, 3673
Hamilton, Bernard, 288
Hamilton, Franklin, 289
Hamilton, Harry, 1160
Hamilton, Robert W. , 2684
Hammond-Innes, Ralph, 3182, 3674
Hanes, Frank B. , 1955

Hanley, Gerald, 3183
Hannay, James O. , 2905
Hansard, Luke J. , 969
Hanson, Joseph M. , 1731
Harben, William N. , 1732
Harcourt, A. F. P. , 2455-2456
Harding, Bertita, 2141
Hardman, Ric, 2906, 3675
Hardwick, Mollie, 822
Hardy, Rene, 3184, 3676
Hardy, Ronald, 3677
Harkins, Philip, 3185
Harper, Robert S. , 1475
Harris, Clare W. , 2225
Harris, Credo F. , 2685
Harris, Cyril, 1298
Harris, Edwin, 290
Harris, John, 1565, 2686, 2907-2908, 3186
Harris, Leonard, 3678
Harris, MacDonald, 3187
Harris, Margaret, 1956
Harris, Thomas, 3679
Harrison, Charles Y. , 2687
Harrison, Constance, 1733
Harrison, Frederick, 291, 2225a, 2319
Harrison, William, 3680
Hart, J. Weley, 626
Hart, Scott, 1734
Hartley, A. B. , 3188
Hartley, M. , 970-971
Hartmann, Michael, 3681-3682
Harvey, Frank, 3683
Harwood, Alice, 627-628
Hasek, Jaroslav, 2688
Hassel, Sven, 3189-3191
Hastings, Peter, 53
Haugaard, Erik C. , 629-630
Haverfield, E. L. , 631
Havill, Edward, 1735
Havinghurst, Walter, 1299
Haworth, Paul L. , 1159
Hawtrey, Valentina, 242
Hay, David, 2689
Haycox, Ernest, 1300, 1736-1737, 1957
Haycraft, Molly C. , 293, 2321
Haynes, Herbert, 632, 972-974, 2142-2148, 2457-2458
Hays, Wilma P. , 1160
Heaven, Constance, 974a

Hebden, Mark, 3684
Heckelmann, Charles N., 1958-1959
Heinemann, Larry, 3685
Heinrich, Willi, 3192-3194
Heinz, Max, 2690
Heinzman, George, 1960
Heller, Joseph, 3195
Helm-Pirgo, Marian, 633
Hemingway, Ernest, 2691, 2909-2910, 3891
Hemingway, Leicester, 3196
Hempstone, Smith, 3686-3687
Henderson, Daniel M., 2149
Hendryx, Gene, 3197
Henri, Florette, 1301
Henriques, Robert D. Q., 2911, 3198-3201
Henty, George A., 54-55, 294-301, 634-637, 823-826, 975-982, 1161, 1302, 1730, 2082-2083, 2227, 2322, 2395-2397, 2459-2466
Herber, William, 3202
Herbert, Alan P., 983, 2692
Herrick, William, 2912
Hersey, John, 3203-3205
Hewes, A. D., 2323
Hewes, J. V., 3206
Hewlett, Maurice, 302
Heydensu, Friedrich, 3207
Heygate, W. E., 303
Heym, Stefan, 3208, 3688
Hibbert, Eleanor, 303a-305, 638-639
Hicks, John, 1739
Hill, Susan, 2693
Hillary, Max, 640
Hillman, George S., 2228
Hinkson, Henry A., 641, 827
Hinsdale, Hariet, 1085
Hirschorn, Richard, 3209
Hoare, E. N., 306
Hocking, Joseph, 642
Hodge, Jane A., 1476
Hodges, C. Walter, 307-308
Hodson, James L., 2694-2695
Hoehling, Mary D., 1740
Hoffenberg, Jack, 3689
Hoffman, William, 3210-3211

Hogan, Pendleton, 1566
Hogan, Ray, 1741-1746, 2696-2701
Holberg, Ruth L., 2324
Holland, Cecelia, 309-313, 642a-643, 2325-2326
Holland, Rosemary, 2327
Hollands, Douglas J., 3690
Hollis, Gertrude, 314, 2328-2330
Holmes, Roy J., 2702
Holt, Emily S., 315
Home, Michael, 3212
Homer, 2229
Hood, Alexander, 56, 984
Hooker, Forrestine, 1961
Hooker, Richard, 3691
Hoole, Barbara, 2467
Hooper, Byrd, 1747
Hope, Graham, 644
Hopkins, Joseph G. E., 1303-1304
Hopkins, Tighe, 985
Hoppus, Mary A. M., 1305
Horan, James D., 1306
Horback, Michael, 2468
Horgan, Paul, 1962
Horne, Howard, 1307
Horne, Roland, 316
Horsley, Reginald, 1748, 2469
Horton, S., 645
Hosford, Dorothy, 317
Hosmer, George W., 1749
Hough, Frank O., 1308-1309
Houghton, Eric, 57-58
Household, Geoffrey, 59
Houston, June D., 646
Howard, Clark, 3213
Howard, Elizabeth, 1477
Howarth, Anna, 2470
Howath, Ferdinand H., 2703
Howe, Charles, 3692
Howe, George, 3214
Huard, Francis W., 2704
Hubler, Richard G., 3215-3216
Huch, Ricarda O., 986-987
Hudson, Charles B., 2084
Hudson, W. H., 2150
Huffaker, Clair, 988
Huggett, William T., 3693
Hughes, Beatrix, 318
Hughes, Paul, 3217-3218

Hughes, Rupert, 2085
Huie, William B. , 3219
Hunt, E. E. , 2705
Hunt, Frazier, 2706
Hunt, Howard, 3220
Hunter, Evan, 3893
Hunter, Mollie, 647
Hurley, Victor, 2231
Hurst, John S. , 2913
Hurwood, B. J. , 3221
Hutchinson, Graham S. , 2708
Hutchinson, James, 2914
Hutchinson, Roy C. , 2709
Hyde, M. P. , 319
Hyman, Freda, 320, 2232
Hyman, Mac, 3694

Icenhower, Joseph B. , 1750
Inchbold, A. C. , 2398
Ingersoll, Ralph M. , 3222
Ingram, Grace, 321
Ingram, Hunter, 1567
Innes, Norman, 648, 828-829
Iogolevitch, Paul, 2710
Ipcar, Dahlov, 322
Iroh, Eddie, 3695
Irwin, H. -C. , 2471
Irwin, Margaret E. F. , 649-
650
Israel, Charles E. , 323, 2233

Jack, Donald, 2711-2712
Jacks, Oliver, 3696
Jackson, Dorothy, 324
Jacob, Violet, 830
Jacobs, Thornwell, 1751
Jahn, Mike, 3223
Jahoda, Gloria, 1310
Jakes, John W. , 1752, 3894
James, G. P. R. , 325-330,
651-653
Jameson, Storm, 3224
Jamieson, Leland S. , 3225
Jarman, Rosemary H. , 331-
332
Jeal, Tim, 989
Jeans, Alice, 990
Jefferies, Barbara, 2331
Jeffries, Graham M. , 2086,
2151, 2332, 2555
Jeffries, Ian, 333
Jenkins, Burris A. , 2713
Jenkins, Guyn, 2234

Jenkins, R. Wade, 2235
Jennings, John E. , 1162-1163,
1311, 1568, 2087, 3895
Jeske-Choinski, Teodor, 60
Jessup, George H. , 654
Johannsen, Ernest, 2714
Johnson, Annabel and Edgar,
3896
Johnson, C. F. , 1753
Johnson, David, 991, 2715
Johnson, Gillard, 2235
Johnson, Owne M. , 2716
Johnston, Jennifer, 3226
Johnston, Mary, 334, 831,
1312, 1754-1755
Johnston, Myrtle, 992
Johnston, Paul, 335
Johnston, Ronald, 3697
Jokai, Maurus, 655-656, 993-
997
Jolly, Andrew, 3897
Jonas, Carl, 3227
Jones, Douglas C. , 1963-1965
Jones, Janies, 3228-3231
Jones, Juanita N. , 2237
Jones, Justin, 1569-1571
Jones, Peter, 1313
Jordan, Roland K. , 3232
Josika, Nicholas, 336
Judson, Edward Z. C. , 1314,
1572
Julitte, Pierre, 3233
Just, Ward, 3698

Kadish, M. R. , 3234
Kaler, James O. , 1086, 1315-
1336, 1478, 1756-1757, 1966
Kane, Harnett T. , 1758-1761
Kantor, MacKinley, 1337,
1573, 1762-1765, 1967, 3699
Kapusta, Paul, 3235
Kark, Leslie, 3236
Karl, S. W. , 3237
Karlin, Wayne, 3700
Karp, Marvin A. , 3238
Kata, Elizabeth, 3239
Katcher, Leo, 3701
Kauffman, Reginald W. , 2717
Kaye, Mary M. , 2472-2473
Kazakevich, Emmanuil G. ,
3240
Kazantaakis, Nikos, 998, 3702
Keable, Robert, 2718

Mano, D. Keith, 3751
Marbo, Camille, 2754
March, Anthony, 3333
Margulies, Leo, 3334
Marlowe, Stephen, 3335
Marquand, John P., 3752
Marriott-Watson, H. B., 699
Marsh, Frances, 1013
Marshall, Beatrice, 700-701
Marshall, Bernard, 1481
Marshall, Edison, 376, 2096,
2248, 2341
Marshall, Emma, 845
Marshall, Rosamund, 702
Marshall, William L., 3900
Marston, William M., 70
Masefield, John, 377, 703
Mason, Alfred E. W., 2490
Mason, Colin, 3753
Mason, Francis Van Wyck,
1090-1091, 1358-1361, 1801,
2341, 3901
Masselink, Ben, 3336
Masters, John, 2402, 2491,
2755, 3337, 3754, 3901a
Masterson, Graham, 3338
Mathai, K. Easo, 3339
Mather, Berkely, 2342, 2923
Matheson, Richard, 3340
Maugham, A. Margery, 378
Maugham, Robin, 2492
Maurois, Andre, 2756-2757
Maxwell, Anna, 1014
Maxwell, Herbert, 71, 379
Maxwell, Patricia, 2156
Maxwell, W. H., 1015
Maxwell, William B., 2758
May, Stella B., 2097
Mayer, A. I., 380, 1482
Mayer, Tom, 3755
Mayran, Camille, 2759
Meader, Stephen W., 1167,
1803, 3756
Meadowcraft, Enicel M., 1352
Meakin, Neville M., 2343
Meding, Oskar, 1016
Meisels, Andrew, 2249
Meissner, Hans, 3341
Melchoir, Ib, 3342-3343
Mellard, Rudolph, 1804
Melville, G. J. Whyte, 2250-
2251
Merejkowski, Dmitri, 72

Merle, Robert, 3344
Merrell, Leigh, 73
Merrick, Gordon, 3345
Meyer, Annie N., 381
Meyer, Karl H., 3346
Meyneng, Mayette, 3347
Michelaard, B., 3902
Michner, James A., 3757-
3758, 3903
Middleton, Jan, 3349
Miers, Earl S., 1092, 1805
Milis, J. M. A., 704
Miller, E. F., 3350
Miller, Elizabeth, 2252
Miller, Helen T., 1363-1364,
1806
Miller, Mark, 2011
Miller, May, 1807
Miller, Merle, 3351
Miller, Patrick, 2760
Miln, Louise, 2560
Milne, James, 846
Minto, William, 382
Mirdrekvandi, Ali, 3758a
Mitchell, Margaret, 1808
Mitchell, S. Weir, 1365
Mitchison, Naomi M., 74-75
Mitford, Bertram, 2493-2499
Moberg, Vilhelm, 1809
Mockler-Ferryman, A. F.,
1017
Molander, Harold, 705
Momaday, N. Scott, 3759
Monaco, Richard, 383
Monsarrat, Nicholas, 3352,
3760
Monsey, Derek, 3353
Montague, Margaret P., 2761-
2762
Montgomery, R. G., 3354
Montupet, Jeanne, 2500
Moore, Arthur, 1093, 1810
Moore, Donald, 3355
Moore, Gene D., 3761
Moore, John T., 1483
Moore, Robert L., 3762-3765
Moore, William, 2501
Moray, Ann, 2253
Mordecai, Alfred, 1811
More, E. Anson, 2254
Morgan, Barbara E., 2255
Morgan, John H., 2763
Morgan, Michaela, 1018, 2561

Morgulas, Jerrold, 2924
Morley, Iris, 706
Morris, Edita, 3766
Morris, Walter F. , 2764
Morris, William, 384
Morrison, Gerry, 1812
Morriss, Mark, 3356
Morrow, Honore, 1813
Moss, Sidney and Samuel, 3357
Motley, Annette, 2345
Mott, F. B. , 1586
Mott, Michael, 3358
Mottram, Ralph H. , 2765-2766
Muddock, J. E. , 847
Muir, Robert, 1484
Mullally, Frederic, 3359
Mullins, Richard, 3360
Mulville, William, 3361
Mundy, Talbot, 76, 2256, 2502-2503, 2562, 2767, 2925
Munroe, Kirk, 1168, 1587-1588, 2098
Muntz, Hope, 385
Murciaux, Christian, 2926
Murdoch, Iris, 2768
Murfree, Mary N. , 1169-1170
Murphy, James, 848
Murphy, John, 3767
Murray, D. Christie, 1019
Murray, David L. , 849, 1020
Mutswairo, Solomon M. , 2504
Myers, L. H. , 2346
Myrer, Anton O. , 3362, 3904
Myrivilis, Stratis, 2769

Nablo, James B. , 3363
Nadaud, Marcel, 2770-2771
Napier, Charles, 386
Nason, Leonard H. , 2772-2779, 2927
Nathan, Robert, 77, 387
Nathanson, E. M. , 3364
Neale, J. M. , 388
Neihardt, John, 6, 2012
Neill, Robert, 707
Nelson, Truman J. , 1589
Neumann, Alfred, 1021
Nevins, Albert J. , 2099
Newberry, Perry, 2780

Newbolt, Henry, 389, 2781
Newhafer, Richard L. , 3365
Newman, Bernard, 2782
Newsom, J. D. , 2928
Newsome, Edward, 2013
Nicholls, William J. , 708
Nicholson, Christopher, 2505
Nicholson, Meredith, 1485
Nicole, Christopher, 2157, 3366
Niles, Blair, 2100, 2158
Noble, Hollister, 1814
Nolan, Frederick, 3367-3369
Noller, Ella M. , 2257
Nordhoff, Charles B. , 2783, 3370
Norton, Alice M. , 390, 1590, 1815, 2258, 3371
Norway, Nevil Shute, 3372-3373

O'Byrne, M. L. , 391
O'Byrne, W. L. , 392
O'Connor, Richard, 393, 1816-1817, 2506
Odell, Katherine, 1022
O'Dell, Scott, 1591, 2101
Odom, John D. , 1818
O'Flaherty, Liam, 2784
Ogilvie, Charlton, Jr. , 3376
O'Grady, Standish, 709
Olden, Balder, 2785
Oldenbourg, Zoe, 394, 2347-2348
Oldham, Henry, 1819
Ollis, Robert, 3375
Ollivant, Alfred, 2507
Olson, Alton M. , 3376
Olson, Lloyd E. , 3377
Olson, Theodore V. , 395, 1592-1593
Oman, Carola, 396
O'Meara, Walter, 397, 2349
O'Neal, Cothburn, 2350
Ooka, Shokei, 3378
Opitz, Karlludwig, 3379
Orczy, Emmuska, 710-711
O'Rourke, Frank, 2786-2787, 3380
Orr, Myron D. , 1486
Orrmont, Arthur, 1366
Osborne, Duffield, 78
Osgood, Claude J. , 398

Oswald, E. J. , 399
Overholsen, Wayne D. , 2014
Oxley, J. MacDonald, 1094
Oz, Amos, 2351

Page, Elizabeth, 1171
Page, T. N. , 1820
Paine, Ralph D. , 2929
Palmer, Bruce, 1487, 1821, 2930
Palmer, J. L. , 2788
Palmer, Marion, 400-401
Paretti, Sandra, 1367
Pargeter, Edith, 402
Park, Mrs. Kendall, 403
Parker, Gilbert, 850-851, 1172-1173, 1594, 2259, 2508
Parkhill, Forbes, 2015
Parrish, Randall, 1174, 1488, 1595, 1822, 2016
Partington, Norman, 1368, 2403, 2824
Pashko, Stanley, 3381
Paterson, A. , 712
Patten, Lewis B. , 2017-2020, 2563
Patterson, Burd S. , 1175
Patterson, Henry, 3382-3383, 3773
Patterson, Sarah, 3384
Patton, Oliver, 2021
Paul, Elliott H. , 2789
Paul, Louis, 3385
Pauli, Hertha, 713
Payne, Pierre S. R. , 2022, 2404, 3774
Payne, Robert, 2260
Peacock, Jere, 3775
Pearce, Charles E. , 2509-2511
Pearce, Richard E. , 1596-1597
Pearl, Jack, 3776
Pearsall, Robert B. , 2159
Peart, Hendry, 404
Pease, Howard, 852, 3386
Peck, Robert N. , 1176, 1369-1370
Peck, Theodore, 853
Pei, Mario A. , 405
Pelfrey, William, 3777
Pemberton, Max, 854-855,

1023, 1026
Pendeleton, Louis, 2261
Pender, Mrs. M. T. , 856
Pendexter, Hugh, 1177, 1489-1490
Pepper, Dan, 3387
Percy-Graves, J. , 2405
Perdue, Jacques, 79
Pereny, Eleanor, 1822
Perna, Albert F. , 3388
Perowne, Barry, 3778
Perry, Robin, 3779
Pertivee, Roland, 2790
Perutz, Leo, 1027
Petrakis, Harry M. , 1028
Pick, John B. , 714
Pickering, Edgar, 715, 857
Pike, R. E. , 1178
Piper, David, 3389
Pirro, Ugo, 3390
Plantz, Donald J. , 3391
Plievier, Theodor, 3392-3394
Plowman, Stephanie, 80, 2791
Polland, Madeline, 716
Pollard, Eliza F. , 81, 406-407, 1029, 1371, 2406, 2512-2513
Polley, Judith, 2160
Pollini, Francis, 3780
Pollock, Alyce, 2161
Poole, Lynn and Gray, 82
Pope, Edith E. , 1598
Porter, Jane, 408
Potter, David, 1599
Potter, Jeffrey, 3395
Potter, Margaret H. , 2352
Pottinger, Henry, 409
Powell, Anthony, 3396-3397
Powell, Richard, 2262, 3398
Powers, Alfred, 83
Powers, Anne, 410-412, 1030
Powys, John C. , 413-414
Poyer, Joe, 3781
Prada, Renato, 3782
Pratt, John C. , 3783
Pratt, Rex K. , 3400
Prebble, John, 1824, 2023
Preddy, George, 858
Prescott, H. F. M. , 2353
Prescott, John, 1825
Price, Anthony, 717, 3402
Price, Eleanor C. , 415
Price, Olive, 2354

Stein, Evaleen, 2374
Stephens, Eve, 741, 872, 1044
Stephens, Peter J., 464
Stephens, R. N., 742
Stern, Emma G., 1394, 1856
Stern, Philip V. D., 1855
Stern, Richard M., 3833
Sterrett, Frances R., 2828
Stevens, James, 2829
Stevens, Sheppard, 2108
Stevens, William, 3469
Stevenson, Burton E., 1190, 1395
Stevenson, John P., 743
Stevenson, Philip L., 744-745, 873
Stevenson, Robert L., 462, 874-875
Stewart, Charlotte, 876
Stillman, A. L., 1103
Stimson, Frederick J., 1396
Stoddard, William O., 463, 1397-1400, 1499
Stone, Grace Z., 1104
Stover, Herbert E., 1191, 1401-1402, 1957
Stowell, Gordon, 2830
Strabel, Thelma, 2168
Strackey, J. S., 1045
Straight, Michael, 1858, 2034
Strain, E. H., 746
Strang, Herbert, 467-470, 877-878, 1046, 2411, 2525
Strange, J. S., 3470
Strange, Stephen, 3471
Stratemeyer, Edwards, 1192-1193, 1608-1610, 1859
Stratton, Clarence, 2375
Street, James, 1500, 1860, 2169
Strong, Anna L., 3472
Strong, Charles, 2831
Stuart, Esme, 1047
Stuart, Frank S., 2273
Stuart, Henry L., 747, 1105
Stubbs, Jean, 471
Stuchen, Eduard, 2109
Styles, Showell, 1048-1049, 1403
Styron, William, 1611, 3834
Sublette, Clifford, 1106
Suhl, Yuri, 3473
Sullivan, James A., 1404

Surdez, Georges, 2941
Surry, George, 748
Sutcliff, Rosemary, 96-99, 472-478, 749-750
Sutcliffe, Halliwell, 751-752, 879-888
Sutherland, Joan, 2526
Sutton, Henry, 3835
Swann, Edgar, 479
Swanson, Neil, 1194-1196, 1405
Swarthout, Glendon, 2832-2833
Syers, William E., 1861

Tabor, Michael, 3474
Taboureau, Jean, 2834
Takeyama, Michio, 3475
Tamas, Istvan, 3476
Tapsell, A. F., 2274
Tarbet, W. G., 881
Tarr, Herbert, 3836
Tarrant, John, 3477
Tasaki, Hanama, 2942
Tassin, Ray, 2035
Taylor, Allen, 1406
Taylor, Anna, 100, 480
Taylor, David, 1407-1410
Taylor, Geoff, 3478
Taylor, Georgia E., 481
Taylor, H. C., 1050
Taylor, Irene S., 753
Taylor, James G., Jr., 2110
Taylor, Philip M., 2412-2414, 2527
Taylor, Richard, 1197
Taylor, Robert L., 1612
Taylor, Thomas, 3837-3838
Taylor, Ward, 3479
Taylor, Winchcombe, 2415
Teague, J. J., 882
Tebbel, John W., 1198
Teilhet, Darwin, 2170-2171
Tenenbaum, Joseph, 2836
Terlouw, Jan, 3480
Thayer, James S., 3481
Theiss, Lewis E., 3482
Thomas, Cenethe, 2376
Thomas, Craig, 3839
Thomas, Donald, 1051, 1199
Thomas, Harlan C., 3484
Thomas, Leslie, 3840
Thomason, John W., 1862-1863, 2036, 2837-2838, 2943-2944, 3909-3911

TITLE INDEX

A-18, 3837
Able Company, 3690
Absent Without Leave, 3017
According to Orders, 2587
Ace of the White Death, 2696
Achilles, His Armor, 50
Across the Crevasse, 1804
Across the Delaware, 1315
Across the Range, 1966
Across the Salt Seas, 785
Action at Aquila, 1620
Action at Beecher Island, 1907
Adam, Where Art Thou, 3018
Adobe Walls, 1909
Adria, 984
Adventure in the Sky, 3535
The Adventurer, 760
Adventures and Discoveries of
    Marco Polo, 2380
The Adventures of Arnold
    Adair, American Ace, 2650
The Adventures of Count
    O'Connor, 2410
The Adventures of Gerard,
    915
The Adventures of Harry
    Rochester, 1110
The Adventures of Humphrey
    Chatteris, 158
The Adventures of Private
    Gaust, 3256
The Adventures of Robb Roy,
    814
Adventures of the Night, 2905
Aegean Adventure, 3309
An Affair of State, 3728
The Affairs of the Generals,
    2916
Afgar the Dane, 185
Afghan Assault, 3733

Africana, 3680
Against the Fall of Night, 2284
Against This Rock, 770
The Age of Death, 3900
Agincourt, 325
Agnes de Mansfelt, 615
Agrippa's Daughter, 2208
Ahira, Prince of Naphstali,
    2257
The Aide-de-Camp, 956
Aide to Glory, 1696
Air Bridge, 3674
Air Force Girl, 3445
Air Force Surgeon, 3147
Air Ministry Room 28, 3142
The Alamo, 1552
Alaric, the Goth, 163
The Aleph Solution, 3652
Alexander and Roxana, 2240
Alexander the God, 2238, 2260
Alexander the King, 2241
Alexander the Prince, 2242
Alfred the King, 518
The Algonquin Project, 3367
Alice of Old Vincennes, 1412
Alison Blair, 1138
Alkibiades, 12-13
All Else Is Folly, 2569
All God's Children, 1634
All Men Tall, 506
All My Laurels, 3107
All Night Long, 3051
All Our Yesterdays, 3912
All Quiet on the Western Front,
    2798
All the Brave Rifles, 1613
All the Young Men, 3554
Allan Quartermain, 2451
Almost Midnight, 3592
Alps and Elephants, 27

The Big Pick Up, 3491
The Big Red Ball, 3059
The Big V, 3777
The Big War, 3362
Birds of a Feather, 2770
Bitter Victory, 3184
The Black Arrow, 465
The Black Bull, 541
Black Camelot, 3277
The Black Camels, 3697
The Black Camp, 3060
The Black Colonel, 846
The Black Council, 673
The Black Cuirassier, 744
The Black Danes, 303
The Black Disc, 351
The Black Douglas, 213
Black Falcon, 1498
Black Fox of Lorne, 204
The Black Hunter, 1140
Black Ivory, 1447
Black Partridge, 1473
Black Rain, 1112
The Black Rose, 2302
Black Sheep Squadron: Devil
   in the Slot, 3223
Black Sunday, 3679
The Black, the Gray, and the
   Gold, 3644
Black Thunder, 1451
The Black Watch, 957
Blackcock's Feather, 758
Blade of Picardy, 2155
The Blazing Sun, 1524
The Bleeding Land, 1580
The Blind Bull, 3537
The Blind Journey, 1343
Block 26: Sabotage at Bucken-
   wald, 3233
The Blockhouse, 3086
The Blond Beast, 2597
Blood and Guts Is Going Nuts,
   3297
Blood Brother, 1894
The Blood of the Brave, 2059
Blood Reckoning, 2032
Blood Red, Sister Rose, 339
The Bloodiest Bivouac, 3345
Blood-Stained Footprints,
   3339
Bloody Baron, 2931
Bloody Beaches, 3463
The Bloody Field, 402

Blow Bugles, Blow, 1621
Blown In by the Draft, 2706
Blue and Green, 409
The Blue Banner, 2292
The Blue Flag, 640
Blue Leader, 3859
The Blue Max, 2707
Blue Meadow, 1432
The Boat of Fate, 85
Bob Hampton of Placer, 2016
Body Count, 3693, 3743
A Body Fell on Berlin, 3278
The Bold and the Lonely, 3729
Bold Raiders of the West, 1639
Bomb Run, 3119
The Bomb That Could Lip-
   Read, 3810
Bombardier, 3067
Bomber, 3111
Bomber Pilot, 3185
Bombers in the Sky, 3536
Bombs from the Murder Wolves,
   2698
The Book of Merlyn, 512
Boots and Saddles, 1906
The Border, 1699
The Border Guidon, 1841
The Border Trumpet, 1736
Border War, 2115
The Borgia Prince, 544
Borgia Testament, 132
The Bormann Brief, 3124
Boston Boys of 1775, 1318
Both Sides of the Border, 295
Bottletop Affair, 3092
Bounty Hunters, 2007
The Bowmen of Crecy, 239
The Boy and the Baron, 344
A Boy at Gettysburg, 1845
Boy in Blue, 1659
A Boy of the Lost Crusade,
   2323
The Boy with a Gun, 3805
The Boys of '45, 1086
Boys of the Border, 1108
Boys of the Light Brigade,
   1046
Brakespeare, 348
The Brave and the Blind, 2881
The Brave and the Damned,
   3254
Brave Company, 3539
Brave Eagle's Own Account of
   the Fetterman Fight, 1948

Brave General, 954
Brave Journey, 3471
Brave Mardi Gras, 1830
The Brave One, 3236
The Breach, 3782
Breast of the Dove, 2137
The Brethren, 2318
Bridal Journey, 1429
Bride of Fortune, 1758
Bride of the Machugh, 739
The Bride of the Nile, 2205
Bridge on the Drina, 2968
The Bridge Over the River
  Kwai, 3024
The Bridges at Toko-Ri, 3757
The Brigade, 2989
Bright Battalions, 1125
The Bright Face of Danger,
  1106
Bright Feather, 1615
Bright Sword, 1823
Bright to the Wanderer, 1578
The Brink, 3812
Brinton Eliot, 1270
The British Legion, 972
Britton of the Seventh, 1905
Broad Margin, 3005
Broken Arc, 3347
Broken Dykes, 573
Broken Shackles, 934
The Broken Soldier and the
  Maid of France, 2843
The Broken Song, 2637
The Broken Sword, 229, 1770
Broncho Apache, 2044
Bronze Drums, 3285
The Bronze God of Rhodes,
  29
The Brother, 3438
Brother Against Brother, 1712
Brothers Five, 663
Brothers in Arms, 2319, 3258
Brothers of the Sword, 395
The Brown Mask, 550
Buddy Boy, 3486
Buffalo Soldiers, 1824
Bugle in the Wilderness, 1668
Bugles and Brass, 2024
The Bugles Are Silent, 1574
Bugles Blow No More, 1700
Bugles in the Afternoon, 1957
Bugles West, 1951
Builders of the Waste, 243

Britain's Greatness Foretold,
  107
Burma Rifles, 3020
The Burning Cresset, 852
The Burnished Blade, 440
Burnt Offerings, 3830
Bury Him Among Kings, 2841
The Bushwackers, 1728
By Antietam Creek, 1832
By Command of the Viceroy,
  2481
By Dim and Flaring Lamps,
  1788
By England's Aid, 634
By His Own Might, 317
By Pike and Dyke, 635
By Right of Conquest, 2082
By Sheer Pluck, 2460
By the Eternal, 1492
By the Ramparts of Jezreel,
  2199
By the Rivers of Babylon, 3625

The Cactus and the Crown,
  2135
Cadet Days, 1340
Cadmus Henry, 1707
Caesar of the Narrow Seas, 44
Calico Bush, 1074
Call It Treason, 3214
Call of the New World, 3895
Call of the Soil, 2601
Call to Battle, 3315
Cambria's Chieftain, 279
The Camp Grant Massacre,
  1895
A Candle at Dusk, 120
Candle in the Night, 1477
Candleshine No More, 861
Canolles, 1256
Canton Barrier, 3660
Caoba, the Guerrilla Chief,
  2131
The Cap of Refuge, 369
The Capsina, 900
Captain Apache, 2047
Captain Bacon's Rebellion,
  1087
Captain Blackman, 3916
Captain Blake, 1971
Captain Close, 1972
Captain Comstock, U.S.M.C.,
  2603

Courage to Command, 1088
Court Martial, 3540, 3637, 3765
The Court Martial of Daniel Boone, 1262
The Court Martial of George Armstrong Custer, 1964
Court of Honor, 3478
The Court of Rath Croghan, 391
Courts of the Lion, 2475
Courts of the Morning, 2884
Cousin Isabel, 533
Covenant with Death, 2686
The Coventry Option, 3047
The Cowards, 3456
The Cowboy and the Cossack, 988
Cowboy of the Ramapos, 1294
The Crack of Doom, 3192
Crag-Nest, 1694
Crecy and Poictiers, 227
A Creek Called Wounded Knee, 1965
The Crimson Chalice, 168
The Crimson Conquest, 2084
The Crimson Field, 751
The Crimson Gondola, 258
Crimson Moccasins, 1260
The Crimson Sign, 667
The Cromwell of Virginia, 1073
Cromwell's Boys, 629
Cromwell's Own, 712
The Cross and the Arrow, 3330
Cross Bearers, 2672
The Cross of Baron Samedi, 2892
Cross of Fire, 2580
The Cross of Iron, 3193
Cross to Bear Proudly, 2985
Crossfire, 3821
The Crossing, 1253, 1714
Crouchback, 355
A Crown for Carlotta, 2149
Cruel Easter, 2936
The Crumbling Fortress, 3194
Crusade, 2291
The Crusaders, 3208
Cry of Dolores, 2138
Cry Wolf, 2939

The Crystal Cornerstone, 1226
Cumberland Rifles, 1468
The Curious Career of Roderick Campbell, 839
The Curse of Jezebel, 2271
The Curse of the Nile, 2521
The Curved Sabre, 674
Custer's Last Stand, 1886
Cyborg, 3593
The Czar, 888

The Dahomean, 2533
Damascus Lies North, 2839
The Damned Wear Wings, 3058
Dan Monroe, 1397
Dance Back the Buffalo, 2008
Danger Patrol, 3432
Daniel Boone, 1281
Daniel Boone, Wilderness Scout, 1204
Daring Destiny, 2095
The Dark Angel, 500
The Dark Comes Early, 1566
The Dark Command, 1666
Dark Finds the Day, 3523
Dark Forest, 2848
The Dark Island, 102
The Dark Mile, 781
Dark Moment, 2882
The Dark of the Sun, 3827
The Dark Rose, 759
The Dark Stranger, 558
Dark Torrent of Glencoe, 620
The Darkness and the Dawn, 184
D'Artagnan, 542
Daughter of New France, 1071
A Daughter of the Sioux, 1975
The Daughters of Suffolk, 708
The Dauntless and the Dreamers, 1950
David Maxwell, 795
David of Jerusalem, 2202
David, the King, 2266
David, Warrior of God, 2237
David's Stranger, 2267
Davis, 3906
Dawn Attack, 3056
Dawn Command, 3232
Dawn Falcon, 2253
Dawn Over the Amazon, 2996
Dawn Wind, 473
Dawn's Early Light, 1225

Five Days in June, 3688
The Five Fingers, 3789
Five Signs from Ruby, 3746
Fix Bayonets, 2837
Flame and the Shadow, 3065
The Flame Gatherers, 2350
The Flame in the Dark, 153
Flame in the Sky, 2183
Flame in the South, 969
The Flame of Courage, 1151
The Flame of the Borgias, 552
Flames of Empire, 2151
Flames of Moscow, 1009
Flaming Sands, 2947
Flamingo Prince, 1563
Flare Path, 3084
Flash for Freedom, 1720
Flashman, 2443
Flashman at the Charge, 949
Flashman in the Great Game,
  2444
Flashman's Lady, 2445
Flawed Blades, 2952
The Fleet in the Window, 3001
The Fleet Rabble, 1955
Flemington, 830
Fleur-De-Camp, 908
Flicker's Feather, 1113
Flight Deck, 3532
Flight from Natchez, 1392
Flight from the Grave, 2699
Flight of the Bat, 3664
Flight of the Eagle, 1051
The Flight of the Heron, 782
Flower O' the Lily, 711
A Flower of Araby, 2307
The Flowers of Adonis, 97
The Flying Artillerist, 1569
Flying Death, 2879
Flying Poilu, 2771
Flying Wildcats, 3334
Flying with the Air-Sea Rescue
  Service, 3482
Foes in Ambush, 1976
Foes of Freedom, 833
Follow My Black Plume, 1053
Follow the Drum, 2477
Follow the Free Wind, 1519
Follow the Gleam, 642
Follow the Leader, 2639
Follow the River, 1482
The Fool, 127
Fool of Venus, 2306

The Foothold, 2981
For Church and Chieftain, 668
For Flag and Freedom, 1480
For Freedom, 985
For Freedom and for Gaul, 1
For Infamous Conduct, 2917
For King or Empress, 508
For King or Parliament, 645
For Love and Hanover, 860
For Love and Loyalty, 866
For Love and Ransom, 1047
For Name and Fame, 2461
For Rupert and the King, 632
For Sceptre and Crown, 1016
For the Emperor, 1029
For the Honour of His House,
  536
For the King, 581, 597
For the Liberty of Texas, 1608
For the Love of Dying, 3817
For the Temple, 2227
For the White Christ, 141
For the White Cockade, 847
For Three Kingdoms, 570
For Whom the Bells Toll, 2910
The Forayers, 1384, 1730
Forbidden City, 2551
The Forbidden Ground, 1405
Force 10 from Navarone, 3324
Foreign Devils, 2553
Forest and the Fort, 1111
Forest Cavalier, 1077
Forest Days, 328
The Forest of Swords, 2575
The Forest of the Hanged, 2796
The Forest Prince, 502
The Forest Runners, 1215
Forging of the Pikes, 1617
The Forgotten Army, 3158
The Fort, 3224
Fort Amity, 1181
Fort Everglades, 1606
Fort Frayne, 1977
The Fort in the Forest, 1164
Fort in the Jungle, 2953
The Fort of Missing Men, 2955
Fortress Fury, 1286
Fortress in the Rice, 2969
The Fortune Hunter, 705
Fortune Made His Sword, 430
Fortune's Castaway, 590
Fortune's My Foe, 2068
The Fortunes of Colonel Torlogh

The Gift of Paul Clermont,
2642
Gilded Spurs, 321
Girl Soldier and Spy, 1740
The Girondin, 776
Girty, 1197
Gitana, 1531
Give Me the Daggers, 2674
Give Me Tomorrow, 3617
The Gladiators, 63, 2250
Gladiators' Revolt, 64
The Gleam in the North, 783
The Gleaming Dawn, 131
Glendower Country, 431
Glide Path, 3082
The Glider Gladiators, 3388
The Glory and Sorrow of Nor-
wich, 148
The Glory and the Dream, 658
Glory Is Departed, 2735
The Glory Jumpers, 3464
God Have Mercy on Us, 2806
The God of Clay, 773
God Save King Alfred, 268
God Wills It, 2308
God's Angry Man, 1545
The Gods Are Not Mocked,
100
God's Men, 2541
The Gods of Yesterday, 2596
Gods on Horseback, 2058
Going After Cacciato, 3770
Gold from Crete, 3137
The Golden Blade, 2299
The Golden Chain, 259
Golden Eagle, 1557, 2087
Golden Exile, 442
The Golden Fleece, 531
Golden Hawks of Genghis Khan,
2359
The Golden Hope, 2214
The Golden Horde, 2902
The Golden Lyre, 2217
The Golden Pilgrimage, 2807
The Golden Princess, 2060
Golden Strangers, 103
Golden Warrior, 385
The Golden Wildcat, 1207
The Golden Yoke, 226
The Goldsmith's Wife, 304
Gone to Texas, 1862
Gone with the Wind, 1808
A Good Day to Die, 1904

Good Gestes, 2569
Good Soldier Schweik, 2688
The Good Sword Belgrade, 195
The Gooney Bird, 3561
Gorgo, 38
Goshawk Squadron, 2800
Gossip from the Forest, 2720
The Governor's Daughter, 1206
Graham of Claverhouse, 762
The Grail and the Passing of
Arthur, 418
The Grain of Mustard, 214
Granada, Surrender, 341
The Grand Defiance, 3144
Grapes of Wrath, 2622
Grave Doubt, 2979
Gravity's Rainbow, 3404
Gray Canaan, 1723
The Great Adventure, 1560
The Great Amulet, 2434
Great Axe Brewwalda, 340
The Great Betrayal, 1721
The Great Captains, 485
The Great Crusade, 2865
Great Heart Gillian, 936
The Great Locomotive Chase,
1709
Great Maria, 312
The Great Santini, 3607
A Great Treason, 1305
The Great War in England of
1897, 1005
The Great White Army, 1024
The Greatest Rebel, 1102
The Green Berets, 3763
Green Centuries, 1153
Green Cockade, 1213
The Green Fields of Hell, 3063
The Green Flag, 918
The Green Man, 486
The Green Mountain Boys, 1371
A Green Tree and a Dry Tree,
2179
Greencoats Against Napoleon,
1048
Greenmantle, 2619
Grey Dawn, Red Night, 2694
The "Grey Fox" of Holland,
545
Grey Maiden, 3908
Grisley Grissell, 528
Guard of Honor, 3093
La Guerra, 2898

Guerrilla, 3121, 3627
Guerrilla Girls, 3868
Guerrilla Padre of Mindanao,
   3177
Guerrillas, 3768
The Gun Garden, 3465
The Gun Runner, 2493
The Gunner, 3469
Gunner Asch Goes to War,
   3260
Guns Along the Brazos, 1968
The Guns Boom Far, 3007
Guns for Rebellion, 1358
Guns Forever Echo, 231
The Guns of Bull Run, 1625
Guns of Burgoyne, 1344
Guns of Chickamauga, 1817
The Guns of Europe, 2576
The Guns of Navarone, 3325
The Guns of Palembang, 3744
Guns of Quebec, 1142
The Guns of Shiloh, 1626
The Guns of Vicksburg, 1805
Guns to Sonora, 2544
Guy Gilpatrick's Flying
   Stories, 3890

The Haigerlock Project, 3341
Hail Hero, 3867
Half-Breed, 1931
The Hallelujah Trail, 1952
The Hammer, 2192
The Hammer of God, 2516
Hammer on the Sea, 3508
Hand of the King, 2255
A Hand Raised at Gettysburg,
   1753
Hang for Treason, 1369
Hang My Wreath, 1801
Hanging On, 3272
Hankow Return, 2970
Hannah's Hessians, 1209
Hannibal of Carthage, 31
Hannibal's Elephants, 83
Happy Foreigner, 2589
The Hard Men, 3591
Harm Wulf, 687
Harold, the Last of the Saxon
   Kings, 365
Harold the Norseman, 507
Harold Was My King, 356
Harp into Battle, 373
The Harp of Burma, 3475

Harry of Monmouth, 378
Harry's Game, 3813
The Harvest, 3724
Hastings the Pirate, 189
Hatchet in the Sky, 1150
A Hatful of Gold, 1297
Havelock the Dane, 509
Hawk of Como, 223
Hawk of Normandy, 129
The Hawks of Noon, 1927
He Went with Hannibal, 61
The Head of Iron, 1175
The Healing Blade, 792
Heart of Danger, 3386
The Heart of Hope, 1828
The Heart of Hutton, 803
Heart of Jade, 2074
Heart of Wales, 424
Heart's Conquest, 375
Hearts of Hickory, 1483
Heaven Knows, Mr. Allison,
   3447
The Heights of Zervos, 3434
Heike Story, 2385
Heir to Kings, 800
Heir to Kuragin, 974a
The Heirs of the Kingdom,
   2346
Held Fast for England, 824
Hell Bent for Blitzkrieg, 3376
Hell in Georgia, 1818
Hell to Halleluhah, 1742
Hellbent for Glory, 3073
A Helluva War, 2659
Helmet and Wasps, 3358
Helmet of Navarre, 728
Hengest's Tale, 499
The Hepburn, 763, 505
Her Majesty's Captain, 1109
Her Private We, 2753
A Herald of the West, 1443
Here Come the Marines, 3076
Here Comes a Candle, 1476
Hereward the Wake, 343
The Heritage, 1395
Hermanos, 2912
The Hero, 3353
Hero in the Tower, 3261
A Hero in Wolfskin, 9
A Hero King, 406
The Hero Machine, 2998
The Hero of Iwo Jima, 3219
A Hero of Lucknow, 2418

Red Cross Barge, 2741
The Red Daniel, 2486
Red Dickon, the Outlaw, 147
The Red Doe, 1388
Red Eve, 287
Red Falcons of Tremoine, 404
The Red Fleur-de-Lys, 835
The Red Fountain, 2500
Red Fox of the Kinapoo, 2025
Red Hawk's Account of Custer's Last Battle, 1949
Red Heritage, 1214
The Red Lances, 2172
Red Lanterns on St. Michaels, 1751
Red Lion and Gold Dragon, 463
Red Man and White, 2050
Red Men in Blue, 2035
Red Morning, 1149
Red Orm, 140
Red Over Green, 3200
Red Pants and Other Stories, 2838
Red Queen, White Queen, 106
Red Rain, 3236
The Red Republic, 913
Red Beverage, 2510
Red Road, 1177
Red Rose and White, 124
Red Rose on the Hill, 1795
The Red Sabbath, 2020
The Red Saint, 209
Red, White, and Green, 974
The Red Year, 2529
Reds of the Midi, 816
Refugees, 564
The Regiment, 3907
The Regulators, 1461
Reluctant Rebel, 1427
Remember the Alamo, 1515
Rendezvous with Hell, 3576
Renée, 571
Renegade, 1944, 2535
Renown, 1309
Requilda, 403
Rescue Mission, 3567
The Reservation, 1662
Respite, 3311
Restless Are the Sails, 1072
Restless Border, 1597
The Restless Land, 1935
Retreat, 890, 2598

Retreat from Rostov, 3218
Retreat from the Dolphin, 2171
Retreat, Hell, 3064
Retreat to Glory, 1579
The Return of Gunner Asch, 3266
Return to the Wood, 2695
Reveille, 1898
Revolt Along the Rio Grande, 2102
The Revolt of Gunner Asch, 3267
The Revolt of Zengo Takakuwa, 2980
Revolt on the Border, 1526
The Rhinemann Exchange, 3314
Rhodes of the Leathernecks, 2918
Richard and the Knights of God, 2287
Richard Chatterton, V.C., 2588
Richard Montgomery, 1415
Richard III: The Last Plantagenet, 495
The Richmond Raid, 1657
Ride a Paper Tiger, 3563
Ride East, Ride West, 411
Ride for Old Glory, 1800
Ride Home Tomorrow, 2370
Ride into Danger, 489
Ride Proud Rebel, 1815
Ride the White Tiger, 3603
The Ride to Panmunjom, 3841
Ride with Danger, 412
Ride with Me, 919
The Rider and His Horse, 2226
Rider on a White Horse, 749
The Rifleman, 1240
Rifleman Dodd and The Gun, 947
Rifles for Washington, 1390
Rifles for Watie, 1766
The Right Hand, 786
The Right Line of Cerdic, 222
The Ring Has No End, 892
Ringan Gilhaize, 606
Ringed by Fire, 964
The Ringed Castle, 587
Rio Bravo, 1601
Riot at Gravesend, 525
The Rise and Fall of Carol Banks, 2825
The Rising, 992

BATTLE, WAR, AND WARRIOR INDEX

549, 570, 636
Braddock's Defeat, 1117, 1162,
1165, 1175, 1177, 1190,
1193
Bragg, Braxton, 1868
Brant, Joseph, 1214, 1237,
1239, 1247-1249, 1251,
1263, 1265, 1284, 1306,
1314, 1398, 1419-1420
Brims of Coweta, 1096, 1101
Bristol, Siege of, 661, 688
Britain, Battle of, 2979,
3036, 3047, 3082, 3111a,
3142, 3159-3160, 3170,
3182, 3206, 3235, 3247,
3291, 3410, 3489, 3493,
3538
Britain, Roman invasion and
occupation of, 2, 7-8, 21,
39, 45, 48, 54, 66, 69,
71, 76-77, 81-84, 87-89,
95-96, 98-102, 105-107,
110, 113, 240
Brown, John, 1545, 1547,
1580, 1582, 1586, 1589
Buena Vista, Battle of, 1508,
1531
Bulgarian Uprising, 931, 1055
Bulge, Battle of the see
Ardennes, Battle of the
Bull Run, 1st Battle of, 1625,
1648, 1752, 1830, 1844,
1859
Bull Run, 2nd Battle of, 1723
Bunker Hill, Battle of, 1222,
1257, 1277, 1302, 1335,
1356, 1397, 1438
Burgoyne, John see Sara-
toga, Battle of
Burma, Japanese occupation
of, 2959, 2967, 2991,
2993, 2995, 2998, 3020,
3024, 3032-3033, 3045,
3106, 3128, 3254, 3339,
3374, 3395, 3398, 3441,
3475, 3485, 3510
Burmese War, 2463, 2467

Caesar, Julius, 1-3, 8, 12a,
25, 34, 37, 54, 66, 70,
75, 81, 84, 100, 102,
110, 112-115
Calais, Siege of, 179, 348

Cambrai, Battle of, 2665, 2860
Cambrai, Siege of, 711
Camden, Battle of, 1385-1386
Canadian Rebellion, 1537, 1578,
1594, 1616
Cananae, Battle of, 73, 78
Canute, 185
Caradoc, 39
Carausius, 44
Carcassonne, Siege of, 176
Carlist Uprisings, 920, 948,
972, 980, 1040-1041
Carlo Alberto, Battle of, 970
Carroll, Anna E., 1814
Carson, Kit, 1591
Catherine the Great, 859
Catiline's Revolt, 65
Cavalier, Jean, 787
Cawnpore, Battle of, 2418,
2444, 2510
Cevennes Revolt, 787
Chalons, Battle of, 432
Chancellorsville, Battle of,
1685, 1708
Charlemagne, 141, 225, 241,
319, 347, 390, 423
Charles I, 559, 572, 575, 578,
581, 585, 597, 601, 610, 622
641-642, 649-650, 741
Charles II, 610, 707, 727
Charles V, 574, 770, 2330
Charles XII, 838, 884
Charles the Bold, 444, 449
Charleston, Siege of, 1363,
1386
Chateau Thierry, Battle of,
2599
Chattanooga, Battle of, 1798
Cherokee Removal, 1549, 1551
Chickamauga, Battle of, 1628,
1659, 1683, 1726, 1778,
1817, 1860
Chief Joseph see Nez Percé
War
Chile, Liberation of, 2062,
2143, 2146, 2171
Chile, Spanish conquest of,
2097
China, Japanese occupation of,
2970, 3066, 3217, 3302,
3398, 3458, 3463, 3534
Chinese Revolution, 2885,
2890, 2894, 2902, 2907,

2943-2944
Chippewa, Battle of the, 1471-1472
Chirchua, 1885
Chivington, John M. see Sand Creek Massacre
Choiseul Island, American invasion of, 3215
Churchill, John, Duke of Marlborough, 553, 608, 658, 778, 788-789, 804, 819, 823, 844, 877-878, 882
Civil Air Patrol, 3108, 3567
Clark, George Rogers, 1253, 1267, 1299, 1342, 1350, 1382, 1389, 1412-1413, 1429-1430
Claudius, 39
Claverhouse see Graham, John
Cleopatra see Antony, Mark
Clive, Robert, 2390, 2397, 2403, 2411-2412, 2415
Clontarf, Battle of, 157, 313
Cochise, 1894, 2003, 2051
Colchester, Siege of, 567
Commandos, 2971, 3013, 3040, 3056, 3069, 3124, 3140, 3184, 3187, 3198, 3201, 3209, 3214, 3245, 3268, 3272, 3277, 3285, 3289-3290, 3299, 3309, 3318, 3324-3326, 3341-3343, 3364, 3367-3369, 3382-3383, 3407, 3412, 3432-3435, 3481, 3523-3528, 3530, 3534, 3543, 3552
Congolese Civil War, 3557, 3706
Constantine, 90
Constantinople, Fall of, 212, 362, 388, 441, 498, 500
Coomassie, Battle of, 2460
Cornish Uprising, 699
Cornwallis, Lord, 1258, 1293
Cortez, Hernando see Mexico, Spanish Conquest of
Corunna, Battle of, 893, 979, 1031, 1046, 1048-1049
Courtland, David, 1353
Courtrai, Battle of, 181, 565
Cowpens, Battle of, 1224,

1436, 1440
Crecy, Battle of, 216, 227, 239, 281, 287, 293, 300, 348, 466, 470, 489, 506,
Cree Indian Rebellion, 1922
Creek Indian War see Horseshoe Bend, Battle of
Crete, German occupation of, 2961, 3139, 3418, 3428, 3514
Crimean War, 889, 905, 914, 929, 933, 943, 949, 958-959, 962, 990, 1019-1020
Crockett, Davy, 1483, 1500, 1522, 1588
Cromwell, Oliver, 558, 572, 593, 598, 607, 642, 681, 693-694
Crusades (General), 2284, 2293, 2331
First, 315, 2289, 2300, 2308-2310, 2316-2317, 2324, 2332, 2334-2335, 2341, 2347, 2351, 2356, 2364, 2366, 2376, 2381
Second, 2304, 2348, 2362, 2376
Third, 2287, 2296, 2305, 2315, 2318-2322, 2345, 2348, 2365, 2367-2371, 2374, 2382, 2386
Fourth, 2284, 2306, 2338, 2372
Sixth, 2292, 2314, 2325, 2327, 2339, 2353
Eighth, 2291, 2329, 2384
Cuchulainn, 474
Culloden, Battle of, 775, 781-783, 790-791, 820, 832, 837, 839, 846-847, 849, 852-853, 860, 861, 863, 865-866, 871-872, 874-876, 879-881
Custer, George A. see Little Big Horn, Battle of the; Washita, Battle of the

Daedalus, 5
Danzig, Battle of, 1039
David, King of Israel, 2189, 2198, 2202, 2234, 2237, 2239, 2247, 2259, 2261, 2266-2267, 2277
Deerfield Massacre, 1104

DeGuesclin, Bertrand, 574
De Lacy, George, 980
Delaware Valley Campaign,
    1227, 1367
Delhi, Battle of, 2418, 2448,
    2455, 2512, 2525
De Maltroit, Fulke, 172
De Montfort, Simon, 158, 209,
    220, 228, 277, 280, 501-
    502
Derry, Siege of, 636, 667,
    715, 746
Detroit, Fall of, 1448, 1459,
    1475, 1477, 1496
Detroit Indian Siege of see
    Pontiac's Conspiracy
Dettingen, Battle of, 786
Devereux, Robert, Earl of
    Essex, 591, 676-677, 724
Devil's Bridge, Battle of, 1002
Dionysius of Syracuse, 28
Domitian, 53
Dover, Siege of, 195, 527
Drogheda, Battle of, 540, 560
Drusus of Lyonesse, 10
Dudley, Robert, 1108a
Duke of Burgundy, Charles,
    333
Dunkirk, Evacuation of, 3117,
    3150, 3161, 3344, 3397,
    3484, 3491, 3496, 3511,
    3514

Easter Rebellion, 2590, 2667,
    2768, 2784, 2819
Eaton, William, 1455, 2423
Edgehill, Battle of, 579, 619,
    626, 689
Edmund, King, 128, 264, 303
Edward I, 270, 277, 280, 283,
    502
Edward II, 119, 199, 379,
    425
Edward III, 148, 216, 281,
    287, 300, 348, 412, 470,
    506
Edward IV, 229a, 304, 318,
    433, 519-522
Edward VI, 627
Edward, the Black Prince,
    143, 148, 179, 466, 470
Egyptian Campaign, French,
    2387-2388, 2392-2393

2395, 2398-2399
El Cid, 275, 398, 458, 481
Eleusis of Crete, 16
Ems, Battle of, 663
English Civil War, 540, 558-
    559, 572, 575, 578-581,
    596-597, 600-601, 610, 612,
    619, 622, 625-626, 629-632,
    650, 661, 665-666, 669,
    688-690, 700-701, 717, 720,
    723, 741, 749-750, 752-753,
    757
Ethelred the Unready, 510
Eugene of Savoy, Prince, 788,
    810, 825, 842
European War of 1914, 2569-
    2873
    Aerial Operations, 2577,
    2584, 2591, 2596, 2620,
    2623, 2647, 2650-2652,
    2658, 2661-2663, 2673, 2681-
    2682, 2696-2701, 2707, 2711-
    2713, 2730, 2770-2771, 2783,
    2797, 2800-2801, 2812, 2817,
    2823-2825, 2847, 2854-2861,
    2870
    Tank Operations, 2665, 2860
Eutaw Springs, Battle of, 1383
Evesham, Battle of, 158, 277,
    291, 483, 501

Fairfax, Thomas, 622, 749
Fallen Timbers, Battle of,
    1444, 1460
Ferdinand and Isabella, 305,
    341, 351, 366, 407, 443
Ferguson, John A., 2023
Fernando I, 275
Fetterman, LTC see Fetter-
    man Massacre
Fetterman Massacre, 2034,
    2038
Field of the Cloth of Gold,
    Battle of the, 571
Finnish War of Independence,
    2674
Fitzgerald, Edward, 792-794
Flodden Field, Battle of, 602,
    605, 722, 751, 763
Fontenoy, Battle of, 868
Forrest, Nathan B., 1682-
    1683, 1716, 1726, 1815
Fort Alden, 1261

Guerrilla warfare (post-1945),
3553, 3563-3564, 3566,
3569-3570, 3584, 3591,
3598, 3621, 3623-3624,
3627, 3630, 3634, 3636,
3639, 3681, 3715a, 3727,
3754, 3760, 3768, 3782,
3792, 3794, 3802, 3816,
3829, 3831, 3833, 3854,
3856, 3861, 3868-3869

Haarlem, Siege of, 624, 635
Haitian Revolution, 2065,
2071, 2073, 2083, 2086,
2110
Hampton, Wade, 1622, 1787
Hannibal, 6, 11, 27, 21-32,
40, 43, 55, 58, 61, 67-68,
73, 78, 83, 91
Harald of Norway, 138, 487,
490, 492, 507
Harmon, Joshua, 1482
Harold, King, 186, 188, 285,
289, 356, 358, 365, 371,
385-386, 460, 463, 468,
479, 488
Harrison, William H. see
Tippecanoe, Battle of
Hastings, Battle of, 186, 188,
285, 289, 301, 315, 356,
358, 365, 369, 371, 385-
386, 460, 463, 468, 479,
488
Hastings, Warren see Ali,
Hyder
Heiligerless, Battle of, 663
Henry II, 127, 321, 392, 446,
504
Henry IV, 198, 244, 295,
389, 402, 413, 424, 431,
435
Henry IV see Navarre,
Henry of
Henry V, 261, 288, 294, 314,
324-325, 378, 430, 435,
467
Henry VI, 282, 465, 522
Henry of Guise, 742
Hofer, 1056-1057
Horseshoe Bend, Battle of,
1463, 1469, 1483, 1485,
1487, 1500
Hospitallers, 152, 298, 532

Hotspur, Harry, 320, 389, 402
Houston, Sam, 1555-1556,
1559, 1579
Hugo V, 253
Huguenot Wars, 583-584, 613,
637-638, 644, 646, 654,
675, 698, 728, 732, 742,
745, 754, 767
Hundred Years War, 171, 231,
380, 411, 440
Hungarian Uprising (1848), 971,
993-997
Hungary, Mongol Invasion of,
336
Hussite Wars, 130-131

Indian Wars (post-1865), 1884-
2052
Inkerman, Battle of, 935
Irish Civil War, 2888-2889,
2895, 2905, 2914, 2917,
2920, 2936
Irish Republican Army (IRA),
2888-2889, 2895, 2905,
2914, 2917, 2920, 2936,
3626, 3810, 3813
Irish Revolt (1798), 777, 779,
792-795, 812, 827, 841,
848, 851, 856, 870
Ironside, Edmond, 511
Isandhiwana, Battle of, 2425
Italian Campaign, French, 772-
773, 784, 817, 854-855
Italian Unification, Wars of
see Garibaldi, Giuseppe
Italy/Sicily, Allied invasion of,
2974, 2989, 3003, 3008,
3022, 3026, 3043-3044,
3096, 3099, 3123, 3167,
3173, 3203, 3234, 3237,
3305, 3310, 3321, 3353,
3358, 3363, 3390, 3416-
3417, 3422, 3435, 3438,
3488, 3516, 3519, 3539,
3552
Ivan the Terrible, 587
Ivry, Battle of, 653

Jackson, Andrew see Horseshoe Bend, Battle of; New
Orleans, Battle of
Jackson, Stonewell, 1629, 1678,
1754-1755, 1759, 1851

Leyden, Siege of, 573, 624,
635, 697, 702
Limerick, Battle of, 598, 636,
691, 695-696
Little Big Horn, Battle of the,
1886, 1889-1890, 1893,
1901-1903, 1905, 1926,
1934, 1937, 1942-1944,
1945-1951, 1954, 1957,
1963-1964, 2016, 2019-
2020, 2028, 2039, 2041
Llewelyn ap Gruffydd, 200,
373
Londonderry, Siege of, 533
Long Island, Battle of, 1269-
1269a, 1275, 1282, 1321,
1323, 1346, 1435
Lookout Mountain, Battle of,
1656
Lopez, Francisco see Paraguayan Civil War
Louis XI, 444, 449
Louis XIV, 531, 553, 564,
654, 657
Louisbourg, Colonial capture
of, 1071, 1080-1081, 1085-
1086, 1088, 1091, 1093,
1095, 1124
Louvain, Battle of, 352
L'Ouverture, Toussaint see
Haitian Revolution
Lucknow, Battle of, 2418,
2448, 2456, 2509
Lundy's Lane, Battle of,
1471-1472

Maccabees, Wars of the,
2192, 2209, 2211, 2235,
2268, 2283
McGillivray, Alexander, 1366
Mafeking, Siege of, 2437
Magdeburg, Siege of, 705
Malplaquet, Battle of, 878
Malta, Battle of, 3012, 3352,
3467
Manassas, Battles of see
Bull Run
Mangus Colorado, 1929
Maori War, 2422, 2438,
2462, 2469, 2531
Marathon, Battle of, 18, 22,
93, 108
March to the Sea, Sherman's,

1651, 1656, 1667, 1757,
1767, 1818
Marengo, Battle of, 817
Marlborough, Duke of see
Churchill, John
Marignano, Battle of, 571
Marion, Francis, 1212, 1232,
1234, 1244, 1266, 1288-
1289, 1325, 1331, 1334,
1338, 1341, 1345, 1349,
1379, 1384, 1388, 1410
Marne, Battles of the, 2572,
2575, 2600, 2741, 2803,
2851
Marston Moor, Battle of, 601,
642, 645, 688, 712
Martel, Charles, 273
Masada, Siege of, 2215, 2226,
2243, 2263
Matilda see Stephen and Matilda
Maximilian see Mexico,
French Occupation of
Mecklenburg, Battle of, 1034
Medici, Lorenzo de, 523-524
Mercenaries (post-1945), 3557,
3574, 3591, 3595-3596,
3597a, 3629, 3647, 3666-
3680, 3682, 3701, 3720,
3733-3737, 3739, 3741-
3745, 3748, 3771-3773,
3778, 3785, 3819, 3821,
3827-3828, 3845, 3862,
3865, 3870-3871
Merrill's Marauders, 3020,
3254, 3374
Metz, Battle of, 938, 1026
Meuse-Argonne, Battle of the,
2603, 2780
Mexican Revolution of 1910,
2536, 2540, 2544, 2547,
2561, 2563, 2565-2567
Mexican War, 1505, 1508,
1513, 1520, 1526, 1530,
1534, 1540, 1542, 1546,
1553, 1557, 1561-1562,
1569-1572, 1575, 1584,
1591, 1599, 1601-1604,
1609-1610, 1612, 1617
Mexico, French occupation of,
2115-2116, 2118, 2122-
2123, 2126, 2130, 2135,
2137, 2141, 2144, 2149,